IDOLS OF THE 'HALLS'

H. CHANCE NEWTON
(" CARADOS ")
Photo by Elliott & Fry)

Frontispiece

IDOLS of the 'HALLS'

Being

My Music Hall Memories

BY

H. CHANCE NEWTON

("*Carados*" of *The Referee*)

AUTHOR OF "THE LIFE OF CHARLES MORTON"

"CUES AND CURTAIN CALLS," ETC.

WITH A FOREWORD BY

SIR OSWALD STOLL

ILLUSTRATED

EP PUBLISHING LIMITED

and

BRITISH BOOK CENTRE, INC.

1975

Republished 1975
by permission of the copyright holders

by

EP Publishing Limited
East Ardsley, Wakefield
West Yorkshire, England

and

British Book Centre, Inc.
996 Lexington Avenue
New York, NY, USA

First published 1928 by Heath Cranton Ltd.

ISBN 0 7158 1047 2 (UK)
ISBN 0 8277 3351 8 (USA)

Please address all enquiries to EP Publishing Limited
(address as above)

Printed in Great Britain by
Redwood Burn Limited
Trowbridge & Esher

FOREWORD

As the World is a Stage, so is the Stage a World. It has its greater and its lesser lights, its peculiar atmosphere, its many forms of life, its wide range and variants of mood and social status: and a strange psychology, sometimes worthy of the cloister and sometimes of the slum.

If, in a humble, human way, it has its all-seeing eye, or its recording angel, to whom in our day could the honour of that office be better assigned than to Carados, the grand old man of *The Referee*, H. Chance Newton?

Age cannot wither, nor custom stale his vision or his pen.

Not only has he, like Hamlet, realized that "the play's the thing," either on the World-Stage, or in the Stage-World, but, like Jaques, he has gathered much wisdom from his vast experience. Like Polonius, too, he has given much sage advice, to the well-being of those who have taken it, and the ill-being of those who have been its "stony ground." Like Yorick, he has proved himself "a fellow of infinite jest"; and now—as the following pages will prove—a fellow of "most excellent privilege and the pleasure of learning."

OSWALD STOLL.

PREFACE

In submitting this rather extensive selection from my varied experiences and adventures in front and on the stages of Music Halls from my earliest boyhood to the present time, I can at least make one especial claim. Which is that they are not derived in any way from any books of reference but are entirely personal and all true.

Naturally in such a long theatrical and variety career as mine, I have witnessed many strange changes, both as regards entertainments and entertainers, particularly in the Halls. These changes of course have been quite startling as regards the entertainment places themselves.

Those who are only old enough to have been patrons of the Variety Palaces of the present, or even of such popular Halls as the London Pavilion, the Canterbury and the two (alas ! now defunct) namely, the Tivoli and The Oxford, would indeed be startled could they be transplanted into the pot-house music halls, or Free-and-Easies, of the past.

In those days every music-hall was but the chief room or at best, a mere annexe, of this or that tavern or gin palace. They were run entirely on drinks, or what is usually known as " Wet Money." Indeed, at some admission was by a so-called ' Refreshment Ticket,' half of the cost of which was given back to the patron in the form of liquids !

Equally of course ' Lion,' ' The Mammoth ' and other strangely labelled but still more strangely garbed Male Comiques, and Lady ' Serios,' could they re-visit the Palaces, Hippodromes and so forth of to-day would seem to Kind Friends in Front, very much what the author of the phrase ' Infinite Variety ' calls ' Fearful Wildfowl.'

But although these Stars of a former firmament were mostly, like their songs and ' business,' boisterous and blatant, yet the majority of them were chockful of comic singing and acting ability. Moreover, they gave larger slices of that ability per Turn than is vouchsafed by our modern Variety folk. And yet it must be borne in mind that in those days the most swollen salary was generally a Tenner a week ! Indeed, when George

Leybourne was suddenly given £30 per week by William Holland, the excitement and amazement in the Halls knew no bounds!

Among our present-day 'Artistes' (to give them their own 'Hall' mark) there are several who remind old timers of certain great favourites of the past. This is especially the case with our Comic Singers and 'Patter' Comedians. Such cases of resemblance quite unknown to the Modern Resemblers, are treated in the Chapter on 'Pro.'s and Their Prototypes.'

On the music-hall platforms, (for they were then scarcely stages), the Present Writer soon 'appeared' in this or that Comic singing 'Turn.' Anon he grew up to become for many years, a very lavish provider of Songs, Skits, Sketches, Ballads and Ballets for those Shrines of Song.

It now remains but for me to tender my most grateful thanks to the respective Editors of *The Referee*, *The Era*, *Harmsworth's Popular Music Weekly*, and *The Performer* for their kind permission to reproduce Articles which I had the pleasure to contribute to their popular periodicals. It should be mentioned that it was in the last-named journal (the organ of the Variety Artistes Federation) a Series of these experiences and adventures were published under the title of *My Music-Hall Memories*.

I would also like to thank my esteemed old friend, Sir Oswald Stoll for his very generous Foreword, and my *Referee* colleague, Mr. W. J. Collins, for his exhaustive Index.

And now in the words of the old-time Chairman who used to shout from the table at which he hammered, and around which so many patrons paid in Liquid form to sit:

"Order please. . . . We are just about to commence!"

And at this utterance some of us can still hear the echoes of the shambling harpy-like waiters, who all night haunted us in those Halls with the sepulchral command:

"Hany Horders? . . . Give yer horders, Gents!"

H. CHANCE NEWTON.

CONTENTS

LIST OF ILLUSTRATIONS

IDOLS OF THE 'HALLS'

CHAPTER I

The Music-Hall Chairman—Early Comic Singers—The Great Vance—Vance's Song Successes—The First Coster Carols—Vance's Tragic End.

At the time when, at a very tender age, I was initiated, so to speak, into theatrical and variety life and work, I travelled almost nightly, for years, from playhouse to playhouse, and from hall to hall with sundry immediate ancestors and relatives, all professionals in these two entertainment departments. Then, and even a little later, when I began to be engaged in the theatrical and variety mummer medium myself, music-hall matters were vastly different from what they are nowadays.

In the first place we had none of the Empires, Palaces and Hippodromes and such-like huge and handsome variety theatres such as have been dumped down in every district, metropolitan and provincial, in later years.

Certainly there was at Regent's Park, or in what Gasfitter Gerridge in "Caste" would call "the immediate neighbouring vicinity," a biggish place called the Colosseum, where comic singers, and others, of what has since been labelled the Variety "Industry," appeared from time to time. But its "seasons" were fitful and brief, and, in fact, Destiny soon did away (in my young days) with that London Colosseum.

No; nearly all the music-halls of my youthful period—even those of the important kind—were, more or less (generally more), transformed "pubs" or pothouses, run to draw that since fast dwindling asset of the variety houses—"Wet Money."

Some of the music-halls had a stage apiece—of a sort—but most of them had little more than a platform with a pianist, sometimes plus a fiddler, by way of "orchestra," and some places had orchestras of five or six instrumentalists. The conductor of such "augmented orchestras"—or "leader" as he was mostly billed then—waggled the stick with the right hand and punished the piano with the left, at a salary of thirty shillings—seldom more than two pounds—per week.

True, the " leader " could, by alert diplomacy, acquire quite a useful amount of " bunce," firstly by farming his poorly paid little band and getting commission out of those whom he engaged for it. Moreover, that maestro could earn a little more booty, or " bustle " (as the highwaymen heroes used to call it), by extracting—not to say exacting—backsheesh from the artistes engaged.

" Believe me, or believe me not "—as Dear Old Dan Leno used to say—I have known many of these artistes suffer a good deal from such " leaders " and their orchestras through not weighing in with weekly tips, or through failing to weigh in enough. Also I have known artistes' " band-parts " become accidentally injured or mysteriously lost in order that such maestri could get a job to re-score those necessary articles.

I can vouch for this state of things, for I, too, have suffered in my time from such tip tyranny, both in theatres and halls alike, as an (alleged) entertainer, song-writer, sketch-writer and playwright.

Another bold backsheesh-absorbing music-hall magnate of the halls was " the Chairman," which official, as many middle-aged folk will remember, occupied a sort of throne chair at the head of a table against the stage ; a table around which sat many privileged habitués or guests, who deemed it the greatest of honour to load that official with drinks and cigars. Really the ability of most of the Chairmen I knew (and I knew all of them of my time) to absorb these relays of free liquid and nicotiney " refreshments " was, I mostly found, more than equal to the passion of poor Mrs. Todgers's commercial young gentlemen lodgers for gravy !

Now, our friend the Chairman had at least one other passion, and that was, as I have hinted, a passion for the taking of tips. In his case this " palm-oiling " was in return for services rendered, in the shape of hammering on his sacred table for applause, or the encore (or " obliging again ") of the artiste concerned, together with special hammer-knocks invoking applause for this or that wheeze, warble or " feat."

Neglect or refusal of this Chairman's tip-ful " rights " was speedily visited upon the heads or " turns " of the neglecters or refusers. No weekly tip, no nightly " hammering " was the rule.

As I propose to describe the general habits and customs of several such Chairmen of my extensive experience later in these " Memories," I will conclude this chapter with an early effusion of mine (published many years ago in *Fun*) concerning this kind of music-hall magnate.

THE MUSIC-HALL CHAIRMAN.

" You'll doubtless wonder why it is I've given you a call—
You must know that I'm the Chairman at a well-known music-hall ;
I hammer on the table and announce each artiste's name.
And in knocking down their ' choruses ' I've gained no end of fame.

Chorus—I occupy the chair, boys,
By jingo, I'm all there, boys,
With my rap-tap ' Order, please ! '
I'm the Idol of the Hall !

When eight o'clock is striking, the performance I begin
With a sentimental song or two to sing the people in,
And having done my turn I take possession of the chair,
And all admire my shirt-front, showy studs and curly hair.

Chorus—I occupy, etc.

The youthful swells that nightly come and lounge about the stalls .
For numerous cigars and grog indulge in frequent calls.
I patronise them all around (a most successful fake),
For feeling highly honoured, they all ask me what I'll take.

Chorus—I occupy, etc.

Besides, I'm always petted by all artistes of renown,
They know that I'm a ' caution ' in the way I knock them down ;
I listen for their ' bits of fat,' and knowing all their ways,
I gaily lead the choruses in all their ' leary ' lays !

Chorus—I occupy, etc.

Whene'er I take my ' ben ' all noted artistes gather round,
All lion-comiques, acrobats, and lady stars renowned ;
My *next* occasion's advertised—so, pray you, make a ' mem '—
We've got a drinking licence up till two o'clock a.m.

Chorus—I occupy, etc.

The chairman was not without his more or less poetic historian or lyrical worshipper. I feel I must refer to a very eye-opening ditty of the kind by someone else—whose name I forget.

This song—a striking proof of the hold that this hammer wielder had upon the music-hall patrons of that age—showed that the person impersonated by the singer had taken his wife to the " halls "—and, of course, the fair sex then seldom dared to go to such haunts !—and that his hitherto blameless bride had been smitten by the resplendent personage who did the " hammering " and the lavish liquor absorption !

The refrain of that pathetic ballad ran thus:

> "She said she loved the chairman!
> That most attractive chairman.
> With his rap-tap 'bravo' and 'encore'!
> 'The artiste will oblige once more!'"

As to the artistes, or "turns," of these early halls, their respective abilities, however brilliant (as they often were), were not rewarded by any specially swollen salaries. Indeed, my own beginning in such entertainment resorts synchronised with the approaching end of a period when many, even of the "tremendous favourites" of that branch of Mummerdom, counted themselves, or were compelled to count themselves, adequately paid at five shillings, or even three shillings and sixpence per night!

Certainly sometimes the popular comic singers of the time received extra solatium in the shape of as many free drinks as they could consume—or as many of the management cared to supply. They were also allowed, however, to receive as many such liquid tokens of esteem as they could get from patrons in the auditorium or at the bars.

In sundry special cases, moreover, such great stars as Sam Cowell, J. W. Sharpe, Tom Penniket and G. W. Ross were kindly permitted to "make a bit" by hawking in the halls cheap copies of their chief song-hits.

I never saw Sharpe. He finished up just before my time, in poverty and a poorhouse. My many professional relations and others, who often saw him and knew him well, used to tell me all about him.

From these descriptions of poor Sharpe, I should think that his method was very much like that of my "Variety Veteran" young friend, Arthur Roberts; and I should imagine that he was quite as clever and quite as comic.

Although personal experience of Comedian Sharpe was denied me, I very soon learned from my pro-relations, and others, certain of his chief songs. One of Sharpe's most popular ditties was one which has lasted until our very latest pantomimes. Anyhow the "Air" of it has thus survived, as it is always utilised to accompany the antics of the harlequinades. This song—a very clever lyric—had for its refrain:

> "Pity the downfall of Poor Old Punch and Judy.
> Pity the downfall of Poor Old Punch."

The songs of Cowell, whom I first remember hearing when

I was a mere youngster, soon "grew up" with me, and were especial favourites of my stage-chortling youth.

Sam, who had been in opera and in "straight" comedies in the West End long before his music-hall days, was really a remarkable man. He was descended from both the great Siddons and the Kemble families, and must have been a richly droll comedian, and the quaintest of comic singers.

As I write these lines, several fine portraits of Sam Cowell lie before me—both in "character" and in private. A striking one of the latter kind shows him with his quaint quizzical "mug" bearing a startling resemblance—even to the droll turn of the eye and the very turn-up of the nose—to the comical visage of his brilliant little low-comedy grand-daughter, Sydney Fairbrother. Sam Cowell was also an ancestor of the fascinating Fay Compton.

Later I will return to the subject of Sam Cowell's songs: character numbers like "Billy Barlow," "The Ratcatcher's Daughter," and "Vilikins and his Dinah."

It was at the then not long-opened "Sun," Knightsbridge, that I saw my first big new stars. Undoubtedly the best, certainly the most versatile, of these music-hall artistes of these middle 'sixties was the one who was always billed as—

"THE GREAT VANCE"

he who always professionally signed himself "Alfred Glanville Vance" but who was really Alfred Peck Stephens. When I first saw this comic singer at the Sun, it was early in my nightly prowls round the "Halls" in company with certain members of my family, who, with several friends of theirs, gained their livelihood upon the theatrical and variety stages of the period.

When Vance thus first came into my view I was, of course, too young to form any reasoned opinion of his abilities. I know that I soon learned from him and from my "people" that he had been an actor in the "legit," and that at the time when I first saw him, he had not long left off being a clown in the "regular" theatres—which, in those times, were far more marked off from the music-halls than is the case in these latter days.

I soon grew, however, to find that Vance impressed me very much by the way he came out at the Sun, and later in other popular halls, in many "character" songs. He was totally distinct from most of the "comics" I saw then, and for some years later.

These other comic singers appeared usually in evening dress, or mostly in a frock coat, and they "changed" for this or that ditty, by simply putting on—or leaving off—a top-hat, or exchanging the usual "topper" for a white hat—and sometimes, by way of an extra touch of "character," banging a battered hat well over their eyes, and indicating extra subtlety by dabbing the nose with a splodge of red, which meandered somewhat over each adjacent cheek-bone.

Indeed, in those early days of the "halls," I can recall only Ross, Vance, Arthur Lloyd, Tom Maclagan and the still-surviving Harry Liston, who really attempted to emphasise their portrayal of "character" by properly and thoroughly changing both costume and countenance.

And even Maclagan—truly versatile artiste though he was—would often content himself by adopting the somewhat dilatory disguise of Sam Cowell, whose chief songs he so bountifully borrowed. That is to say, while retaining the comic frock-coat of the comic singer—or such a variant of that garment as George Robey wears, as a trade mark—Maclagan would suddenly don an old white hat, trimmed with long black streamers, such as were wont to be worn by funeral "mutes." But, of course, Mac always took care when thus "changing" to add the "usual" artistic blood-red blotch on the boko!

Now Vance, as I say, went in for more or less suitable complete "character" changes—even more so than Ross, of whose mock-tragic impersonations I have written elsewhere. It must be confessed that Vance's "swell"-song klobber (like Leybourne's, and that of their respective many imitators) ran to quite a startlingly variegated assortment of colours in each such impersonation. Thus the "Great" Vance and "Lion Comique" Leybourne rejoiced to pose for certain songs in puce coats, green vests, and trousers which resembled the "poppy show" of the juvenile carol in that they were "All sorts of colours, Oh!"

Vance's variegations in this sumptuary regard were certainly often less flamboyant and less "banged at you" so to speak, than Leybourne's. (But more of the brilliant but often blatant George in his place.)

Although when I first saw Vance I was rather too young to sort out his merits or demerits, yet, as I had altogether about twenty-five years of him, I was soon able to appraise his great ability and to regret his defects.

For though I can testify that Vance never, in all my long experience of him and his work, indulged in the carelessness and monotony evinced by some whom one could name nowadays, yet he had one regrettable fault which he shared with so many of his contemporary " comics." That is, he dropped from time to time into the double entèndre, or " blue bag" habit, which was thenadays so common and which is not quite dead even now.

Vance was perhaps at his worst in this regard, in his otherwise richly humorous, thoroughly praiseworthy impersonation of the fat old bathing-tent woman with a song, the raggedly rhymed refrain of which ran:

> " Come to your Martha, come, come, come,
> The water is hot in the sun, sun, sun."

It is only fair to add, however, that in this "blue-bag" using, Vance was a long, long way behind most of his comic-singing contemporaries.

So strongly, always, did Vance's and Leybourne's many-coloured costumes for their " dude " ditties impress me, even in my callow youth, that whenever their respective names meet my eye, or whenever I begin to think of them, I at once (thanks doubtless to what the author of " The Essay on the Human Understanding" calls "The Association of Ideas") think first of those singers' gaily-assorted rainbow-lined coats, vests and " bags," and especially of their yellow-topped glistening boots. Vance's fascinating footwear, indeed, filled me with awe, when I was a mere boy in the " halls," and just about to venture on becoming a juvenile comic singer myself!

Many of Vance's swell songs—always with the exception of the phenomenally foolish " Slap Bang!"—better than the similar ditties of the day, were highly popular. Like Leybourne's swell songs, the refrains of Vance's were often very tuneful—thanks to the many excellent melodies composed (or sometimes stolen) by the highly useful alert musicians and " arrangers " of that time.

Vance's swagger songs, or dudish ditties, included the following, of which I give (for the most part) only the " choruses "—as far as I can remember them.

And you will soon see how very " repeatful " and how full of " lines " of least resistance these refrains were.

Here is the chorus of one of Vance's greatest song successes:

> " Walking in the Zoo—
> Walking in the Zoo—
> The O.K. thing on Sunday, boys,
> Is walking in the Zoo.
> Walking in the Zoo—
> Yes—that's the thing to do.
> The proper game on Sunday, boys,
> Is—er—walking in the Zoo!"

The above interjected "Yes" and "Er," like the addition of "Boys" or "My Boys" or "Sirs," were considered very effective, not to say highly artistic, touches in those days.

Here is another of Vance's swell songs, one for which, however, his dress was somewhat sobered, perhaps because this especial lyric was, in effect, one of what were then known as "motto" songs.

Its refrain ran thus—also rather repeatfully:

"Act on the square, boys!
Act on the square!
Honest and fair, boys,
Act on the square!
Act on the square, boys!
Act on the square—
Always be fair, boys!
And—er—act on the square!"

The silliest song Vance (or anyone else) ever chortled was, of course, the hereinbeforementioned "Slap-Bang; or Jolly Dogs are We!"

This doggy ditty—which had its idiotically inane duplicate in Leybourne's "Champagne Charlie is My Name!"—had this ridiculous and more than usually repeatful refrain:

"Slap bang! Here we are again!
Here we are again! here we are again!
Slap bang! Here we are again!
Such jolly dogs are we.
Yes—We always are so jolly—Oh!
So jolly Oh! *Quite* jolly Oh!
We always are so jolly Oh!
Such jolly dogs are we!"

Then came this continuous catch of cachinnation:

"Ha! Ha! Ha! Ha! Ha! Ha!
Ha! Ha! Ha! Ha! Ha! Ha!
Ha! Ha! Ha! Ha! Ha! Ha!
Ha! Ha! Ha! Ha! Ha! Ha! Ha! Ha!
Slap Bang!"

and so on:

Silly as some of our modern music-hall songs are, and uncatchy as many of their melodies are, yet it is really difficult to imagine how people could possibly tolerate such tip-top tommy rot! And yet I have seen and heard huge audiences yell themselves hoarse and speechless with delight at such blatant, brainless bosh.

And that reminds me that the same volcanic appreciation was wont to be lavished in the pothouse "halls" of those days on such refrains as these, or even worse.

Here is one "chorus" that used to be chortled by a comic singer called Sidney Barnes, who closely followed Vance and Leybourne in their ditties, and in their startling "kadies" and coloured "klobber." Barnes lacked the commanding ability of those two comiques—still he was a smart and attractive young fellow, with something of Vance's low comedy "mug." Sidney Barnes' most popular chorus was as follows:

> "I'm bound to win, when I go in—
> Tommy Dodd ! Tommy Dodd !
> Glasses round, cigars as well.
> Tommy Dodd ! Tommy Dodd !
> When I go in, I'm bound to win.
> Tommy Dodd ! Tommy Dodd !
> So shout aloud in all the crowd,
> Hurrah for Tommy Dodd !"

I remember that Sidney Barnes' Tommy Dodd hat was much idolised by the young "bloods" of the halls of those days. It was of white beaver, and was far more glossy and had a far curlier brim than any chapeau that Vance, or George Leybourne, and I might add, even Harry Liston, ever dared to sport in the pursuance of their art. And the last-named cheery chirruper had the most astonishing array of curly "kadies" that I ever met, even in the music-halls of the middle 'sixties.

When Vance went in for his character studies, then you saw something quite out of the common—the then often very common—music-hall ruck. Soon after my early experiences of that comedian I was able to see how great an asset Vance's several years' work on the dramatic stage was to him in his music-hall character studies.

Year in and year out Vance did some of these fine impersonations. For example, "Costermonger Joe," "Going to the Derby" (which was featured for so many years later by J. W.—or "Over" Rowley) and "The Chickaleary Cove," to name no others of the more or less "Coster" kind—were universally and deservedly successful. Each of these rorty sketches of real life was absolutely a distinct and cleverly differentiated impersonation—a perfect portrait.

Even those later-day "Coster"-carolling comedians—Walter Laburnam, Gus Elen, Alec Hurley, Teddy Mosedale,

Albert Chevalier (and why leave out the late quaint little "slangster" Hyram Travers?)—never did anything of the coster kind to beat Vance in the above-named three ditties.

As to "Costermonger Joe," although its refrain was as repeatful as most of those of the contemporary carols, yet, in Vance's hands, the song became memorable for its realistic acting. Moreover, the whole song had a tuneful air.

Here is its "chorus" (again from memory):

"I'm Costermonger Joe!
And as my rounds I go,
For many a mile
The gals all smile
On Costermonger Joe.
With mind devoid of care,
And sperrits as light as air,
I whistle and I sing,
And cabbages bring
From Covint Garden—Oh!"

Chorus— "I'm Costermonger Joe."
(Repeat first four lines.)

And this ballad of the barrow had a most delightful "symphony," to which Vance did a remarkable silent-footed step-dance. And, believe me, Vance could dance!

As the "Chickaleary Cove," that was quite a fetching replica of a New Cut, or Lower Marsh, dandy crook dressed up fit to kill, and certainly to "paralyse," his donah. In fact, Vance often sang this song, causing "a phenomenal furore" (as the adverts of the time put it) not only at the Canterbury, at Westminster Bridge Road end of the "Cut," but also sometimes at the "Old Vic," at the Waterloo Road end of that still thrillful thoroughfare.

And speaking of the New Cut, the "Great" Vance, garbed, I remember in a very shiny beaver topper, an extraordinary yellowish skirt-coat, and a startling pair of light nankeen trousers, was wont in this song of slanguage, to boom or boost the then also "Great" cheap tailor of the Lower Marsh—one Edward Grove.

This merchant had, just before, put up an extensive "emporium" (as it was called) a few doors from the Vic, and another in Shoreditch, a few doors eastward of the Standard Theatre, now the Gulliverian Variety Temple, known as the Olympia.

Here is a more or less "elegant extract" from the "Chickaleary Cove" (or "Bloke") with a little sidelight on Grove the Tailor who, be it noted, used to reciprocate by giving Vance all his "klobber" for this—and for several other songs:

"I'm a Chickaleary bloke, with my one—two—three—
Vitechapel was the willage I was born in;
To catch me on the hop,
Or on my tibby drop,
You must vake up wery early in the mornin'
I've got a rorty gal, also a knowing pal,
And merrily together we jog on.
And I doesn't care a flatch,
So long as I've a tach,
Some pannum in my chest—and a tog on!"

Chorus—

"I'm a Chickaleary Cove."
(Repeat first four lines.)

Here is the "Great" Grove stanza:

"Now kool my downy kicksies—they're the style for me,
Built on a plan wery naughty;
The stock around my squeeze is a guiver colour see!
And the vestat with the bins so rorty!
My tailor serves yer well,
From a perger to a swell,
At Groves's you're safe to make a sure pitch.
For ready yenom down,
There ain't a shop in town
Can lick Groves in the Cut, as well as Shoreditch.
For I'm, &c."

The rhymes "sure pitch" and Shoreditch may, perchance, pain the poetic purist. It must be remembered, however, that Bard Browning sinned as badly in rhyming many-a-times, besides his startling "Tommy Make Room for your Uncle" poem.

It was when that at-one-time handsome and smart comic singer W. B. (or "Billy") Fair was taking the town with the above named avuncular ballad that the great Robert Browning burst forth in one of his great poems, thus referring to certain rowdy folk of the time:

"Troop! all of you Man or homunculus!
Who, treading down, rose and ranunculus.
All Tommy Make Room for your Uncle' us."

Fancy that! as the very non-variety Ibsen would say.

Always a true and earnest worker—resolved to do his duty to his public and his manager at whatever cost to himself, (as I and others who knew him knew so well)—poor Vance, although a comparatively steady fellow at last, overstrained his physical powers.

And so, as will be remembered by a good many music-hall pro.'s and patrons—it was on the Boxing night of 1888, while he was singing a very successful topical song, entitled, "Is he Guilty"—good old "Great" Vance, then barely forty-nine years of age, dropped dead on the very stage where I had first seen him nearly a quarter of a century earlier—namely, the Sun, Knightsbridge.

After the inquest "a strange thing happened" as certain modern manneristic novelists are so fond of saying. A few days before Vance's funeral, my old friend, the late Theophilus Dunkley, (himself given to comic singing, and to dressing like Vance and Leybourne when he was not engaged in "undertaking" for the music-hall profession) received a strange and mysterious letter at his funeral-furnishing premises, in the Westminster Bridge Road—premises afterwards very ably carried on by Dunkley Junior.

The late Mr. Dunkley read the letter to me in due course. It asked that undertaker to request the relatives of the late Mr. Vance to allow the writer—a Church of England clergyman—the privilege of conducting the Burial Service over that popular favourite, that is, if other arrangements had not already been made. The writer of this letter added that he had a special "personal reason for asking this great honour."

The privilege asked for was given (or "accorded"—as most music-hall folk prefer to say)—and the ecclesiastical applicant duly performed the beautiful service, in the presence of many thousands of people, including, of course, a vast number of Vance's fellow professionals.

The mysterious clergyman having finished the "committal" part of the service suddenly besought those present to remain a few moments longer while he made what he called "a personal confession."

And then, amid the solemn hush of the thousands of hearers, that parson made a really sensational statement. And this (in effect) was what he said:

"I ask your permission" (said he) "to tell you, the troops of friends and admirers of the late Mr. Vance—to give him his professional name—that the reason why I sought permission to conduct the service over his grave is a deeply personal reason.

" My parents, reverent Christian folk, had resolved to have me educated for the Church, in fact, to give me every chance of becoming a true minister of our Blessed Lord and Master. To this end my dear father and mother, well-born, but by no means wealthy, stinted themselves to send me to Oxford so that I might gain the learning and training necessary for that sacred calling.

" Unfortunately, during my visits to London, I became mixed up with a gay and giddy set of young fellows. And although I had shown a good deal of application and promise at first, I soon began to drift into neglect of my studies, and even into drink and other forms of dissipation.

" Some time later, being again in London with some of this fast set—most of them with parents far wealthier than mine, I chanced one night to be with my fellow roysterers in the bar of the Oxford Music Hall.

" I'm afraid I was in a rather uproarious state—a very noisy young chap, and using language which I should not. Anyhow, suddenly I felt a tug at my coat. I turned and found a man, evidently a stage professional. He compelled me to go aside with him—saying as he did so : ' My dear lad, evidently you're with people who are no good to you. Pull yourself together, you young fool, and come out with me ! '

" He made me go with him in a little brougham, took me to his lodgings, pulled me round and sobered me. Indeed, he was so earnest and so kind and cheery that he made me feel ashamed. I told him who I was, and how my parents were paying and praying for me to study to serve my God !

" ' You shall do it yet, my lad ! ' said my mysterious awakener and helper. That awakener and helper, dear friends, was the man whose body we have just committed to the grave. Week after week, night after night, he took me about with him, around the music-halls—to do his ' turn '—and then home to his place.

" He never left me till he had set me on my feet again, and had seen me pull round, resume my studies, and at last gladden my dear parents by achieving that for which they had shown such constant self-denial and such ceaseless prayer.

" Can you wonder then that I asked to perform this funeral service ? I'm sure you cannot. For, under God, the man who brought me back to Him, and who was in fact the cause of my reclamation and my salvation, was he who lies in this grave—

Alfred Peck Stephens—the Comic Singer—the favourite known to thousands whom he has delighted as the 'Great Vance.'"

There's an epitaph for a Music-hall Comedian!

And I could tell of several similar kindnesses Vance did, especially to foolish young fellows about Town. And one of them is now a very big 'pro'!

CHAPTER II

My Chairmen—Their Emoluments and Effusions—Ross, the Rude and Rowdy—Detachments of Duettists—Harry Clifton, a great Personality of the Halls.

In the previous chapter I have given some account of that strange announcer of turns and acts who, with 'is 'ammer in 'is 'and (as the song puts it), would "knock down," and invite applause, and indeed would force encores, for the artistes concerned. Also, I have hinted at a habit of this class of music-hall official to "acquire eleemosynary emolument" (to use a Micawberian metaphor) by means of tips from the pro.'s thus hammered, and hammered in proportionate noisy ratio to the amount advanced per week.

And now it is perhaps fitting to give some account of some specimens of the chief chairmen whom I knew, or with whom I had to do.

The first chairman with whom I was personally acquainted was William Anderson, who officiated with the hammer at the "Sun," Knightsbridge. In addition to artiste-announcing, Anderson, like several of the chief chairmen of those days, was also a kind of manager for the proprietor—who was in nearly every case a full-fledged licensed victualler, running the "pub" which always formed the not always too nice nucleus of the entertainment premises.

Anderson was a kind of a sort of relation of mine by marriage. Or, to put it more clearly, his wife, Caroline, a resident-ballad singer at the said "Sun"—and then seldom anywhere else—was related by marriage to one of my aunts, stage-named Annie Addison, who was a serio and dancer not only often at the "Sun" but at most of the London and provincial theatres and music-halls of the period.

Chairman Anderson was a man of rather imposing appearance. The portraits of Blondin will give you Anderson's face pretty correctly, for his visage strongly resembled that of the great French funambulist. Anderson was of a taciturn type, singularly unloquacious, decidedly undemonstrative—and extremely "temperate" for a chairman in those days. He was also very kind and helpful to me as a youngster, but very early in my teens he died. His wife—a lovable lady—went on ballad singing for some few years, when she, too, "passed over."

I can remember noticing in my childhood's days that both William and Caroline Anderson, while treating me so kindly, always seemed to regret having no little kiddies of their own to make a fuss of, as they made of me, God bless them!

Anderson was succeeded at the "Sun" by Theodore Gordon, whose "chairmanship," both there and in after years at the Washington (afterwards the Battersea Palace), lasted so long that even many of the now not very middle-aged will remember him.

Gordon was one of the best and breeziest of baritoney chairmen, and a right good manager to boot. In his later years, he often came to see me at the *Referee*, and there (and elsewhere) we would exchange experiences of our respective lives and adventures in the halls; wherein, he, of course, had worked as a full-grown man years and years before I was born. Like most of the chairmen of the good old days, Gordon would not only do a turn or two a night (as "nominated in the bond" —or contract), but also he would be able to fill any kind of gap or stage wait.

And, let me tell you, that we had a good many such waits and gaps in those days, for, music-hall—or variety——artistes were not then, as they certainly have been for many years, the most punctual of pro'.s.

Undoubtedly the most popular and most picturesque of the chairmen of my young days was the famous Harry Fox, who so long "hammered" comic-singers, serios, duettists, acrobats, and so forth at the old Mo—or Mogul—for so many years afterwards known as the Middlesex. And now it is the beautiful Winter Garden Theatre.

It was when W. E. Winder was towards the end of his proprietorship of the Mo, and "Jimmy" Graydon was a kind of bar or "refreshments" manager, that I first began personally to know the great Harry Fox. From my youngest youth up, however, I had gazed often and often upon his wondrous visage and listened in rapt fashion to his stentorian admonition to "the gods"—his awesome, thunderous rebuke of "Order, gents!"

Old Friend Harry had indeed a marvellous "mug." It was of purple hue, thickly-veined—and emphasised by a big bulbous "boko." Many were wont to say that Harry Fox's "physog" suggested that of Bacchus. But I knew that face in a more modern form than that of the deity of Drink!

For I, look you—young as I was, when Fate, in the necessity of adding to my then slender means of livelihood drew me to the Mogul—I had already had a good deal to do with the dramatic stage, and especially with such blood and thunder dramas as "Jack Sheppard." That being thus, I at once recognised Harry Fox's "chivvy" as being that of Blueskin's in that very crimeful melodrama. Therefore, it was not in the least surprising to me to find a little while after I first saw Chairman Fox, that, although when he sung, he usually sang "The Warbling Waggoner," he sometimes condescended to oblige with Blueskin's very own bacchanalian ditty, namely, "Jolly Nose."

By the time I became more associated with the Middlesex Music Hall—on a business basis (you will learn anon what that "business" was)—I found Magnate Harry more often alternating "Jolly Nose" with "The Warbling Waggoner" (I never heard of him singing any song but those two). In fact, so impressed did the Mo pit and gallery habitués—flower-girls, hawkers, cab-touts, etc.—become with Blueskin's ballad, as voice by the full-throated flaming beaked Harry, that ere long, whenever he admonishingly roared "Ord—er, gents," those gay "gods" would almost unanimously and sternly retort: "Jolly No--oo-se!"

And here is a morceau of Harry Fox's bucolic ballad.

"THE WARBLING WAGGONER."

"When first I went a-waggoning—
A waggoning did go;
I filled my parents' hearts
Full of sorrow, grief and woe,
And many were the hardships
As I did undergo.
Sing, wo, my lads, gee wo,
Drive on, my lads, he ho.
Who wouldn't lead the life
Of a jolly waggoner!"
Chorus ad lib.

The last verse is even more inconsequent than the others. It runs:—

"Now Michaelmas is coming,
What pleasures shall we find!
'Twill make the gold to fly, my boys,
Like chaff before the wind—
And every lad shall take his lass
And sit her on his knee—
Singing "Wo, my lads," etc.

Chairman Manager Harry Fox had a daughter, a beautiful young brunette when I knew her. She became a clever serio and skipping rope dancer—chiefly the latter—and played as Rose Fox. After appearing at the Mo and other halls, she went to join John Hollingshead at the Gaiety.

Poor little Rose! She soon had a very unhappy life, for she had—suppose we say the "incompatible" fate—to marry Hugh J. Didcott (of whom more anon). One of her (and Diddy's) daughters became popular as a clever actress, staged named Violet Raye, and married that excellent actor, Harry Nye Chart son of the famous Brighton theatrical manager of that name.

One of the other early days chairmen I remember was Donald Kerridge, the father of a then popular serio, named Emma Kerridge. He was a kindly old gentleman in those days—not unlike Charles Morton in appearance. Donald, like the rest of his fellow-table rappers, was wont to warble whenever needed. I first met him at the Raglan, then in Theobald's Road, and run by that quaint little music-hall manager, Harry Hart, who subsequently transferred the Raglan name to the Salmon Music Hall, in Union Street, Borough. (N.B.—Of rum little Harry Hart I shall have a few stories to tell later.)

Another famous chairman of my youth was Pat Corri—a fine singing member of a very fine singing family. Pat was chairman at Weston's—afterwards Sweasey's, afterwards the Royal, and now the Holborn Empire. Pat was a true Irishman, and therefore a true humourist. I have a realistic portrait of Pat in a comic picture, in which he is shown acting as a second with that peculiar old German basso, Ferdinand Jonghmans, to Charles Morton and Edward Weston fighting in a ring.

This picture was intended as a satire on Manager Weston (then running his Holborn hall), having sought to prevent Charles Morton opening his new music-hall, the Oxford. C. M., however, gained the day, and as all well know, the Oxford was opened and remained a music-hall up to the time when Charlie Cochran turned it into the New Oxford Theatre. And now, alas! there is no Oxford! It has been acquired for a Lyons Restaurant.

Corri "hammered" away for a good many years, leaving several descendants, all of whom were brilliant. One of them was the late clever composer and conductor, Clarence Corri, who collaborated so often in musical plays by my late famous *Referee* colleague, George R. Sims. Another descendant of Pat's is Clarence's brilliant brother Charles, who succeeded him, and is still the musical director at the now Shakespearean Old Vic.

It will be interesting to sportsmen to learn that my fellow

THE "GREAT" MACDERMOTT
AND
CHARLES GODFREY
(From an "Entr'acte" Drawing by Alfred Bryan)

ARTHUR ROBERTS

BRANSBY WILLIAMS
(Photo by Hana)

National Sporting Clubber, the great boxing referee 'Gene Corri is a descendant of Pat's.

At the Winchester music-hall, locally known as "The Grapes," after the sign of its pub—in the Southwark Bridge Road—I knew and worked with several quaint chairmen. One of them was Rodney Polglaze, a Cornish man. He afterwards filled the chair at the Parthenon, Greenwich.

Another cheery chairman at "The Grapes" was "Tommy-make-room-for-your-Uncle" Fair, who afterwards acquired those "licensed premises," but soon wished he hadn't, for down down derry down went all that Billy Fair put into it. As a matter of fact, however, W. B. F. was never a good business man—nor did he ever attend to business more than he could possibly help.

I knew Fair well, alike as comic singer in the halls, as comedian and panto-actor at the Surrey and elsewhere, and I always found him erratic, wayward and irresponsible, but bright and clever right through his professional career. As a chairman he was quite of the "hail-fellow-well-met" type, and was very popular at his table, among patrons who were in no sense true friends, but would lead him on to foolish excesses. Not that I ever found Billy Fair wanted much leading in that line. As dear old Dan'l Peggoty said, when the lone-lorn creeter Mrs. Gummidge deplored that she was drivin' him to the public house. "Lor, bless yer 'eart, old woman, I don't want no drivin', said Dan'l, I goes natural." And the funny, lovable, upstanding, handsome Billy Fair also went bar-ward "quite natural."

This exceeding bright and smart comic-singer-comedian-chairman rose and fell, and fell and rose again and again, and I (among others) gladly got him fresh chances of work from time to time. At last he dropped out of the actual stage work, both of the theatrical and variety kind. I fancy that the last job he had was as a janitor and cab-door opener at the Coliseum. At least it was the last post I found him fulfilling—and a majestic figure he still was.

One of the most notable chairmen of the halls in my younger experiences was the functionary at the South London—or "South," as it was called locally, for short. This very impressive magnate—one might almost say "magnet"—was the one known as "Baron" Courtney, by reason of his glorious get-up. His glossy, wavy (and well-greased) hair, his noble and beautifully trained moustache, his lavishly-studded shirt front, and the gorgeous manner in which he waved and whacked his "hammer" —each of these attributes was what Bard Keats would call "a thing of beauty." And if not a joy for ever, the "Baron" was certainly a joy at the moment of watching.

Courtney, who sometimes ran a local business (I remember him specially running a barber's or hairdresser's), was compelled, like the other chairmen I have described, to sing a song whenever called upon—in fact, to fill any "wait" in the programme.

One ditty which "The Baron" most favoured was one in which that splendid comic singer and actor Arthur Lloyd had previously made a great success. It was based on an old Scottish song, showing how a miller—fond of his glass—excused his non-Pussyfoot proceedings by declaring that he heard his mill wheel continually saying to him, in what was the song's refrain :

"Take it, Bob, take it, Bob,
Take it, Bob, take it, Bob—
Take it, Bob, take it,
It's better than tea.
Take it, Bob (*da capo*)—
That's what I fancy the mill says to me!"

ROSS THE RENOWNED BUT ROWDY

That really comic comic singer and splendid character actor, W. G. Ross, has never recovered from what I might call his "Sam Hall" mark. All who are at all interested in the history of the music-halls have read, or have heard, of W. G. Ross, and his vile, not to say blasphemous song, "Sam Hall," which he was wont to exude at such rowdy sing-songs as the Cyder Cellars, in Maiden Lane, off the Strand, and the Coal Hole, in the Strand. The last-named low-life resort was near the site of Terry's Theatre, so long bereft of dramatic in favour of kinematic shows. Terry's itself was pulled down in December, 1923.

Readers of Thackeray will remember that in his great story "The Newcomes," the grand old Colonel, sitting with his young son Clive in one of these old-times "Caves of Harmony," heard a comic singer "oblige" with this foul ditty. That, indeed, is clearly the song which the great novelist flays so unmercifully and so deservedly.

It will be remembered, also, that the old Colonel arose in his place, volcanically denounced both singer and song, and stalked out indignantly with his fine young boy.

"And then," adds the novelist, "as he marched out, we all felt as if the Colonel's cane had been laid about our shoulders."

Now, Ross never repeated this disgraceful ditty in my time. In fact, so far as I have been able to ascertain, he abandoned it before I was born. I have, however, a couple of versions of

"Sam Hall," which I came across later in life. The singer is supposed to impersonate a criminal of the worst class under sentence of death.

Here are a few extracts from the version which was usually printed. They ran thus:

SAM HALL, CHIMNEY-SWEEP.

"Oh, my name it is Sam Hall,
Chimney-sweep, chimney-sweep!
Oh, my name it is Sam Hall,
Chimney-sweep!
My name it is Sam Hall.
I have robbed both great and small,
And now I pay for all,
——my eyes!

I goes up Holborn Hill
In a cart,
At St. Giles's takes my gill,
And at Tyburn makes my will,
——my eyes!"

. . . . .

"And now I goes upstairs,
Goes upstairs.
And now I goes upstairs.
Here's an end to all my cares,
So tip up all your prayers,
——your eyes!"

I have, however, another version, which is in manuscript, perhaps because it is too horrible to be printed. Anyhow, it is absolutely unprintable for these "Memories." If Ross ever did dare to say such a version as this latter one in public, or even in private, then he must have been more daring than I ever knew him to be, and I soon grew to learn that Ross could be very audacious.

I came across Ross for some few years before he vanished from the variety stage, but when I first heard him I was a very young lad.

Anyhow, I well remember his giving then, and several times later, a remarkably clever burlesque medley, in which he impersonated Richard the Third. I know that it was a remarkable and, indeed, brilliantly written medley, for I secured a copy in my later years, and studied it for my own use.

This "Richard the Third" stunt was a companion musical monologue to another and even smarter specimen called "The Life and Death of Bad Macbeth," and both had been originally written for Sam Cowell, who, I was told by my "pro." relations and others, was "absolutely great" in both characters.

However great, "absolutely" or otherwise, Cowell may have been in these two travestied tragic rôles, to this day I have a vivid recollection of Ross's mock Crookback King, and his alternatively humorous and intense outbursts of Shakespearean snippets, sandwiched with little parodies of popular songs and pathetic ballads.

Later it chanced that W. G. Ross came to play at the Standard Theatre, Shoreditch (now the Olympia), where at that very time I was also concerned with my several herein-before-mentioned professional relations, some grown up and others of similar youthhood to myself.

At the Standard the great Ross appeared in a burlesque which formed the afterpiece to our usual drama, which, I think, during that week or so, was the then immensely popular play, "The Gipsy Girl," with that really great actress, Miss Marriott, in the name-part.

This burlesque, if I remember rightly, was called "Lalla Rookh." Anyhow, I recollect Ross surprising me with his comical singing, dancing, and spouting as a sort of "villain," scoring especially in a number called "Hoop-de-dooden-do!" After this I saw but little of the remarkable but still rather rowdy Ross, and soon I lost count of him—at least, for many years.

For I *did* see him later—perhaps fifteen or twenty years after I had last seen him "bringing down the house," as he always did with his unforced, if often undisciplined, drolleries.

The place where we thus met again was Astley's Theatre, where I was then engaged in rehearsing a certain early play of mine, a burlesque named "Giddy Godiva; or The Girl who was Sent to Coventry."

"Do you know that man?" said our veteran stage-manager, Jack Doyne, to me, pointing to a poor old blotched and bloated, raggedly dressed "super" among a crowd of such. The face, although sadly changed, seemed familiar to me, but I could not "put a name to it."

"That man," continued the stage-manager, "is, or was, the great W. G. Ross."

I soon learned that this seedy "super," so long the idol of the night clubs and night houses of London, had been leading a very down-and-out life, and had drifted into the direst poverty.

Ross died not long after, and in sore need—just as his great predecessors and contemporaries, J. W. Sharpe and Sam Cowell had ended.

Alas! how often was it in those days that even our biggest

stars, both the theatrical and variety, male and female, so lived that, when they died, they left those belonging to them, as the subsequent benefit billing matter used to put it, "totally unprovided for."

And (alas again!) one is bound to add that such sad billing matter or subscription lists are by no means uncommon, even in these days of tremendous salaries.

DOZENS OF DUETTISTS

In the days that were earlier, the music-halls were literally laden with what were called "duettists." In fact, they were thus labelled whether they sang or only "sketched"—and many of these couples were really sketch-players—or "duologuists." This kind of double turn or act—as such pros. are now billed, has shown, during the last few years, quite a recrudescence—as the picturesque paragraphist would call it. But such popular present pairs of players as Kirkby and Hudson, Lake and Barrasford, Billy Mayerl and Gwen Farrar, Lorna and Toots Pounds, the Brothers O'Gorman, the Duncan Sisters and the Dolly ditto, would all, in those early days, have been lumped together under the label of "duettists."

From my childhood's days onwards—and indeed, well beyond my teens—I saw literally, hundreds of pairs of these "duettists." In fact, there used to be several couples per night on one bill!

Among the earliest of my "duettists" were John and Emma D'Auban, and John and Emma Warde. John D'Auban, who recently passed away an octogenarian, was, when I first saw him, a smart young fellow, dancing and singing with his sister at the Sun, the Raglan, Gatti's, the Winchester (or "Grapes"), Weston's, etc. I remember that the first duet turn in which they impressed me—and I grew anon to love it—was called "Ain't She Wery Shy!" They were a quaint little couple, garbed (for this especial turn) in semi-quaker fashion. John used further to inspire me with admiration by his being able to draw and colour his own window posters for this and other of their duets.

John D'Auban's subsequent long and honourable career as arranger of Old Drury's splendid ballets is a matter of theatrical history.

John and Emma Warde were a couple of a more strenuous or vigorous kind, with the accent on the dancing, but both very comic, especially the brother. In due course, this John married Miss D'Auban, and the other John married Miss Warde. Later, these respective "duettists" became what I might term "quartettists," and figured in the theatres and halls as The D'Auban and Warde Troupe.

In this form I saw them many years in one piece—a kind of rollicking farce, at which I always laughed till my sides ached. Ever and anon the two Johns broke into a kind of dirgeful chant—with the refrain—"I'm a Married Man Myself."

This pair of double duettists are represented on our stage to-day by Ernest D'Auban, the now retired Drury Lane stage manager, son of the John of that surname, and of the aforesaid Emma Warde, and by the ex-Gaiety and Daly's actor, Willie Warde, a much younger brother of the other John. Willie is still a funny comedian, a wonderful dancer and ballet arranger, and quite a champion fly-fisher.

Among the other popular "duettists" of my youth and my adolescence were Mr. and Mrs. Mark Johnson—he a tall, saturnine man, she a handsome actress, quite what the man in Dickens described as "a fine figure of a woman." Mr. and Mrs. J. were wont to indulge in dramatic sketches, mostly (as I could tell even then) borrowed from, or suggested by, stage plays. Sometimes they added a "statuary act" to their turn, with Mrs. Mark posing as Venus, Juno, Diana and other mythological madams.

For a while, in their later career, these "duettists" became trio-ists, by bringing into turn, a Miss Mattie Mitchell—a niece, if I remember rightly, and quite a pretty and clever girl. Ere long, however, Mr. and Mrs. Mark re-drifted into "duettism."

A very favourite "duet" turn of my early period was that provided by George Fredericks and Carrie Julian, his wife. This pair for a good while managed Wilton's Music-Hall (the old "Mahogany Bar"), Wellclose Square, E. There, and at all sorts of halls, I saw this clever couple, who afterwards ran the Bedford Camden Town, for a while. George Fredericks, a very smart, well-set-up and clever artiste, died comparatively young. His widow became the beloved Mrs. O'Brien, so long the hostess of that ancient and accepted hostelrie, "Rules," in Maiden Lane. Mrs. O'Brien, the once idolised "serio," semi-"duettist" and "principal boy" is now living in retirement.

Other very popular pro's in the "duettist" line in my youth included Mr. and Mrs. Bland, who seldom, if ever, sang;

Mr. and Mrs. Hal Hemfrey, a quaint farcical couple; and Alf George (a very crude and blatant actor), at first with Nellie Glover, and after with Nellie Griffiths, both clever and attractive damsels. Also Harry Rickards (afterwards comic singer on his own, and anon the great Australian variety manager), with him Carrie Tudor, a dashing artiste, far cleverer than Harry, who was never really very artistic—that is, on the stage. His chief song in my young days was " Oxford Joe," in which he dressed in cap and gown. He also had a rather clever ditty called " Mugby Junction," suggested by Dicken's story of that name, which had just then been issued as a Christmas annual, price fourpence !

Likewise we had that alert and artistic pair, Fred Evans and his wife, Amy Rosalind, who had been respectively clown (and sometimes Harlequin), and Columbine at Drury Lane and other theatres. Fred and Amy became the parents of Fred Evans, of the Florador Troupe, and of that screamingly funny comedian and knockabout, Will Evans, who has of late blossomed forth as a dramatist and serious novelist, forsooth !

Harvey and French (afterwards Harvey and Connelly), with their funny dancing duet " Nerves," and " Sandy, He Belongs to the Mill." Little Levite, and Jessie Nina (he a quaint Yid and she a delightful dumpling of a Yiddess), Leggett and Allen (who sometimes figured as " pedestal " dancers), and John Ryley and Marie Barnum (The Dancing Quakers), were also tremendously popular duettists of the period.

I really think, however, that the most attractive duettists of my youthful era (to me, anyhow) were Harry and Katty King. They were the children of the then—and long after—popular tragedian, T. C. King, who, when I was concerned with him a few years later, at Drury Lane and the Adelphi, was wont to make those theatres' rafters ring again by means of his rolling, thunderous tones.

Harry King, I remember, was about seventeen when I first saw him at the then newly opened McDonald's Music Hall, in Hoxton, when he became so great a favourite that he was often re-engaged there for the remainder of his life, which (alas !) ended about two years later. He was one of the handsomest young fellows I have ever seen—dark-skinned and dark-eyed, like his sonorous father. Young Harry had a fine singing voice, and was a capital dancer.

As for Katty King, she was a darksome darling—a sweetly pretty, nay, fascinating colleen. I call her a colleen because she and Harry (after generally starting their turn with the duet called "The Gipsy Countess," composed by "Jimmy" Glover's ancestor Stephen) always deviated into Hibernian ditties and jigs.

Poor Harry, as I have said, died young, else would he have become a fine actor—aye, a "matinée idol" to boot, had such idols been objects of flapper worship in those days.

Dear Little Katty King a few years later married and toured with Arthur Lloyd, which clever all-round comic singer and actor, is treated fully by me in "another place."

But alas! Katty King also died too young!

Of course, as Father Time rolled on—and I rolled on with him—I saw and admired (mostly) such deservedly renowned "duettists" as the Sisters Leamar (both saucy and lively!) the Sisters Bilton, one of whom—a lovely lady—married Viscount Dunlo, the Sisters Mario (Minnie and Dot), the Sisters Vaughan (the late famous Kate and the still surviving Susie), not to mention other precious "pairs" of the period.

Kate Vaughan in later years was the famous Gaiety dancer and Old Comedy actress, who, after many vicissitudes, went to South Africa and died there. Miss Susie, now a fine actress of comic grandes dames, sent me a most kindly farewell message recently on embarking for Australia.

Minnie Mario, a splendid-figured girl, became a fine principal boy at Drury Lane under Gus Harris, and married Augustine Healy, the variety agent. Dot Mario, who joined sister Minnie at the "Lane," acting as principal girl, wedded that friend of everybody, namely, the late Alfred Gibbons, so long editor of the *Lady's Pictorial*. One of the Leamar Sisters espoused Billy Bint, a quaint but erratic comic singer; Alice Leamar, a sweetly pretty girl, became one of our best and brightest serios and dancers. She introduced to the London halls that popular ditty "Her Golden Hair was Hanging Down Her Back." This saucy song was afterwards used by Seymour Hicks, thirty years ago, in "The Shop Girl," at the Gaiety. He also re-introduced that Leamar lyric on the play's comparatively recent revival at that theatre.

A REALLY REMARKABLE HALL IDOL

Anon I will review Harry Sydney's career. But, now let me present to you an artiste who was even cleverer—certainly much more versatile, namely, Harry Clifton.

In the first place, for some time the first-named Harry supplied the second Harry with his song material. In due course, however, Clifton wrote his own songs, both of the "Motto" and the merry kind, always excepting those few written by that prolific poet-comic-duettist-singer-manager agent, George Ware. (N.B.—Of this blithe Bohemian, so deservedly nicknamed "The Old Reliable." I shall have more to discourse *in loc.*, as they say in the classics.)

Harry Clifton, like so many of the best artistes of the "halls," had been on the "legit." boards. For nearly ten years I saw all his impersonations, and in the course of all my varied experiences I have never seen or known a cleverer or more conscientious comedian-caroller.

As to the so-called "motto" songs, I venture to assert that Harry Clifton's specimens thereof are the very best that our "halls" ever had. Among the most striking of these were those with the following respective refrains :

"Do your best for one another,
Making life a pleasant dream ;
Help some worn and weary brother,
Pulling hard against the stream."

And this (with the "my boys," so characteristic of the period) :

"Then try to be happy and gay, my boys,
Remember the world is wide ;
For Rome wasn't built in a day, my boys,
So wait for the turn of the tide."

And this (to the tune of "Tramp, Tramp, Tramp, the Boys Are Marching") :

"Work, boys, work and be contented,
As long as you've enough to buy a meal,
For that man, you may rely,
Will be wealthy by and by,
If he'll only put his shoulder to the wheel."

Lest those who never saw Harry Clifton should imagine that he was like so many stage folk, writers and actors, a runner on "one pair of rails," I hasten to put it on record that, besides being a "motto" or "topical" vocalist, Harry was also a splendid comic and character comedian.

In this connection I challenge anyone in the music-hall profession (or "industry," as some now prefer to call it) to produce in evidence any comic songs more comic or better written than the few I am about to quote from Harry Clifton's repertory of such lyrics.

Take this one, which was tremendously popular in its day:

"PRETTY POLLY PERKINS"

"A broken-hearted milkman, in grief I'm arrayed,
Through keeping of company with a young servant-maid,
Who lived on board-wages, the house to keep clean,
In a nobleman's family at Paddington Green."

Chorus.

"Oh, yus, she was
As beautiful as a butterfly and as proud as a queen
Was pretty little Polly Perkins of Paddington Green."

Very popular, also, was a ditty of Clifton's, written at the time of the introduction of the sewing machine from America into England, in the last century's early or middle sixties. This song had the following chorus set to a remarkably catchy and comically plaintive air:

"She fairly broke my heart—
Oh, I wish I never had seen
That fair young girl,
With her hair in curl,
Who worked a sewing machine."

And note these two of Clifton's best-written and cleverest "character" songs.

The first was a gardener's ditty, and the first verse and chorus ran thus:

"My name is William Simmons, I'm a gardener by trade
I served seven years in one situation;
First I lost my *heart*, then I threw away my *spade* (note the puns here)
Oh, listen to my sad lamentation!
Oh, my, the world is now to me
A garding of great desolation:
I'm a stem without a flower since I lost my Mary Ann
And was plunged into a state of agit-ation!"

Chorus—

"Oh, my, look upon me now!
Will you take a quiet observation?
I've been down to Camden Town for to look for Mary Ann.
And returned in a state of agit-a-a-tion."

And, by way of final illustration of the Cliftonian Comic Carols, take this sailor specimen verse:

"My love was not no foolish gal, her age it was two score;
My love was not no spinister, she'd been married twice before;
And you could not say it was her wealth as stole my heart away,
She was starcher at a laundress's at eighteen-pence a day."

Chorus—

But I never thought she would be false or ever prove untrue;
When I sailed away a month to-day on board of "The Kangaroo."

To sum up, Harry Clifton left the regular music-halls for some time, and went touring with an entertainment, in which he was assisted by Fanny Edwards, a smart singer and actress, of a more refined "serio" type than was prevalent at that period. Harry died in the height of his powers, at forty years of age. He was a great loss to the stage, both theatrical and variety.

Chapter III

Another popular Harry—The Grecian—" Old Vic " Varieties—The " Wells " ; the Bower, the Cosmotheka and the "Dusthole"—Numerous Niggers (with Mackney as Monarch).

Another highly popular comic of the middle sixties was Harry Liston, who, although he is happily still among us at the age of eighty-six, I must venture to submit was not quite so finished, and certainly not so versatile, an artiste as Harry Clifton, Vance, or Arthur Lloyd, nor was he so good an actor-singer as his surnamesake—Victor Liston.

Harry Liston, when I first saw him, was scoring in a very extravagant ditty called " The Tin-Pot Band." For this song, which made this Liston's name, he was garbed in a suit of armour made up of tin dishes and ditto saucepan lids, with a saucepan by way of helmet. With a couple of smaller saucepan lids, Harry banged himself all over, as he chortled the following chorus, the two lines being repeated twice :

" Bang ! Bang ! Ain't I mighty grand,
I'm the Tip-top man in the Tin-pot Band."

This comic singer, bearing the surname of one of England's most famous theatre comedians, namely John Liston, the original Paul Pry, etc., anon came out with a couple of songs, of which these are, as I remember, the respective refrains :

" Ginger ! Ginger !
They always call me Ginger.
When I go out, the people shout,
' Howdy do, Gingah ! ' "

The other refrain ran thus :

" Naughty Mary Ann,
Naughty Mary Ann,
How could you be so very unkind,
And false to your young man ? "

The first verse of this—all I remember of the song—was as follows:

"Naughty Naked Cupid,
With his Bow and Ar-row
Has settled me, who used to be,
As gay as a young Cock Spar-row.
Once I was as happy as
A Marquis or a Nearl,
But now I'm broken hearted,
And all through a false young girl."

The hilarious Harry used to make one striking "point" in the refrain of this song. That was when repeating it. When he came to the last lines, he made it:

"How could you be so very unkind
And false to your young—Chorus please."

But perhaps Harry Liston's greatest song-success in those days was one called "Nobody's Child," of which I append the first verse and chorus (again from memory):

"They found me 'neath a Gooseberry Bush,
At the tender age of three,
I don't belong to Nobody—
Yet he belongs to me!
Some horrid blunder has been made,
By somebody or other,
And I am not myself at all—
But somebody else's brother."

Chorus—
"For I never had a father,
I never had a mother.
I'm Nobody's Child, I'm Nobody's Child—
I never had a sister,
I never had a brother,
In fact, I'm Nobody's Child."

Here again Harry would, on repeating the refrain, vary it thus:

"In fact, I'm Nobody's—Orfspring."

For the benefit of future historians of the "halls"—I might add that "Nobody's Child" was suggested by a drama of the same name, written by Watts Phillips, and then running with enormous success, as the playbills put it, at the Surrey, with the popular tragedian and part-manager of the theatre, William Creswick, in the name part.

And thereby hangs a tale.

One night, while Creswick was acting the parentless hero—a character I often saw him play—a strange thing happened.

Creswick had just reached the big scene where the heroine, played by Miss Georgina Pauncefort, had caused the hairy waif to wash himself, and she then combed his matted locks to teach him to be smart.

At this point a gallery patron, noting poor Joe's woolly visage, yelled, sympathetically, "Hi, mum, Why don't yer also give 'im a blinkin' shave."

As to Harry Liston, he left the regular music-hall stage a great many years ago. Since then, and indeed, for over forty years, he has toured continuously with a bright little entertainment entitled "Merry Moments."

Truly a wonderful record; and may good luck still attend this ever hilarious Harry.

MUSIC-HALLING THE THEATRES

For a good many years I saw, and often was concerned with, a great deal of music-hall matter sandwiched between the plays at sundry so-called "regular" playhouses. In fact, these hybrid experiences of mine lasted from my early boyhood to my ditto manhood.

At these playhouses variety turns were blended with dramas, melodramas, and even, ever and anon, with Shakespeare's plays! Such theatres included Sadler's Wells, the "Brit" in Hoxton, the Standard, Shoreditch, the City of London in Norton Folgate, the Pavilion and the Effingham, both in the Whitechapel Road, the Grecian, the "Vic," the Surrey, and even the Princess's in Oxford Street!

Undoubtedly the most extensive outbursts of music-hall turns and acts "between the pieces"—and for a run, mark you—were found at the "Brit," where that renowned actress-manageress, Mrs. Sara Lane, ruled so long and so lucratively. This dear old friend—not to say mentor of mine—knew me from my early childhood to the day of her death, nearly twenty-five years ago. So far as I can remember she was the first leading actress I ever saw, and I remember being quite startled at her strange appearance—for she was showing her legs! I soon learned from my "people," several of whom were over and over again under engagement to the much worshipped Sara, that, on that occasion, she was pretending to be a *Boy*!

"Incidentals" was the name given to these turns imported from the halls to Mrs. Lane's playhouse, and she served them up with such sensational shockers as "Sweeney Todd: the Barber Fiend of Fleet Street," "Maria Martin: or The

TALBOT O'FARRELL
(*Photo by Claude Harris*

VANONI
(*Photo by W. & D. Downey*)

BESSIE BELLWOOD

KATE CARNEY

Facing page 46

Murder in the Red Barn," "The Miller and His Men," "Guy Fawkes," "The Scalp Hunters," "The Skeleton Horseman," "Alone in the Pirates' Lair," and so on.

The music-hall favourites who came to the "Brit" and to several other East End, City Road, Northern and Surrey side theatres to give a show "between the pieces" in those days included Mackney (described in my chapter on him and his contemporary "nigs"), Tom Sayers, who used to show his belts and other "trophies" and spar a bit; Tom Sayers, junior, who became a circus clown (if I remember rightly), and was afterwards "converted" (like that other prize-fighting missionary, Bendigo), and Tom Maclagan and Constance Loseby.

Both Tom and Connie started with Mrs. Lane by singing songs about the then current American Civil War. Tom usually opted for the Slave ditty, "Pity Poor Uncle Sam," and Connie, when not engaged in duets with her mother (billed as Madame Losebini), for a long time nightly thrilled the "Brit-uns" with that stirring song with the refrain:

"On a bright May Morn in 'sixty-three
And ready for the action;
On the battlefield for Liberty
Fell General Stonewall Jackson!"

Even Mackney (among others) was wont to contribute to the American War song output, for he from time to time chipped in with that original old "Dixie" song, the air of which served him (and many more, even up to now), for comic carols, such as "I Wish I was With Nancy."

At the "Brit" and other of these suburban or central playhouses, I also heard such stars as Vance, Leybourne, Macdermott (who was then oscillating between the theatres and the halls), Annie Adams, Louie Sherrington, Amy Ellis (who was billed as "the Northern Star"), Harry Sydney, Harry Clifton, Billy Randall, Teddy Mosedale, Hyram Travers, Jolly Nash, Arthur Lloyd, and many others.

At the Hoxton House, at the Grecian, the Surrey, and so forth, there were also some clever "resident" comedians and comedianesses, who turned their hands (not to mention their voices and feet) to comic singing, "duetting," and dancing between the pieces. Among these doubly-equipped histrions were G. B. Bigwood, George Lewis and his clever, quaint little Yiddish wife, Adelaide Downing, Edward Elton, and Julia Summers, who, like Adelaide, was long the "Brit." chambermaid or soubrette.

This theatre possessed a remarkable resident tenor, who played in all the plays besides singing between 'em. His name was Joseph Plumpton, and he was the father of my late lamented dear old friend, Alfred Plumpton, so long musical director at the Palace Theatre, where he was succeeded by Herman Finck.

Joe Plumpton, whom I knew so well from my boyhood at the "Brit" and elsewhere, always cultivated a physical resemblance to Sims Reeves. Unlike S. R., however, J. P. always kept his professional engagements. Sims Reeves had a hobby of sending a doctor's certificate to take his place. Joe, like his great carolling contemporary, had a beautiful voice, and, moreover, although not a particularly good actor, he could act far better than Sims Reeves.

Plumpton, when acting in the drama or dramas of the evening—for we had several plays per night at the "Brit" —had to sing, and to find his own songs. His own particular pet ballad was, I remember, "Tell Me, Mary, How to Woo Thee." This he chortled in many a play; when he didn't chortle it "between." But what used to amuse me, even in that very youthful period of mine, was that Joe Plumpton was often compelled to drop into Mrs. Lane's Shakespearean revivals sundry songs, by no means concerned with Shakespeare's original scripts!

Other popular Britannia varietyarians included the D'Aubans and Wardes; Fred Evans and Amy Rosalind; Mr. and Mrs. J. F. Brian, and, in later times, Ada Reeve (then very young); Chirgwin, and Marie Lloyd, who made her professional stage début at the "Grecian" (or Eagle), for which see later.

In dropping the curtain on the "Brit." I might add, as likely to be of interest to some, that the brilliant little Ada Reeve eventually married the then very young grandson of the Britannia's remarkable resident playwright, Colin H. Hazlewood, who was formerly a low-comedian at the "Wells," the City of London, and the "Brit." Later she espoused Manager Wilfred Cotton.

Much music-hall "mixed grillery" was also sampled by your humble at that famous entertainment place, the Grecian Theatre, which, when I first was concerned therewith as a youngster, still retained something of its more than local fame as the "Eagle," of that badly rhymed, but quaint quatrain:

"Up and down the City Road,
In and out the Eagle;
That's the way the money goes—
Pop goes the Weazle."

When I first struck the Grecian it was being run, as it was to its finish, by that really wonderful actor, author, acrobat and manager, the late George Conquest, who, some years before my birth, had succeeded to his Uncle Benjamin Oliver Conquest. Here I saw many an excellent variety turn or act, not only in the theatre itself, but also in the adjacent hall, or "Assembly Rooms."

The other Grecian variety favourites of my time, reaching up to the end of its time, included Jenny Hill (afterwards known as "The Vital Spark"), the hereinbefore-mentioned Tom Penniket, James Hillier (who had been low comedian at the Surrey before I was born), and many other music-hall "comics" and serios of the period. The latter group included my aforesaid pretty little aunt, Annie Addison.

But Conquest's resident theatre company comprised several clever and then young theatrical people, who could also score by doing a variety bit "between." Among these were the Sisters Vaughan (the late Kate, the survivor Susie, and another), all dancing pupils of Mrs. Conquest; clever and comical little Emma Chambers; that afterwards great West End favourite low comedianess, Miss Victor; and John Manning, a truly humorous low comedian and comic singer, father of that fine character-actor, Ambrose Manning.

One of the most versatile theatrico-variety persons in George Conquest's Grecian company at that time (one who afterwards did all sorts of acting and singing "stunts" at the "Brit.") was a wild young Irish fellow, who had not long previously served before the mast. He was born Farrell, but was staged named G. H. Macdermott. This remarkable pro. soon blossomed into a regular variety star, as "The Great Macdermott," and will be found treated in fuller detail later in these "memories."

At the City of London Theatre, Norton Folgate, then run by the wonderful old manager and most prolific of pantomime concocters, Nelson Lee; also at the neighbouring Standard, Shoreditch (the local St. Leonard's 'Hall'), at the Whitechapel Pavilion, still a successful theatrical going concern under Councillor Rosenthal; at the Effingham Theatre close by (afterwards the pugilistic "Wonderland," so long managed by the late Jack Woolf, father of Gipsy Woolf), and at the Surrey there were also variety shows from time to time.

Owing to the rapid increase of music-halls in and around London from the middle 'sixties to the late 'seventies, theatrical managers, acting on the defensive, began to interlard their dramatic fare with variety "trimmings." Herein they took a leaf out of Mrs. Lane's book.

Thus, at the "Vic," now the Home of Shakespeare—but even then a frequent "house of call" for the Bard—sundry managers, but especially the famous impresario, old Joseph Arnold Cave, all sorts of music-hall stars, even including Leybourne, Vance, the great little Jenny Hill, and the then enormously popular Nelly Power, and others, were wont to do turns between the pieces.

One of the turn-ers was Joe Cave himself, who had been one of the earliest of music-hall artistes. Cave had started as a sort of imitator or understudy to "Jump Jim Crow" Rice, the American nigger minstrel, whose antics in this song (the silliest of songs to read) had caused a furore both in his nation and ours.

Cave afterwards became a regular nigger minstrel; a ballad singer, and warbler of operatic excerpts (with really a very pleasant voice). In fact, good old Joe's singing was always far better than his acting. By this time I became actually associated with Cave (I was about fifteen and he about forty-five), he had only just started managing the "Vic." Anon he became a sort of relation of mine by marriage—but that is a mere matrimonial detail.

At the "Vic" Manager Cave went in for helping in the "Incidentals" pretty often, confining himself, however, to a few favourite ditties of his, including "Kathleen Mavourneen" (which he had long trilled in a very successful drama of that name) and "Villikins," which he had sometimes chortled as I have done in the Great Little Robson's character, namely Jim Baggs, in "The Wandering Minstrel."

One of the most successful songs which Josephus Arnoldus (as some called him) sung was an exceedingly clever comic "patter" ditty, called "Bradshaw's Guide." This had been written for him by Henry S. Leigh, that funny and finished writer of light verse on *Fun*—a brilliant, if not too industrious "Savage" and poet. I became associated with Leigh when I was about twenty-one, as a verse-spinning colleague on that comic journal. Leigh's epitaph, alas, I soon had to write therein, and I succeeded him on that staff as general bardling!

"Bradshaw's Guide" was one of the best comic songs I ever heard. Even Cave, harmonious enough—but by no means a humorist, couldn't kill it! I would advise George Robey, or somebody, to get hold of this brilliant, bewildering roundelay of the railways and revive it.

Cave's other "Vic" music-hallers included James Hillier (who had been a popular low comedian at the Surrey before my time). There and at the "Vic," Hillier's music-hall career was comparatively brief—but at the chief halls in London he had achieved quite a decent amount of fame by his quaintly humorous kind of comic singing. His chief "number," I remember, was called "Tickling in the Tunnel."

The refrain ran thus:

> "A tickle in the tunnel is a lark, my boys,
> A tickle in the tunnel in the dark, my boys;
> 'Tis nice to take your Mary Jane
> A riding in a railway train,
> And have a jolly tickle in a tunnel O!"

Jimmy Hillier, who had quite a distinguished appearance—not unlike that of George Leybourne—and a handsome, humorous face withal, dropped dead at a comparatively early age, but not during his turn, as Vance did. If I remember rightly, Hillier had been working just before, between the Royal Holborn, the "Vic," and the Royal Surrey Gardens, where a really varied variety show was often in full blast.

Variety at Sadler's Wells is so bound up with merry memories of my esteemed old friend, George E. Blanchett (better known as George Belmont), that many people know variety at the "Wells" chiefly through him—that audacious lessee who dared not only to transform that historic Temple of the Drama into a twice nightly music-hall, but even to rename it "Sunny Old 'Sads.'"

The "Wells" started having songs and dances of the regular music-hall kind under the management of Mat Robson, whose first partner there was a clever young actor, E. N. Hallows who died just as he was making a name.

Mat, whom I first knew as a singing low comedian (chortling in and between the pieces) at the Surrey, dropped in a good deal of variety business at the "Wells." He had a light tenor voice, and was a far better comic singer than he was a comic actor.

After the Belmont règime—in the nineties—the "Wells" retained all—or nearly all—its variety form under the Macnaghten management—with Fred Baugh in charge. Only occasionally did the Real Drama pop up in the programme—and then mainly the R.D. was represented by "Dick Turpin," "Sixteen String Jack," "Sweeney Todd: The Barber Fiend of Fleet Street," "Maria Martin" and "The Shade; or Blood for Blood."

By the time I began to know that celebrated blood-and-thunder playhouse, the Bower Saloon in Stangate, the management had been fain to interpolate between the dramatic "shockers" a lavish amount of music-hallism to compete, as it were, against at least three big variety enterprises close by. One was the Canterbury, then just taken over from Charles Morton by "Billy" Holland, and the other two (then comparatively new) were Gatti's, "in the Road" (meaning Westminster Bridge Road), and Gatti's "Arches," meaning Hungerford.

All three of these once famous London "Halls" have long been "picture" houses. The Canterbury, however, still infuses a decoction of music-hall matter into its filmatic fare.

At the Bower the music-hall turns, like the melodrama there at my time, were mostly of the "minor" order. Still, as in the case of the blood-boltered dramas there, a good many struggling pro.'s became strong favourites—and even stars—elsewhere in due course.

One of the turns then beginning to loom large in these Surrey-side halls and theatres was a merry and later massive serio named Selina Seaforth, for whom, in my early muse-wooing days, I wrote songs, as indeed I did for so many others—but of those more or less poetic outbursts I shall speak in their proper place.

Serio Selina, as many may remember, afterwards joined a tremendous popular singing, acting and pugilistic act, labelled Seaforth, Daltry and Higgins, and in this Selina proved conclusively that she, too, could "scrap."

Another minor Surrey-side resort where music-hall turns were blended with "blood and thunder"—chiefly short "Ghost" plays of the kind afterwards seen only at the New Cut and East End gaffs—was the Rotunda.

This strange entertainment house—the name of which is still plain to see outside—was between Blackfriars Bridge and Stamford Street. Its shape—which led to its name—was not unlike that of that neighbouring pugilistic palace the Ring, where, when it was the Surrey Chapel, I have often heard several of the greatest of Non-conformist preachers.

Another instance by way of the "conversion" of places of worship into resorts for theatrical music-hall, and other entertainment seekers, is the South London, which is on the site of a Roman Catholic Church, and the Clarence (later Cabinet) Theatre, King's Cross, and often a variety house, formerly a dissenting chapel.

That strange, theatrical-cum-variety house, the Cosmetheka, in Bell Street, Edgware Road, was (like the Rotunda) just about to finish its chequered (and, alas! often cheque-less) career when I began to know it. That was when it was under the direction of Joe Cave—some years after several of my "people" had appeared there in their early professional flights. The Cosmetheka shows were always of a most mixed blend, and the language of "kind friends in front" was often anything but kind. When, however, the audience were specially pleased to approve of an artiste's efforts, they would often mark their appreciation by showering pennies on the stage!

This same volcanic language, plus the hurling of coppers at masculine or feminine artistes, was also habitual at several other theatre-music-hall or hybrid halls which I attended—front and back of the stage—in my younger period.

"The Dusthole," you must know, was the nickname given to a certain theatre devoted to tragedies and "turns," and was in its last throes when I was a youngster. Young as I was, however, I was concerned, in a measure, with that then fading dramatic and music-twice-nightly twopenny-gallery temple.

In the course of its career—which started, it seems, nearly a century and a half ago—this theatre had been named variously the Fitzroy, the Tottenham Street, the Clarence, and sundry other names, culminating in the Queen's. It had long been the Queen's, and, indeed, it had for some years been known as "The Dusthole" when I first struck it. In its time many a then—or afterwards—famous pro. had graced its boards, and many a popular play had been presented there. During my brief experience of "The Dusthole" only the most minor pro.'s—theatrical and music-hall—were engaged there—strugglers all!

Then "The Dusthole" had its lid put on, and remained thus for a little while. Suddenly, lo! it arose from its ashes (or dust) and became a most beautiful band-box theatre—namely the Prince of Wales's, where its re-openers, the Bancrofts, made their fortune. After the Bancrofts left for the Haymarket, the Prince of Wales's dwindled down again. Anon, however, it resurged once more, and became that beautiful theatre of my old friend, Dr. Distin Maddick, namely, the Scala!

NUMEROUS NIGGERS

Many will remember that in the earlier history of the "halls" and other "places where they sing," Niggers were billed either as "Negro Entertainers" or (more often) "Ethiopian Serenaders"—always excepting the time when they were

Somebody's "Minstrels"—Christy's, Moore and Burgess, Mohawks, Mohawk-Moore-and-Burgess, the Mastodon, Haverley's and what not.

It was in Haverley's Ministrels, by-the-bye—when that troupe was managed by Charles Morton (afterwards "The Father of the Halls")—that I first met—as a "minstrel"—that subsequently great little theatrical manager and noble-hearted man, Charles Frohman.

In my younger days in the halls, as patron and as "pro.," "Ethiopian Serenaders" were far more numerous than they are now. In proof thereof I may mention that in the lists of variety artistes which I have tabulated for several years—from the "sixties" onwards—the average number of nigger turns alone, per year, was over a hundred!

Now, amid all these "blacked-up" entertainers—for I do not call to mind any one of them that was a real negro—there stood out one who was in every way the finest all-round artiste of the numerous nigger group, and that was the one who was always billed as

"THE GREAT MACKNEY"

I saw Mackney for many years, until he retired and went to live on a little farm at Enfield. I saw him again when he returned to the stage, and again retired. And I resampled his versatile turn, when, as an old man he was compelled by losses to reappear on the boards, and had reached a very advanced age indeed.

As a proof of this brainy, temperate, alert veteran's condition, I may mention that when Mackney was about eighty-three years old—or rather, say, eighty-three years young—he called on me one day for a chat. Chaffingly, I dared him to do his famous "Such a gitting up stairs" song and dance, such as I had so often seen him do from the time when I was a youth and when then he must have been getting on for sixty.

And I assure you that the octogenarian Mackney at once broke into that song and dance in quite his former form!

All he lacked was his famous fiddle—for Mackney also was a famous fiddler, and in most of his songs he used the instrument with wonderful effect.

The refrain of this special song ran:

> "Such a gitting up stairs and a playin' on de fiddle,
> Such a gittin' up stairs I nebber did see!
> Some lub coffee—some lub tea—
> Some lub a lubbly gal, just like me.
> Such a gittin' up stairs, etc."

Mackney's other enormously popular ditties included: "Ladies, won't You Marry," "I wish I was with Nancy" (to the tune of "I wish I was in Dixie") and "In My Garret near the Sky."

The most noteworthy "number" of Mackney's, however, was for many years the one entitled

"THE WHOLE HOG OR NONE"

which had been written for him by the versatile George Ware.

Mackney, with the assistance of the poet Ware, kept "The Whole Hog or None" right up to date.

The topics worked by Mackney into this silly-looking, stupid-sounding, but always effective "darkey" ditty were of any and every kind conceivable and inconceivable, political, scientific, "society" theological and theatrical.

I can remember well that when that wonderful and deeply discussed foreign actor Fechter startled London with his daring but illuminative impersonation of "Hamlet" Mackney was quickly "on the job" in the "Whole Hog" with the following verse—which again I quote from memory:

"Just now you white folks hear a lot
Ob Hamlit and the Ghost,
Cause Massa Fechter's turned de part
All inside out, almost.
Dere's Sammy Phelps and Charlie Kean
Have made their Hamlits run,
But Fechter swears that his shall go
De whole hog or none!"

The other popular "Ethiopian Serenaders" of my earlier and middle music-hall days included Will West, Unsworth (both with "stump speeches" with the then popular query-refrain, "Am I right, or any Udder Man?"), and Sam Redfern, then singing nightly at the "Pav.," week after week, for months together, that Cruikshankian carol, "Any Excuse for a Booze."

Other celebrated "nigs" of my youthful days included Herbert Campbell, the later comic singer and panto actor, then a member of the blacked-up trio, Harman, Campbell and Elston. Among other burnt corkers who "have gone where the good niggers go," but who were then great favourites, were the duettists, Will Orkins and Cyrus Bell, and Paul Deulin.

There was also a quaint "nig" called Dick Penny whom I used to hear week in and week out at McDonald's Music Hall in Hoxton and sundry other such resorts. He had some very strange songs, to most of which he did a big boot dance.

There was, I remember, a good deal of monotony about Dick Penny's singing and acting, but his dancing would have taken a lot of beating.

And of course, even in those early days, we had the young brothers Chirgwin, that droll darkey trio Brown Newland and Wallace (for a long time plus the screamingly funny little Gus Leclercq), in full blast. And in that, so to speak, far-away past, I saw "cullerd" comedians and other troupes of the kind play "Black Justice," "The Mummy," based on the old theatre farce, "The Virginian Mummy"—which I had seen even earlier—together with all sorts and sizes of "nigger" sketches. Indeed, so often did I see these nigger pieces that I was able to go on for any part in any one of them.

Wallace in later years, at least twenty years after I had first seen him, acted with Charles Coborn, the Two Macs, and other old variety pals of mine, in a "Cinderella" pantomine, written by "Richard Henry" (Richard Butler, then editor of the *Referee*) and myself, and produced at Her (now His) Majesty's Theatre.

And there were other "niggers" in those earlier days whose names would rather surprise their admirers in their later "white" turn times—then and now.

Among these then other blacked-up artistes were Edward Terry (afterwards the famous actor-manager), Jimmy Fawn, who presently came to be low comedian at the Vic, (when my family and I were concerned there), and anon took to high comedy and then to comic singing. There was also Tom Maclagan, which fine all-round artiste often blacked up. I remember Maclagan, especially as a burnt cork turn, about the middle of the American Civil War time.

In later years came another brilliant blacked-up pro. He was then billed as "Little Tichborne." That early "nig" was the late Little Tich, and, happily, he retained his big-boot dance from his burnt cork period.

CHAPTER IV

Leybourne—The Lion Comique—Leybourne's Song successes—Henry J. Byron's Burlesque of Leybourne—Some " Serio " Stars—and some Lesser Twinklers.

Although George Leybourne died far earlier than he might have died—at forty-two, in fact—yet I saw and met him at all sorts of halls and theatres, and under all kinds of circumstances throughout his professional career, which lasted about twenty years.

Much as I, like so many other admirers of his, objected to the frequent unpleasant tone of a good many of his songs, I do not hesitate to say that brilliant artiste as George Leybourne was, he could easily have been far more brilliant had he taken a little more trouble. That is to say, as to improving his education and his singing and acting gifts.

Vance was superior to Leybourne—especially in characterisation. He was not only better equipped as a humorous, keen-eyed observer of " character," but also had the advantage of a previous dramatic and general stage training.

The great George, as a matter of fact, always relied a good deal for his attractiveness on the fact that he was one of the finest-looking, upstanding men on the stage of his time. His lithe, splendid figure, his handsome, semi-Jewish visage, the majestic sweep of his hand-play, and his really fine, though untrained voice always compelled attention directly he started his turn. And George well knew it !

As a proof of what I say—for those who never had the privilege—yes, I say, the privilege, of seeing this fine young music-hall favourite—I may add the testimony of the late Sir Charles Wyndham !

" Good God ! " exclaimed Wyndham to some of us one day, when Leybourne had just finished a turn for a charity matinée at the Crystal Palace. " If that comic singer had only been educated and better trained, he would be the finest light comedian on the English stage!"

And I think you will agree that Charles Wyndham was no mean judge of light comedy.

George's music-hall rise was meteoric. He had not been long upon the boards before he was taking the town with that idiotic song, "Champagne Charlie," and from that time right on to his last appearance, the week of his death at the Queen's, Poplar, I knew and learned—and often chortled in public—nearly every song Leybourne ever warbled.

While yet a youngster—perhaps because even then I was familar with the best theatrical and music-hall work—I always squirmed against the inane and idiotic "Champagne Charlie" with its ridiculous, repeatful refrain.

Despite its appalling "words," however, "Champagne Charlie" proved so hugely to the liking of the patrons of the music-halls of the period, that Leybourne became quite a warbler in praise of wines of different kinds, and in that degree George, not altogether unmindful of certain advertisement fees, hilariously hymned forth in turn the praises of sundry popular vintages.

In these "boosting" ballads, the chief lines in the respective refrains came out thus:

> "Whenever I'm going upon the spree,
> Moet and Chandon's the wine for me."
>
> "I'm Burgundy Ben": "Sparkling Moselle," etc.

Vance, as what might be called a lyrical-liquor-pusher, couldn't hold a music-hall candle to Leybourne.

Leybourne, I remember, came into the halls after being a "hammerman" at Maudslay's, the marine engineers, then in the Westminster Bridge Road—about where the North Lambeth Bakerloo station now stands. He appeared first in the halls for a little while as "Joe Saunders," but he quickly dropped that name. He was quite an Apollo among men, and able to "carry" the most distinguished apparel. Mostly, however, he flaunted the broad-check suits, the puce jackets, widely-striped trousers and lurid vests of his so-called "swells."

Yet with all his imposing appearance and deeply interesting face George, the "Lion Comique," never quite divested himself of his "mechanic" manner; and to the last he displayed flashes of illiteracy quite amazing to those who saw or who spoke to him for the first time.

A remarkable asset Leybourne had, one that, when he cared to use it, marked him off as above his music-hall rivals, was a splendid voice for ballad singing.

I have known occasions when George Leybourne would startle the worshippers of his mostly brainless " swell " songs by suddenly appearing in perfect evening dress, a striking figure of an English gentleman stepping quietly down to the footlights and singing, in rich deep tones, a perfectly " straight " song or ballad. His favourite lyric in this regard was—as in Sir Harry Lauder's case—" Rocked in the Cradle of the Deep."

At once, however, the waggish cockney George would revert to his " leonine comiquerie," and blatantly roar forth some love ditty, or a ridiculously written, if melodiously composed, song of supposed West End swelldom.

Soon after Leybourne's early successes, such as " Champagne Charlie," " Up in a Balloon," and " The Little Eel Pie Shop "—of which something more anon—he came, I remember, to the Canterbury, which had just been taken over from Charles Morton, its founder, by William Holland, who always billed himself as " The People's Caterer."

Holland engaged Leybourne at a salary—then enormous—viz., £30 per week—on the strict condition that the " Lion Comique " was to drive to and from the Canterbury in a brougham with four white horses. And George did it ! Night after night did I see him careering to the Canterbury, arousing great excitement and bold advertisement en route.

The still surviving Harry Liston (now eighty six) soon burlesqued Leybourne by driving about with four white donkeys—or as near white as he could get them.

One of Leybourne's earliest song hits of the " swell " sort was, of course, the then far-flung brainless ditty called " Champagne Charlie."

The chorus of this runs as follows :

Chorus—
" Champagne Charlie is my name !
Yes, Champagne Charlie is my name !
Good for any game at night, my boys !
Yes, good for any game at night, my boys—
Champagne Charlie is my name !
Champagne Charlie is my name !
Good for any game at night—boys !
So, who'll come and join me in a spree ! "

This refrain is very noteworthy in one sense, that is, for being so very " repeatful," seven or eight lines being almost exactly the same, barring the occasional " yes " and " so," which form quite a stroke of genius in the way of variation.

Perhaps even a still more "repeatful" refrain is found in this other of Leybourne's:

> "She was the belle of the ball, dear boys!
> She was the belle of the ball, dear boys!
> *Yes*, she was the belle of the ball, dear boys!
> She was the belle of the ball. Pom! Pom!"

The additional "Pom! Pom!" to vary the "repeats" is again a flash of lyrical genius.

Another of Leybourne's most popular ditties was also repeatful in its "chorus," which was set to a very delightful and catchy air. It ran thus:

> "My Lancashire lass! Sure, none can surpass
> My Lancashire lass for style and beauty;
> So stay, ere you pass, and fill up your glass,
> And drink to the health of My Lancashire Lass."

Some of the Leybourne lyrics, however, really had an idea in them, and some even had a distinct dash of humour.

One of these had the following chorus in which Leybourne worked a little "advt." for himself, thus:

> "Oh! She danced like a fairy and sang like a bird,
> She did, on my word, though rather absurd.
> But she fancied George Leybourne, a singer you've heard—
> And with him she skeddaddled away!"

Another song, called "The Mousetrap Man," was "chorused" as follows, to a delightful air:

> "Mousetraps! Mousetraps, I cry!
> Mousetraps! a penny, who'll buy?
> Strong as a house, just have one and try!
> Mousetraps a penny! a penny who'll buy!"

"Up in a Balloon" opened thus, with somewhat of a ragged rhythm:

> "One night last week I went up in a balloon;
> On a voyage of discovery to visit the Moon,
> Where an old man lives, so some people say,
> For cutting his toe-nails on a Sund*ay*!
> Up, up we went, still higher and higher—
> Over house-top, chimney-top, steeple and spire!
> We knocked off the Monument top very nigh,
> And made a hole in the cross of St. Paul's passing by.
>
> *Chorus—*
> While up in a balloon, boys,
> Up in a balloon!
> All among the little stars and round about the moon,
> Up in a balloon, boys, up in a balloon,
> It's something awfully jolly to be up in a balloon!"

"The Little Eel Pie Shop" was a really quaint comic love song, the chorus of which was set to a part of Rossini's "Carneval de Venise." The refrain ran as follows:

"Oh, Sarah Jane is the girl I love
And behind the counter you'll see—
At that little Eel Pie Shop near Temple Bar—
Well, that girl she belongs to me!"

Many another strange song of Leybourne's could be quoted, but those given, being really representative of his prolific output, will doubtless suffice.

It is enough, perhaps, to add that this most phenomenally favourite music-hall star, who speedily rose from a few shillings a night to what was then a very swollen salary, namely, thirty pounds per week, and a few years later to £120 per week, died forty years ago at the early age of 42. He left a widow, a son and a daughter, the last named long popular in the "halls" as Miss Florrie Leybourne. She was the beloved wife of the late lamented "coster" and "character" comedian, Albert Chevalier.

There is no denying that George Leybourne, in a good many of his songs, went "very near the knuckle," to use a phrase adopted by Arthur Roberts.

In fact, when I take my still serviceable memory back to some of George's ditties, really I shudder at the absolute audacity of their double meanings, their sly hints and their even positive statements.

Some of these songs were so daring, especially when our "Lion Comique" found himself in halls West or East where he could "let it go," that I cannot venture to quote them.

In one of these very "shady" songs a charming air ditty called "If Ever I Cease To Love," and in another with the refrain "They All Do It," Leybourne went to the "bluebag" limit.

There were times when this greatly daring "Lion Comique" had to be "spoken to severely" by the myrmidons of the law. Indeed, I knew of cases in those days when the singer was warned. The managements concerned were admonished to keep an eye upon the offending artiste on pain of licence-losing, and so on.

And there wasn't the slightest necessity for Leybourne to indulge in this kind of "unpleasantness." Like several others who sometimes descended to it, he was far too clever to need this sort of thing.

Leybourne's other songs, brainless as some of them were, were at least inoffensive and often interesting. For example, there was his "Up in a Balloon, Boys," which, like most of his best songs, was sung in the so-called "ladies' versions" of those days by such stars as the lovely Louie Sherrington, the majestic Annie Adams, and the fascinating and versatile Nelly Power.

Leybourne's "Mousetrap Man" and his "Scarecrow" impersonation for his modernised old Crow carol were distinctly clever character bits. This "Crow" song was effective, although it may look very ridiculous in cold print. Here is an excerpt—as far as memory serves me:

"Once there was a tailor cutting out a coat—
Fol-de-rol-de-riddle-ol-de-ri-do!
There came a great big crow and he sat upon an oak—
With his Quah! Quah! Quah! Quah!
Fol-de-rol-de-riddle-ol-de-ri-do!"

I have laid some stress upon this strange folk song because I have never forgotten how the audience used to "Quah!" that part of the refrain.

It was soon borne in upon me that dear old Henry J. Byron, the actor-dramatist (whom I, of all men, had so much reason to love and honour), had been much attracted by this Quah-ing chorus of Leybourne's. For not long afterwards Byron, who was singularly like Leybourne in size, face and general appearance, deliberately burlesqued George, not only in his flamboyant, gaily coloured garb, but also in his still more flamboyant song refrains.

The play in which the sly Byron carried out his skit was "The Prompter's Box," at one time called "The Crushed Tragedian." The leading character, Fitzaltamont, written for Sothern, but first played in London by Byron himself, starts as a small-salaried "legit." actor who anon becomes an "interlocutor," and finally a "mammoth comique."

"This mammoth comique business has been my greatest success," proudly asserts the erewhile crushed tragedian. "I have four turns a night, and brougham and four. My greatest hits are my appealing ditty, 'Never Pay Your Taxes Till You're Summoned, My Boys!' and especially my startling song 'Hurrah for the Dog of the Fire Brigade!' That is encored many times for the audience to bark the chorus."

There was a remarkable fascination about Leybourne. He was a real good hearted pal, was this "Lion Comique," ever ready to stand by—or to "stand" for—a friend. Like most pro.'s, he was generosity itself, and, alas! like a good many such, he was easily persuaded by so-called well-wishers into going beyond the bounds of moderation. But even on such

" Bohemian " occasions George would never leave a chum who chanced to be more " overcome " than himself. Often have I seen him at the Canterbury's long bar, or at Kennington Oval, or at some roadside hostelry, and especially at the Albion in Drury Lane resolutely stand by a pal in (alcoholic) distress.

And at some such times that " Lion Comique " would airily beguile the time by quaffing champagne out of a pewter pot, by way of washing down a few plates of whelks !

As in the case of so many hail-fellow-well-met, generous-hearted, lovable fellows, broken health set in all too early. In his last few months this became more and more painfully apparent. How he struggled through his last engagement—the one at the Queen's Poplar—a few days before his death no one will ever know.

SEVERAL "SERIOS"

A very popular kind of artiste in my young days was the serio-comic lady, and they abounded in those times. The first of the several " serios " who impressed me in my youth —and whom I have ever remembered with pleasure—was Mrs. F. R Phillips, a stately lady who, possessing true dramatic ability, could always " put over " her songs with no uncertain " put." I heard her first, in my boyhood, at Collins's, but afterwards, for a good many years, I met her in all sorts of halls, ending I fancy, either at the Old Mo or at Weston's (now the Holborn Empire).

Mrs. Phillips, like many serios and so-called " descriptive " singers of those days, was wont to chortle what were then known as " ladies' versions " of certain songs made popular by the " motto " singers and " comiques " of that time. For example, among her hits were feminine variants of Sam Collins's song, " No Irish Need Apply," to the tune of " The Spider and the Fly " (immortalised by Silas Wegg), also " It's Just as Well to Take things in a Quiet Sort of Way ! " : " The Captain with his Whiskers took a Sly Glance at Me ! " and " I'll Ask My Mother and I'll Let You Know Next Sunday Afternoon ! "

Mrs. Phillips's great song, however (by Harry Sydney, I fancy), was a descriptive ballad entitled " The Shadows on the Wall."

One of the merriest little serios I remember in my youth was a little dumpling of a damsel named Emma Chambers, who afterwards married an old boyhood's chum of mine, viz., the late Lyceum actor, Frank Tyars. Little Emma was quite a girl when I used to hear her sing her chief ditty, which opened:

> "That nice young fellow there
> Keeps winking at me shocking."

But, small serio as she was, I caught up Emma Chambers a couple of years or so later, sharing the leads and the success with Mrs. John Wood at the St. James's, where she played the hero, Harry Halyard, to Mrs. John's Mary Maybud in that splendid burlesque, "My Poll and My Partner Joe." Miss Chambers's subsequent career is a matter of stage history.

Two other famous "serios" of my early days—also singers of sundry "ladies' versions"—were Louie Sherrington and Annie Adams.

Louie was, I remember, a lovely creature, and she came into vogue in the early Vance-Leybourne period, and sang versions of many of their respective song successes, such as "Up in a Balloon, Boys" (changed to "Girls," etc.). I can see this beautiful girl in her (generally) rich green dress even now in my mind's eye, and I can hear her sweet voice in my mind's ear.

These "ladies' versions" were comparatively easy to write. (I know, for I soon began to be engaged to vamp several such ditties.) You took, say, "Champagne Charlie is My Name," and you popped in "his" for "my," perhaps added a little "patter"—or "spoken," as it was then called—indicating the feminine view of this or that escapade set forth in the male version, and thus (for about half-a-crown) you wrote your "ladies' version."

Annie Adams, however, was a stronger and more strenuous kind of "serio." She was a strapping woman with (if I may be pardoned for mentioning such a matter) a very big "bust," and a big voice to match. She had, withal, a jolly, laughing face, and a wonderful way of banging her choruses right at you! In fact, full over the Chairman's table in such sort as to make not only the glasses but also the welkin ring!

Annie Adams, who worked for a good many years after I first heard her, at Collins's, the Sun, the Canterbury, the Winchester, the "Brit.," etc., was the wife of a quaint, quizzical and very shrewd little man named Harry Wall. He was long known as "The Copyright Demon," from his habit of dropping down on any singers and instrumentalists who, all unwittingly, warbled or strummed sundry airs, such as bits of "The Bo' Girl," etc.—the then existing rights of which Harry, or the firm which he represented, had bought up.

CHAPTER V

"Dan"—Dan Leno's early days—His merry songs—My "Referee" notice of Leno and London Managers—Dan Leno "Blackballed"—"Diddy"—Didcott and the "Great" Macdermott.

"What do they know of Leno, who only Leno knew?" is the question which—paraphrasing Rudyard Kipling—I might very well ask of those who knew or remember him only in his days of "stardom" in the halls, or in Druriolanean pantomime.

Properly to know the great little Dan was to know him as I (and some few other "intimates") did, from being with him and working with him in his early struggling days. It was to know him from his boyhood's time, when his parents, calling themselves Mr. and Mrs. Johnny Wilde, appeared at such forgotten music-halls and cheap theatres as "gaffs" as the Rotunda in the Blackfriars Road, the Cosmetheka in Bell Street, Edgware Road, and so on.

When Dan was but a youngster his father, Galvin (alias Wilde), died, and his mother married soon after a music-hall performer, William Grant, whose stage name was Leno. So Dan's name was changed again.

HOW LENO BEGAN

Very soon the child Dan had to assist the family in getting its collective livelihood. He started as a kind of combination of acrobat or contortionist—plus comic singing, chiefly of an Irish kind.

For this Hibernian purpose our little friend (born Galvin) was billed as "Dan Patrick Leno."

From this time forth, Dan sometimes worked as co-duettist either with a younger brother, but mostly with his boy uncle, who was younger than himself, namely, the still surviving and still-working Johnny Danvers! Anon, much of the youthful

Dan's vocal, acrobatic, and saltatory abilities were utilised in "busking" outside public-houses or at street corners, just as we see so many poor fellows doing in the theatre queues nowadays.

As he grew to early manhood, Leno dropped the comic and "character" singing which he had worked from his childhood, and went in almost solely for dancing, and especially clog-dancing. In this "clogging" line he became—as many will remember—the champion of his time, winning a marvellously ornate thing in the way of a belt—or "trophy," as they always called them in the halls.

It was with great difficulty that some of us persuaded Dan to take to what we felt would yet be his professional trump-card, namely, comic singing and "pattering." It was felt that he would come out especially strong in patter, as he was so full of quaint turns of speech and thought in his usual talk, and so keen an observer of quaint character.

Eventually he came out in the comic singing line; at first, very nervously in the provincial "free and easies" or "sing-songs," and anon in the minor metropolitan music-halls.

Directly he started this line in London, I caught Dan up at that long-defunct Islington New River-side music-hall named Deacon's. This was some few years after, in my early theatre and hall-working days, I had taken an engagement at that very resort, as a duo-sketch artiste, with my cousin from the Sadler's Wells Theatre on the opposite New River bank. For that engagement I wrote my own sketch (a skit on "Hamlet," if you please!) and played the Ghost. The joint salary for myself and cousin—*and* sketch—was thirty-five shillings!

I feel compelled to mention this, because, I fancy, Leno was getting very little more than this sum when I caught him at Deacon's.

A WONDERFUL PERFORMANCE

But what a performance little Dan gave that night at Deacon's! It was quite a revelation of real, wild, but basically natural domestic humour! Never shall I forget two of his songs especially. One was called "When Rafferty Raffled His Watch," the long chorus of which contained the following graphic lines:

> "The tables and chairs were tumbled downstairs,
> We'd plenty of Irish and Scotch;
> And the divil's own fight there was on that night,
> When Rafferty raffled his watch!"

His most startling hit that night, however, was with a screamingly comic ditty, in which he gave the first of his extensive gallery of "funny female" impersonations. He appeared as a sort of nursemaid—a cross between Dickens's two "servant" specimens, Tilly Slowboy and Miggs. That Lenonian and ceaselessly dancing damsel carried a huge kitchen pail on each arm, and, breaking off into much extraordinary patter, periodically dashed into the startling refrain, "I'm off to get milk for the twins!"

Many merry ditties were given off by the great little low comedian. One has only to mention such "screamers" as "All Through a Little Piece of Bacon," "The Horseshoe on the Door," "The Waiter," "The good Old Tower of London," "My Wife's Mother's Gone Away" and "Buying a House," to see Dan rise up before us, the very embodiment of hearty honest fun.

By the time I first saw Leno in his lyrical form I had, while keeping up my connection with the stage in the song, sketch and play-writing line, also become a journalist, doing dramatic and variety criticisms, articles and gossip for the *Referee* and other newspapers. Now I was so tickled with Dan's comic singing act, a kind of line which several of us had long wished him to adopt as his professional sheet-anchor, that I wrote a very enthusiastic descriptive notice of him in the *Referee*, in which paper, by the way, I started eventually its first separate variety article in addition to my "Carados" work.

The *Referee* notice brought the chief London theatrical managers swooping down on Dan, all fighting each other as to which should secure him for panto use. The combat for little Leno eventually was confined to the afterwards Sir Augustus Harris (who wanted Dan for the "Lane") and George Conquest, who pined to secure Leno for the Surrey—and Conquest conquered.

The managerial rush after Leno included, of course, several of the big music-hall magnates of the day, and thus between his two Surrey and subsequent many Drury Lane pantomime engagements, he was kept constantly in work at the "halls." His first salary—a joint salary to include his wife—was, if I remember rightly, £22 10s. per week! Afterwards he went up and up in his music-hall and theatre salaries (Mrs. Leno soon retiring from the "boards") to £100, then £200, and £250 weekly. His last "Lane" salary, I think topped £300!

Leno's wonderful career in the halls is—or should—be still remembered with affectionate regard as well as regret by many. How his funny little snatches of songs and his patter (so much of both being the work of the still-going-strong actor-manager, Herbert Darnley) leap up in the memory!

Who can forget his "Shop-Walker," with its quaint bustling little refrain:

"Walk this way, step this way!
Sale now on, there's a grand display!
Upon my word, we're giving 'em away!
Step this way, madam, walk this way!"

Think again of such extraordinary lyric and chatterful outbursts as "Our Stores" (written for him by good old Harry Wright). One can almost hear Dan chortling:

"Our stores! Our stores!
Our nineteenth-century stores!
We've new marmalade,
And eggs overlaid,
In our nineteenth-century stores."

In due course "Gus" lassoed young Leno for Old Drury, and Dan's successes at both theatres, reaching at the "Lane" to the end of his too brief life, are also on the dramatic records plain for all to see.

All I need add on this point is that droll little Dan's gratitude to me for my *Referee* notice, which he always declared "made him," was expressed in all sorts of strange ways. In vain I kept telling him that he had earned that criticism or "boost" by his own remarkable talents, and that he would not have got it from me if he had not thoroughly deserved it.

Indeed, Dan followed me about, and kept with me whenever practicable, with dog-like fidelity. As a matter of fact, the golden-hearted little chap would do anything I asked him, even in the unhappy time when, thanks to well-meaning but foolish "treating" friends, he had become too fond of the often devastating "another with me" habit.

Many a time was I able—when other equally loyal friends had failed—to get Dan away from his "bar" companions both of the well-meaning kind and of the ear-biting and slavering sort. Many a night, for months together, did I "capture" Dan when he had finished his night's work, and carry him off straight away to his home.

Yet I caused Leno to be blackballed!

This awful affair happened thus. Dan, just then beginning to score as the leading comic in Druryolanean pantomimes, and getting a larger salary than ever he dreamed of, but nothing

VESTA TILLEY
(LADY DE FRECE)
(Photo by Brown, Barnes and Bell)

DAN LENO

SIR HARRY LAUDER

DOROTHY WARD

Facing page 68

near so large as he received later, came to me one day and asked me to put him up for one of the clubs of which I was a member.

Now, Dan was then not only—as he was always—working his utmost to do his duty, and to give his very best to the British public, but also he was then the most temperate-living and careful pro. of the hundreds I have known.

This being thus, I selected what I felt to be the quietest and most cosy of my clubs—one most suitable to Dan, who had told me that he wanted a club not for what is called "Bohemianism"—which so often means booze—but for rest and proper meals and refreshment, especially between the shows. For then Leno was acting twice daily at the Old Drury in pantomime.

I selected the Yorick, then a comparatively new club, of which I was one of the original members, and I proposed Dan, who was glad and grateful.

To my utter amazement, *Dan was blackballed* !

On my asking the reason for this astounding decision, I was told by the Committee that "Mr. Leno was inelegible for Yorick membership as he was a variety, or music-hall artiste!"

I notified that Committee at once that, as persons concerned with variety or music-halls had been suddenly declared to be ineligible, this decision, also, automatically blackballed or ejected *me*, as I was then still gaining part of my livelihood in or from the halls, as well as the theatres.

Also I called the attention of this variety-phobe Committee, or its strange majority, to the fact that, to be consistent, they would have to eject our Yorick president, that splendid actor-manager, Edward Terry, for he, too, had been a variety artiste, although, like Leno, he was now acting in the "legit."

I rubbed it in a bit more by showing that my old and esteemed friend Edward Terry had even been a "blacked-up" turn in the halls about the time I started business in that line.

Edward Terry and other Yorick members anon overruled the blackballers, but Leno and I refused to be concerned with the club.

We both exclaimed—in effect—"Alas, poor Yorick!" and left the club severely alone.

It was not till long after Dan's death that I resumed hob-nobbing with my old Yorick chums.

And so ends the strange story of the blackballing of Dan Leno.

Little Leno and I were wont to go about a good deal together, and at one time I was anxious to secure him for the lead in a new burlesque which I had written with Richard Butler.

Dan, being as I have indicated, almost my very shadow, wanted very much to play in this new burlesque in which I had collaborated. Gus Harris, however, who had just captured Dan from Conquest, laughed me to scorn!

"You should not have written such a fine *Referee* notice of Leno at first," remarked Augustus. "It was you who caused all us managers to go after him, and now you can't have him!" And Gus gloated over me—with no uncertain gloat.

And so I never secured Leno for any play of mine, though sometimes I gave him a "gag" or two for his songs, or wrote songs for him. And what a wonder he was at working up a song or a gag!

Also I had to do with Dan when he edited the *Sun* by way of a stunt, but that is another story.

Friend Dan had one absorbing passion which became crescendo as his salary rose. That passion might well be called a consuming passion for it was for fried fish! And, mark you (as he would say), fried fish of the richly redolent, glistening, greasy, shop sort!

Over and over again when Dan and I used to go home together in his brougham, for he would insist on thus carrying me home as I dwelt near him for some years—he would always stop his chariot at a certain fried fish emporium near Clapham Common, and go in and select a huge amount of middle-pieces, tail-pieces, and so on, plus masses of chips, and bang the lot in a huge oleaginous parcel into his brougham! Anon, when reaching home he would dump his precious parcel down on the table in the dining-room, as he made his triumphant entry thereto, beaming all over his funny little face.

Here is another little story concerning Leno, which, like those already told herein, has never been printed. Well do I remember this occurrence. It happened in this wise. There was a certain clever little Cockney—or "coster" serio (happily still surviving and working)—at the period mentioned, and e'en now, prosperous in her profession. Well, she invited Dan to "come round one Sunday to tea," as the handsome Dora Lyric was wont to warble in her winkley and watercressey carol.

Dan accepted the smart little Cockney serio's offer of the hospitality with one of his profoundest bows (I can see him now performing it), and in due course Daniel presented himself at that lively lady's suburban "palace," for such it proved to be.

Leno, dressed in his Sunday best, rattatted at the door. The rattatter then nearly fell back down the steps into the beautifully kept hedge-rowed gravel path, for lo, at the portals stood two statuesque flunkeys garbed in gorgeous array.

On recovering, Dan was ushered in by these sumptuous servants and planted in a magnificent chair in the ditto drawing-room. While perspiring all over and striving to pull himself together so as to be on his best and most dignified behaviour, the little visitor was suddenly swooped down upon by the serio's young brother, now in startling "attire," a thing hitherto unusual with him.

The effusive and effulgent young welcomer, explaining that his sister had not yet finished her "toilet," began to invoke guest Dan's attention and admiration, not to say adoration, of sundry articles of furniture, bric-a-brac, and so forth, recently acquired by his serio-sister.

"Look at this yere pianer, Dan," quoth the juvenile enthusiast, "all dekerated wiv gold, gold things to hold the blooming candles, and gold between the blinking keys. Don't it dumb yer?"

Dan silently assented.

"And jest tyke a lyker at these 'ere pictures on the walls! There's gorjus frames—them frames cost a lot of spondulics, I give yer *my* word. Don't *they* dumb yer?"

Leno, quite overcome, made further signs to express his voiceless worship.

"And yer's fire-irons for yer; gold plated and wif all kinds of coloured stones in the handles and fings! And yer's so and so and such and such," the good little lad continued, again ejaculating after each specimen, "Don't it all dumb yer?"

"And then—believe me, or believe me not," Dan used to say (using his well-known music-hall catchphrase). "In due course down came that serio in all her glory. She grandly took the head of the Sunday tea-table, her dainty little nob surmounted by huge feathers, her bare chest and chubby little arms and hands smothered in trinkets. And as the two flunkeys behind her chair motioned grandly to the two equally gorgeous parlourmaids to hand round the winkles, I noticed that to pick 'em out with we had *gold pins*!"

"And then," added Dan, "when I saw those gold winkle pins I collapsed, indeed, saying: 'Don't it all dumb yer!'"

It was not long before Dan's final breakdown in the course of the malady which caused his untimely end, that his ever good friend Arthur Collins, and several of us, by careful and sympathetic encouragement gradually helped him to make his reappearance at the "Lane," where he had so long been a tremendous and thoroughly deserving favourite.

The dear little fellow, in a manner most pathetic to those of us who knew and loved him, was working hard and quietly at rehearsals, keeping off the drink, and, indeed, doing his utmost to get back to his proper form.

One afternoon, however, poor little Dan was lured off between the interval rehearsals.

On resuming the rehearsal, Arthur Collins, now getting alarmed after waiting for Dan for some time, 'phoned to me at the *Referee*, saying "If anyone can bring him back, you can."

On learning from Arthur the names of one or two pro.'s who were supposed to have persuaded Leno to "join them in a couple," I guessed that the place that these persuading pals would make for just then was the canteen under the London Hippodrome, so I drove there at once.

Sure enough there was the droll Dan with quite a little gang in that canteen, and he was just beginning to get "fresh," and, of course, was preparing for his old impersonation of the "drinks round" man.

Happily my old influence over Dan came out all right once again, and at my wish he came away at once and went back to the "Lane" with me.

Happily I had caught him in time to prevent his being unfit for rehearsals, and on he went all right for some time.

Alas, it was not long before Dan Leno had his final breakdown, and passed away at the early age of forty-three from a world in which he had worked so terribly hard from his merest childhood and which he had done so much to cheer and to exhilarate.

We often hear nowadays the phrase "Brighter London." If the droll, kindly hearted, truly charitable, brave-souled little Leno were still with us, it would indeed be a Brighter London—and a Brighter Britain!

"DIDDY"

When I use the word "Diddy" many variety patrons and professionals will grasp that by that diminutive I mean that extraordinary character, that many-sided man known to most of his contemporaries as "Hugh Jay Didcott."

"Diddy," however, had been known to me by several other aliases—theatrical, managerial, variety and private—from my boyhood time onward.

To most people, even to professionals of experience reaching a good way back, "Diddy" was known only as a music-hall or variety agent. And many such pro.'s have good cause to remember him as an agent, for he was what, alas! too many agents then were not, and some still are not—that is, a splendid worker for his clients.

I first knew "Diddy" when I was very young, and often did he recount to me then—and also in his (and my) later years—his prowess in undertaking Shakespearian "leads"—Hamlet, Othello, Shylock, Macbeth and so forth, in the chief theatres in England and America. Did "Diddy" not, for example, play the Dane at the "Lane"? He did.

I soon gathered from him that he was chiefly enabled thus to "strut and fret his hour upon the stage" (as he always Shakespearianly said) by reason of his having at that time inherited money. I did not see "Diddy" in any of these impersonations, but in spite of his always giving himself a fine "Press" for these things, some who did see him told me that with exception of his reverence for the text, his actual acting was the "limit."

Nevertheless, it was in the strictly theatrical, or "legit." line that certain of my relations and I first had to do with "Diddy." He was then starting in co-management of the famous Surrey Theatre with Charles H. Ross—then and long after editor of the comic journal *Judy*. The plays they began with were respectively a strange and wobbly melodrama called "Clam," and a very smart, if crude, burlesque called "The Beggar's Uproar."

This, burlesque had been written by "Hubert J. Morice." That was Didcott's alias at that time.

After "Hubert Jay Morice" had finished—or had been forced to finish—running the Surrey Theatre with Charles H. Ross, he went round the halls for some time as a comic and topical singer.

As in the case of his ventures in Shakespeare, his Hamlet, Othello, Richard the Third, and so forth, so "Diddy" did not shine even as a "comic" of the music-halls.

Anyhow, in due course, and the York Road—hard by "Misery Junction" or "Poverty Corner" as some called it—this versatile professional and certainly very variable "private person" set up as a music-hall agent. To do "Diddy" justice he not only began to prosper amain, but he really deserved his prosperity, for not only did he show true diligence and acumen, but he was one of the best workers the artistes of the "halls" ever had. It was largely due to Didcott that variety people—minor as well as major—began to be paid properly and to rise to the princely pay (or as some say swollen salaries) which they now receive.

And now, having followed my old crony Didcott up to his early successful career as an agent, I will proceed to tell you a somewhat strange story concerning "Diddy" and the "Great" Macdermott—that is, if you will, as our music-hall comedians say, "Kindly give me a few minutes to change."

The true story which I am about to relate occurred in the last century's early eighties. I having by then spent some few years working in and for the halls—(details later)—had by now become chiefly a theatrical and variety critic and chronicler—at the same time still (as now) keeping up my older work as a play, playlet, song, sketch, and revue writer.

It so happened that among my journalistic output was a series of dramatic and variety articles contributed in collaboration with Richard Butler—the "Richard" of our subsequent play-writing "Richard-Henry" combination.

These especial articles (written for the *Weekly Dispatch*, and signed "Autolycus") started with one called "Misery Junction."

In that article, which emanated chiefly from me, as I had had the stage and other inside experiences—and Butler hadn't—I treated very fully the motley crowd—so full of poor "shopless" music-hall people—which were then to be found daily haunting the York Hotel corner of the Waterloo Road—the Misery (or Poverty) Junction of the period.

Alas a similar state of things may be found nowadays in the thousands of poor "small part people and supers" haunting the corners near the Cinema agent's quarters!

In describing some of these in the habit of congregating on that rum Rialto—the comic singers, topical and motto vocalists, acrobats of all kinds, old and young dramatic actors and actresses eager to be shopped for song or sketch, together with the agents, the poor devils whom poverty compelled to pester daily—of course I drew a veil (more or less) over their names and general identity. Nevertheless, many of my "Misery Junction" dramatis personæ came out pretty obviously for many readers.

Now, you must know that just before the time when "Misery Junction" appeared, the "Great" Macdermott (to be fully described in a chapter or so to himself), although then gaining in the "halls" perhaps ten times the salary he had ever gained in the "regular" theatres, thought fit to set up an agency against and, indeed, almost adjacent to that of the great "Diddy"!

Very naturally, not only was there no love lost between these rivals, but really a good deal of hatred was gained by both. And it so happened that my "Autolycus" statements concerning "the dapper little Semite" and the "Great" Jingo Songster fell like a bomb-shell on both! But the strange thing of all was that "Mac" and "Diddy" charged each other with having written thus about each other!

Their many mutual accusations as to the authorship thereof culminated in their terrific denunciations of each other at a Music-hall Association meeting, when, alas! the "Great" Macdermott and the great Hugh Jay Didcott, the "Daddy" of all agents, very nearly came to blows and had to be parted by a number of their respective bands of well-wishers.

Now, mark the sequel! Eventually on finding that each combatant was (as the heroes and heroines of melodrama say) "in-no-cent!" "Diddy" and Mac shook hands, and swearing eternal friendship (for the time being), united to go to the *Weekly Dispatch* full soon—and to demand, in effect, the blood of the writer who had dared thus to satirise them.

I chanced to meet them on or near the aforesaid Rialto, when they had just made the compact, and chaffing them for their having so fiercely acted Bombastes Furioso to each other, I at once—emulating the late Coriolanus—exclaimed, "Alone I did it."

Both the Great Mac and the ditto Didcott fumed at me at first, but eventually they simmered down. Although I boldly confessed to the soft (or rather hard) impeachment which those two then giants of the "halls" had made to each, I did not apologise, for all I had said in that article about them (and the others) was true, and in their respective heart of hearts they knew it!

Didcott being of Russian-Yiddish extraction was wont to call himself in conversation "Your old father," and I am deeply sorry to have to add that, with all his keen business intellect, his great gifts as a linguist and his really unquenchable diligence, poor old "Diddy" met at last with a debacle, that —to use a latter-day locution—"did him in."

There was no doubt that this really remarkable man, fascinating in manner, cultured to his very finger tips, thoroughly conversant with the literatures of Europe and not unacquainted with those outside thereof, did anon (as I often told him) become too lofty for his job !

It is enough to say that at last this really many-named man —with whom I was so intimately associated from my boyhood's days to the day of his death—dwindled from prosperity to adversity.

Unfortunately, Didcott was himself largely responsible for his fall. After having the monopoly (or something very like it) of supplying all the so-called "syndicate" and other halls for some years with artistes great and small, he became so unbearably autocratic in his demands and conditions that he quarrelled with the "syndicate's" organiser and chieftain, the late Herbert Newson-Smith. H. N. S. failing to bring Didcott down to weight, severed his and his co-syndicators' association with him and issued advertisements setting forth that "Mr. Hugh Jay Didcott has now no connection with the London Pavilion," etc.

"Your old father"—after a stiff and staunch fight (for "Diddy" was nothing if not courageous)—never really recovered from this sudden and severe set-back. His once vast variety influence and his once extensive variety business began to droop. I grieve to say, that as he drifted and dwindled from prosperity to adversity, there were (to quote from the author whom "Diddy" worshipped) "few so poor to do him reverence."

Certain members of Didcott's family and relations helped to look after him in his drooping days. One of his daughters— especially the late pretty little Maudi Darrell—I have seen help our "old father" several times in truly sympathetic and practical fashion.

The few others who kept with "Diddy," helping and cheering him to the end, included two of his old cronies, namely, the late Harry Hibbert and your humble servant, who had known him far longer.

I have hereinbefore mentioned an author whom H. J. D. worshipped. That author was Shakespeare. Indeed, Hugh Jay had such a verbatim acquaintance with the whole of that writer's plays and poems that even those of us who fancied that we knew a bit about the Bard dreaded to take him on as regards that so-called Swan of Avon.

I know I shuddered whenever "Diddy" seemed likely to challenge me on that author's lines—although, like "your old father," I had had to learn a good many Shakespeare plays and parts—alike for stage work and literary use.

One day, however, it was just after his rumpus with and his dismissal from the "syndicate" halls, and before he had severely "felt the draught" of that dismissal, I did manage, to "down" Didcott over a Shakespeare quotation!

"Diddy," said I, with a sort of sudden Bardic brain-wave, "Isn't it wonderful how your old pal Shakespeare foreshadowed your recent 'row' with the syndicators."

Of course, I imagined, from old experience, that "Diddy" would at once give the quotation. "Instead of which" (as the magistrate said to the master of arts who would go about stealing ducks) "Diddy" replied thus:

"Oh, my boy, and what does the Divine William (raising his hat, as he always did in speaking of that author) say about those dissensions and your old father?"

"What, don't you know?" (I exclaimed, somewhat cock-crowingly, I fear), "Why, Diddy, overhaul your 'Troilus and Cressida,' and when found make a note of Pandarus's exit speech towards the end of the play."

"'Lord, Lord, Lord' (says Pandarus). "How is the poor agent despised!"

"Diddy" didn't turn a hair, but simply replied, again reverently raising his hat: "Wonderful William! Thus to spot your old father!"

And so now I bid adieu to a man with something of genius, sometimes ill-directed, a man of the most remarkable gifts of commerce and of culture, of one who, whatever his faults and follies, had, thank God, that unquenchable trait of his great and so long oppressed Race—contempt for the proud, but kindness for the poor.

CHAPTER VI

The "Great" Macdermott—He buys the Jingo song for a guinea—Macdermott's other Song Bargains—The Sketch Squabbles—Charles Morton in Court—Charles Godfrey and "On Guard"—William Holland, "The People's Caterer."

The "Great" Macdermott, the one-time enormous favourite in the music-halls, was of Irish extraction. He was born Farrell, and christened Gilbert Hastings. He came out on the dramatic stage at first under those two names, but soon re-named himself for "billing" purposes G. H. Macdermott, whereupon some people, seizing on the "G," gave him the front name of "George"—though, of course, most of his intimates, throughout his career, always addressed him as "Mac."

When I first knew him, Mac had not long given up serving before the mast, and had just then come into the theatres and halls where I, then about fifteen, had been working—and having the run of—in one way or another, from my childhood's days.

After knocking around sundry "halls" and booths of the "free and easy" type, Mac came along, first to the Grecian, off the City Road, and later to that famous theatre whereat the most nerve-racking "blood and thunder" drama was sandwiched with Shakespeare—a solid slice of each being often dispensed on one evening! I allude to the "Brit." or Britannia in Hoxton, then, and so many years before and after, directed by the renowned—and locally idolised—actress-manageress, Mrs. Sara Lane.

That other celebrated "outlying" playhouse, the Grecian, was in Shepherdess Walk, City Road, London, and was a wonderfully popular resort, then run by that before-named, many-sided actor-author-manager-pantomimist and incredibly startling acrobat, the late George Conquest.

The Grecian, which stood a stone's throw from where Mr. Wilkins Micawber "resided" in Windsor Terrace, had been famous locally in a previous generation as "The Eagle." It has been lyrically handed down in history by the haunting quatrain:

"Up and down the City Road,
In and out the 'Eagle,'
That's the way the money goes,
Pop goes the weazle!"

Later—early in 1885, in fact—we shall find little Marie Lloyd making her variety dêbut at the Eagle—or Grecian Assembly Rooms, in the "Gardens" of this entertainment temple. These licensed premises came anon into the possession of the Salvation Army!

But to return to Mac. It so happened that both at the "Brit." and the Grecian several theatrical and music-hall members of my own family were engaged at the time. And I also, engaged at these and other theatres in play-copying, song and sketch writing—prompting, playing, and so on, soon knew all there was to know about the subsequently "Great" Macdermott.

At the Grecian and the "Brit." young Mac did "yeoman's service." For example, the young Irish ex-mariner played all sorts of parts—heroes, villains, "dialect" characters, low-comedy, burlesque and pantomime leads, with songs and dances. He also wrote and stage-managed many of the dramas, farces, and panto's put on at those two busy theatres, where as a rule, the programmes—containing two and three plays per night—had to be changed weekly!

In fact, Mac and I (much his junior) learned every shade of the "business" at those two theatres, and at the West End, before we both drifted into the "halls."

Strangely enough, Mac eventually gave up playwriting, although he had done so much of it, and had done most of it so well. His stage version of the much-discussed novel, "The Mystery of Edwin Drood" (Dicken's last work, and left unfinished by him) was the best of the many "Drood" dramatisations I have seen or have been concerned with. Mac also wrote a very effective melodrama entitled "Racing." It was produced in 1887 at the Grand Theatre, Islington (now the popular Gulliver Variety house, the Islington Empire).

In that play of Mac's there appeared two pushful lads—

one of them serving as call boy, the other as a very minor part player. The call boy was Seymour Hicks! The small part "walker-on" was Cyril Maude!

Macdermott's taking to the "halls" arose in this way. After achieving a remarkable success at the Grecian (where he had returned) in acting, singing and big-boot dancing in a pantomime written around the much-married Henry the Eighth, he was engaged for the first time at Covent Garden. There he played the name-part in a "Bluebeard" pantomime, and again scored in the song and dance line.

Ere long, Macdermott saw his chance and took it. Finding there was room in the halls for one who could be alike a "comic singer" and a "topical" and "descriptive" vocalist, he made a start in variety land with a song which he had acquired for half a guinea from Henry Pettitt, then a budding playwright, who was being trained by that best of all such trainers, the hereinbefore-mentioned George Conquest.

That song was called, "If Ever there was a Damned Scamp," and its refrain ran as follows:

> "If ever there was a damned scamp!
> I flatter myself I am he;
> From Brigham to Odger,
> There isn't a dodger
> Who can hold a candle to me!"

"Brigham" was, of course, the famous (or in-famous) Brigham Young, then Chief of the Mormon sect. Odger, was George H. Odger, a contemporary notorious demagogue—a journeyman shoemaker. Cobbler Odger's Socialistic harangues (as I can personally vouch) were milk-and-watery compared with those of his political descendants.

Of course, as this refrain was repeated other contemporary alleged "Damned Scamps" were mentioned—the whole ditty seeming to the much more easily pleased and less-educated music-hall patrons of nearly half a century ago—quite a marvel of topical rhyming!

Yes, Mac got quite a fine financial harvest out of that half-guinea's worth of Henry Pettitt's. Pettitt used to tell me that he never received any additional honorarium from Mac for this ditty, although that rapidly growing idol of the halls was receiving five times and presently ten times the salary he had been paid for all his hard, clever and versatile work in the outlying theatres! At those busy houses Mac's salary seldom exceeded five pounds a week!

His next big lyrical coup—though he had several successes "in between"—was the phenomenally popular piece of music-hall song jargon, bearing the following "patriotic" refrain:

"We don't want to fight, but, by Jingo, if we do—
We've got the ships, we've got the men, we've got the money, too.
We've fought the Bear before, and while we're Britons true—
The Russians shall not have Constantinople."

Doubtless it will startle many who are not in the know to learn from one who is in it, that the Great Mac—by then well up to his hundred pounds per week—paid for that blatant but prosperous "patriotic" masterpiece the munificent sum of one guinea!

And that epoch-making lyric's author, good old G. W. Hunt, the "poet" who supplied Leybourne's and Vance's biggest song hits, used to tell me that Macdermott never "sprung" a bit extra! Still, Hunt was bountifully rewarded by being called "Jingo" Hunt all the remainder of his life.

This "great" vocal apostle of Jingoism also achieved a good deal of music-hall popularity by his songs respectively entitled, "Up Went the Price of Meat!" and that ballad of infinite "rot" entitled, "I'll strike you with a Feather!"

The refrain of this precious poem ran thus:

"I'll strike you with a feather,
I'll stab you with a rose.
The idol of the ladies,
Is Hildebrand Montrose!"

One of Macdermott's best songs—and one in which he displayed much of his earlier dramatic and humorous force—was "Jubilation Day," the air conveyed from the French tune, "Père La Victoire," and this was written in honour of Queen Victoria's Jubilee.

Mac also blossomed forth as music-hall manager on his own account, notably at the Forester's (off the Mile End Road), and other resorts of the type. He was always a most cheery fellow, though given to ebullience of manner.

Mac died highly respected and comparatively well-to-do in 1901, at the age of fifty eight. Speaking for myself, I shall always remember with the deepest appreciation the early remarkable dramatic playing and play-writing of the afterwards so-called—or so-billed—"Great" Macdermott.

SQUELCHING THE SKETCHES

Many may think that enough, or even more than enough, has been written upon the Sketch Squabbles. Inasmuch, however, as both sides erewhile appeared to be included to emulate Hamlet's remark as to his love for Ophelia, and to talk with each other upon this theme "until their eye-lids shall no longer wag," I propose to set forth the true history of the evolution of this silly squabble. I can at least claim expert knowledge upon this subject, for from my youth up I have either produced, stage-managed, written or written about, large numbers of such sketches as were lately the dry—often very dry—bones of contention.

In the first place, a great many people are in error in supposing that the sketch trouble is of comparatively recent origin. The first actual anti-sketch prosecution of the modern form took place over *sixty years* ago. The prosecutors in that case were certain envious theatrical managers on the Surrey side, and the defendant was the late Mr. Charles Morton, who, only a year or two before, had made of an old, and not too reputable, Lower Marsh tavern, known as the Canterbury Arms, a magnificent music-hall, which often drew to its mixed musical entertainments such far-seeing judges as William Makepeace Thackeray and his brother novelist, whose full name was Charles John Huffham Dickens. Morton was ever audacious even in his early youth, and so, as he often told me, it chanced that in the year 1855 he produced at the Canterbury Music-Hall a short sketch (or mimetic entertainment) which was entitled "The Enchanted Hash." For this awful act Morton was summoned to the Lambeth Police Court, where, after a good deal of discussion and much adjournment, the wicked defendant was

FINED FIVE POUNDS!

The finer in this case was no other than the then celebrated Hon. Mr. Norton, who had taken the advantage of the adjournment to go to the Canterbury and see the sketch for himself. It is noteworthy that he expressed regret at having to give his verdict against the defendant. Mr. Norton was the husband of the Mrs. Norton, the poetess, who was utilised by Meredith as the heroine of that great story, "Diana of the Crossways."

By one of those remarkable coincidences which sometimes happen even in real life as well as upon the stage, not long before his death (and just as I had written his Life!) Charles Morton, then eighty-four years of age, was again haled before the Bench on a charge of producing at the Palace Theatre an alleged stage-play, entitled "La Toledad." This sketch was simply a boiled-down version of a comic opera of the same name, which had been adapted by Augustus M. Moore and J. Hickory Wood, both since passed away.

Long before the above-mentioned sketch prosecution of sixty years ago, however, there had been a serious upheaval in theatrical circles, an upheaval which, in effect, was responsible for the genesis of the "sketch" as we now understand it.

The only music-halls in existence at that period (say, about the Pierce-Egan-"Tom and Jerry" epoch) were, of course, mere sing-songs of the low, and indeed often loathsome, "Cyder cellars" and "Coal-hole" type. About that time, however, there began to spring up in and around London quite a large group of what were then called "minor" theatres.

Minor as those playhouses were they included such popular resorts as the Surrey (just then transformed from the "Royal Circus"), the Adelphi, the Coburg (afterwards the renowned "Vic"), the even then ancient Sadler's Wells, and the Lyceum, which had already had a chequered career.

These so-called "minor" theatres, in most cases, had excellent companies of players, such as old Buckstone, Ben Webster, and Mr. and Mrs. Keeley (to name just a few seen and remembered by the present writer). Although, however, the players concerned in many of these houses were good class, the law did not allow them to have plays to match. The works of Shakespeare and other so-called "legitimate" dramas were sternly forbidden to these theatres, and their presentation was restricted only to the two big patent theatres, namely, Drury Lane and Covent Garden.

As most people know, there is always a way of setting the law at nought if one puts one's mind to it. The prohibited playhouse managers soon set their minds to it, and in the course of a few years found means to evade the law. In order to achieve this (to them) devoutly wished-for consummation they began to produce a series of short plays, called "burlettas." This description proved very elastic in the case of the managers concerned, for almost everything in a dramatic shape was served up in "burletta" form.

Oftentimes these burlettas even took the form of mutilations of Shakespearian, Dickensian and other famous classics condensed to two acts or one, with musical "improvements" in the shape of comic and serious songs and duets. These "additional numbers" were mostly contributed by the theatre's own resident lyrist or dramatist, who was paid the magnificent sum of two or three pounds per week to keep such things going. Even as the great little Douglas Jerrold and the lesser but clever Colin Hazlewood were so long glad to do to gain their respective families' livelihood.

The above-mentioned prohibition in favour of the two patent theatres has not really been repealed. But whether or no, it was not until some three years after the marriage of the late Queen Victoria that there was introduced a kind of a Bill of not too sweeping a nature by virtue of which the legislature graciously permitted certain of the so-called "minor" theatres to play so-called "legitimate" drama. As far as I can remember, that late glorious actor, Samuel Phelps, was the first to avail himself of the opportunity to present Shakespeare, "by kind permission" of the new Bill, as it were. He started doing so at the old Sadler's Wells, where he gave such a wonderful series of Shakespearian and other revivals for eighteen solid years.

A few years later, that is to say when the New Canterbury Music Hall was in full swing, the success of that hall caused many of the other halls to arise in London and the suburbs. Then the "burlettas" banished from the "minor" theatres bobbed up in various shorter forms and adaptations in these other music-halls. These halls included the Sun at Knightsbridge, Sam Collins's, the old Colosseum at Regent's Park, the Middlesex (or Mogul), the South London, and so on.

These "burlettas" or sketches, mostly reduced by this time to carry very few characters, went on for some years unchecked. By about the end of last century's seventies or early eighties, however, a good many theatrical managers again grew envious of their music-hall managerial brethren, and threatened to apply to the law, not only for prohibition, but even for the total abolition of all such sketches, or, as they called them, stage-plays.

At the head of these threateners and prosecutors in the 'eighties were the late George Conquest and the late Augustus Harris, who was not then knighted. These twain, to name no others, made things very warm for all sorts and conditions of music-hall managers. Most of the prosecutions appeared to many of us to be very vexatious in character.

At the time the *Referee* (per yours truly), alone among the papers of the period, stood forth on behalf of the smaller sketch-producers, always, of course, providing that the sketch produced was not audaciously borrowed from some "copyright" play.

Augustus Harris and George Conquest soon began to be

abashed somewhat by these prosecutions being labelled as trivial or paltry, and for a time the poor little sketch culprits again enjoyed some immunity, while managers ceased from troubling and prosecutors were at rest.

In due course, however, Gus Harris (always in other respects the kindest of men) did a very foolish thing. He had just been elected a county councillor and no sooner had he entered upon his county councilling duties than he made a strenuous proposition for the abolition, or, at all events, for a considerable reduction, of the sketches in the music-halls. This proceeding brought down upon this managerial county councillor much variety and journalistic denunciation, whereat poor Harris grew very wroth and signified his more or less righteous anger by withdrawing his advertisements from sundry journals. And he kept them out for a long time, especially from the *Referee*.

After a while, however, this generally shrewd impresario not only saw the error of all his ways, but on taking over from the late Mr. Richard D'Oyly Carte the Royal English Opera House (which he renamed the Palace Theatre), Harris started with three sketches or brief plays in one evening, and I wrote one of them!

It was in 1888 that the London Entertainments Protection Association was formed with Henri Gros as chairman, George Adney Payne as vice-chairman, and J. L. Graydon as hon. secretary, with a view to the better protection of the variety theatres and music-halls. These places, as the Association's Society's manifesto pointed out, were licensed under an obsolete Act of 1752 (25 George II. c. 36), entitled " An Act for the better preventing thefts and robberies and for regulating places of public entertainment and punishing persons keeping disorderly houses." A nice sort of Act, forsooth, under which to run our modern variety theatres.

Again, for some time the sketchers went on their way rejoicing and causing their variety audiences to rejoice also, more or less. And all would doubtless have gone on peacefully had not certain sketch-mongers taken to making their sketches not only out of " copyright " dramas but also out of plays, then touring and even booked in the immediate neighbourhood. Thus certain sketch companies brought trouble on themselves and involved their more innocent and equally hard-working sketch brethren not only in loss of repute but also in loss of employment.

The prosecutions of the Palace Theatre, of the Oxford and the Coliseum, the Palladium and other leading variety houses will be fresh in the memory of all who are at all interested enough to follow the somewhat tortuous course of these unhappy dissensions.

For some time Beerbohm Tree, George Alexander and certain other leading lights of actor-managerdom, and certain magnates of the variety world were at (legal) " daggers drawn " upon this subject. Later, however, the T.M.A. proposed a compromise, permitting sketches not exceeding thirty minutes' duration, with the dramatis personæ limited to six principals and twenty supers. The variety contingent accepted these propositions, with some slight reservations and few suggestions of amendment.

WILLIAM THE WONDERFUL!

The appropriator, and for many years the proud possessor of that lofty label, "The People's Caterer," was William Holland, who undoubtedly was one of the most extraordinary theatrical and variety managers that ever presented programmes to the public.

I make this statement without fear of contradiction, for in my time I have known and often worked with several extremely strange, not to say startlingly eccentric stage impresario, including E. T. Smith, " Joe " Cave, " Gus " (afterwards Sir Augustus) Harris, Charles Morton and that most mysterious of managers, W. H. C. Nation!

All these, like Holland, put in a good deal of their time as theatrical managers, and, of course, that part of their respective careers does not come within the scope of these Music-Hall Memories.

I might point out, however, for purposes of reference, that Edward Tyrrell Smith (who had been a policeman and, anon, a publican), Joseph Arnold Cave, etc., put in long periods apiece in variety, both of them on different occasions at the Alhambra and Cremorne and Cave, ever and anon at the Old Vic, the Marylebone and Elephant and Castle Theatres, and also at that extraordinary Marylebonian music-hall and playhouse so classically called the Cosmetheka!

Now "The People's Caterer," otherwise Holland (who sometimes even audaciously billed himself with Gladstone's popular label, " The People's William " !), was the most extraordinary of all these personages. He impressed me on this manner when I first began to know him personally: that was when I was not quite fifteen. Holland, originally concerned with an "Emporium" in Newington Causeway, soon 'verted to the variety line of business and became assistant, and afterwards co-manager, with William Sweasey, of Weston's Music Hall, afterwards the Royal and now the Holborn Empire.

When I first met William late in 1868 he had just become manager of the still-surviving, if somewhat "screen"-ish, Canterbury Music Hall. Here he succeeded Charles Morton. Morton had run that amusement temple (so long known, from its pictures, as "The Academy Over the Water") from 1848 in partnership with his brother-in-law, Frederick Stanley, head of the famous firm of theatrical and variety solicitors, Stanley, Woodhouse and Hedderwick. I knew Stanley until his death some years ago, and always found him like his brother-in-law, Morton, the true embodiment of a Fine Old English Gentleman.

William the Wonderful had not been long at the Canterbury before he started in connection therewith what was thenadays regarded as a startling "stunt," and (N. B.) Holland was the most stuntful entertainment purveyor I have ever met. Perhaps the nearest approach to W. H. in these "bold advertisement" gags—although in a smaller way—was my dear old, ever-alert advertiser, friend George Belmont (born Blanchett).

Holland's first big "boom" at the Canterbury was his engagement of the then enormously popular "Lion Comique," George Leybourne, at a very swollen salary for those days, namely, at the rate of £1,500 per annum.

Holland, in fact, boomed the Canterbury sky-high, laughing to scorn the competition of the then new music-hall, Gatti's ("in the road"), nearly opposite William's amusement temple. He e'en pooh-poohed the crescendo rivalry of the South London Music Hall (locally called "The South" for short), which had thus converted out of a Roman Catholic place of worship!

During a most remarkable five years' management—or sole lesseeship—of the Surrey Theatre, where his variety engagements were chiefly confined to his fine pantomime productions, the irrepressible and ubiquitous People's Caterer also undertook a vast and largely variety enterprise. In point of fact, he ran the North Woolwich Gardens!

Here, as at the Surrey, William was assisted by his brother Charles as Ruler of the "Refreshments." At those then celebrated pleasure gardens he presented many "mammoth spectacles," as he called them. In these gigantic productions, William mostly worked in the splendours of "10,000 additional fairy lamps," and always ended with "a gorgeous display of fireworks."

In fact, Holland, who never believed in spoiling the ship for a few thousand pounds' worth of tar, did things on princely—not to say, kingly—fashion at North Woolwich, always sandwiching daily with his alfresco and indoor attractions sundry "grand spectacular ballets," "marvellous aquatic performances," and all the best and brightest variety turns and acts of the period.

But, alas, at North Woolwich Gardens William Holland suffered (as Charles Morton always suffered there) from a persistant foe, a relentless rival, namely, the Rain God!

It would seem almost incredible were I to attempt to give an idea of the countless occasions on which Holland's shows (and "returns") were ruined by what Mr. Mantalini would call "the demnition moist" state of the weather. In fact, by the awful downpours which either kept patrons away or so damped and depressed them that they vowed never again to seek entertainment in those continually sodden "gardens."

So, often indeed, was Impresario Holland thus foiled and frustrated by these waterspouts that ere long, in making announcements of old friend William's North Woolwich shows, in the then young *Referee*, etc., I mostly took care to add, by way of cautionary tag, "Jupiter Pluvius permitting."

The dauntless William, however, (adopting this "tag") continued to "put forth the tender leaves of hope"—until at last stern fate downed him—at all events, in the North Woolwich part of that district, which a more than usually observant poet has described as "England—Where it rains!"

Yet he poured forth programme after programme, production after production, of the most vast and varied kind, always adding at the end of each printed bill or poster, "Your obedient caterer, William Holland."

One of the most remarkable ventures of Holland's was his taking of Covent Garden Opera House in the mid-'eighties and running it as a circus-cum-music-hall. Here he presented an entertainment quite on his gigantic North Woolwich Gardens lines, and, of course, without needing to pray (as it were) against rain!

At Covent Garden, Holland put on several artistes then new to London. These included the late lovely wire-walker, billed as the Beautiful Jessica (who subsequently became the wife of Joe O'Gorman). Another artiste whom William introduced to the British boards at that theatre was that fine and not yet beaten conjuror, the great Cinquevalli. Another courageous, but, alas, not too cashful, venture of Holland's was his running of that huge building, the Royal Albert Palace, Battersea Park, on the banks of the more or less silvery Thames. He speedily made things hum there, but this amusement temple was a little too swagger for the local hard-working music-hall goers, and was rather too far out of the way for the general London amusement patron. And so it dwindled—quite undeservedly, certainly, through no fault or neglect on the part of the intensely hard-working Holland!

A few months before the outbreak of the Worst of Wars, in fact, in the early summer of 1914, a good deal of enthusiastic Press comment was called forth by what was regarded as the great novelty of giving a big variety show in a specially prepared music-hall aboard ship! This was given at the launching of the huge Cunarder called "Aquitania," then described as "Britain's Largest Liner."

I was present at this entertainment amidships, which was presented by Moss' Empires, Ltd., and directed by its then managing director, Frank Allen. The artistes included George M. Saker (as musical director), George Robey, Vesta Tilley (afterwards Lady de Frece), Violet Essex, Arthur Prince, John Tiller's Eight Sunshine Girls, Barclay Gammon, David Devant and R. G. Knowles.

I have good cause to remember that variety show afloat, for on quitting it alone on a tender, and disembarking at the Liverpool landing stage, I found all that town in a state of awful grief and horror at the news just then received of the wreck of the "Empress of Ireland." Nearly all the crew and many of the passengers were Liverpool people. My own grief was concerned with the fact that two of the drowned passengers were my dearly loved young friends, Lawrence Irving and his wife, Mabel Hackney.

Putting aside this tragic happening, however, it is both necessary and just to tell you that more than thirty years before that "Aquitania" variety entertainment given at the mouth of the Mersey, William, "The People's Obedient Caterer," started a similar show, and what is more, he started it on the Main—or Ocean itself! And, characteristically, he selected for his Floating Music-Hall and General Amusement Temple, the vastest vessel he could find—that then monster of the deep—the "Great Eastern!"

Despite sundry failures, William Holland had many big successes. In most cases, however, he profited but little himself. The seat of my ever-enthusiastic old friend William's work was always in his heart—never in his pocket! In fact, he had a perfect genius for making money—for other people!

Good-hearted, breezy, ever-optimistic "Bill" Holland, spent his last years at Blackpool, where his great and successful ventures, both in the huge entertainment line and also municipally, caused it to be said of him then, and ever since, that he "made Blackpool." After all his vast variety and other output, he died at the height of his powers—aged fifty-eight.

These few mems, personal mems and experiences, of a most remarkable and many-sided manager, may be of some use in stirring up researchers in the future. It is certainly strange that so little has been written of such a man as William Holland.

CHAPTER VII

Arthur Roberts—Arthur Roberts meets James Fawn—Marie Lloyd—Her artistic gaiety and her golden heart—Arthur Lloyd and Jolly Nash—J. H. Stead and " The Perfect Cure "—The Music-Hall War.

Mr. John Roberts, afterwards, Mr. Arthur J. Roberts, but later (and still) Arthur Roberts, was a young amateur comic singer when I first knew him. He was about twenty-one, and was in business in the City. In those days he always wore a little black moustache and imperial and red tie, which in later years would have made him look very much the Socialist which he *isn't*.

He used to come and see me from time to time when he was chortling on certain nights a week, especially on Saturdays, at the Town Hall, Shoreditch, and similar local and temporary (yea and e'en " Temperance ") temples of amusement. Arthur then used to tell me how he longed to be a full-blown professional, and I am afraid I broke, or helped to break, his amateur status by causing him to be engaged at Carter Street, Walworth, the Theatre Royal, Greenwich, and one or two similar places, where I was strutting and fretting as an alleged low-comedian.

I got the then Arthur J. Roberts the swollen salary of half-a-guinea a night. He retaliated for this kindness by playing me " off the stage." Although I was acting leading low-comedy parts (plus stage management) and Arthur sang between our pieces, the amount of laughter which he received, compared to that meted out to me, was so lavish and insistent that my father (a very kind man) told me that I had made a great mistake in causing the engagement of such a really funny fellow to run against myself !

Later I retaliated on Mr. A. J. Roberts by writing him his first original song—no, it wasn't the one in which he made his professional name, but quite another sort of song—for which he retaliated by paying me 7s. 6d. !

In after years I revenged myself upon him by writing one of his most successful burlesques and four or five of his skitlets. But as this vengeful business occurred in the theatres, it does not call for further comment in these variety stories.

It will be remembered by all who know anything at all of music-hall matters that the song which made Arthur's fame had the refrain :—

> "If I was only long enough, a soldier I would be,
> And fight for my country and be revenged on she,"

and so on. And thereby hangs a tale.

Some time after Roberts started this pathetic ditty, a half a century ago, he chanced to go to Day's Music-Hall, Birmingham, on a starring engagement. After opening in one of his general songs, the orchestra struck up the opening bars of "If I was only long enough," but presently when about to make his entrance for that song, he was stopped by the resident manager, who said, "Mr. Roberts, you mustn't sing that song here."

"Why not ?" said Roberts. "It is my own song."

"Never mind," replied the manager. "You are not going to do it on this stage."

"But there is no harm in it," added Roberts. "Besides, it is the song by which I am chiefly known, and, of course, I shall sing it."

"If you do," retorted the manager, "I will have the curtain rung down upon you. I am not going to have any disturbance in this house."

"Disturbance !" echoed Roberts.

"Yes," said the boss. "Joe Lawrence, the nigger, came here last week, and sang your song on his head ! Now, as you cannot do that," he continued, "our Brums will only guy you, so just you cut it out."

"And," said Roberts, "I had to cut it."

All who know anything about Joe Lawrence know that he did some of his songs upon his head. Also that he was the father of Lawrence Barclay and Vesta Victoria.

A couple of years or so after Arthur started in "the halls" he 'verted to the so-called "legit.," but anon he returned to his first love, and increased his popularity therein. During his early time in the theatres he went to Drury Lane, where, in a pantomime which Gus Harris had stocked chock-full of variety people, he (Arthur) met James (or "Jimmy") Fawn.

In due course this comical couple took to duetting in the halls, especially at the Pav., and therein they warbled some few numbers which were (to use a phrase invented by Roberts) "very near the knuckle."

Indeed, as the irrepressible Arthur will tell you even now, the pair very often got into trouble and had to be warned by the authorities.

But as Arthur said to me a week or two ago, "All that is past; I am now a reformed character."

Speaking of the reformation of Roberts, here is another little tale.

One night A. R. gravely informed me, after a long spell of Pelican-Clubbing, that he intended to give up these long nights, which lasted till milk-time in the morning. In short, that he was going to turn over a new leaf, go to bed earlier, and take to having a constitutional before breakfast.

Arthur kept his word, and actually *did* go home *one* night, and, rising at early morn, left his Maida Vale mansion and went for a spin round the park.

On returning for breakfast, he was met at his outer portals by the usual policeman, who, knowing Arthur's strange nocturnal habits, and therefore, of course, reckoning that he had just come home, said very respectfully, "Good*night*, Mr. Roberts!"

"This," said Roberts, "was all the encouragement I got for new-leaf turning, so all that was left to me was to relapse into my bold bad Bohemianism."

The above-named association of Roberts and Fawn was really a very happy and hilarious one, as naturally two such real humorists, so unlike in method, were able to bring down the house between them, as, indeed, either of them could do separately.

When I first knew Fawn (who was born Simmons), he had just left off being a blacked-up turn, and had come to the Old Vic, as first low-comedian to Manager Joe Cave.

Although "Jimmy" was then only about twenty-two, he was a wonderfully clever fellow. Not only did he play all the low-comedy leads, making an especial hit in Cave's remarkable revival of "Tom and Jerry"; he also sang between the pieces when required, which was pretty often.

Fawn's versatility was further proved by the fact that, after another course in the halls, he made a great hit in leading low-comedy characters in the most famous old comedies at the Royal Aquarium Theatre, Westminster, with such stars as those late acting giants, William Farren (father of the present clever

William), the famous Miss Marie Litton, Lionel Brough, Mrs. Stirling, and even that greatest of actors, Samuel Phelps.

As to Arthur, he voltefaced from time to time between the theatres and the halls. In the latter he gave many a remarkable show, not only in comic singing, but in pantomimic or silent acting. One of his finest variety stage feats was his side-splitting burlesque of the quick-change artiste, Biondi. In this turn, Roberts's quick-changing was quite as quick as that of the Italian whom he skitted.

As a master of lightning retort, I know of no one to beat Roberts.

It was not long ago that the eccentric Arthur and I, standing at the Cavour Bar and talking over old times (with a little soda), a couple of Jewish-looking co-refreshers began pointing at him and arguing excitedly. At last one of these anxious Hebrews plunged between us and said, "I beg your pardon. Mithter Roberth; my friend and I have been arguing about your age, and I say you *must* be seventy odd."

"No, I *mustn't*," flashed Roberts.

Dear, droll old Arthur, now one of the youngest in manner of "The Veterans of Variety," recently returned to the Pav., it will be remembered, to appear in revue under that enthusiastic theatrical and variety student and alert impresario, Charles Blake Cochran. It so happened that in the latest revue in which he appeared there Arthur was cast for a character in which he entered at eight o'clock and finished about ten minutes past!

Arthur and I were colloguing as to this revue the day after its production, when he made the following remark:

"I hope this revue will be a success," said he, "but, if it should turn out to be a failure, no one can blame me for it. *I can prove an alibi.*"

Good old Arthur! Long may he wave—and warble!

"MARIE"

The lamented passing of England's greatest variety comedienne—meaning, of course, Matilda Alice Victoria Wood—otherwise Marie Lloyd, evoked so much Press comment that it would almost seem that very little more could be written about that not easily replaced idol—or goddess—of the "halls."

Knowing dear Marie, however, as I knew her from her "coming out" on the variety boards at the age of fifteen until what might well be called her premature end, I feel that I can impart some intimate details of her meteoric career, and especially of her inner life not yet made public.

Her outside family life and her numerous and, in some cases, remarkably clever professional relations are well known. Her father and mother, Mr. and Mrs. Wood, Johnny Wood, Daisy Wood, Alice Lloyd, Bella Lloyd and the rest have all been set forth as far as is necessary in the various obituaries of dear old Marie. Much of this chronological matter, however, was really forced into the public ken by something with which I had a great deal to do. This is how it happened.

Marie Lloyd, who made her dêbut at the Grecian Assembly Rooms, in 1885—when she was fifteen—started so early and became celebrated so soon that many of her public admirers, not knowing her real age, were led to think that she was much older than she was.

This same mistaken idea as to the real age of this or that stage favourite has often been repeated, notably in the respective cases of Ellen Terry, Mrs. Kendal, Nellie Farren, Fred Griffiths and Vesta Tilley (Lady de Frece) all of whom began to tread the boards, or to sniff the footlights, in very early infancy.

And so it fell out that before Marie was, say, five-and-twenty, and then ten years a favourite, there were those who asserted to believe that she must be at least fifty! Arguments began to grow rife and far-flung as to Marie's age, and men (and women) began to write to the *Referee* in large numbers, imploring to be told "the real age of Marie Lloyd."

In due course the repetition of the now historic reply in that journal's "Answers to Correspondents" oftentimes to several querists per week, namely, "Miss Marie Lloyd was born February 12, 1870," became quite a joke, and I, the answerer, had to undergo a good deal of chaffing as to that reply's continuous cropping up! There were e'en those, doubtless, who believed—or affected to believe—that I, or we, "worked up" this Marie Lloyd answer in order to cause talk.

As a matter of fact, every answer was strictly genuine. At an early stage in these age questionings, Marie gave me a copy of her birth certificate, although I, of course, knew her exact age. Later these queries as to Marie's age developed abundantly into questions concerning her family, her relations, her real name, etc., all testifying to our dear old friend's tremendous popularity.

When these queries with more of the "family" touch began to increase and multiply, the great little Marie Lloyd called at the *Referee* office one day and told me that she had just had a "brainwave."

Thereupon she dumped down a kind of combined certificate of the respective ages—private names, stage names, etc. of all her family, and begged that that interesting document should be published in the *Referee* for the belief of these insatiable and increasingly sceptical querists.

Herewith please find (as they say in commercial correspondence) copy of same:

COMBINED CERTIFICATE, 1908.

MISS MARIE LLOYD

NOTICE TO ALL

Miss Marie Lloyd has one daughter—and she is not on the stage.

IN ANSWER TO ALL INQUIRIES.

MARIE LLOYD, born February 12, 1870.
The following are her brothers and sisters and their respective ages:
JOHN WOOD (not in the profession), born December 7, 1871.
ALICE LLOYD, born October 20, 1873.
GRACE LLOYD (not in the profession), born October 13, 1875.
DAISY WOOD, born September 15, 1877.
ROSIE LLOYD, born June 5, 1879.
ANNIE WOOD (not in the profession), born June 25, 1883.
SYDNEY WOOD, born April 1, 1885.
MAUD WOOD, born September 25, 1890.

This is final. Will anyone disputing this, kindly apply at Somerset House?

Wood is the family name, Lloyd stage ditto.

Many well remember that some of the smart ditties that our Marie warbled were more or less tinged with squeezes from what the dear girl herself called "the blue bag."

There was really no need whatever (as I often told her) for an artiste so really gifted both in humour and the way of "putting it over," to descend to this ceruleanism of song. Little Marie, however, chucklingly chaffing any of us who rebuked her for what we regarded as a blot upon otherwise wonderful work, was easily persuaded to drop into this thusness by some of her song-writers and certain of her so-called friends.

There came a time at last, however, when even at the "Pav.," where such "shadiness" of song and jest seemed to be encouraged in those days, Marie was "warned" by the management, but not until that management had been "warned" by others, including your humble memoriser.

MARIE LLOYD
(*Photo by Hana*)

Facing page 96

(Your H.M. by the way, had been partly responsible a few years before for an alleged "libel" in the *Referee* against the Pav. management of the period, for allowing sundry songs, wheezes and other matters *not too* conducive to the cause of public morality.)

That "libel" cost the *Referee* a large sum of money by way of "damages and costs." But that "libel" started a campaign for purifying the then often very unpleasant state of the "halls." Moreover, the alleged aggrieved manager afterwards secretly apologised to the *Referee*, and confessed his real reason for bringing that action!

But, dropping digression, let us return to our Marie.

The above-mentioned "warning" from the London Pavilion's manager to Miss Lloyd aroused in her quite a volcano of indignation. She started by denouncing me as partly, if not chiefly, responsible for the sudden moral managerial manifesto, because I had so often rebuked her both in prattle and in print for what I regarded as the one blot on her undoubted genius for true humour and "character" acting.

Marie next declared that she would quit the "halls"—for a time, anyhow—and go on the "regular" stage, and she ended her denunciation of me by demanding that I should try to get her a theatrical engagement at once!

It so fell out that by one of those strange happenings which are, like truth, stranger than fiction, I met a theatrical-minded friend who wanted to embark in a good "spec." I mentioned Marie's wish, and he caught her at one of her "turns" that very night, and at once engaged her at a vast salary to go on tour in a new play which he would write for her.

Who really wrote that play, and how it really came to be written at all, and the strange adventures thereof will appear anon.

In the meantime I must give you some account of a startling eye-opener which our beloved Marie received in administering a decoction from the Blue Bag to a toiling, moiling East End audience.

This is how it happened. Chatting with Marie at the good old Tivoli one day with the lamented manager, Vernon Dowsett, and the happily still surviving Angelo Asher, then the Tiv.'s musical director, her little ladyship said to me: "Chancey" (that was her usual form of addressing me—when she didn't call me something else!) "I'm going to the Paragon next Monday. It's the first time I've ever appeared there. I reckon I shall have to 'lay it on a bit thick' down Whitechapel way, what?"

"My dear girl," I replied, "I marvel at *you*—an East End native—making such a statement to *me*, with all my inside knowledge of East End shows and show-goers."

"Now, speaking from that experience," I continued, "and from the manner in which I have seen Hoxton, Whitechapel and Mile End playgoers and music-hall goers treat 'blue' singers and undressed actresses, I warn you that if you dare to sing at the Paragon any of the very 'shady' songs you are now singing in the West End, that East End audience will balloon you off the stage!"

"My God! What rot you talk," said Marie, "don't be a blinking idiot."

"Righto, dear old friend," quoth I, "we'll leave it at that."

Again, thanks to what my lamented old friend, dramatist Haddon Chambers, called "the long arm of coincidence," on the very Monday when Marie opened at the Paragon I chanced to be in the very near neighbourhood, having been called to see some new dramatic show—Yiddish or Goy—most probably the former, and at about 10 o'clock at night I turned into the Paragon.

As I entered I heard a noise. It was the sound of an audience giving a not too favourable reception to our wonderful little pal. In fact, so unfavourable was it that Marie dashed off in a mixed state of rage and weeping.

Happily she pulled herself together and returned to give one of her cleverest character studies. At once the erstwhile sibilant audience took the brilliant little Marie to their hearts. Indeed, they would hardly let her go!

MY PLAY FOR MARIE

The theatrical starring engagement which Marie Lloyd made me (so to speak) engineer for her started under the management of my friend, whom I mentioned in the previous chapter. I cannot name him, for he would never have his name mentioned, billed, or announced in any way. He "bought her time," as they say in America, for the whole of her variety vacation. After which she was compelled to return to the Halls, as per her contracts.

My mysterious friend also stipulated to write the play in which Marie was to "star." He at once advertised in the *Era* and the *Stage*, setting forth in bold type the attractive statement, "Marie Lloyd to Tour in a New Play."

Naturally, the mere announcement of Marie in such a novel

environment drew dates at once, for her theatrical appearances up to then had been made only in pantomime.

And then a strange thing happened. Week by week rolled by, and Marie's opening date drew closer and closer; but, lo! neither Marie nor the important resident managers who had readily booked her could get any tidings about the play in which she was to tour!

Marie kept worrying me, and I kept worrying her engager for news regarding that eagerly awaited script. But all was silence!

At last, this was the strange outcome. Marie came to me in a volcanic state, and declared that my managerial friend had suddenly brought her *three* plays of his or somebody's. "And," exclaimed Marie, "they all turned out to be blinking Bernhardt plays—all right for Sarah, but no earthly use for Marie!"

An ominous lull then set in for some few days. Next—about a fortnight before Marie's advertised opening date—epistolary and wireful bombs began to be dropped by the provincial managers concerned.

To come to cues, this is what occurred. Exactly a fortnight before that long-booked opening date, I might have been observed rehearsing a new burlesque of mine, called "Julius Tree-Sir," for the Moore and Burgess Mohawk Minstrels, when suddenly there dashed into the theatre the play-promising (and-now-perspiring) engager of Marie Lloyd.

Expressing thanksgiving that he had traced me, he called me aside, and said: "Old Friend, you must help me—you alone can help me out of this awful difficulty. *You must write this play for Marie Lloyd.*"

"What! Are you dotty?" I replied. "Why, Marie's starting date is a fortnight hence! You must find something ready made. No new play can be written, rehearsed, and produced in such time for such a Star!"

The upshot of it all was that, as my friend was (and is) one of the noblest-hearted of men, and being anxious to help little Marie out of this terrible difficulty, I agreed to do the best I could in the time.

And so I wrote that play for Marie, scene by scene, and song by song, at a series of day and night rehearsals, with the composers, scene-painters, dress designers, chorus, etc., by my side, and engaging people as I went along. Anyhow, we got through! And on Monday, a fortnight after I had been roped in (as it were), Marie Lloyd and "Her London Company" started her tour with my dear old lovable friend, E. H. Bull, at the Grand Theatre, Wolverhampton.

The music was by quaint George Le Brunn (who, as usual, kept leaving his core of my lyrics at sundry "houses of call" en route), also by Gustave Chaudoir (maestro of the aforesaid Minstrels). Likewise I dropped in a few numbers by a young beginner who insisted on being billed as "Graban." He is now the great composer and conductor, Dr. Granville Bantock!

I almost forgot to add (in case of need for reference) that the name of this musical mixture—which is still my property—was "The A B C Girl; or Flossie the Frivolous."

Marie played an A B C Tea Shop Girl—who turns out to be somebody of note—and those two brilliant and still surviving humorous theatrical and variety players, W. H. Thompson and Marie Wright (sister of Haidee, Huntley, Fred, etc.) were the two broad low comedians.

MARIE'S BOUNDLESS BENEVOLENCE

Now I, like many others, had always known and been impressed by little Marie's unfailing kindness to, and sympathy with, the poor, struggling and the anxious, but during the day and night (and sometimes all night) rehearsals of this hastily improvised play, Marie continually beat even her own record for thoughtfulness, loving kindness, and self-sacrifice. The way in which our ever eccentric little friend and star behaved to the chorus girls and men—the supers and other so-called "minor" people—the manner in which she unswervingly helped them, secretly arranged for food and refreshments, for cabs, etc., in the small hours of the morning, will never be erased from my memory.

Since then, too, and right on to her fatal illness, which robbed the stage of one of its most artistic and most deserving of artistes, Marie Lloyd never lost—but even made—opportunities to help and succour the needy, the starving, and those stricken for death.

In fact, Marie was one of three lady theatrical-cum-variety Stars who not only gave their money lavishly to the poor and the suffering, but who gave (as I well know) active service to such unfortunate folk, by clearing up their poor rooms, or watching by their bedsides, etc.

The other two were Florence St. John and Bessie Bellwood.

And so I come to my last chat with Dear Old Marie! It was at the Cavour Restaurant, and the poor lass was just getting about again after a very severe attack of illness.

"Well, Chancey," said she. "I hope I shall soon be at

work again, for God knows I need it—as you well know, all my oof has gone!"

"My Dear Girl, I don't wonder at it," I replied, "for what money you haven't given to poor pro.'s and others you have been 'bled' of by so-called friends. Anyhow, it will take me a long time to believe that the ceaseless benevolence of such a God-given heart as yours will go unrewarded, even in this world."

Poor Marie was moved to tears, as she patted me on the arm, and said, "That's all right, old pal, I couldn't help wanting to help them that couldn't help themselves! Well, anyhow" (she added with something of her old defiant manner), "I don't intend ever to send round the blinking hat!"

A very little while after that our Beloved (if foolish) Little Friend was called to meet There the real reward for her quenchless charity and self-sacrifice.

The epitaph which reached me from the poor old variety folk at Brinsworth, while I was writing her obituary for certain journals, was a true one. It ran: "The passing of Marie Lloyd robs poor variety artistes of their best and kindest friend."

One of the best epitaphs, however, on the ever unselfish charity of "The Empress of Serio-Comedy" (as she was often billed) was given to me at the end of the week in which she died, by good old Joe Elvin, who has done so much himself for needy pro.'s.

"What ho! Chancey" (he, too, like Marie, always addressed me thus), "this is a blooming sad Saturday night for poor pro.'s, I give yer *my* word! No, Marie, my boy, no little Marie with her little bag, giving out her usual bits of money to the hard-up-'uns! My God! What a Saturday night for *them*, eh, sonny."

Can you beat that for an epitaph on Marie Lloyd!

May God rest her dear soul!

MORE "COMICS"

In the halls of my early days and nights there were numerous gay dogs of more or less "stellar rank" (as they say in the American language). Some went on to long life and others dropped out early—far earlier than most of them need have done had they taken reasonable care of themselves.

One of the most notable of stars was Arthur Lloyd, who, like his father before him, had been on the dramatic stage. Although Arthur Lloyd was really a clever "character" comic singer, droll alike in acting and in dialect, he clung obstinately to the old-time pro.'s moustache of G. V. Brooke, Charles Dillon and Sims Reeves pattern.

He had an excellent voice, and mostly he selected, or had composed for him by Alfred Lee and others, some excellent tunes wherein to exercise it.

The most popular of Lloyd's songs included "The Dark Girl dressed in Blue," "Not for Joe," "Immensikoff," "Madame Rachel" (meaning the lady who professed to make her all too trustful feminine clients "Beautiful for Ever") "Bandy-Legged Borachio" (who had a large moustachio), "The Beauty of Brixton," "Seringa-patam-tam-tam," and a quaint yokel yodel, the refrain of which ran thus:

> "I fancy I can see her now"
> Down at Farmer Fenn's,
> Picking up the new laid-eggs from the cow
> And milking the cocks and hens.

Arthur Lloyd married that sweetest of serios and dancers and dainty little colleen, Katty King, daughter of that tremendous organ-voiced tragedian, T. C. King, who so long raised the roof even of Old Drury by his thunderous tones. Arthur and Katty toured with their own musical party for some years. Then little Katty died, still very young, and good old Arthur anon passed away. With him passed one of the very best artistes that ever chortled in the halls of harmony. Another fine and extremely comic singer, one who died some years before Lloyd, was W. T. (or "Billy") Critchfield. When I heard "Billy" (as I did many times, whatever he chanced to sing), there were certain ditties which his audiences always demanded of him. One was a kind of Chelsea Pensioner's song which "rubbed it in" as regards certain military authorities of the period. Another very elastic topical song was called "Freedom of Opinion." This lyric was set to a tune, used for a good many other ditties of the day—including another topical one called "So said Mr. Johnson." Critchfield sang it in the garb of a cobbler, and I assure you that it was one of the most rousing and rollicking topical songs of the thousands I have heard.

Jolly Nash was another of the most popular comics of the days that were earlier. My earliest remembrance of him was at the Strand Musick Hall (they were very particular as to the "k" in the "music"). Many people have never even heard of this hall. In fact, though it was quite a gorgeous resort for those somewhat pot-house music-hall times, it didn't last long to be seen or heard about. It achieved one useful purpose, however, it served as the site of the Gaiety Theatre!

Nash having cultivated a most infectious laugh—or series of

chuckles—became known as the "Laughing Comic," and had carols fitted to his cachinnations. Some of these ditties lasted for years. They included "I couldn't help laughing, it tickled Me So!" "The Little Fat Grey Man," and "Ho! Ho! Ho! He! He! He!"

"Jolly" Nash, as he was always subsequently billed, became quite a favourite with the then Prince of Wales—afterwards King Edward the Seventh—and on several occasions he chirruped and chortled in the presence of Royalty with Vance and other "stars" of the day.

A comic singer, who after a comparatively unremarkable career, suddenly became the "sensation" of his time, was J. H. Stead. His sudden and strange rise was due to having found a song called "The Perfect Cure." This was written by one of the cleverest, but most poorly-paid music-hall bards of the period, namely, Fred Perry. The air belonged to a previous successful (and very sultry) song called "The Monkey and the Nuts."

In this "Cure" song Stead, garbed in a strange streaked tight-fitting dress surmounted by a high fool's cap, did a sort of jumping dance—and jumped so many times throughout the verses and "chorus" that the habitués of the "halls" used to bet as to how many times Stead would jump up and down per turn.

Stead's success was phenomenal, and his song was sung and the air whistled all over each town in which he appeared. When at last he retired, it was thought that, although salaries were by no means the size they became in later years, he had saved a comfortable "little bit."

Some variety chroniclers have stated that Stead left "quite a fortune." Other chroniclers have asserted that he died in poverty. Neither statement is correct! Here is the true story of the end of "Perfect Cure" Stead.

Some months before Stead died he wrote, or induced some friends to write, to me at the *Referee*—which is always running "appeals" of one kind or another—and requesting that we would help him in this way, as he was in a sadly needy state!

An appeal was made at once, and in rolled the donations. Very soon we got several hundreds of pounds.

Suddenly it was discovered that poor old "Jemmy" Stead, who had evidently gone off his head, had been secretly hiding his money away like a miser, and that he really had a good many hundred pounds already!

In fact, it was found that the old "Cure" had quite enough

to see him "through." And he went "through" very soon after.

Of course, we, the fund-raisers, returned the donations so kindly sent.

Another "comic," and a really comic little chap he was, was "Billy" Randall, one of those who never changed their dress, but did all his warbling and wheezing in a frock-coat and top hat.

Night after night at the Sun, Knightsbridge, the Raglan, the Canterbury, the Britannia, Deacon's, the "Mo," etc., did I hear little Billy give off his droll ditties.

Randall's cleverest songs included "The Charming Young Widow I Met in the Train," "Two in the Morning," "The Hole in the Shutter," and "The Goose Club" (all about the goose in which the winner, failing to carve it, "danced a hornpipe on its back, and it bore it like a Briton!").

Three other of Billy Randall's domestic songs were of that minutely biographical and circumstantial kind so common in the "halls" of the time. They were entitled respectively "Sarah's Young Man," "Bob Fubbs, or the Love Chase," and "Isabella with the Gingham Umbrella."

Towards the end of Billy Randall's long stage innings (sometimes in duets with his "serio" daughter Polly) he chanced to meet another Randall, who had just begun making hits in the halls. This was our dear old friend Harry Randall, who, happily, is still with us, only writing comic songs instead of singing them.

It was then that the veteran "Billy" Randall sternly denounced the young Harry for daring to use the surname Randall, which he (Billy) had made so renowned.

Whereupon Harry replied very respectfully, "I'm sorry you feel so upset about it, sir, but really I can't help it. Randall happens to be my own name, and I don't think it is yours!"

Three of the most popular early comics of the rorty or slangster type were Teddy Mosedale, Hyram Travers, and Walter Laburnum (otherwise Joe Davis). Teddy had an excellent singing voice, a deucedly funny "dial," and the nimblest of feet. I have often seen him dance a jig on a pocket handkerchief placed on the stage and never ruffle it.

Mosedale had a very bright and clever daughter in the halls, namely, Amy Lyster, who married the popular mimic, George Fairburn.

Dear little old Hyram Travers was long popular, especially as a "patter"-singer of back slang and rhyming slang songs. Like Vance, Mosedale, and Laburnum, he was a costerial caroller long before the coming of those other renowned exponents of such argot "studies," the late Albert Chevalier and the still surviving Gus Elen.

Walter Laburnum (Jewish born) came out at McDonald's in Hoxton, and returned there over and over again while the hall was there to return to. At first he adopted the method of George Leybourne, whom he resembled strongly in his fine appearance, although his features were heavier.

Three other deservedly popular comics of the early halls were Fred French, Henri Clark, and Victor Liston. All three had been actors—in fact, Henri (like Sam Cowell) had been e'en in grand opera. Fred French had, I remember, several very striking ditties, including "The Wreck off London Bridge."

Fred could show true pathos when needed, as was proved by his rendering of a very clever "broken-down swell" song called "When These Old Clothes Were New."

Victor Liston, who used to be billed as "the Robson of the Music-halls," was also very strong in pathetic acting, as was evidenced for years by his singing a very touching song called "Shabby Genteel"? Henri Clark's chief success was in quite a dramatic mock scena entitled "The Mad Butcher."

I will finish this mixed bag of celebrated artistes of the old-time halls—with all of whom I associated intimately—by mentioning two very smart "character" and chiefly costerial comic singers and dancers, namely, Nat Ogden and Tom Kirby. Their "material" was not particularly noteworthy until suddenly they both broke out with a song apiece all about a workhouse casual ward. And thereby hangs a strange little story. Towards the latter part of last century's sixties a very alert young journalist named James Greenwood, engaged upon the then new and recently defunct *Pall Mall Gazette*, wrote a special article concerning the Lambeth Workhouse Casual Ward. Greenwood, having disguised himself as a starving, ragged tramp, contrived to pass through that Union's still grim portals as a "casual." But see a strange story later.

THE MUSIC HALL "WAR"

Before making my exit after this "Memories" turn of mine, it is fitting, methinks, that I should chronicle some personal experiences of that remarkable and now historic volcanic variety eruption, which soon became described as "The Music-Hall War!"

I do not propose to give any specially definite details of the causes and consequences of the many battles which raged in halls and streets during that excited campaign—especially as "twenty years have elapsed"—as they say on playbills.

This brief, but battle-ful, campaign started in January, 1907, and all concerned (including your humble) were speedily in the thick of it. In fact, it soon fell out that just after the opening episode at a certain suburban theatre, then temporarily turned into a variety hippodrome, I was requisitioned by the more moderate mal-contents on both sides to act as sort of ambassador to the then young variety (and now very distinguished) manager, who was then running that transformed variety house.

This manager was alleged to have precipitated the dissensions and discontents by delaying to carry out a certain verbal promise he had made to the artistes whom he had engaged for that enterprise.

That young magnate "received me most politely," as poor Fragson used to warble. He told me, however, that he didn't see his way to carry out that promise, and that as a matter of fact he had changed his mind and would not meet the artistes concerned.

For a long time I remained with my (in my opinion) ill-advised friend, and implored him over and over again to reconsider the decision he had just pronounced. Like Sheridan's Governor of Tilbury Fort, however, that young magnate was "adamant." So, alas! there was no help for it but for me to come away and duly and dolefully report the failure of my pacific mission.

And lo! in due course the artistes arose, and struck first against my young friend's halls, and then against those of several of his friends and his relations, who thought fit, rightly or wrongly, to support him.

The campaign now began in real earnest. The Variety Artistes' Federation, which had started about a year before, and *The Performer*, which started a little later, very naturally supported the music-hall favourites and the smaller turns in their demands for various improved conditions. These conditions included, it will be remembered, payment for the additional and fast-increasing matinées; for the better remuneration for playing twice-nightly, instead of once; the reduction or betterment of the then over-stringent Barring Clause, and the amendment or abolition of the "split" and double commission scandal. Also the stoppage of the then far too prevalent transference of artistes from one hall to another, and even from one town to another often far off, directly they had started to fulfil their respective dates, and they had taken their respective "digs."

All these truly necessary suggestions of improved conditions were duly set forth, first in a Memorial and afterwards in a very definitely worded Charter. For a while the then Mr. (now Sir), Oswald Stoll, at that time representing the Moss Empires, Ltd., was the only manager who took the trouble to reply to the Memorial. Of course, he replied from the managerial side. He did so, however, in his usual temperate, commonsensible manner.

In due course the other variety magnates, including George Adney Payne, Henri Gros, Henry Sutton, and other responsible chiefs, very naturally, I suppose, joined the anti-Artistes battalion.

Then things began to rule very lively. The Tivoli, the Pavilion, the Oxford, and other important variety theatres were "struck" against. In fact, all manner of variety houses and music-halls were "proclaimed," so to speak, and were picketed by artistes and variety stage folk of all kinds.

These insurgents were led by the leading stars, who orated at meetings not only within doors, but also out in the streets from lorries, cabs, and e'en from the kerb!

Prominent among these speakers working day and night for the artistes were our dear little friend Marie Lloyd, Wal Pink, and W. H. Clemart.

Among the happily still-surviving workers in the V.A.F. cause were: Joe O'Gorman, Joe Elvin, Frank Gerald, George Leyton, Gus Elen, Monte Bayley, R. A. Roberts, Charles Coborn, W. H. McCarthy, Harry Mountford, Harry Blake and George Gray. The last named is at the moment of writing prospering amain financially and filmatically in the Channel Islands.

The picketed halls were in what Touchstone calls "a parlous state," for the time being. At those places which were kept open, strange little programmes were provided, made up of all sorts and conditions of comparatively minor turns, aided and abetted by sundry concert artistes, and even by many a raw beginner. In point of fact, on going round these stricken halls night by night, I found most of them as desolate as the strange Ossian's Halls of Balclutha!

As for me, I was kept busy, not only journalistically, but also oratorically, for I was asked to speak at many a meeting, where, I am proud to say, I was welcomed cheerily and in most friendly fashion by both sides of the disputants.

And not only so. If you will kindly pardon a touch of not utterly unreasonable egotism, I will add that I was the first person asked by both sides to act as arbitrator !

Of course, I declined this great honour, and suggested that someone much more expert in arbitration, and especially one not at all connected with either wing of the disputants as I was, should be approached for this most delicate post. As will be remembered, this pacific duty was undertaken by that brilliant arbitrator, George R. Askwith (then acting for the Board of Trade), who has long been a very distinguished member of the (up to now) still existing House of Lords.

" The War " finished in about a month, after many meetings of what was called the Conciliation Board, which meetings I was asked to attend from time to time. This C.B. consisted of Adney Payne and his son Walter, Oswald Stoll, Henri Gros, T. E. Browne (a very expert lawyer), Wal Pink, Isaac Mitchell (a very commonsensible trades unionist), the then Mr. (and afterwards Sir) Henry Tozer, Henry Sutton, and Arthur Roberts. The last-named conciliator not only made many useful business suggestions, but added to the proceedings what Lord Beaconsfield would call " the spirit of gay wisdom ! "

In due course, Arbitrator Askwith (one of the noblest of such officials I have ever met) issued his Award. Also, in due course, we all celebrated what was very properly, not to say poetically, called Peace Night !

Alas ! there were some few managers, especially in the provinces, who sought, more or less, to evade this most just and sensible Award. Eventually, however, things simmered down, and the many favourite " turns " went on turning in tip-top fashion.

Again, as for me, the only other thing I was able to do on behalf of the artistes and others with whom I am proud to have been so long associated was to engineer (some time later) and to be greatly responsible for the licensing of agents. In fact, I was summoned to the L.C.C. on several occasions to show cause why this licensing should materialise, and I showed it !

In reviewing the above-mentioned temporarily troublous times it is sad to think that so many who were concerned therewith, both artistes and managers, have passed away.

Dear little Marie Lloyd ; good old Wal Pink (straight as a die) ; poor Clemart ; the impulsive but noble-natured Henri Gros ; the quaint, quizzical and generous Henry Tozer ; brisk and business-like Henry Sutton ; the breezy, outspoken Adney Payne—all gone, and all deeply lamented.

As to my old friend, George Adney Payne, I would like to add a little story, one which I shall always remember with the deepest thanksgiving.

It was on the very morning of the day in which Mr. Payne met with the accident which so soon led to his death that, in wishing me good-bye after lunching with him and several other friends at the Adelaide Gallery, he called me aside and spoke the following words:

"Chance, my boy," he said, "we have known each other many years, and many a time you and I have disagreed very strongly. You have often pitched into me as to this or that show or view of mine, and we did not see 'eye to eye' at all over the music-hall strikes. But to-day I want you to know this, that however much we have disagreed on certain points we will try to drop that attitude. I think you know I have been honest and straight, and I am d——d well sure *you* have."

Those were the last words George Adney Payne ever spoke to me. Could there be a nobler or more touching farewell than this? I think not! Anyhow, it will always be a memorable one for me.

Chapter VIII

Jenny Hill—" The Vital Spark "—Charles Godfrey and his songs—Chirgwin—" The White-Eyed Kaffir "—Some Coster Carollers—Albert Chevalier—Vesta Tilley—Some Irish Comic Singers

Although it was not regarded as *de rigeur*—nor indeed was it at all desirable—to take one's feminine folk to the music-halls of the earlier times, yet a great many ladies were engaged in these frivolous resorts.

Most of the ladies thus engaged acted as " duettists "—that is, as partner either to a male or a female singer. There were scores of these pairs of " duettists " in those early halls. In fact, the professional advertising columns of the journals of that period teemed with them. The other damsels who were in the halls were what were known as " serios "—which was short for " serio-comic-singers."

About that time, or a little later, there began to appear fitfully at sundry London " free-and-easies " a child " serio "—a quick, sharp, keen-eyed Cockney little damsel, named Jenny Hill.

Jenny made her professional dêbut—for a shilling or two per night—at the Doctor Johnson Concert Room—a very ordinary pot-house sing-song in Bolt Court, Fleet Street. This " Haunt of Harmony " disappeared from Music-halldom nearly sixty years ago, after becoming a celebrated resort for racing men, known as the Albert Club.

Jenny Hill, like most other hall-folk of her time, especially the beginners, sang other people's songs for a while. Just when she was reaching young womanhood, however, she chanced to come into the ken of a very alert and busy music-hall agent of the day, one Maurice de Frece, father of the present Sir Walter de Frece, M.P., who married that other great star of the halls, Vesta Tilley.

Little Jenny was speedily booked by Maurice de Frece at the Oxford, the Canterbury, and other leading halls of the period;

and just as speedily did Jenny " make good." In fact, from that early chance of hers to the end of her five-and-twenty years' career, Jenny Hill was rightly regarded as the most humorous and most artistically " realistic " comic and pathetic singer on the music-hall boards.

She was soon labelled " The Vital Spark," (Didcott was the labeller) and Jenny fully acted up to this label of Vitality and Sparkishness.

Jenny Hill's principal song successes included " 'Arry " (written by the late veteran music-hall bard, E. V. Page, author of so many such " hits ") and " The Boy in the Gallery " —a ditty also warbled by Nellie Power, and later on by Marie Lloyd, when she was very young.

Miss Hill (how that old friend of mine would laugh me to scorn at addressing her as " Miss ") had several other and somewhat more domestic song hits.

The husband-nagging, semi-pathetic chorus of one of these was as follows:

" I've been a good woman to *you*,
And the neighbours all know that it's true ;
You go to the pub,
And you " blue " the kids' grub,
But I've been a good woman to you."

Another of Jenny's " husband " ballads had the following " sad story " refrain:

" He's out on the fuddle, with a lot of his pals,
Out on the fuddle, along with other gals ;
He's always on the fuddle,
While I'm in such a muddle,
But I mean to have a legal separ-a-a-tion ! "

At the height of her music-hall fame, Jenny Hill was engaged by the late astute theatrical manager John Hollingshead for the Gaiety Theatre, where for a time she played the Great Little Nellie Farren's " line of business."

Some of us wondered how the saucy little Jenny—who could be (and so often was) " rather sultry " in the halls—would get on without what we used to call her " blue bag " on appearing at that famous West End theatre.

Jenny contrived to conceal her cerulean method at the Gaiety, and although she seemed to chafe under these restrictions, she did her new burlesque work like the real little artiste she was. She soon felt, however, that she would rather be a star " on her own" again in the halls. So back to the halls she went, and again shone under the title which she couldn't use in her Gaiety environment, namely, "The Vital Spark."

In her later years Jenny Hill made her mark as a really intense pathetic—as well as a quaint—comic actress. This feat she achieved in sundry dramatic sketches, but especially in a very successful specimen called "The Little Stowaway."

This sketch was dramatised by Fred Bowyer (the still-surviving author of that delightful recent dainty fairy play, "The Windmill Man") from Clement Scott's poem, "The Stowaway" and a very effective little drama "The Little Stowaway," was, running at the Canterbury, the Paragon, and other variety houses for months at a time. Jenny Hill's performance of the name-part was wont to hold vast audiences spellbound!

My little friend and fellow-worker, Jenny, finished up at about forty-seven years of age in 1897.

She had been ill for a long while before she had to give up her work. And no wonder, for, like so many women in her profession (and out of it), she had been very unlucky and unhappy in her two or three marriages. She left a daughter, who did some excellent variety work under the stage name of Peggy Pryde.

To sum up, it may safely be said that no "serio" or "serio-comedienne" in the history of the "Halls" has ever beaten—or even equalled—Jenny Hill, alias "The Vital Spark."

CHARLIE GODFREY

Like his predecessor and sometime contemporary G. H. Macdermott, Charles Godfrey had been an actor on the so-called "regular" theatres before he appeared in variety. When I first knew Godfrey, he started stage-playing under his own name, Paul Lacey, in the East End theatres. For some few years he was what we used to call in those days a "general utility man" at the Pavilion Theatre, Whitechapel, under that splendid producer and stage-mentor, the late Isaac Cohen—father of the still surviving Lady Lyons, widow of the brilliant organiser, Sir Joseph Lyons, the chief founder of Lyons & Co., Ltd.

Godfrey's salary at the Pavilion was generally about a pound a week—rising to twenty-five shillings or so. For this very unswollen salary Charlie put in a lot of work, mostly of a very intelligent, if not exactly of an epoch-making kind. Often Charlie played "Hamlet" and "Sweeney Todd" in one night!

It was not long before young Godfrey felt the call of the "halls,"

JENNY HILL
(*Photo by Sarony*)

Facing page 112

and he joined them at what was for him a very fortunate time. Those places just then had a plentiful lack of dramatic descriptive singers, and Charles, full of force—not to say fire—soon seemed quite a *rara avis* on the music-hall stage, when he wouldn't have shined overmuch in the "regular" theatres.

His earliest great hit in the halls was, of course, in that soon phenomenally successful sketch entitled "On Guard."

Godfrey's vigorous acting of the neglected old soldier in this sketch really raised vast audiences to an almost incredible pitch of enthusiasm. Alike in London and the Provinces have I seen him move the patrons of the "halls" to volcanic excitement and to thunders of applause!

This was especially the case when he came to the part where the now starving old tramp warrior applied for a night's shelter at the workhouse casual ward.

"Be off, you tramp!" exclaims the harsh janitor. "You are not wanted here!"

"No!" thunders the tattered veteran. "I am not wanted *here*! But at Balaclava—I was wanted *there*!"

So deep was the effect of this "On Guard" sketch of Charlie's, and especially his showing up of the then all-too-prevalent neglect of many of those who had fought for King and Country, that the War Office people of the period took steps to have the sketch "barred" in some quarters, as it threatened to be "prejudicial to recruiting."

Godfrey's most popular songs—or musical monologues—included "The Masher King," "Across the Bridge He Goes," and that spirited soldier song, "Fighting With the Seventh Royal Fusiliers."

Here is the chorus of that Inkerman song which was written for Charlie by the late universally esteemed Wal Pink:

> "Oh! Fighting with the Seventh Royal Fusiliers!
> Famous Fusiliers! Gallant Fusiliers!
> Through deadly Russian shot and Cossack spears,
> We carved our way to Glory!"

And how Charlie used to let this chorus go!

It always thrilled the house, and was repeated vociferously by all "kind friends in front."

As to the "Masher King," Godfrey dressed in the so-called "aesthetic" velvet costume, just then—in the early eighties—brought into vogue by George du Maurier's Postlethwaite drawings in "Punch," and soon made still more far-flung by reason of the male garb in Gilbert and Sullivan's æsthetic skit "Patience: or Bunthorne's Bride."

The refrain of this "Masher King" number ran with:

> "A stroll down the Strand-ity—
> Cane in my hand-ity—"

Rather forced treble-rhymed form. Really, it was not a song of genius, but Charlie always "put it over" with no uncertain "put."

Another song hit of Charlie's was "Hi-tiddly-hi-ti," another swell ditty, in which the singer was supposed to be rather confused through taking too many "tiddleys." Lest any should be ignorant of the derivation of this word, I should mention that it is an abbreviation of "tiddley-wink"—which is rhyming slang for "drink." The refrain of this blatant Bacchanalian ballad ran as follows:

> "Hi-tiddley-hi-ti-hi-ti-hi,
> Come with me and wet your eye!
> Everybody here's invited!
> Come with me I'll see you righted.
> Hi-tiddley-hi-ti-hi-ti-hi—
> Hi-tiddley-hi-ti-hi-ti-hi!
> Come with me and have a spree,
> For I'm all right!"

"Across the Bridge" and "My Shadow is My Only Pal," were full of rugged pathos, and in this always difficult part of any stage impersonation "Good old Charlie" could always score, by sheer earnestness.

In fact, deep earnestness and unquenchable enthusiasm in his work—not too common in music-hall stage-folk—or even in dramatic stage-folk, especially in the eighties—were strongly embedded in my old friend and fellow-worker Charles Godfrey.

In connection with his many heavily-staged sketches, historical and otherwise—examples of his work which do not call for detailed description in these song stories—Godfrey would study and indulge in the deepest and most patient research day and night.

I have frequently found him buried beneath a mass of documents, books, drawings, engravings, and maps for this "study" of his historical music-hall impersonations, such as Nelson, Drake, General Gordon, and so on.

Certainly I have known the time when Charlie's carelessness between business hours caused a good many alarums and excursions. For example, he and his composer, dear old George

Le Brunn, would sometimes take to the open road, starting, say, from the George Canning at Brixton, on their way to, we'll suppose, the Oxford. Now, it so happened that on these pilgrimages, which involved calls at sundry "licensed premises" Charlie would leave his (and Le Brunn's) band parts at one or another hostelry.

On arriving at the hall which was their objective, and discovering that those band parts were missing, Charles or George or the management, had to send an emissary all the way back, taking the different hostelries in turn, until they found the precious package.

Good old George Le Brunn was often known to mislay, in this manner, certain musical morceaux which he owed me, for this or that musical play or sketch of mine. But that is another story, which need not be recounted at present.

Poor Charlie was also a bit of a gambler and a good deal of his money went in that way, but this I can and will say, from the time that Godfrey began to earn anything like money he was one of the most benevolent people to professional and other needy folk that I have had to do with, and, thank God. I have had to do with many such generous-hearted pro.'s of both sexes.

While still comparatively young, his health failed, and Godfrey, after a voyage to Australia, came back worse than he went—thanks to the foolish "hospitality" out there, and on the out and home voyages.

He died a wreck at the age of forty-nine, while trying to fulfil an engagement at Birmingham. And that was the premature end of a real good kindly fellow, a true friend, and one of the most phenomenally successful artistes ever seen in the British music-halls. Such was the "finis" of one who, in his earnest little speeches of thanksgiving for his "reception" o' nights, always described himself as "Your grateful humble servant—Charlie Godfrey."

THE WHITE-EYED ONE

This title, of course, belonged to the late G. H. Chirgwin, who, through unconsciously rubbing around one of his optics one night in the early part of his career, removed a portion of his burnt cork make-up and went on without re-blacking up. His appearance caused such convulsions of laughter that young Chirgwin resolved to leave that part of his countenance burnt-corkless henceforward and for evermore!

He soon adopted for his billing matter the name of "The White-Eyed Kaffir," although (as I often heard him say) he "didn't Kaffir it."

This most inveterate of punsters and wickedest of word-twisters, was of Cornish extraction and of Cockney rearing. Like many another stage favourite both of the dramatic and of the music-hall kind, he started on the very lowest rung of the professional ladder, and he started very young. In fact, the future White-Eyed Star began to chortle and to play instruments as a mere child with his brother Jack and a boy friend—all three being known as the Brothers Chirgwin.

What is more, they started as buskers! That is to say, they gave a taste of their quality at this or that street corner, in that or this metropolitan district, or on the sands at certain seaside resorts, wherever they could find, or were allowed, a "pitch."

In this busking and pitching in childhood Chirgwin resembled many another who, like him, subsequently became stars of great magnitude, from great little Edmund Kean down to great little Dan Leno!

While yet in his boyhood, certainly in his early and middle 'teens, the Cornish-Cockney Chirgwin managed to obtain "indoor work" of the variety kind, in certain music-halls, mostly of the minor sort.

These halls, or sing-songs, included such places as the Swallow Street Hall, off Regent Street (where I, too, worked and wrote some time after boy Chirgwin); Deacon's, on the New River bank at Islington; and even the Cosmetheka.

Anon, Chirgwin passed to that capital testing place, the Old Mo!—or Middlesex Music-Hall (now the beautiful Winter Garden Theatre), and eventually reached the Oxford! Here the White-Eyed One also reached his first "swollen" salary, viz., four pounds! Before he left the Oxford, however, Chirgwin mounted e'en to seven pounds per week for seven performances.

In his later days my old crony Chirgwin received for sundry special engagements as much as £100 per week! And, after some spell of the then far too common so-called "Bohemianism," Chirgwin began to take more care of his earnings.

In due course, he began to dabble in house "property"—even eventually in "public"-house property. For example, not long before his lamented death, a couple of years ago, my White-Eyed Friend became Mine Host of that popular old truly-rural hotel, the Anchor, at Shepperton.

For about thirty years Chirgwin's hold over his audiences was really phenomenal—not only in the music-halls but also in the "regular" theatres. In those latter houses I have seen him, and been with him, when in pantomimes, especially at the famous Britannia (or "Brit.") in Hoxton, he has held the vast audience in the hollow of his hand, so to speak. I have seen him play upon them as easily as he played his fiddle, which he so often tunefully declared was his "sweetheart." Many will remember the refrain of this brief ballad of Chirgwin's :

> "My fiddle is my sweetheart,
> And I'm her only beau ! (bow) ;
> I take her by the waist, like that (*Grasping the middle of the fiddle*)
> Because I love her so !"

In this song, as in his perennial ballad, "The Blind Boy," Chirgwin used a remarkable falsetto voice. This voice, he used to confess, he acquired by accident in his youth, through having suddenly to understudy a real and well-known falsetto singer.

"The Blind Boy," with its really pathetic words and air used to arouse considerable interest in more ways than one. Some people were wont to assert that he wrote and composed it himself ! As a matter of fact (as he confessed much later) Chirgwin bought the words and melody from Pony Moore, the early Christy Minstrel "corner man."

Another extraordinary point of interest regarding "The Blind Boy" was that for some time, in Chirgwin's later career, it was widely rumoured, and believed by many, that he sang it because he had a blind son of his own !

Myself, I have been called upon, over and over again, to clear up this question by way of "Answers to Correspondents" in the *Referee*. Happily, I was able to prove that friend Chirgwin and his wife had been spared such an affliction.

Chirgwin as a pantomime actor, singer, and dancer, was "an unknown quantity" to those who only saw him in his music-hall "turns." He appeared in six pantomimes at the Britannia (or "Brit.") alone, for Mrs. Sara Lane, that loved actress-manageress, who for her boundless benevolence to the local poor was affectionately termed "Queen of Hoxton."

The leading characters played by Chirgwin in these pantomimes included Daddy Longlegs, Idle Jack (in "Whittington"), and Svengali, in which he gave a funny burlesque of Beerbohm Tree !

It is not generally known that one of Chirgwin's early successes was as a kiddie trying to get his father home from a public-house, which he "used" too lavishly and too late o' nights. This was in a kind of "living picture" arrangement of the famous temperance and tear-extracting ballad, "Father, Dear Father, Come Home!"

The first verse and refrain of this once-phenomenally successfully ballad ran thus:

> "Oh, father, dear father, come home with me now;
> The clock in the steeple strikes One;
> You promised, dear father, that you would come home,
> As soon as your day's work was done.
> The fire has gone out, and we are all cold,
> And mother's been watching since tea—
> With poor brother Willie so ill in her arms,
> And no one to help her but me!
> Come home! Come home! Come home!
> Oh, father, dear father, come home!"

Simple, nay, crude, as all this song seems, it had that true touch of domestic pathos which never fails to appeal in large "popular" theatres and halls. I have seen vast audiences moved to tears by its words, and its simple but striking melody, especially in that terrific Temperance melodrama "Ten Nights in a Bar Room."

And now to sum up as regards my gay, good-hearted old chum Chirgwin. I think I might well add that we could well do with another such always vivacious and ever-versatile entertainer on our halls and variety theatres nowadays. Surely all of us who saw his work will always remember his astonishing readiness in topical allusions, fresh up to the moment of his stepping on the stage, with his "'Arf a mo, cocky!" Allusions such as his appealing up-to-date verselet, in which, preceding his clever long-pipes dance, and set to the air of "Pop Goes the Weazle," he let fall the following stern truth:

> "Everyone has his political views,
> And everybody backs his;
> But whether you win or whether you lose,
> Up go the taxes!"

COSTER CAROLLERS

Those—and there are many—who hold that Albert Chevalier was our first "Coster" comedian are not quite correct in their belief. I have already instanced Vance.

Undoubtedly "Chivvy" (of whom more presently) was the most finished, the most artistic impersonator of what one might call the idealised, Coster. Several music-hall comedians before him, however, have I seen do splendid humorous and realistic work in such "character" songs.

One of the best and brightest of these, starting way back in the late sixties, was "Teddy" Mosedale, who was not only a rattling good strong-voiced vocalist, but a really astounding "step" dancer. I have often seen Mosedale dance, either in the usual shoes or "pumps," or in clogs, on a pocket handkerchief (placed upon the stage) without ruffling it!

"Teddy" Mosedale had quite an extraordinary batch of coster and other "slummy" songs. They included one called "My Chestnut 'Orse," "Sarah," and "My Isabelle!"

The choruses of the first and third Mosedale song ran respectively thus:

"Like a hengine he could go
To 'Ackney, 'Ampstead Eaf, or Bow,
I never shall survive the lorse
Of poor old Jack, my Chestnut 'Orse!"

and—

"This was the toast that Joe would cry—
'My charmin' belle, my scrumptious gel,
Oh! Search the country thro' you shall,
But yer won't find a gel like my Isabel!'"

Presently, however, this "slang-slinger" (as he was called) was faced by a dangerous rival in crook's rhyming and "back slanguage." This rival was a quite gentle little fellow named Hyram Travers.

Hyram, who died only a year or two ago, was, I venture to think, absolutely "the limit" in coster, hawker, and crook slang.

A good example of the "coster" or humble hawker or illiterate operative character singing was also indulged in from the seventies onwards by J. W. Rowley—usually known as "Over" Rowley, because of his wonderful somersault-dance.

Rowley having (like Hurley) a beautiful singing voice, used to deviate into an "idealised" form of coster carol. These included such then tremendously popular and melodious ditties as "A Starry Night for a Ramble," and "It Was Only the Way it was Done on the Stage," and that fine ringing working-class ballad with the chorus:

"Down in a coal mine, underneath the ground,
Where no ray of sunshine is ever to be found;
Diggin' dusty di'monds, all the seasons round,
Down in a coal mine, underneath the ground."

"CHIVVY"

This lamented character comedian and coster singer had to sustain a heavy burden as a mere babe! His father, a Frenchman, and his mother, a Welsh woman, bestowed upon him fourteen baptismal names!

Wisely enough he only used one—that was Albert. But often with that merry twinkle in his eye he used to run over these names with me. I wish I could remember them all. But there, space is short and time is fleeting.

I first knew Albert of the numerous names, when at sixteen years of age he made his stage début at the old Prince of Wales's (now the Scala Theatre), with the afterwards Sir Squire and Lady Bancroft. Young as he was, "Chevalier" showed such promise that he was snapped up later by those great impresarii, Mr. and Mrs. Kendal.

For about fourteen years in England and in America the young Chevalier played on the legitimate stage, and worked nobly.

Perhaps his biggest hits in the drama proper were made at the Avenue (now the Playhouse), with the afterwards knighted George Alexander, who started in management at that theatre, and thereby hangs a tale—and a strange tale it is.

Now it so happened that "Chivvy" was cast for an Anglo-French character in (I think) "A Struggle for Life," at the Avenue. Of course he had to adopt the Gallic accent.

Now it also happened that the late distinguished critic, Clement Scott, wrote a notice of this play for the *Daily Telegraph*. In that criticism "Clemmy" declared that the young actor Chevalier was totally unable to speak the French accent!

Well do I remember little Albert's rage at this extraordinary notice. Anon he rubbed it into Scott by writing to the papers pointing out that he (Chevalier) ought to be able to speak that accent as his father was a Frenchman, and that French was mostly the language of his household!

It may not have been due entirely to Clement Scott's statement, but whether or no, soon after that, little "Chivvy" was for a long, long time "out of a shop" (as the actors say).

In the meantime, bearing his adverse circumstances with characteristic courage, he began to fill in time by writing songs of a distinctly homely and especially "coster" type. These songs I found him singing at the piano of this or that club, just to amuse his brother members. In fact, "Chivvy" often gave these and other friends copies of his delightful lyrics to do as they liked with!

Continually did I and other comrades of Albert's urge him to keep these songs, and to use them himself—and indeed it was I who advised him over and again to try his luck with them on the " halls."

But " Chivvy " had always a rather lofty idea of dramatic art, and for a long time he shied at the idea of " letting himself down " by turning to the variety stage.

Chevalier's view of the " descent " from the drama to the halls was shared at that time by a great many players of the so-called " regular " theatres. Many of them have since " listened to reason "—and large salaries.

Happily, after I and several other friends kept pegging away at Albert, and after one of his earliest clever low-life songs, namely, " Our 'Armonic Club " had been sung by Charles Coborn on the halls, and by E. J. Lonnen at the Gaiety, Chevalier evidently thought he might as well take our continuous advice, and go on the music-hall stage !

He took to it at the Tivoli one night in 1891, and everybody who knows anything of the history of entertainments knows what a great and instantaneous success he made. I was there, and well remember the deep impression Chevalier's quaint and semi-pathetic manner and his finished acting made upon the usually rollicking Tivolians.

Two of his chief hits that night were respectively " Mrs. 'Enry 'Awkins," (with its sweet melody by the late fine composer John Crook), and " Knocked 'Em in the Old Kent Road." His subsequent successful songs, such as " The Little Nipper," " Our Bazaar," " The Fallen Star," " Blue Ribbon Jane," and more than all, " My Old Dutch," are of course well in the memory of all lovers of the truly artistic.

It must be confessed that despite his great triumphs in the halls, " Chivvy " never quite had a proper affection for that style of entertainment. Whenever he could he would either run a series of " recitals " at some high-class concert hall, or return for a while to the regular drama—sometimes writing his own plays !

In England and America Chevalier was alike successful, and was accompanied on these tours by his brother and manager, stage-named Charles Ingle, and by Alfred H. West, his pianist, both of whom wrote several of his best melodies.

To the day of his death " Chivvy " would never cease to indicate to me that he loved the " legitimate," and felt he was " playing down" in the halls. And yet, happily for him, he chose his wife from those " halls," namely the long celebrated "serio," Florrie Leybourne, daughter of the late George Leybourne, the "Lion Comique." That estimable lady survives, although, alas, too often in a delicate state of health.

Albert Chevalier made (and deservedly) a lot of money. He also lost a lot. These losses were chiefly incurred by speculation in entertainment ventures. This was especially the case at the Trocadero Music Hall (now the Restaurant), where he was partnered by the late Hugh Jay Didcott, who certainly had done a good deal for "Chivvy" in the agency line.

Chevalier's greatest financial success was the drama based by him and Arthur Shirley, on the famous domestic monologue, "My Old Dutch." The dramatic and cinematic rights brought in a lot of money.

Albert Chevalier left something over £7,000. But for more or less unwise speculation it might easily have been £70,000!

"THE LONDON IDOL"

In the year 1868 a tiny tot of a girl, then between three and four years of age, might have been observed, dressed as a man and chortling a ditty, on the stage or semi-stage of a music-hall in the Midlands. This miniature artist was Tilly Ball, daughter of that hall's resident chairman and comic singer, Harry Ball, who had been born Powles.

Then, and for some years later, the tiny Tilly, who seemed to have a Peter Pan-ish idea of not growing up, worked in and around the Midland halls and sing-songs. She was still in male attire and billed as the "Pocket Sims Reeves." Later she became advertised as the "Great Little Tilley," and ten years later Tilly Ball, then fourteen, made her London débût at the Royal Music Hall, Holborn, now the Holborn Empire. That was in 1878.

At that hall and on the same evening, also at the Mile End Hall, then called Lusby's (afterwards named the Paragon) the young débutante sang, among other songs, the "Pet of Rotten Row," "Rose May," "Strolling Along with Nancy," "Squeeze Her Gently," and other songs, most of which had been written by Papa Harry Ball.

From that time little Tilly Ball, otherwise Powles, flashed forth as Vesta Tilley, and, dropping her previous billing matter titles, stood forth as "The London Idol."

The present writer, who had known little Tilly almost from her cradle, after following her career around the halls in her early teens, suddenly found her blossoming forth in the theatres as principal boy in pantomime, when she was seventeen! It will be a convincing proof of the striking ability and versatility of Tilly, otherwise Vesta, that a year later, at the age of eighteen she was principal boy at Drury Lane Theatre.

Well do I remember Vesta's first appearance at Old Drury. It was in a pantomime, "Sinbad the Sailor," if I remember rightly, for which that great impresario, Sir Augustus Harris, had engaged not only the vivacious Vesta, but all the other music-hall artistes he could think of.

Amid all this competition, our little heroine contrived to score as the hero. Of course, after the panto was over, away went Vesta on her variety wanderings. She went from success to success, and it was not long before she was lured to America. On that tour, and on several others, through the States, the "London Idol" was perhaps the greatest success of any English artist either from our theatres or the music-halls.

As the delightful little Tilly started her stage career so early in life, so comparatively early was she "booked" for matrimony. And thereby hangs a tale.

I don't think it has ever been mentioned before in print that dear little Vesta, then as sweet and as modest as she has remained to this day, beloved by all who have the privilege of knowing her, was sought in marriage by several suitors. While she was playing in Liverpool from time to time, either in the halls or the theatres, the suitors for Vesta's hand and heart were anon narrowed down to two very eligible young fellows. One was Walter, the scion of a famous theatrical and variety family named de Frece, the other was a youthful variety manager, whose name I shall not mention, but will only add that he has since attained world-wide fame.

In this race for the charming "London Idol," Walter won, having then and ever since, as he so often tells me, blessed his lucky stars! As indeed well he might.

As one who has known the bride and bridegroom from their early years, they did me the privilege of inviting me to their silver wedding, which they celebrated a few years ago at their delightful riverside dwelling, The Homestead, Maidenhead. We all had a right joyous time, and found our dear little friend, the silver bride, sweeter and more gentle than ever.

During that twenty-five years of happy married life, and after, Walter de Frece, since knighted and M.P.-ed has been a wonderful helper on the business side to his enchanting partner, and many of Vesta Tilley's best songs have been written by her husband.

It is now just over thirty years ago that Vesta Tilley, feeling (as I have shown that Marie Lloyd once felt) a strong urge for the dramatic stage, sent for me to write her a burlesque. Vesta, Walter and I at once chatted this matter out, and in the course of a few weeks, as time was short, I delivered to my friends the script of a burlesque entitled "Cartouche and Co., or The Ticket-of-French-Leave Man."

In the character of Cartouche I managed to fit Miss Vesta Tilley very closely, but well do I know what I owed to her splendid acting of the character. Her lyrics, and the others in the piece, all written by myself, were set to music by that brilliant but erratic master of melody the late George Le Brunn.

The subsequent career of Vesta Tilley is, or should be, well known to all true enthusiastic patrons of variety. Therefore, these will remember, without my going into special details, such enormously successful songs of hers as "Burlington Bertie," "Sweetheart May," "What Shall We Do With Our Daughters?" "The Midnight Son," "By the Sad Sea Waves," "Following in Father's Footsteps," and "Algy, or The Piccadilly Johnny with His Little Glass Eye." Other immensely popular ballads of Vesta Tilley's include, of course, those two variants "Jolly Good Luck to the Lass Who Loves a Sailor" and "Jolly Good Luck to the Girl Who Loves a Soldier," and especially her quaint little martial study, given in the war-time, namely, "The Army of To-day's All Right."

In between these lyrics of a light kind, our brilliant little heroine from time to time showed her true dramatic gifts in songs and monologues of a stronger and far more difficult nature. Among these Tilleyan essays in the "legit." was her fine performance of the ill-fated boy poet Chatterton, at the old Tivoli and elsewhere.

A few years ago this really great variety artiste retired from the stage, and her farewell performance for which Sir Oswald Stoll gave the London Coliseum, was indeed a memorable affair. Since then Lady de Frece (to give her her proper title) has had to spend the winters more or less at Monte Carlo.

The members of the theatrical and variety professions are famous for one attribute in private life: that is, that they are continuously and consistently generous to the poor and needy, both in their professions and out of them. Among all these truly benevolent folk, of whose kindnesses it falls to me to have special knowledge, not one has been more benevolent or fuller of loving kindness than my dear little friend of whom it is my privilege to write. I could, indeed, give many an instance of her wonderful help to the distressed, but I know what she would say to me if I did, so I refrain.

I can best sum up this great little artist's career in this regard by saying, with the World's Greatest Dramatist, she always

> "Had a tear for pity, and a hand
> Open as day for melting charity."

ERIN IN THE HALLS

Hibernian minstrels and merrymakers have always been popular on the music-hall stage, where at one time they seemed to roll up, as it says in Thackeray's "Battle of Limerick,"

> "In squadrons and platoons,
> With their bands a-playing chunes."

That these songful sons of Erin are still enormously popular in varietyland is proved by the continued success of that tuneful warbler and glib patterer, Talbot O'Farrell.

One of the greatest favourites in this line of business in my boyhood's extensive experience of the halls was one who was billed as Sam Collins. He was really born Vagg, and his first profession was that of a chimney sweep, though nobody would ever have guessed it in his after life. Sam was a fine, upstanding, genial comedian, far better educated than many of his contemporaries on the halls. Also, he was a capital comic singer and a splendid dancer.

While I was but a boy, Sam Collins took a public house on Islington Green. It was called the Lansdowne Arms, and of it he made one of the most popular music-halls of the period. He called it Sam Collins's. It soon became Collins's for short, and Collins's it remains, although for some time past its music-hallism has been transformed into melodramatics, and twice-nightly blood-and-thunder thrillsomeness, now plus "pictures."

It was at Collins's, just after it opened, that Sam, a friend of many of my theatrical and variety relations, used to teach me little snatches of Irish songs and sundry steps of Irish jigging. As I was entering my teens, Sam passed away, and his funeral was one of the biggest I ever saw, for Sam was not only an excellent entertainer, but a splendid fellow. So much so, that the then famous song writer and "motto" singer, Harry Sydney, himself a noble character, whom all of us loved, wrote this epitaph for Sam's tomb:

> "Farewell, brave honest-hearted Sam,
> Until we meet before the Great I Am."

Sam, like many other comic singers of his time, dug out several of the songs which had been sung half a century or so before his time by such famous theatrical stars as "Irish" Johnstone, Hudson, and the great Tyrone Power. Among these songs were two well worth quotation. One was "The Sprig of Shillelagh." One verse of this runs as follows:

"Did never ye go to Great Donnybrook Fair?
An Irishman all in his glory is there,
With a Sprig of Shillelagh and shamrock so green;
He goes in his new clothes without e'er a speck,
With a nate Barcelona tied round his nate neck;
He darts round the fair and he spinds half-a-crown;
He meets with a friend—and for love knocks him down
With his Sprig of Shillelagh and shamrock so green."

Sam Collins' other big songs included "Limerick Races", "No Irish Need Apply" and that quaint ditty "The Rocky Road to Dublin."

As time rolled on I caught up large numbers of these Irish comedians and step-dancers. By that time most of them called themselves Paddy or Pat. For instance, the greatest of the favourites of those days included Paddy Fannin, and later still Pat Rafferty and Pat Feeney.

Another very popular Irish singer of my earlier days was Peter McHaffie, a very tuneful warbler and excellent character actor. I remember that Peter, whom I had been a good deal with at McDonald's music-hall at Hoxton (then the resort of all the stars) was wont to arouse a great deal of controversy with a song which he sang in the costume of an Irish squireen. It had the following somewhat provocative refrain:

"Why can't Paddy be a gintleman
A gintleman, a gintleman?
Oh, why can't Paddy be a gintleman?
Come, tell me the reason why."

One of the sweetest, daintiest Irish colleens that ever appeared on the halls was little Katty King, who sometimes used to sing duets with her equally fine-looking brother, Harry King. More often, however, she used to make the whole audience and company (including myself) fall violently in love with her by her charming vocalisation and arch acting in those glorious Irish ballads "Katie's Letter" and the "Whistling Thief."

Many will remember the opening of "Katie's Letter," which runs:

> " I sint my love a letther
> And I put a seal upon it,
> 'Twas almost as big
> As the crown of my best bonnet.
> For I would not have the post masther
> Make his remarks upon it;
> For I said inside the letther
> That I loved Pat dearly.
> But he knows it—shure he knows it,
> And widout one worrd from me."

And who, who knows anything of the halls, can forget that late and always lamented breezy genial generous Irish comedian and dancer, Walter Munroe?

Not only was Walter a master of step-dancing, in every form, but his comic-singing was a sheer joy.

Can't you hear him now chortling in the funniest frenzied fashion, the following tragic chorus?

> " First we mopped the floor with him;
> Dragged him up and down the stairs;
> Then we lugged him round the room,
> Under tables, over chairs!
> And then we jumped upon his face,
> Before he'd time to say his prayers
> (Pom, pom, pom)
> Rags and bones were all we left
> Of the man who struck O'Hara."

CHAPTER IX

Some Music-Hall Managers—Managers of the "'sixties" and "'seventies"—"Pony" Moore—Frederick Burgess—"The Mahogany Bar"—"Bill" Bailey—Sam Adams, a many-sided Manager.

Naturally in the long course of my experiences in the "Halls," I had to do with a great many Proprietors, Lessees and Managers generally of such places, on both sides of the curtain. That is to say, when there *was* a curtain, which in the old days was not often, for of course, the stages even in some of the best known Variety houses, were but platforms. Sometimes we had a pianist and a violinist on the stage, sometimes blossoming out into something like an orchestra, down in front of the boards, and giving off their twiddley bits at the back of the then always necessary functionary, the Chairman.

In these days variety theatre managers are quite magnates in their way, mostly of financial renown, and they delegate their managerial duties to specially engaged managers who have in effect very little to do with the managing itself. In the early days of the halls, the proprietor who was mostly his own manager was in every case a licensed victualler. This meant that his music-hall was in nearly every instance a kind of adjunct, or annexe, or even an actual part of his tavern, and the hall was often named after the sign of the house.

Before proceeding to describe sundry heads of the halls, both past and present, it will perhaps be enough for me to group up a batch of such entertainment-runners, whom I knew, and in most cases respected from my boyhood's days to until say my middle manhood.

One of the earliest of these was Edward Williams who ran the long celebrated Sun Music Hall at Knightsbridge, close to an older rival house of harmony, called the Trevor. The Trevor a very fine hotel, still stands where it did, like Scotland. The Sun has long since disappeared under the clouds of time, but in its day, it was far superior as a hall to the Trevor.

If I may drop into personal matters, I might here add, that dear old Williams, quite a fatherly benevolent kind of chap was exceedingly kind to me, from the time when I was a little boy onwards, and also to little Nellie Power, who was exactly my own age, and with whom I used to travel a great deal when she was a child serio-comic.

Those who knew the Battersea Hall will remember that its most interesting period was that during which it was run by the then wealthy and always extraordinarily eccentric "minstrel" generally known as "Pony" Moore. Indeed it was re-named the Washington, after "Pony" himself, whose initials G. W. stood for George Washington. Patrons of that generally rollicking, but sometimes then very rowdy resort, will also remember that G. W. M. really took that hall for Charlie Mitchell, the eminent pugilist, who had by then become "Pony's" son-in-law.

Another daughter of Moore's married in earlier years the great Legmania dancer, Fred Vokes, of the renowned Vokes family.

"Pony" was so strange a character that he deserves a little more detail all to himself.

I had known him for a good many years before he came to the Washington, that is, when he was running that historically successful nigger company, known as the Moore and Burgess Minstrels. From my earliest associations with G.W.M. and this troupe at the St. James's Hall, which is now the Piccadilly Hotel, and was long known as St. Jimmy's. I always found that Washingtonian warbler a most audacious person . . . even for an American.

Many will remember him as chief corner-man as well as part proprietor of these Minstrels, and some, like myself may recollect that he brought forth several big song hits of the nigger type. Perhaps the drollest and most popular of these ditties, were those respectively entitled, "Over On The Surrey Side," and "Hunky Dorum, We Are The Boys."

As I have previously given some indication of strange songs current in the earlier days, I may as well here append a verse and chorus of the latter Darkie ditty.

If my memory serves, it ran thus:

> " I went out one day for a lark—
> Hunkey Dorum, we am de boys
> I met with a lubly gal in de park—
> Hunkey Dorum doodle dum dey.
> Her hair it was frizzed all over her head—
> Hunkey Dorum, we am de boys.
> She nearly killed dis darkie dead
> Hunkey Dorum doodle dum dey!
> *Chorus*—
> Her hair was frizzed all over her head,
> She nearly killed dis darkie dead—
> Her maiden name she said it was Brown,
> And she lived wid her mudder in Camden Town."

This outburst was accompanied by bones, tamborines, banjos etc., by Moore and all concerned.

I may finish up with regard to "Pony" by saying that much of his hard-earned wealth was poured out for the most part on all sorts of "parties" which he gave on his own and his family's birthdays, and all sorts of other occasions, real or manufactured at his fine old house in the Finchley Road.

Often times have I visited him there during these outbursts, and also in the few quiet times that intervened. In between these Finchley Road Festivals, and his flamboyant banquets elsewhere, good old "Pony" had a regular habit of coming into collision with the police, either on account of furious driving or "slogging" in the street, and other diversions which always seemed to please the poor old chap.

Despite these volcanic outbursts, and "seeing it out" nightly until the small hours began to grow large, "Pony" Moore lived to a good old age, certainly to eighty odd.

Moore's partner in the Minstrels, that is after "Pony" had dropped his original partner Crocker, was a very dear old friend of mine named Frederick Burgess. He was what might be called the "practical partner" and indeed but for his sound business tact, and steadiness of temperament, "Pony" would never have made the money that he did, nor would the Minstrels have lasted so long.

Part of my knowledge of Burgess was acquired in the "regular theatres," for while I was engaged at the Adelphi as a youth, Burgess used to come there, courting a tall and graceful young actress named Ellen Meyrick, a niece of those strong Adelphi players, Mr. and Mrs. John Billington. The last-named lady died some time ago at the ripe old age of ninety-four.

Burgess was the very antithesis of "Pony" Moore, for not only did he attend strictly to business, but he was also a lover and collector of books of great value. He left a library which realised what our old friend Shylock would call "A good round sum."

Among other highly esteemed, sometimes also highly eccentric music-hall proprietors whom I knew and often worked with, were James Laurie Graydon, otherwise "Jimmy"; J. S. Sweasey, who at one time ran Weston's, afterwards the Royal, and now the Holborn Empire; Robert Preece, who was as good a violinist as he was a licensed victualler, and for years ran that popular Surrey side hall, called The Winchester, but mostly referred to by its public house sign, The Grapes; Richard Wake, who so long managed the Royal Standard, Pimlico, known now as the Victoria Palace.

Also worthy of honourable mention are such managers and proprietors as Will Riley, who, being a well-to-do publican and bookmaker, elected not only to run the Cambridge Music Hall in Commercial Street, Shoreditch, but also to fill in time by doing a bit of comic singing. Good old Will, a delightful and straight comrade, long preferred in his singing bouts that delectable "If Ever There Was a Damned Scamp" which Henry Pettitt, afterwards the eminent dramatist, wrote for the great Macdermott for half-a-sovereign, a song which I have quoted in a previous chapter.

Proprietor Riley had for his manager the late popular song writer, E. V. Page, who was the first manager of the Empress, Brixton, and who afterwards became concerned with a large motor works and garage in Acre Lane, Brixton, a firm now run by his sons.

Another proprietor and manager somewhat of Riley's type, but of a nautical cut rather than race-coursey, was Frank Maltby, a very rum chap, who bought and ran a music-hall or two, including Wilton's, the Wellclose Square Hall, which was mostly called by those who patronised or worked in it, "The Mahogany Bar."

Also the quaint but business-like and loyal little Wilton Friend, was at the "Mahogany Bar." I might also mention the much esteemed J. J. Poole and his wife (so soon, alas, his widow), who both directed the South London Music-Hall following upon the management of Edwin Villiers who was its ruler almost, if not quite, from the time it was converted from a Roman Catholic Chapel into Music Hall-ism.

Concerning Villiers, who was at first a light comedian at

the Haymarket Theatre, and the uncle of the famous War correspondent Fred Villiers, I shall have more to say in connection with my chapters on the London Pavilion, etc.

One of the most remarkable of the many music-hall managers, I have known so intimately, was William Bailey, whom I knew as a full-grown comic singer in and around his native Midlands when I was a tiny boy, and afterwards the manager of the Metropolitan, (or "Met.") in the Edgware Road.

Bill Bailey and I collogued recently at a meeting of the Theatrical Managers Association, for William had to deal with dramatics as well as variety and film-atics at the Met. He died a few days before I wrote these mems and was nearly a nonogenarian.

A merry many-sided manager, very extraordinary person, and a most ebullient example of manhood, namely, Sam Adams, died about thirty years ago, when he really ought to have been living now.

I first met Sam when I was a youngster, and he was the Manager and Chairman of the Philharmonic Music Hall, or "Phil" as it was called, a resort which afterwards became the Philharmonic Theatre under Charles Morton.

Sam, a joyous golden-curled, handsome, dashing fellow, became for a while concerned with the Phil as a theatre, but afterwards deviated to resorts which were devoted both to dramatic and variety fare. In due course he became a manager-director at the South London, and was for some time at the Canterbury. His last venture however, was at the Trocadero Music Hall, which was for some time called The Eden. This resort which before it music-hall days was known as the famous (or infamous) Argyll Rooms, is now of course the famous Lyons' Restaurant.

It was during the volcanic, vivacious Sam's management of the "Troc" Music Hall that he died. The early death of this valued friend was due to too much work, and too little proper refreshment. During his brief illness of a day or two the hall was besieged by callers and by telegrams, for few men, if any, has ever been so popular as Sam in any profession.

The theatrical profession especially owes a debt to Sam Adams, for by his wife, the tuneful singing actress, Cicely Nott, he had three clever singing and acting daughters, one of them being that smart Drury Lane principal boy and musical comedy player, Ada Blanche. One of the daughters was the first wife of Robert Courtneidge. Another married that highly esteemed theatrical manager, William Peacock of the Harrogate Opera House, and *his* daughter, the niece of Sam, is that beautiful and accomplished actress Marie Blanche. A son of Sam became a very reputable music-hall manager himself, but alas, also died very young.

Chapter X

A famous Hebrew Manager—Sir Henry Irving and Harry Hart — Joseph Cave — The Cosmotheka — Workhouse Official as Variety Act—The "Syndicaters"—Herbert Newson—Smith, Henri Gros and Sir Harry Tozer as Managers—J. L. Graydon and the Old Mo.

When I mention a famous Hebrew manager, Harry Hart, concerning whom many, like himself, always dropped the two "aitches," there will be many readers of these lines who will remember that quaint but lovable little fellow. I say little, because 'Arry was perhaps the shortest music-hall proprietor within the memory of man. I knew him from the time he ran the Raglan Music Hall in the Theobald's Road, Holborn. I followed him along when eventually he went over to Union Street, Borough, and acquired a slummy old hall called the Salmon, at which at least four of my own relations regularly appeared.

Hart soon re-christened the Salmon, the Raglan, after his popular place up Holborn way, and there as at the former house he not only made things hum, but he also made things pay. Anon, still keeping on the Surrey side, he took over that old established tavern music-hall, the Star, Bermondsey, and it was there during his regime that Bessie Bellwood, (born Mahoney,) up till then a local rabbit puller or fur dresser, took to the music-hall stage. Bessie's adventures there and elsewhere will be found treated in another chapter.

As to Hart, that indefatigable little chap busied himself in this or that music-hall and similar speçulations, licensed victualling and otherwise, till the day of his death.

And that death I assure you was mourned far and wide, for he was one of the kindest as well as one of the most business-like men ever known in the entertainment world.

And thereby hangs another tale!

I always found that one of the many noble qualities of

the late Sir Henry Irving's personal character was his warm brotherliness towards his fellow managers, in what he always described as "Our Beloved Calling."

This esteem for the work and this anxiety regarding the prosperity of his fellow managers was also extended to those of the music-hall side of the entertainment world.

A very popular object of Irving's affectionate regard was little Harry Hart, and it was a quaint experience to see these two together, the gaunt Irving, the head of the Drama, towering over this 'Arry of the 'Alls.

I remember that one day Irving ran up against Harry, in the Strand, and, as his custom was, slapped Harry on the back, expressing the hope that business was "going on well," at Harry's Hall, the Star, Bermondsey. Hart replied in somewhat pessimistic mood that "bithneth was bloomin' bad."

Irving to comfort him retorted, "Well, my boy, we managers all have our ups and downs. We at the Lyceum have felt the draught a bit, for you see just now a good many of our patrons are going to the opera."

"Yeth," exclaimed little Harry. "And all my blinkin' customers are going 'opping!"

Irving knew a good man when he met him, in whatever line of business that man might be, and it didn't take the great actor-manager long to find out that his hard working music-hall friend Hart was also one of the best, both as regards his business and his behaviour.

A CASUAL WARD COMEDIAN

Many will doubtless say, why drag in Cave? Even as Bernard Shaw once remarked, "Why drag in Shakespeare?"—but as a matter of fact, although Joseph Arnold Cave (to give him his full name) was chiefly a theatrical manager, I have known him to dabble a good deal in music-hall managing, and also to appear in such places in sketches and things of that sort. Indeed, I have already quoted proofs of Joe's very useful labours in the variety world in a previous chapter. These labours included his running a variety season, even at the Old Vic. some time before the late Miss Emma Cons turned that former blood and thunder playhouse into a temperance hall, pending her esteemed niece, Lilian Baylis, M.A., running it on all Shakespeare lines.

I had a good deal to do with Cave, who was a relation of mine by marriage, at the aforesaid Vic. and at the Elephant and Castle, and also when later he blossomed forth, if you please, as manager of the Alhambra, Leicester Square. Here he mingled the drama with variety, and of course presented many big ballets, which in those days formed the chief staple in that theatre's entertainment.

Cave ran more theatres than most people ever ran, and as to his variety activities, these were really remarkably numerous, considering the antagonisms which existed in those days between the so-called "Legit." and the halls. Those were days when it was thought derogatory for any theatrical professional to have anything to do with the halls. This always seemed a strange thing to me, even as a youngster, for happily I belonged to a rather extensive theatrical family, and when things were bad in the theatres we migrated to the music-halls.

But to return to Joe Cave.

This story relates to the time when Joseph was running one of his most successful theatres, namely the Marylebone, in the Edgware Road, a theatre which afterwards became the West London, and is now a cinema.

I have known strange things occur there, both as regards performances and patrons. The latter had two ways of expressing their views. If they appreciated your artistic efforts, they hurled coppers at you, if they didn't, they hurled curses!

It was while Joseph was looking about for extra attractions for the Marylebone that he made an engagement of a very peculiar kind. This engagement was with a very humble official, who had worked for years at Lambeth Workhouse!

I was very young at the time, but I had already become very familiar not only with the plays of the period, but also with the comic songs and their singers. I had scarcely entered my teens when a journalist named James Greenwood wrote that very sensational article (slightly alluded to earlier) to the then brand-new journal, *The Pall Mall Gazette*, and in this essay he described a secret visit he had paid, while disguised as a casual tramp, to Lambeth Workhouse.

This article was permeated with references to a poor official whose duty it was to receive and to bath the wretched casuals applying for a night's shelter and also, to see that they behaved in conformity with the Rules of that Union.

Greenwood's article created such a sensation, that of course this official whom he described as "Good old Daddy," was referred to and quoted in all sorts of plays, burlesques, etc., and very naturally was speedily immortalised, so to speak, in sundry comic and topical songs. I remember especially two of these "Daddy" ditties, in fact I used to sing them myself.

One of them was introduced by a very clever Lancashire comic singer of the time, named Tom Kirby, who died rather young. The other chief song was, if I remember rightly, chortled by a " comic " named Harry Sansom.

I shall only quote a part of these two songs. The Kirby version ran thus :

" If you want good lodgin' and yer board,
Go to Daddy, good Old Daddy ;
At Lambeth Union Casual Ward.
There you'll find old Daddy'O.
If you go to the gate
And the bell you ring,
You'll find old Daddy will let yer in.
If you haven't got a shirt to yer skin
You'll get one from Daddy-O.

Chorus—
Daddy-O. Daddy-O.
Jolly good luck to Daddy-O,
Lambeth Union Casual Ward—
That's the address of Daddy-O."

The other refrain ran as follows ; and had a special reference to the little story which follows :

" No more workhouse for me, boys,
On the stage I can live like a lord,
No more 'lump' then for me, boys
I'm Daddy from the Casual Ward."

The reference " on the stage I can live like a lord " applied to the fact that Joe Cave not only engaged the real Daddy from the Workhouse for the Marylebone Theatre, but also had a special episode with musical effects written around that benign official with intent to send dear old Daddy on tour.

The night arrived when Daddy was to make his start as a star at that famous but generally fusty playhouse which, by the way, had the deepest stage in all London. The time for curtain rise arrived, but alas! Daddy did not. Manager Cave naturally grew very anxious and fidgety (and I assure you Joe *could* be fidgety), and he kept having musical selections chiefly of twiddley bits played pending the overdue arrival of our Casual Ward Hero.

Still no Daddy ! Anon Cave had to apologise to the audience and to ask them to accept a little interlude which he would give (and Cave had a good many such interludes) until such time as the missing star might turn up.

When at last it seemed that this specially written attraction would be Daddy-less, someone brought in the old man, who had been wandering around the neighbourhood unable to find the theatre !

Hurriedly he was ballooned into the scene in which he sat to sit and to receive many casuals, while musical morceaux were emitted all around him !

So the situation was saved, but Joe Cave, as he used to tell me, " had the fright of his life."

Good old Daddy did not remain long on the stage, and some little time later he had a notion to try and go back to Lambeth Workhouse, but if I remember rightly a few friends clubbed together and bought him a little business, a tobacconist's or something, where that even then aged veteran anon passed away.

" THE SYNDICATERS "

By the " Syndicaters " I refer to the chief managerial members of what was called " The Syndicate," which ran for some few years from the early 'nineties those three then highly representative variety houses: The Tivoli, The Oxford, and the London Pavilion.

This combine afterwards took in several other such halls, including the Empress Brixton, The Metropolitan (or " Met."), The Canterbury, and the South London, or " South " as it is called locally. Still later they built or acquired sundry other variety houses ; and indeed the " Syndicate " still runs on, chiefly under the style and title of " Variety Theatres Consolidated." They take in most of the above indicated places, except of course, the Oxford, the site of which has been bought by the Lyons firm for refreshment purposes, and the Tivoli, which long ago disappeared, and was rebuilt as a Picture Palace.

The chief of the " Syndicate " in the 'nineties was the late Herbert Newson-Smith, a very brainy accountant, who on taking to the music-hall side of London's entertainments at first in a financial way, soon began to show managerial qualities of a remarkable kind.

There were two especial matters for which my late friend was responsible. One was that he sent up the " business " of the music-hall " industry " (as many now call it) by leaps and bounds, and earned for his shareholders big dividends as a rule. The other was that he was able to " corner " all the chief variety stars for the " Syndicate halls " by giving them salaries of such a size as to stagger even those recipients. This achievement Newson-Smith was able to carry out in co-operation with that extremely cute variety agent, the late Hugh J. Didcott.

The eventual "split" between Newson-Smith and Didcott is described fully in my earlier biographical notes of the last named co-operator.

Poor Newson-Smith died at the early age of forty-four, leaving behind him a couple of clever sons, one of whom still runs with great success the celebrated Newson-Smith Accountancy firm.

Several other important managers and co-managers also bobbed up with the "Syndicate" and became managing directors of this or that variety hall of the Syndicate group.

One of the most esteemed and most straightforward of this band of managerial magnates was the late Henri Gros, a Dutch Hebrew of most kindly and generous instincts, who had for his own special manager and secretary the still going strong young Israelite, Leon Zeitlin.

Dear old Gros, whose especial pitch was the Metropolitan, was a bit of a volcano in temperament, as well I knew, for he and I had many a "beat up" both personally, journalistically, and epistolarily. Henri was such a grand old chap, however, so fearlessly honourable in all his dealings, that any of us who chanced to fall out with him, on some sincere point of view, very speedily fell in again. In fact, his noble sympathetic nature would not allow him to remain long at odds with any of us whom he had good reason to respect.

Associated also with this syndicatorial combine was a very interesting and equally keen business man, the late Sir Henry Tozer. Tozer, whom I knew from my early youth, was "something in the Law," I'm not quite sure what. He was a very bright and breezy Devonian, who delighted to crack stories with me and others in the dialect of "Dartymoor." Indeed Tozer was very much given to chortle the comical Widdicombe Fair song, all about "Uncle Tom Cobleigh and All."

He had a fondness too for taking me on concerning Shakespearian topics and poets in general, and it was his especial pride to dabble a little in journalism from the time when as a youngster in his native town he had contributed sundry effusions to the "Poet's Corner" of the local press.

Friend Tozer, who was knighted late in life, was at one time Mayor of Westminster, and indeed he had a good deal to do with the L.C.C. and cognate bodies.

His sudden death after an accident was deeply regretted

by all of us who knew him, and great sympathy was expressed with the still surviving Lady Tozer.

One of the chief syndicators, namely that late fine straight fighter, George Adney Payne, also a bit of a tornado in temperament, is described in some detail in my foregoing chapter on the Great Music-Hall War.

Two other very able chiefs of the "Syndicate," were respectively Henry Sutton, and Joseph Davis. These two, though united enough in their work for music-hall shareholders, were as wide as the poles asunder. In their case, as in the case of one or two others mentioned, it was my pleasant privilege to be a sort of peacemaker from time to time, so strongly did they antagonise on many points.

Sutton had been in the financial line, and indeed I believe at one time was not utterly unconnected with the pawnbroking interest. He had been also a director of the Alhambra company, and was altogether a thoroughly equipped if occasionally touchy business man. I have an idea that old pal Sutton was also not utterly unconnected with a certain historical Chosen Race.

Joe Davis was a Scot of the Scots, a very Caledonian of Caledonians. He was not utterly unconcerned with the Whiskey Distilling interest, and before his health unfortunately gave way he was a very fine judge of blends of that somewhat universally consumed "tipple."

A bit of a shoot-ist too, was Joe, and he used to bring down many a brace of birds upon his native moors. Joseph's especial pitches in the "Syndicate" line were the Euston Music Hall (now the Regent Theatre), the Empress, Brixton, and the East Ham Empire. These halls or theatres, together with several others, are now controlled with consummate ability by the late George Adney Payne's son, Walter Adney Payne, who is also a gifted barrister and a fine literary judge. Added to which I may mention that friend Walter is a chief of the West End Managers Association and is a cousin of the distinguished dramatist, Somerset Maugham.

There were some music halls whose successive, and often successful, managers form a little history in a group of themselves, as it were. One of these halls was the famous Middlesex, made out of the Drury Lane Tavern, called the Mogul, and locally known as the "Old Mo'."

These managers or directors included in my time W. E. Winder, and H. G. Lake, both old-time successful licensed victuallers, who had previously run other music-halls, including the Metropolitan, and Weston's, afterwards the Royal.

When I first became connected with the Middlesex (or " Mo' ") I wrote songs for many of its singers, both comic and serious, at very cheap prices. My experiences as a lyrist, sketch-writer, etc. at this and many other variety houses are more fully dealt with elsewhere in this book. Anyhow, when I was first engaged at the Middlesex J. L. Graydon was officiating in the bar, and acting as general supervisor of the refreshment cellars for Manager Lake.

During my first association with that hall Graydon soon became manager on his own account, and eventually proprietor. He retained the proprietorship of that goldmine of a music-hall with its threepenny gallery and so forth, until the place was sold to the now Sir Oswald Stoll, who opened it as the Middlesex Theatre, which was afterwards transmuted to its present state as the Winter Garden Theatre.

Graydon was really a remarkable chap, as will be gathered from the following few remarks concerning his career, with which I had to do right on from his Mogul time on to his co-directorship of the early Palace Theatre, and so on until his death.

When I first became connected with the Middlesex Graydon was assisted in the bars and in his office by his wife, a very pretty young blonde of most kindly nature. She, alas, died while still young, and in due course, Graydon married the widow of Fred Albert, who, as I have shown, was for many years wondrously popular as a topical songster in the halls. Fred Albert was born Howell, and his son by Mrs. Howell, afterwards Mrs. Graydon, is Bert Howell, who runs in Paris, in partnership with F. Baud, a great Anglo-French American Variety agency.

Graydon's son by his first wife is the well known Laurie Graydon, at first connected with the " Syndicate " Halls, but now holding a big position in the Moss Empires' firm.

The second Mrs. Graydon, when I was a youth in the music halls, was very popular as a serio-comic and skipping-rope dancer under her own name, Lottie Cherry. She was the daughter of J. W. Cherry, a renowned composer in his day, alike of ballads and of comic songs.

During her married life with Graydon the former Lottie Cherry proved herself one of the cutest business women ever seen in the halls. Not only did she help to run that ancient cheap priced hall, the aforesaid Middlesex, but also she ran for Graydon and herself that popular sea-coast Variety house, the Alhambra, Brighton, which now, like most such places, is a Picture Palace.

After a very strenuous life, both on the halls and on the hunting-field, Lottie Graydon had to retire through ill-health, caused by overwork.

Jimmy Graydon, during the last years of his life, added to his many activities by helping to found and partly to direct that most useful organisation, the Proprietors of Entertainments Association. He died at a good old age, deeply respected by all who knew him, as one of the straightest of music-hall proprietors and licensed victuallers.

CHAPTER XI

Sir Oswald Stoll's romantic career—His entry into variety—Early Days at the Coliseum—Chatham's Grand Old "Variety" Man—Sir Edward Moss—Opening of the London Hippodrome—An Alligator's Night Out

Doubtless it will be conceded, not only by Variety patrons, but also by other managers, that the Head and Front of them is Sir Oswald Stoll, who directs not only those two huge variety houses—the old Alhambra in Leicester Square, and the comparatively new Coliseum in St. Martin's Lane, but also several vast variety houses in different parts of the British Isles.

These other music hall enterprises of Friend Oswald's include the Chiswick, Wood Green, Ardwick—Hackney and Shepherd's Bush Empires, and those two huge Stoll buildings, the Bristol Hippodrome, and the Bristol Empire. Also, he controls the Chatham Empire and Hippodrome, and perhaps the biggest of all his theatres, the gorgeous Stoll Picture Theatre, formerly the London Opera House in Kingsway.

Oswald Stoll's career is indeed something of a romance, one of those romances which show what real genius can perform in the way of organisation, selection and elimination.

He has just passed his sixtieth year, but he has been in what it is now the fashion to call "The Variety Industry" since he was fourteen years of age, and this is how it came about.

Stoll, who is Irish by birth and was born in Melbourne, Victoria, was the son of Roderick Gray, who died when Oswald was a little boy. After some years his mother married again, this time an entertainer manager named Roderick Stoll, and Oswald, a growing youth, took the name of his stepfather.

I have said that Stoll started his managerial career in his very early teens. This was because his mother's second husband also died young, and it was necessary for Oswald to start assisting his mother, who was then manageress of that then popular music-hall, the Parthenon, Liverpool.

Being ever a glutton for work, the boy Oswald not only managed the Parthenon for his mother, but also started a little variety agency on his own, and soon began to thrive apace. Gradually he increased his mother's property and holdings in the halls, and before he was twenty-three he had acquired Levene's music-hall in Cardiff and turned it into the Cardiff Empire!

Very soon he put up Empires at Swansea and Newport, (Mon.) and before you could say "Encore," so to speak, young O. S. was running eight big music halls in England and Wales!

By this time another music-hall combine had arisen, and it arose up North. It was at first called the Moss and Thornton Circuit.

As many fuller details of the Moss Empire rise and progress will be found elsewhere in this volume, I pass on to show how Stoll got into the Moss and Thornton Combine.

It was when that Combine beginning to spread, made a march towards the Principality, that Oswald Stoll, whose variety interests there were increasing by leaps and bounds, insisted upon certain conditions which necessitated his being taken in to that Northern Combine, which thus became the Moss, Stoll, and Thornton Circuit, and eventually the Moss and Stoll circuit.

After achieving fresh victories for the Moss and Stoll firm, Oswald made his London dêbut therewith in connection with his and that firm's metropolitan variety house, the Finsbury Park Empire, the Stratford Empire and so on. Presently he blossomed forth with that firm in building the London Hippodrome, and he was concerned with the lamented splendid manager Sir Edward Moss and the others of the band, with running that Hippodrome for some years.

My own somewhat strange connection with the opening of the London Hippodrome, by writing its first play at a fortnight's notice is printed in another chapter.

Eventually Stoll came out of the Moss Combine, and started the London Coliseum, and, in due course, the other variety houses which I have already mentioned.

His tremendous success at the Coliseum for many years past is a matter of history, but at first the Coliseum was not a marvel in the way of success, mainly because it took some time to gauge the taste of so large and varied an audience. Even the keen-brained Oswald had to work very hard to discover this; and thereby hangs another tale:

It was during the first Coliseum venture that my friend Stoll, whom I had known all his life in England, sent for me one night, to sit out the programme there with him. "I don't want a notice of the show," he said, "I only want you as an old friend, to sit with me, and when the show is all over to give me your opinion of it."

We sat in a box for three hours, Oswald as usual, being cryptically silent all the time. At last the curtain fell and he said: "Well . . . what do you think?" My reply was brief, but evidently to the point.

"Stoll," said I, "I have sat with you for three hours in this wonderful theatre, and what have I seen? I have seen Mrs. Brown Potter stabbed through the thorax with a long sword, in a very sanguinary sketch. I have seen Charles Warner go volcanically mad, and eventually commit suicide in a short version of "Drink." I have seen my fat friend Rutland Barrington, representing a starving tramp, die on the roadside. I have seen two lovers throw dice at a table as to which should shoot the other dead, for the sake of the lady whom they both love, and would fain carry off!

"All these four plays of doom and gloom," (I added) "have I borne without a murmur. But if this kind of programme of morbidity is to continue in this large and lovely theatre, I shall suggest to you that you rename it!"

"What name do you propose?" asked Oswald.

"The Morgueseum!" I replied.

Stoll stolidly remarked: "That's all I want to know, Chance. Good night!"

And from that time onwards, that kind of "horror upon horror's head," programme, was never again in evidence at the Coliseum!

It is well known, not only by Sir Oswald Stoll's friends and his relations, but also by vast numbers of Coliseum patrons that he installed his mother, Mrs. Stoll, in the Box Office there, from the time of that theatre's opening, until her lamented death, a year or two ago.

In point of fact, Sir Oswald regarded that dear lady for whom he had worked so incessantly, from what one might call his childhood, (certainly from his fourteenth year) as a sort of mascot. So much so that although she might, and did, when she chose, have a night off, by way of a holiday, Oswald would never start a new programme there without his mother being in the Box Office, as a sort of manageress, to welcome all and sundry.

And how delighted we . . . the said all and sundry, were . . . to meet and to chat with that lovable quick-witted Irish lady, as full of cheery anecdotes as she was of her nation's beautiful brogue.

This truly wonderful woman, who idolised her son as he idolised her, became so much a beloved London character, so to speak, that at her death the extent of the sorrow was almost incredible. I shall never forget the profoundly touching Memorial Service held in her honour at the neighbouring church, St. Martin's-in-the-Fields, when a memorable address of eulogy on her character and attainments was preached by one of our most distinguished divines.

To revert to Sir Oswald himself; I now propose to give some description of something which will perpetuate Manager Stoll's memory, more even than his splendid work for the stage, both dramatic and variety.

I allude to that splendid character institution of his, The War Seal Foundation.

This most charitable, far seeing and benevolent organisation was founded by the then "Mr." Stoll towards the end of the Great War, in order to provide for disabled warriors and their families. The affair includes a still increasing number of dwellings and other necessaries for these heroes and their dependants. In addition to the Founder's own munificent donations and continual care, it is supported partly by money raised by the use of War Seal stamps, which you are urged to buy to stick upon your envelopes etc.

It was for this huge philanthropic work and for similar generally unrecorded benevolent work among the poor and needy, not only of the theatrical and variety profession, but outside thereof, that my old friend Oswald Stoll was knighted eight years ago. No man ever deserved knighthood more!

Mention of Sir Oswald Stoll and his many enterprises would be incomplete without giving some details of a very remarkable manager who was his partner in his two Chatham ventures, namely, the Empire and the neighbouring Picture Theatre. This noteworthy man is Captain, or Alderman Davis, who, although he is now nearing the ninetieth year of his age, is as alert and keenly business like as the youngest of them.

When I first knew Captain Davis, he was running that long defunct Islington music hall, called Deacon's, a place where I

SIR OSWALD STOLL

Facing page 146

was engaged as a youngster as a duo-sketchist with one of my cousins.

Davis, who succeeded old Deacon at that Hall, became a captain in a double sense. Firstly, in a famous Volunteer regiment of the period, and secondly, for a very special and very useful purpose. That was as chief of a local Fire Brigade, which really did wonderful work in and around the so-called "Merrie" Islington. Fire Fighter Davis afterwards utilised his anti-conflagration services in a more central part of London, and achieved great renown by his prowess in that regard.

In due course the gallant captain migrated to Gravesend, where also he fought fires and ran various entertainments. Here he became Mayor several times, repeating that municipal feat anon at Chatham. The Alderman, as he now is, indeed became a most valued member of the Municipal life of both those Kentish towns. Nevertheless this versatile veteran finds time to come up and down to assist in the direction of sundry London Variety Theatres. Moreover, it is not many months ago since Captain Alderman Davis, in his Mayoral Capacity, went over to France with all his Insignia on board, to collogue with sundry French and other Mayors.

With regard to the highly successful Moss Empires Combine, I might further state that the hereinbefore-mentioned Sir Edward Moss, formally billed as H. E. Moss, was a man with a far reaching business acumen. His early ventures of a variety form included a wondrous series of performances of all kinds of music halls turns plus a good deal of All the Fun of the Fair kind, at that famous pitch the Waverley Market, Edinburgh. In this enterprise, as in any other of that combine, friend Moss was joined by the late Frank Allen, a much esteemed impresario who succeeded him as Managing Director, and of course especially up North, by that remarkable personality, Richard, otherwise Old Dick Thornton.

"Dick" was a doughty Tynesider, with whom I frequently foregathered, not only in London and the suburbs, but also on what Rob Roy would call his "Native Heath." The Northern spots wherein the breezy Richard and I were wont to hob nob included Newcastle, and that very remarkable place, South Shields.

Dick Thornton, who passed away recently at a very ripe old age, had a rather unique experience in matrimony. That is to say, he celebrated two silver weddings on his own account! And very proud of this was Richard, and indeed we were all very proud of him.

AN "ALLEGORY" ON THE BANKS OF THE TYNE

And speaking of "Teddy" Moss, Frank Allen and Dick Thornton, here perhaps I might relate a little story of an amusing experience, which occurred to me when I visited South Shields on business, connected with the Moss Empires at the time when Oswald Stoll was also concerned therewith.

I had been summoned by that Combine, all of whom knew that I was an experienced playwright and sketchwright, to concoct, at a fortnight's notice, a sort of revue or musical play wherewith to open the London Hippodrome. The opening of this had been postponed from time to time because the directorate had been unable to find a suitable piece for the purpose. In spite of the shortness of notice, I contrived to carry out this difficult job with the valued musical assistance of that late fine conductor-composer, dear old Georges Jacobi.

During the rehearsals I began to notice that we were much in need of a first-class comedian for this play, which by the way was entitled "Giddy Ostend." On my pointing this out, and saying that although we had only a week before us, I could write a big part in to fit a ditto comedian, behold Moss, Stoll and Thornton, suddenly banged me off to South Shields to engage Little Tich. He, owing to sundry disappointments at that time, had vowed never to act in London again . . . at least not in a play!

Reading the new part which I had sketched en route to the popular Tich at the local hotel, that brilliant and most versatile of variety performers speedily arranged to join us at the London Hippodrome. All this in a manner is historical, or shall I say chronicular, if I may use such a word.

What I was really going to relate is, that on arriving at the only important hotel in South Shields, in company with the late Frank Parker, then the Hippodrome's producer, a kind of Captain Kettle chap came banging down the steps, exclaiming: "Who has seen my alligator? . . . I have lost my alligator!"

And sure enough that Kettle-ish Captain had lost one! Great excitement ensued and the town was scoured as it were, to find this missing Saurian. But all in vain, for a time, anyway. In point of fact nobody found that wandering reptile, he found himself! For after much alarm had been manifested at the hotel in the night time, as to whether the awful animal had slunk back, and was lurking in some chamber or other, lo, the next day, as Parker and I were leaving the hotel, straight before us climbing up the steps came that alligator, who had been " out for the night ! "

Evidently that " Allegory " (as Mrs. Malaprop would call him) didn't find our Tyne equal to his native Nile—so he wearily waddled back !

MORE MOSS-ITES

I need hardly state that the present managing director of the Moss Empires is Richard Henry Gillespie. He was once an accountant, and indeed, is something in that line now, anyhow he is concerned with the firm of Gillespie Brothers, Accountants. Very appropriately Gillespie is, like Allen and Thornton, also a Northumbrian, having been born at Morpeth, nearly fifty years ago.

His managerial activities began only about eight years back, when he was appointed managing director of the Moss Empires, and after became joint manager with Sir Alfred Butt of the Victoria Palace Ltd. R. H. G. is also a member of the West End Theatrical Managers Association, by virtue of course of his theatrical productions at the London Hippodrome and other Moss houses. Likewise he is a member of the Entertainments Protection, Provincial Managers and Scottish Managers Association.

Gillespie is by no means a bad cricketer or golfer, and those of us who were more intimately concerned with him can testify to his agricultural and truly rural activities at his delightful farm at Esher.

Myself, when I wish to collogue with Gillespie in the Metropolis, I make it a rule to join him upstairs at the Moss Empires offices, where there is a kind of Secret Club, called after the name of the firm. At this club all the principal members of the huge staff concerned lunch daily with Gillespie, nearly always in the chair.

This very excellent arrangement keeps the staff well together, and I can assure you very merry are those refreshment meetings. The Club is duplicated in another part of the building, for the very extensive minor members of the staff, who however have just the same comforts and comestibles as the major club, as you may call it.

Chapter XII

Sir Alfred Butt and Charles Gulliver—Sir Walter Gibbons and Sir Walter de Frece—Sir George Dance and Colonel Harry Day—Manager and the Muse—A Blend of Business Managers.

Sir Alfred Butt now calls for our consideration in this managerial connection. Like most of the others whom I have named and whom I have yet to name, Butt was trained on strictly business lines. When I first knew him, about twenty-five years ago, Alfred was a very rising young employee at Harrods, where he had the inestimable advantage of being trained by the " head " thereof.

Soon he came into the Palace Theatre to assist the late Charles Morton, with whom I was at that time much associated. Butt proved himself very useful in accountancy matters and in other directions, so much so, that, at the death of the veteran Manager Morton, at a very great age, I was able to be of some slight assistance in advancing Alfred's interests there.

In due course Butt became manager at the Palace Theatre, and two years later joined the Board and became managing director and chairman, and remained so until 1920. Two years before that he had been knighted for political and War Services.

Anon A. B. became managing director of the Gaiety, the Adelphi, and the now demolished Empire Theatre, Leicester Square. He is head of the Globe and Queen's Theatres Syndicates; managing director and Chairman of the Drury Lane Company, managing director of the Victoria Palace and the Glasgow Alhambra. Furthermore, at the time of writing, Sir Alfred is Conservative M.P. for Balham and Tooting.

And now for Charles Gulliver, who undoubtedly is one of the most far-flung managers in the variety fold, and who is also becoming a very wholesale theatrical manager.

I remember Charles when he was a very young clerk in the offices of the renowned theatrical and variety solicitors,

Messrs. Amery, Parkes and Co. There sundry celebrated clients who were variety magnates, soon began to take notice of young Charles who was certainly alert and far-seeing beyond his years. Several of these "noticers" gave C. G. a push or two onwards, and thanks to these and to his business variety associations with his firm, he soon began to know a good deal about what presently became to be known as the Variety "Industry."

His big chance in the music-hall world however, one affording him unbounded opportunities of inside knowledge, was his becoming the first secretary of the Variety Artists' Federation. It was during the so called Music-Hall War that young Gulliver happened on these splendid chances, and right well did he avail himself of them.

A year or so later C. G. made a still greater stride forward by becoming the secretary of the London Theatres of Varieties Ltd., and not long afterwards he succeeded the subsequently knighted Walter Gibbons as managing director of that most extensive combine.

This post Gulliver retained until a few months ago, when he disposed for his company of several of the combine's theatres. Some of these have gone over to the all-devouring "Pictures," others are becoming more theatrical than variety, and as a matter of fact Gulliver himself is more and more veering towards the dramatic from the music-hall, or as some call it, the "vaudeville" form of entertainment.

Also he still runs the Holborn Empire and some few other theatres of the combine. The London Theatres of Varieties comprise the two just mentioned buildings, the Olympia, Shoreditch, the Lewisham, Ilford, Woolwich, Poplar, Willesden, Balham, Putney, Rotherhithe, Richmond and Croydon Hippodromes, the Kilburn, Croydon and Islington Empires, The Hammersmith, Grand, Clapham and Camberwell Palaces. There's a big, bold, batch for you!

Being only forty-five at the time of writing, there is of course still hope that this Gulliver will still further extend his Travels in the Entertainment World.

The aforesaid Walter Gibbons, who was knighted for very striking transport services during the War, was another instance of rapid rise for a youngster, who, having once got his nose into variety circles, soon rose to the top thereof.

Walter, when I first knew him, was in the photographic line, and as such soon became of very expert service in the cinema industry, which was then as one of Dickens's characters said of steam, "yet in its infancy."

It was during these early cinematic experiences, that the very young Walter became associated with the late George Adney Payne, and married that manager's daughter. That dear lady died very early in her married life, and in after years Gibbons married a very charming damsel, who is now Lady Gibbons.

I knew young Gibbons from his early youth onwards, and although I could not see eye to eye with him, during the Music Hall War, for reasons which need not be given in detail, yet happily we have remained very good friends.

After he married into Adney Payne's family, Walter Gibbons soon learned all there was to learn about the variety business, and began to blossom forth into manager of this or that hall, until he became, as I have hinted above, managing director of London Theatres of Varieties Ltd. On giving up that post to Charles Gulliver, the then soon knighted Walter broke out into other managerial directions; for example, in connection with the Golders Green Hippodrome, the Plaza Cinema Theatre in Piccadilly Circus, and so forth.

Another important manager, indeed, one of the most important in variety circles, is of course Walter de Frece, or to give him his full style and title, he has been for some time, since the war in fact, Colonel Sir Walter de Frece, M.P. Here again is a notability whom I first knew when he was a mere youngster at the game. That is to say, when he was budding forth in his native city Liverpool in connection with his numerous relations, who for generations back have been engaged in theatrical, variety and music-hall enterprises, and also with sundry agencies connected with those departments of the entertainment world.

I knew many de Freces, both of the Liverpudlian, and of the London brand; for example, that wonderful old couple, Isaac and Maurice de Frece, Walter's brother Jack, a big variety agent, also that late fine comedian, poor Lauri de Frece, who was the second husband of that brilliant young actress, Fay Compton. In fact all sorts of de Freces all over London and the provinces.

Walter soon went ahead, and after his great good fortune in carrying off the vivacious and versatile Vesta Tilley from the now also great variety magnate, who then was also one of her suitors, he gradually formed a big circuit of his very own, and afterwards ran it into a company under the title of the Variety Theatres Controlling Co. This took in various Hippodromes and such, chiefly from the South Coast, such as Boscombe, Brighton, etc.

Like his fellow variety magnates this Walter also dabbled a good deal in theatrical ventures, but really confined himself more to variety than did his managerial brethren.

Since becoming a Member of Parliament, and being knighted for his certainly very useful War services, Sir Walter has given up all his theatrical and variety interests, and restricts himself chiefly to politics, tempered with an occasional flutter at the tables at Monte Carlo, where he and Lady de Frece are always very popular visitors.

Friend de Frece has certainly done excellent service, not only in matters concerned with theatres and music-halls, but also in more imperial concerns. He and his gifted wife, the aforesaid Vesta Tilley, are undoubtedly two of the most esteemed people who have ever been connected with the variety profession.

Lady de Frece's career is depicted earlier in this volume.

Another variety celebrity who has also entered the House . . . meaning the Political one at Westminster, is Harry Day, who is of course of the same race as his fellow M.P. Sir Walter de Frece. Harry is of Polish extraction. His private name is ever so much more difficult to spell than his professional one. I remember him starting as a youngster, as a sort of stage boy, or bar boy, at the South London Music-Hall, and gradually working his way along, by the hardest of hard work, and always with strict attention to business.

It says a great deal for young Harry's perseverance and pluck that he rose from a state of extreme hard-up-ishness as a little lad to become not only a variety leader and runner of many extensive variety and revue companies, but also for having become of late years a Member of Parliament for that very district in which he first worked as a little boy at the "South" as it is always called.

Harry Day's companies are known and popular throughout these Islands, from the Palladium downwards. During the War time I had the privilege of writing for my old friend H.D. a revue constructed to fit that late most truly humorous low comedian, the Tynesider, Jimmy Learmouth, who passed away at such an early age. That revue was entitled, "Keep to the Right," and it kept there for nearly three years!

Like his vaudeville managerial brethren, Colonel Harry Day, M.P. is branching out more and more into what has long been the fashion to call the "regular" theatres, or as the professionals call it "The Legit."

Another knight who has blended variety enterprise a good deal with his theatrical ditto is Sir George Dance. George and I have been associated ever since he came to this metropolis from the Midlands about forty years ago, when he was of course very young.

Soon after arriving in London this Nottingham youth oscillated between journalism, burlesque building and comic song concoction. Later in life, after his phenomenal success, the thousand nights or so of his travesty, "The Chinese Honeymoon," Dance began to acquire most of the George Edwardes play successes, and other popular pieces of the kind, which he sent on tour, and made a nice little fortune thereby. He has since become interested in various theatrical and variety concerns, both back and front of the stage.

One of his possessions is the now popular little "Magazine Programme," which he invented, and which forms so excellent contrast to the usual programme or playbill, which is mostly smothered with advertisements, with as Sir Benjamin Backbite would say, "A neat rivulet of text (or cast) meandering adown a meadow of margin . . ." meaning the aforesaid "Adverts."

George Dance was knighted in 1923 in recognition of his having lavishly helped with a gift of £30,000 to save that now Shakespearian theatre, the Old Vic, from then pending extinction.

It was in connection with that renowned old theatre in the New Cut, that Dance and I used to meet a good deal. Also it was in consequence of our mutual knowledge of that old-time playhouse, that Sir George commissioned me to write for him my experiences of the Old Vic.

These were embodied in a shilling volume, and the profits of the large sale of that booklet were entirely devoted by Sir George to those two excellent charities, The Actors' Benevolent Fund, and The Theatrical Ladies Guild.

It may be interesting to variety patrons and music-hall lovers generally, to note here that three of the above mentioned stage knights were in their time rival variety lyrists with me.

Both Sir Oswald Stoll and Sir Walter de Frece have written songs for the great little Vesta Tilley, Sir Walter being the author of most of her popular ditties. Sir George Dance's early music-hall song writing took the form of sundry droll ditties for Arthur Roberts and other favourite variety and theatrical comedians. It is enough to add that all three knights scored highly in the lyrical department of their variety experiences, and indeed, several of their respective lyrics have lasted up to now.

So you see that even the most technical and commercial of managerial magnates may also be poets after all! . . . or that at all events, like Mr. Silas Wegg, they can when needed, "drop into poitery."

SOME FIGURES "IN FRONT"

Music-hall goers will, I feel sure, like to be reminded, however briefly, of sundry sub-managers, or, as they call them in the theatres, acting or business managers, who did duty not too far back in the good old days of the Halls.

Those very early ones who mattered are touched upon here and there in previous chapters.

The group which I will here present includes a great many such functionaries, who will be well remembered by large numbers of my readers.

For example, two of the most popular music-hall "lieutenants" of the earlier days were Ted and Arthur Swanborough, who were the sons of Mrs. Swanborough, manageress of the old Strand Theatre for so many years.

By the time that Ted and Arthur arrived in the variety houses they were well primed with theatrical lore, and drew into those halls many a hitherto solely theatrical patron or personage to whom they retailed whole budgets of stories. Both these Swanboroughs had a distinctive, not to say distinguished, manner, and indeed both used to impart to me from time to time, mysterious hints as to their having been way back of somewhat Royal Extraction!

Both Arthur and Ted, each of whom had married a popular actress, Fanny Hughes and Eleanor Bufton respectively, were of a very steady and trustworthy nature. Ever and anon however, we foregathered at certain wigwams, shall I say, where both would very innocently deviate into a little Bohemianism.

I remember on one occasion, when I went in one night to the opening of variety theatres in Bath and Bristol, Ted Swanborough had, with Vernon Dowsett, the dual charge of the arrangements for those openings under the direction of the chiefs of the formerly mentioned Syndicate Halls.

When we parted in the early hours of the next morning at the Clifton Down Hotel (facing the wonderful Suspension Bridge), I remember that Teddy Swanborough stopped on his way upstairs to bed, and solemnly addressed the statue of the Apollo Belvedere, whom he insisted upon regarding as Vernon Dowsett!

But lo! next morning, by the time I got on to the Suspension Bridge and looked far down into the River Avon below—who should approach me but Teddy Swanborough, as fresh as paint, and then finishing a several miles' morning walk.

Vernon Dowsett will be remembered, and his early death regretted by many old haunters of the halls, especially at the old Tivoli, where he started as assistant manager for the great Charles Morton, and was afterwards so long manager himself.

Dowsett was a very kindly and loyal fellow, who married a charming soubrette of the time named Nellie Melnotte. It was Vernon's hobby to hobnob a great deal with famous cricketers, jockeys, and other more or less noble sportsmen, some of whom alas, were not the best of friends to him.

Other exceedingly popular variety business managers included the breezy Harry Hitchens, who for so many years was in front at the now defunct Empire, and the equally popular but ill-fated George Scott, and Dundas Slater, Tom Carlton, of the Royal Holborn, and Walter Gooch, who must perforce have a few words to himself.

I first met Walter Gooch when he was manager for his mother at the hall which became the Metropolitan. After a few other variety experiences, he married a serio-comic, afterwards a stage actress, named Fanny Leslie, who I believe is still living. Walter ran into money, and eventually took the Princess's Theatre, Oxford Street, where he made a big fortune out of Charles Reade's great temperance play called "Drink," in which Fanny Leslie had a part interpolated in for her.

Unfortunately a series of failures followed this, and Walter's luck went down with a bang. This was to be regretted, for despite a habit of fussy showiness, little Walter Gooch had many sterling qualities which I shall always remember.

Some of these music-hall business managers are happily still with us; these include that quaint popular character, Joe Wilson, so long in front at the Tivoli, after he had served as a lancer in a noble regiment, and had taken to the theatre stage playing sailors and such like. At the time of writing Joseph is dwelling on the Dorsetshire coast, sailing about ever and anon in a yachtlet or ketch, or whatever you like to call it.

Another strong survivor is that delightul pal, Frank Glenister, who, after being so many years in front at the London Pavilion, when it was in its variety form, is still installed in that building, watching over the interests of its proprietors, the aforesaid Syndicate directors. Another still strong-going chum is Frank Boor, of the London Hippodrome.

Still another, once manager for the variety houses, and especially for the late Empire, is the hale and hearty Oscar

Barrett, Junior, who, after having served Sir Alfred Butt as manager at the Empire and the Queens Theatre, is at the present moment general manager of London's newest and most beautiful theatre, the Carlton.

Other deservedly popular variety lieutenants include the delightful personality, William Agnew, who was recently appointed by Sir Oswald Stoll as manager at the Coliseum. Also David James, who is not only a business manager for the vast Stoll house, the Wood Green Empire, but is also the grandson of the late famous comedian David James, born Belasco, and is therefore nephew of the renowned American-Jewish manager, dramatist and producer, David Belasco.

One might also mention the popular Harry Hall, business manager of the Victoria Palace, and the many-sided A. G. Andrews, ex-mariner, ex-gymnast, and ex- various things, who presides over the Empress Theatre of Varieties, Brixton, of which that extensive licensee victualler or variety magnate, Billy Grimes, is one of the chief directors.

CHAPTER XIII

The Music-hall Press—Its perplexing Peculiarities—The *Glowworm* and the *Entr'acte*—The *Encore* and the *Performer*—The *Stage* and the *Era*—The *Referee*.

The Music-hall Press has always had its perplexing peculiarities. Before going any further allow me to point out that the "peculiar perplexities" indicated do not apply to the present-day Press, when it treats Music-hall matters, or rather, as they call them now, Variety Entertainments, that is when they are not called Vaudeville Shows (as in the U.S.A.).

But that the Music-hall Press of the past was either peculiar or perplexing, or both, will soon be made obvious by these personal recollections of my own.

Thirty odd years ago some few details as to the Variety Press of the period were given in a very useful little book called "The Variety Stage," complied by A. J. Park, in collaboration with my esteemed old friend, C. Douglas Stuart, who is, at the time of writing, still (I think) the able Secretary of the most useful association for Variety Professionals, the M.H.A.R.R.A. which means, the Music-hall Artists' Railway Rates Association. This was founded a good many years ago, in order to procure reasonable concessions for touring Music-hall Artists, especially when they are in small batches as Sketchists.

This "Variety Stage" book, long out of print, was a small volume, and therefore necessarily, its different chapters as to the old halls, and the new ones of the time, the songs, etc., and especially the Music-hall Press, were brief and sketchy.

Moreover, as the book was financed by certain music-hall folk, naturally it was not too critical in tone. The compilers, however, deserve great credit for this Variety volume, for it was the first of its kind, and very useful for rapid reference.

Now, having been saturated in music-hall, as well as theatrical matters, early in life, I am able to delve rather deeply into the history of the Music-hall Press of my time. I have still by me sundry volumes of a certain very blackmailing journal of my youthful period, a periodical which I shall not name, as there may be still existing certain descendants of the chief contributor concerned.

It was the habit of the editors and critics of such periodicals and the representatives of sundry local papers, to " make a bit " out of their criticisms, both of the theatrical and variety professionals, especially the struggling and would-be rising ones. And this is how they did it.

When the artist or actor, or singer or sketch-player arrived in a certain town or district, it was the weekly habit of those "journalists" to send in to that entertainer a visiting card which the artist was expected to " back " with a little " sub." of half a sovereign, five shillings, or whatever he or she could afford. If the said artist did his "backing" in the approved manner, he received a very gushing notice in the paper represented.

If the artist refused (as happily I always did myself) the critic gave him " socks," and many a frightful pair of that same has the present writer received in consequence. But luckily, like others who refused to be thus bled, there were times when, strangely enough, we were rewarded with appreciative notices, free, gratis, and for nothing !

These revelations of mine may seem strange in these days of a free and just Press, but I can assure the surprised reader that this kind of blackmail was very common in my younger days, and not only among the smaller newspapers of the period.

By the time I was getting into my 'teens, and working and writing for the halls, there started a kind of music-hall Press on its own. I think I am right in saying that the first little sheet that devoted itself (partly, at least) to music-hall matters towards the late 'sixties was a smart thing called the *Glowworm.*

This was speedily followed by that long popular, but alas ! now defunct, weekly, entitled, *The Entr'acte.* For a number of years the late W. H. Combes ran this publication, which it may be remembered was sold in the music-halls, and in each case there was printed thereon the current programme of the hall in which it was sold.

In due course the *Entr'acte* not only dabbled a little in theatre notices, as well as music-hall dittos, but it came additionally popular and much talked about by reason of its remarkable caricature-portraits of theatrical and music-hall folk drawn by the late Alfred Bryan, who was quite a genius at that sort of thing. Bryan was succeeded by his brilliant pupil, Tom Downey, who is now very properly regarded as one of our quaintest caricaturists and comic illustrators.

I had the pleasure to be a frequent contributor to the *Entr'acte*, and especially to its Annual, for which Editor Combes used to rope in many a dramatic, variety, and literary light.

Alas! with the subsequent hermit-like retirement and illness of good old Combes, and in spite of the unfailing night and day devotion to that periodical by Combes's busy little lieutenant, the late lovable W.C. Barber, the *Entr'acte* went off into the journalistic *Ewigkeit.*

Some time before the *Entr'acte* vanished there came out a competitor thereto, a weekly paper called *The Music Hall.* Its name was appropriate, for, unlike the *Entr'acte*, it dealt only with Variety matters. Being also of a subsidised kind, it treated the halls and their artists with great gushiness.

The *Music Hall* was for some time edited, and in a measure owned, by the late extremely careful theatrical and variety chronicler, Harry G. Hibbert, and at one time he was, I fancy, largely assisted financially and otherwise by that remarkable and very keen variety agent, Hugh Jay Didcott.

For some time at a later period the *Music Hall* was run by a very kindly hearted but ebullient Bohemian named Frank Allport. I am afraid that Frank, like Harry, did not come out too well financially by their respective connection with that journal, and as far as I know, it has been for some time *non est.*

One of the variety-treating publications of about that time, however, has contrived to survive, and indeed is, I fancy, better off now than it has ever been. I allude to the *Encore*, which was always, and is, still rather more audacious and critical than its Press predecessors were. It has a habit of asking saucy little questions, which to many of us seem rather of parochial, than of imperial, interest. Still, it has always been a useful sheet, especially for its tiny monographs of suburban music-hall stars and managers. Certainly also it possesses a good deal of real humour although of a very low comedy order.

It is, of course, a matter of common knowledge that one of the best and busiest papers devoted to theatrical and music-hall entertainments is *The Stage.* It may be mentioned in this connection that this very technically correct periodical devotes two or three pages per week to variety matters, treating all such very skilfully, and without any attempt at humour or epigram, and ceratinly without the flamboyance which was generally the habit of writers on music-hall topics.

The *Stage*, in fact, is one of those papers which one can

always safely use for dates and facts set forth with arithmetical correctness and free from all flummery.

Undoubtedly the most comprehensive as well as correctly-chronicling periodicals dealing with the music-hall stage, and standing quite alone in its usefulness to such professionals in the matter of variety and its "politics," is the *Performer*.

This excellently edited little journal has proved of considerable use to all interested in this form of entertainment, especially has it fought bravely for the rights of variety folk and all the wholesome sides of its cause, ever since it came out. That was about the time of the Music-Hall War, which I have described elsewhere in these Memories, many of which appeared in the *Performer* but not, of course, this especial chapter.

The *Performer* is also the organ of that most far-flung charitable scheme, The Variety Artists' Benevolent Fund and Institution, but, of course, this and similar music-halls charities are also well helped by other theatrical and variety organs, as well as by their "trade" papers.

And now it is but fair to consider from a variety point of view, two of the oldest established theatrical newspapers, each of which has done an enormous amount of work, both in pushing and preserving the music-hall stage.

I allude to the ninety-year-old periodical, *The Era*; and the fifty-year-old still more general journal, *The Referee*.

I have a very absorbing affection for the *Era*, for as a member of a very numerous theatrical and music-hall family, it was, of course, the first paper from which I learned to read.

At that time as a mere youngster I had so studied the *Era* announcements and advertisements that I could at any moment tell the whereabouts and the line of business of every actor or music-hall favourite advertised in its columns. This *Era*-reading habit, together with having to study and play many characters on the shortest possible notice, developed a most useful working memory, which I am thankful still to possess.

The *Era* took up the music-halls in some measure directly those entertainment places began to be popular, and while many of them were still in what I might call their pothouse condition. For some time that old journal treated the halls and their people somewhat derisively, but with the coming of the bigger stars, the Vances, the Leybournes, etc., the *Era* began to venture upon somewhat more earnest criticism.

At the present moment that nonogenarian publication devotes a large amount of its space to variety notices, etc. I might here add, as a personal note, that for many years past I have had the pleasure to contribute criticisms, stories, essays, etc., both of a theatrical and variety nature, for the good old *Era*. This, of course, obviously has increased my affection for it.

Needless to add I have an especial affection for the *Referee*, and for its founder, Henry Sampson ("Pendragon"). He engaged me for that paper from its very first number, as he had discovered from my association with him as a comic poet on *Fun* that, young as I was, I was soaked through with experiences of the stage and the music-halls on both sides of the curtain.

At first the *Referee* did not specialize to any extent in music-hall notices, but from my association with those places I was able to persuade "Pendragon" and his editorial successor Richard Butler to devote some space to such matters. Eventually I was also instrumental in causing a blend of the halls with the theatrical notices on the "Carados" page. The regular "Carados" was then the late George Spencer Edwards who was also Editor of the *Era*.

In due course I not only extended my music-hall work for the *Referee*, but later took over the whole of the "Carados" department which I am still running at the time of writing.

I think I am right in stating that in arranging anon for the *Referee* to have a special variety article when the halls were beginning to loom large in the public ken, I was the first to establish such a separate article, certainly in a general paper.

That article devoted to the halls I wrote for a long while, but eventually on my general criticism work in interviews, reviews, etc., increasing, I gave up that variety article to its present very able writer, Mr. Bernard Marks ("Tristram").

In winding up this chapter on the Variety Press, I ought to add that unfortunately a large number of daily papers and weekly ditto, seem still to think it infra dig to have anything in them about the halls, and when they do, manage to "discover" artistes who have been before the public for a number of years. Nevertheless, the general writing of variety criticisms has vastly improved of late years, both as to observation, analysis of "turns" and style of writing.

At one time all the music-hall notices, especially in the so-called "trade" papers, were all exactly alike. To such critics (if I might call them so) one set of words seemed to be quite as good as any other set. Especially there was one particular and unvarying form of tag: as "Mr. So-and-So" still wields the baton as Chef d'orchestre, also that "Mr Such-and-Such still remains the Frontal Representative." This latter strange phrase was really the usual weekly way of describing the business manager.

And now all that remains is to venture on the hope that one of these days even the above-indicated lofty non-music-hall noticing journals will come into line, and will join the rest of us in believing and in acting under the old poetic dictum: namely, that "Variety is the Spice of Life."

Chapter XIV

Charles Morton, the "Father of the Halls"—Stars he introduced to the Variety Stage—His Tableaux Vivants at the Palace—Stars of the Superior Sex—Phyllis Broughton on the Halls—Kate Santley.

"The Father of the Halls" was the term applied for many years to the late Charles Morton, perhaps because during his very long career he was connected much more with theatres than with variety houses. Still, his experience in the music-hall department of the entertainment world was far greater than any of his managerial brethren, before or since.

In fact, his variety knowledge might be said to resemble Mr. Sam Weller's knowledge of London in that it was "extensive and peculiar."

My own personal experience of this famous veteran began when I was a mere boy, and he was then starting to run the Philharmonic music-hall, which he afterwards turned into the Philharmonic Theatre, a place which later became the Grand Theatre, Islington, and is now the Islington Empire.

About this time Morton was also in turn concerned with various opera or opera-bouffe productions at the old Gaiety, where I also came in. I will not, however, dilate upon Morton's very varied and renowned theatrical career, for of course it does not come within the scope of this variety volume.

As regards myself it is perhaps enough to say that my intimate acquaintance with him from my childhood until he died over twenty years ago, when he was getting on for 90, led to my having the privilege of writing in collaboration with his brother William, the veteran Charles's biography, or life and adventures.

This book was called "Sixty Years' Stage Service: or, The Father of the Halls," and was published by the notable military book-issuing firm, Gale and Polden. The reason why those martial publishers took up this book may be explained by the fact that one of the firm, Ernest Polden, was at that time also one of the directors of the Palace Theatre, which was the last variety house managed by the veteran Morton.

Confining myself therefore to the chief music-hall ventures of Charles Morton, I may mention, first, that after he had run sundry taverns of his own, what were then called sing-songs, or "free-and-easies," he took a celebrated tavern or inn at the corner of the Upper Marsh End of the Westminster Bridge Road, and transposed that tavern into the famous Canterbury Music-hall.

From Morton's opening of this long-marvellous place in 1852, and right on to the middle sixties, he made this hall a universally sought pleasure haunt, not only for music-hall patrons generally, but also for some of the most distinguished people in Literature, Art, Music, and the Drama.

It was at the Canterbury that Morton introduced some of the biggest music-hall stars either of that time or since. They included such tremendous favourites as the Great Mackney, first and best of all negro comedians; Sims Reeves, the great tenor and Miss Fitzhenry, afterwards Emile Soldene, both of whom appeared in operatic selections. Also Tom Maclagan, who could do anything on the theatre or music-hall stage from Grand Opera to comic singing and the Highland Fling. Lastly, but by no means leastly, that wonderful comic singer who had also been in grand opera and the drama; namely, Sam Cowell.

It was Cowell who brought out at the Canterbury a couple of songs which he had been giving at the Grecian Saloon, afterwards the Grecian Theatre, which was on the site of the Eagle Tavern, so celebrated in the refrain, "Pop Goes the Weasel." These songs of Cowell's were respectively, "Villikins and His Dinah," and "The Ratcatcher's Daughter," both of which ditties are being sung at the present time in the variety theatres by Muriel George and Ernest Butcher.

These are only a few of the big stars of Morton's at the Canterbury Hall, which towards the end of the 'sixties, was taken over by the wonderful but eccentric manager, William Holland, who has been described in an early chapter.

Early in the 'sixties, Charles Morton swooped down upon another tavern, namely, "The Boar and Castle," in Oxford Street. These licensed premises he transformed into the afterwards famous Oxford Music-hall. A few years later the Oxford was burnt down, but the cheery Charles soon built it up again, and ran it for a good many more years. Here also, as at the Canterbury, Manager Morton was on several occasions, brought "before the Beak," as the saying is, and charged with infringing the law as it then was, by producing sketches, and even duologues, which were held to be of sufficiently dramatic character to infringe the Lord Chamberlain's theatrical licence!

Even when Morton reached the Palace Theatre where he finished his career, he was still often prosecuted for sketch-producing against the law. The strange ramifications of this law, and the manner in which they were finally quelled by the aid of several (including Yours Truly), is more fully set forth in previous pages.

Morton's other variety ventures included entertainments given at the Old Surrey Gardens, Newington Butts; The Alhambra, of which he became manager on several occasions; the Empire, and the Tivoli, which was his last pitch before going to the Palace.

It was at the Palace that Morton introduced, or rather revived in a much more artistic form, the kind of entertainment called "Living Pictures." These shows, which had hitherto been billed as Tableaux Vivants, now and then caused quite a rumpus at the Palace, chiefly on account of the fact that some of the female figures were shown, as Hans Breitmann would say, "Mid Nodings on."

Morton, like his contemporary poet Browning, was "ever a fighter"; and he fought these complainers and others of the sort with characteristic courage. I cannot say myself that I always agreed with Morton with regard to what I called his Nude Departures, but from what I have seen of late in theatres and music-halls, I must say that Charles Morton's Pictures of Venus, etc. were absolute Idylls of Innocence.

Charles Morton was many things besides being a theatrical manager and "Father of the Halls." He was a man deeply read and versed in the Drama and Music. He was also an able and enthusiastic sculler; even a compleat angler, and a bit of a backer of horses. In fact, there were times when Charles "made a book," sometimes on his own, and sometimes in connection with that then famous bookie, Charles Head, who was rich and willing enough to finance Morton at the Philharmonic and elsewhere.

Morton was, of course, by virtue of his position, his integrity and his far-reaching influence, one of the most popular men of his time.

While I was engaged in jotting these memories of my wonderful old friend Charles Morton, a strange thing happened, as they say in fiction. This was that Morton's widow, whom I had not had the pleasure of meeting for a good many years, suddenly turned

CHARLES MORTON
(" THE FATHER OF THE HALLS ")
(*Photo by Samuel A. Walker*)

Facing page 166

up at Drury Lane Theatre if you please, and arranged to have a seat in front to see that new success, " The Desert Song," and all because, forsooth, it was that lady's 101st birthday !

And there Mrs. Morton, whose husband, had he lived, would have been 108, sat and enjoyed herself, seemingly in perfect health and spirits. While correcting these proofs, the news reaches me of that dear old lady's death.

I remember that Mrs. Morton comes from a long-lived race, for her brother, Frederic Stanley, whom I always met with Morton, went on till nearly 90 ! A famous solicitor was Frederic, and in theatrical circles was of great help in many a difficult law action. To his brother-in-law, Charles Morton, Fred Stanley was of especial benefit, for it was he who saw that audacious and frequent breaker of the law, regarding dramatic sketches, through his many troubles, and indeed getting his inevitable fines reduced as far as possible.

The late Frederic Stanley will be remembered by a great many theatrical and variety people as having been the head for so many years of the celebrated legal firm of Stanley, Woodhouse and Hedderwick.

STARS OF THE SWEET SEX

The chief feminine variety stars, all alas ! now passed away, included a round dozen, all of whom either ventured from, or 'verted back to, the dramatic boards, or " legit."

One of the earliest of these to come into the halls was the beautiful Phyllis Broughton—beautiful alike, indeed, in person, and in character. This widely lamented lady, who will or should be remembered for her ceaseless charity to the needy and the suffering, came in her early girlhood from the Grecian Theatre into the Halls. After a few years therein, she blossomed forth into leading-ladyhood in the West End theatres, but ever and anon she returned to Variety Circles. Her Gaiety career is historical.

Another charming and gifted 'vert from the Drama to Variety was the rich-voiced and sweet-natured Evie Greene, one of the cleverest artistes that ever graced the boards of either departments of the professions.

Two of the best and brightest of theatrico-variety artistes were Bessie Bonehill and Bessie Wentworth, both of whom chiefly confined their music-hall work to male impersonations, and continued the same in adopting the Principal Boy-hood of the regular theatre pantomines.

Another famous principal boy and dude player of the theatres and music-halls was that delightful damsel Millie Hylton, who was one of the many sisters of that former renowned dancing soubrette,Letty Lind, born Rudge, and a "Brum." The other sisters, all of whom more or less engaged in variety flutters, sandwiched with theatrical ditto, included Fanny Dango, Lydia Flopp, and Adelaide Astor, who is Mrs. George Grossmith.

Also a chieftain among principal boys, both for success and size, and a favourite on both stages, was Harriett Vernon, a very fine singer, if not a very great actress. I can remember only three fellow favourites of the sort, who resembled poor Harriett, for commanding statuesqueness and, shall I say, plentitude of figure. These were Agnes Hewitt, Helen Barry, both excellent actresses, and the still deservedly popular music-hall and revue star, Florrie Forde.

Perhaps the most historical instance of a dramatic and musical favourite coming into the halls from time to time was the tremendously popular operatic and opera bouffe star, Emily Soldene. It was when I was a little boy in the halls that the finely-formed Emily came to do a trial turn at the Oxford when Charles Morton was running it. She then called herself Miss Fitzhenry, and I remember that as she sailed majestically along the saloon towards the stage, that old music-hall basso Jonghmans, the German warbler so long popular in that period, gazing at this large lady, said to Morton, "Charlie, vot is it?" "I don't know," responded Charles, "but It will be all right if It can sing." And It *could* sing, and sang for Morton for many years, not only in the halls he ran, but also in many of his comic opera successes.

I grew to know the magnificent Emily of the cavernous mouth well, in both departments of the stage, and I must say that she always impressed me, not only with her abounding talent, but also by her very free-and-easy conversation, and the appetising manner in which she could retail strange specimens of *Chroniques Scandaleuses*. In later life the erratic Emily left behind a book or two of reminiscences embodying a good many of these *Chroniques*. They are quite startling volumes I can assure you.

Other popular late favourites of that period included clever little Katie Lawrence, a true artist indeed, who made her chief vogue in Harry Dacre's phenomenally successful song concerning a "Bicycle made for Two." Also poor Victoria Monks, who was as entertaining as she was erratic and good-hearted withal, and whose great hold upon the music-hall public was won by her cheery chortling of very striking ditties, including that long-lived lyric, "Won't You Come Home, Bill Bailey?"

Two other successful damsels of the halls, chiefly as dancers, were Katie Seymour and Lottie Collins, the mother of the melodious Josie. Both Katie and Lottie came in due course from the halls to the theatres, especially to the Gaiety, where the former figured in many a musical play, chiefly with the late droll Edmund (or Teddy) Payne. Miss Collins came into the theatres especially engaged, as the playbills put it, to repeat the strange dervish-like dancing ditty, "Ta-Ra-Ra-Boom-De-Ay."

This effusion which would now be labelled as Jazz, was written by one of our cleverest variety lyrists, namely, Richard Morton, who is, I fancy, at the time of writing, still a valued contributor to our very outspoken contemporary, *John Bull*. Some of Richard's other lively songs were written for another then enormously popular music-hall favourite, namely, the dainty Minnie Cunningham.

Many another past favourite of the variety stage might be described herein, but I think, however, I will add to this present group some reference to a very remarkable lady named Kate Santley, who died a year or two ago, at the ripe old age of 86 !

When I was a little boy I used to hear Kate Santley chortle in such halls as the Sun, Knightsbridge; Gatti's Arches, etc., one especial song. In this she represented a flustered slavey, and the ditty in which she described her troubles had the following repeatful refrain:

"The bell goes a-ringing for Sarah,
For Sarah, Sarah !
The bell goes a-ringing for Sarah
From morning until night."

By the time I reached the Old Queen's Theatre, Long Acre (on the site of which the *John Bull* offices now stand), I, then at the mature age of fourteen, beheld Kate Santley blossom forth into a principal boy ! Her first essay in this line was in a very fine burlesque called very happily, "The Stranger . . . Stranger Than Ever," by that prolific extravaganza writer, Robert Reece whose burlesque writing deputy (to fulfil sundry contracts) I had the privilege to become.

In after years the bonnie Kate, always a pretty fair-haired soubrette, became one of the leading ladies at the Alhambra, then a regular theatre, at which house she had to share the stardom with a fine-figured theatrical and variety singer named Rose Bell. Alas ! this sharing led, I remember, to many rows and ructions or "alarums and excursions" as Warwickshire Will would call them.

I had a good deal to do with the place at that time, and I remember that all concerned (including your humble), used to wait eagerly night by night, for the terrible burst of catcalls and other eldritch cries emitted by the respective partisans of Handsome Rose and Pretty Kate.

These extraordinary ebullitions, which must have cost Kate and Rose a pretty penny apiece, were only equalled by the nightly outburst at the same Alhambra when the respective sympathisers of France and Germany howled forth their " sentiments" during the run of the Franco-Prussian War. Here again, I was in the midst of the fray!

Forty years or so ago Kate Santley became the proprietor and manager of the Royalty Theatre in Dean Street, Soho. Here she produced, among other things, George R. Sims's first musical comedy, "The Merry Duchess," the score of which was by the then popular composer, Fred Clay. She also presented at the Royalty a comic opera called "La Marjolaine," which was based upon the same Boccaccio story which Shakespeare used for his "All's Well that Ends Well."

I may mention in passing that by this time I was writing dramatic criticisms for the *Referee*, and owing to the very unpleasant tone of "La Marjolaine" I had to give it what the poets call "unadulterated beans."

In conclusion I may state that Kate Santley installed in an upstairs room at the Royalty a *chapelle ardente* in memory of a certain benefactor. And that chapel was in that theatre for many years!

One of the most remarkable occasional 'verts to variety from the Higher Drama and Classic Ballet, was the late Isadora Duncan, that extraordinary dancer of what might be called the *Poses Plastiques* type. I say the Higher Drama, because this actress and terpsichorean star made her stage début at the age of fifteen, in 1895, in Augustin Daly's New York revival of "A Midsummer Night's Dream."

Five years later this Belle Americaine (who was born in the glorious climate of California) made her London début, strangely enough, in the same play with The Benson Company at the Lyceum. After a course of Russian and other ballets, and much other foreign choreography, La Duncan began to make considerable fame as a classical dancer. Indeed, she was mainly responsible for a widespread revival of such dancing by means of her schools and classes in France, Germany, Greece, etc.

This gifted, but alas! hapless, dancing damsel, had a very chequered career, but of her it certainly may be said by those of us who knew her well, that like poor old King Lear she was often " more sinned against than sinning."

The terrible deaths of two of her children, and her own awful tragic end, are both such recent events that further details are not needed.

By way of strange sequel to my remarks about this unfortunate lady, so often the victim of an exaggerated form of the artistic temperament, perhaps I may be pardoned for mentioning the insane fact that a lady gambler at Monte Carlo, and such aristocratic resorts, recently bought the fatal scarf which helped to cause poor Isadora's death. This extraordinary purchaser is alleged to have asserted that this article of attire proved a marvellous mascot, causing her to win vast sums at the tables!

Such behaviour, even among mad gamblers, seems almost incredible, but I am afraid that poor Isadora herself would have been rather pleased at this form of publicity, even for her fatal scarf!

A stormy petrel was poor Isadora. May she rest in Peace!

BESSIE BELLWOOD! A SLANGING SERIO

One of the most humorous, and certainly one of the sauciest serios ever seen in even the " saucy " halls of her time, was Bessie Bellwood. Although lacking the versatility and character-acting genius of her great rivals, Marie Lloyd and Jenny Hill, Bessie was a real artist of the brainiest, most alert kind. She would " take on " any of the audience at any time, and on any topic, conducting her arguments in the most voluble slum-slang. Some of her utterances and reports often savoured very strongly of the hereinbeforementioned " blue bag." Although La Bellwood gained her chief stage effects as a " pattering " Irish Cockney, she was no mean warbler. Many even now will remember her chief ditties such as " Woa Emma! ", " Wotcher Ria! ", " Rias on the Job! " and that very clever song " Aubrey Plantagenet " written (if my memory serves me) by that chartered and cheery humorist, poor Willie Goldbery, the " Shifter " of " The Sporting Times " (or " Pinkun.")

I knew poor Bessie thoroughly from the moment she made her music-hall début in Bermondsey, where she had been a " rabbit puller " or " skin-dresser " in a local factory. I always found her really more " educated " than she pretended to be. She was a relative of the renowned literary and poetic priest who signed himself "Father Prout" and was born Mahoney—as Bessie was. She often talked books and poems etc. with me.

Also she confided to me many of her most private matters, especially concerning her association with sundry "aristocrats"—who did her no kind of benefit, either in her profession or out of it. In fact, poor Bessie who thought herself so clever, was always being swindled or "done in" by somebody.

She was a woman of boundless benevolence, and of deep devotion to her Roman Catholic Creed. In fact, I found her always either helping some sad case of distress, or paying (even with her last earnings) for "Masses" for some dying or departed soul. In some cases, these "Masses" (as I well knew) were for those who (as she would have put it), had "done her a bit of no good!" Like Florence St. John, (who we all called "Jack") and Marie Lloyd, dear old Bessie Bellwood would perform the most menial, most trying, and painful offices for the needy, sick, and dying. And to these I have often heard her (like others too) give not only her last coin, but even (what is still harder to such superstitious hearts), her last "mascot." Such was the slangful saucy serio, Bessie Bellwood—born Mahoney! An erratic but noble soul!

CHAPTER XV

Old-time Comic Singers—Sam Torr and Sam Redfern—Fred Albert and Charles Williams—Billy Williams, "The Man in the Velvet Suit"—"Over" Rowley—Harry Fragson, born Potts—Some strange 'Verts to Variety—The Tichborne Claimant as a Variety Turn.

In addition to the great variety stars who have made their exit from the Stage of Life, there were numerous very clever and very humorous "gay dogs" among the comic singers.

One of the funniest of these in his crudely comic way was Sam Torr, who more than once went in for a managerial flutter in London or provincial music-halls, and mostly wished he hadn't! Sam was perhaps one of the last of the comic singers of the red-nosed type, after the pattern of "Jimmy" Fawn, but by no means so finished a comedian as James. A part of Sam's old-fashioness was shown by the fact that he clung to the battered hat, seedy frock coat, and huge bow-cravat, always worn by Sam Cowell and others of the earlier period.

Perhaps Torr's best known, and certainly his most continuously used ditty, was the one with the following chorus:

"The fox and the hare, the badger and the bear
And the birds in the greenwood tree;
And the pretty little rabbits so engaging in their habits,
Have all got a mate but me.
Oh Lor!"

Two other funny fellows very much alike in method, especially in their wilder comic moods, were Henri Clark and Victor Liston. Both had been actors in the "Legit."; always a valuable asset to a music-hall artist. In fact, Clark had also chortled a good deal as a buffo in grand opera. His most famous song, which will still be remembered by many, was the one with the following catchy chorus:

"I'm the mad butcher . . . I'm the mad butcher!
I'm the mad butcher . . . they say I'm insane.
I'm the mad butcher, I'm the mad butcher
Driven to this by my false Mary Jane!"

Very repeatful, but certainly a very rollicking song.

Now Victor Liston in addition to being a very humorous comedian, possessed, as all true comedians do, a very strong vein of pathos. This he exhibited very touchingly in his one big song which he sang year in and year out. It was entitled "Shabby Genteel," and was written by that most finished writer of society verse, Henry S. Leigh. I can see before me now, Victor Liston in his threadbare frock coat, and shockingly bad top hat, as he sang in broken tones that reached the heart, the following refrain :

> "I'm too proud to beg, too honest to steal ;
> I know what it is to be wanting a meal.
> My tatters and rags I try to conceal—
> I'm one of the Shabby Genteel !"

Alas, in his latter days poor Victor, crushed by misfortune, was driven to walking about the streets in something like this very garb, and I fear he was too often "wanting a meal."

Sam Redfern, one of the then multitudinous music-hall niggers, or "Ethiopian Serenaders," (as they used to call themselves) was more of a patter entertainer than a singer. In that respect he resembled the blacked up "stump orators" of a still earlier period ; such "nigs" for instance as Unsworth, and Billy West, each of whom had a similar topical stump speech with the recurring question, "Am I right or any other man ?"

Sam used to reel off his topicalities at engagements which often lasted him over a year at a time at one hall. Many mature music-hall goers will remember that the voluble Redfern seemed really to "live" at the London Pavilion, or "Pav." His topics were always up-to-date, and he generally began and ended his verbose but vivacious orations with a snatch or two of song.

There was one especial "drink" ditty, which Black-faced Sam warbled in season and out of season, and it had the refrain : "Any excuse for a booze."

You could regard this lyric from two angles ; one as a merely comic chortle, the other from a temperance and almost Prohibition outlook ! For look you, Sam's excuses for booze were set forth in exactly the same manner as Cruikshank's terrible picture, "The Bottle ; or The Drunkard's Fate !"

This it will be remembered starts with drinking at the Babe's Christening ; goes on to several of his birthdays ; shows a drinking bout at his marriage ; ditto at each of his youngster's births, and finally a drunken orgy over his coffin ! So Sam used to intone the details as thus! Good old Sam, although not one of the swollen salaried kind, was a very careful liver, and was able to retire among the house properties which he had acquired by saving.

TOPICAL TRILLERS

"In the elder days of Art" as Longfellow would say, topical songsters were very numerous, sometimes they were also labelled "extempore vocalists," which meant that they were supposed to vamp up versicles on this or that kind friend in front, or upon any subject given them.

The great popular topical vocalist of those days was Fred Albert, whose widow subsequently married J. L. Graydon. When I was a youngster, Fred Albert was coming out with such topical ditties as "That's what astonishes me," and "I knew that I'd been dreaming."

Albert had a very rapid manner and a cork leg. Apart from my labelling him one of the most alert and prolific writers and singers of topical songs (for he wrote all his own), I think I may justly add that it was from Fred Albert that I learnt my own subsequently swift and ready habit of writing such songs myself, if I may say so.

Another very successful topical song writer and singer was Charles Williams, who for a few years of his career, which was cut short by a sad accident, ran Fred Albert very close.

Charles made a very great vogue in variety-land with a national topical song, the refrain of which ran as follows:

"The Flag that cheers the sailor on his way;
The Flag that always carries the sway,
The Flag that always carries the Day:—
The Union Jack of Old England."

Poor Charlie's end at a very young age was caused by his reckless driving of a dog cart, late one dark night, when the horse bolted, throwing the poor fellow out, and breaking his neck. This was the more to be regretted for Charles Williams, apart from being a smart songster, had really something of the poet in him.

Two other noted topicalisers in the halls were Tom Vine and F. V. St. Clair. This twain (both I think still with us, but retired), were among the quickest in the up-take, both with regard to topics and in their "improvisations."

Yet another who was very smart in this line with an additional humorous and motto twist, after the fashion of the great Harry Clifton, was Billy Williams, who came over from Australia, and soon became one of the greatest favourites on the variety stage. He adopted a special kind of costume which led him to label himself in his adverts, as " The Man in the Velvet Suit."

So prolific was the blithe Billy, that to this day, you will find at Francis and Day's, whole budgets of songs written by or for Billy Williams . . . songs which are really songs, and not merely the repeatful rubbish which so often does duty for such.

After a few years of great popularity, poor Billy died young, very widely regretted by everybody.

Many will remember that even the popular comic singer and wonderful dancer J. W. Rowley, generally known as " Over Rowley," because of his handsprings in his song called, " Going to the Derby," was also on occasion a very remarkable topical songster.

Rowley had one of the sweetest tenor voices I have ever heard, the only other voice then like it (in the halls) was that of the late Alec Hurley. Each of these entertainers was able to charm you at once by their vocal tones, whatever the song they sang.

Rowley's chief ditties included, " A Starry Night For a Ramble," and " Down in a Coal Mine Underneath the Ground," the refrain of which ran thus :

" Down in a coal mine underneath the ground,
Where no ray of sunshine is ever to be found ;
Digging dusty diamonds all the season round ;
Down in a coal mine, underneath the ground."

It was in many an outside hall, that I used to hear Rowley trying himself at topical ditties, and eventually he made quite a furore wherever he went with a splendid topical song, which if I remember rightly was written for him by Fred Albert.

The topics in this song were introduced in a dramatic form, and each verse ended with the line :

" It was only the way it was played on the stage."

When one thinks of these busy and bright topical song writers and singers, one smiles at recent press-stunt concerning a certain writer of topical verses for a West-End party of entertainers. That press stunt gravely asserted that this new topical song writer was about to do what has never been done before ! That is to write in fresh topics for every performance of that company !

Also it was press agently stated that the chief comedian had bravely arranged to carry out "the formidable task of learning these new verses." Furthermore, it was declared, that so exacting was the writing of these highly topical "gags," that the writer thereof had been compelled to postpone his honeymoon in order to write them !

Speaking as a topical song writer of considerable experience, I can honestly say, for myself, and for all the topical song writers I have met, and also for the large number I have not, that we thought nothing of altering our topics nightly. It was part of our job !

I have mentioned above that one of the favourite topical-isers of the past were also "improvisatores," who would rhyme you on any subject hurled at them from the front of the house. Here is a little story concerning one of these extemporary vocalists.

It happened at a well-known theatre where this artist was singing between the pieces. He had boasted that he would make a rhyme on any word given to him. Suddenly a friend of mine blurted out the word "Mesopotamia."

At first the rhymer looked startled. He was certainly a very illiterate though smart fellow, and evidently that word was a bit beyond him. Soon however, he pulled himself together and stalking gravely to the footlights, addressed the audience thus :

"Ladies and gentlemen, a 'party' in the stalls has given me the word Mesopotimia ! but I beg to state," here he assumed a very reverential air, "that I never rhyme on Scriptural subjects !"

MORE MERRYMAKERS

Two of the most rollicking comedians, comic singers and dancers, of say a quarter of a century ago or less, were undoubtedly Mark Sheridan and T. E. Dunville.

Both were not only rattling good comic singers and champions at the light fantastic, but were also excellent actors in sketches and pantomimes.

Such songs as Dunville's "Umpti doodle di do," and Sheridan's "I Do Like to be Beside the Seaside," were excellent examples of the wilder type of comic song.

Unfortunately both these first class entertainers met with

a tragic end which need not be given in fuller detail. Mark Sheridan is represented by both a son and a daughter in "The Industry."

Another hilarious but hapless singing comedian, who met with a still more tragic end than the above mentioned couple was Harry Fragson, whose long residence in France enabled him to come forth as an Anglo-French comedian of very pronounced gifts.

Fragson was a Cockney surnamed Potts, but he acquired a very perfect knowledge of the French tongue, and his vocal burlesques of scenes of that kind were always of the merriest description. His ditties, too, were of the keenly observant semi-satirical type, his best example, perhaps, being the one about "the Employment Bureau."

Poor Fragson, who was a delightful companion and a very kindly fellow, had two or three flutters on the legitimate stage, especially at the Royalty and Drury Lane. At the latter theatre, he made a start in a "Cinderella" pantomime in which he played the Prince's valet, transformed into an Anglo-French character, called Dandigny.

Dutch Daly with his concertina, which he played so beautifully, Mark Melford, (uncle of the smart young Austin), most eccentric of low comedians; Jack Pleasants, a very delightful droll, and George Formby, the side-splitting Lancashire comic singer, (who has a clever young son on the music-hall stage;) Lancashire Jack of Jack and Evelyn; Ernest Shand, nattiest of comic singers and entertainers; the screamingly funny Tynesider, Jimmy Learmouth, and Phil Ray, a very quaint pattering comic, Slade Murray and that very voluble American chortler R. G. Knowles, can all be truthfully described as among the best and brightest of variety entertainers of the past.

Daly, Melford, and certainly Dick Knowles, for a while had a habit of venturing somewhat too "near the knuckle," as Arthur Roberts would put it.

But their humour was really of a very quaint and infectious kind, and they were always welcome, especially when they used less of the "Blue Bag."

Three of the most successful 'verts to variety from the theatrical stage of course were Alfred Lester, Fred Emney, and Fred Williams, brother of the more famous Arthur Williams.

By the time these three reached the music-hall stage, there wasn't anything they didn't know about the devices and tricks of the "boards." Very naturally each of them took to playing in sketches and in that line each one was very successful.

CHIRGWIN
(*From his " Life "*)

G. S. MELVIN

WILKIE BARD

NELLIE WALLACE

Facing page 178

They were all expert and daring "gaggers"; and Lester in "A Restaurant Episode," Fred Williams in "The Devil Bird," and Emney in "A Sister to Assist 'Er," will be remembered for a long time.

Each of these low comedians was happily what some of their brethren would call "a careful old stick." Fred Williams a very saving character, invested largely in house property, and in music-hall shares. In the latter form, Frederick was largely in partnership with his fellow funny men, and great popular favourites Herbert Campbell and Harry Randall.

Emney, who had a passion for rose growing and other forms of horticulture, always saved money, and must have been pretty comfortable at the time when what seemed but a trivial accident, led to his death at a comparatively early age.

Alf Lester who had gone through the "mill," far more than most theatrical folk, astonished all and sundry by leaving nearly £38,000!

SOME STRANGE 'VERTS TO VARIETY

Sometimes the 'verts to variety from the dramatic stage and from other quarters, were of a very peculiar kind. For example, I used to see such great pugilists as Tom Sayers, Tom King, J. C. Heenan (one of the many husbands of Adah Isaacs Menken), Tom Sayers Junior, and the gipsy fighter Jim Mace on the stage. On several occasions these genii of "the Ring" came to do a turn, sometimes in boxing, sometimes even in comic singing at the Britannia Theatre, Hoxton, and other popular-priced playhouses. It was at the "Brit.", and at the Grecian in the City Road, that I also saw, on several occasions, as an entertainer between the pieces, Arthur Orton the Tichborne Claimant, whose trial lasted for so many years and culminated in his doing what the crooks call "a double stretch," that is to say, fourteen years.

I could tell a good deal about the Tichborne claimant as I have already told, concerning the plays written round him, in my volume entitled, *Crime and the Drama; or Dark Deeds Dramatised.*

All I will add however concerning the Claimant is his remarkable proverb-kind of axiom which runs thus:

"Them as 'as got plenty o' money and no brains, is made for them as 'as plenty of brains and no money."

And the good old Claimant acted on this throughout his remarkable career.

I feel I really must tell you a little about a very extraordinary variety 'vert. He came from the extreme "legit.,' for he was a tragedian of the most thunderous description, and his stage name was Clarence Holt. We who knew him well called him Joe. He used to call *us* all manner of things, always of a most unspeakable or unprintable type. In fact his ordinary domestic language among his dearest ones, was almost enough to take the roof off any house he lived in!

I grew to like him in spite of his expletive habits, and he would often roar into my ear all sorts of strange proposals especially for Shakespearian productions which do not concern us in this book.

The time came however, when even this tragedian of tragedians, stooped or condescended to accept an engagement in the music-halls of the period. Joe Holt made no secret of his profound and everlasting contempt for the "halls," although the salary he asked and for some time got, was much in excess of anything he had ever earned or received on the classic boards.

Well do I remember "The Great Tragedian Clarence Holt" making his variety appearance at the hall which is now the Holborn Empire, in a series of what he called "Cameos from Dickens."

It was a quick change entertainment of the kind, since made so popular by that really fine actor Bransby Williams. I remember Joe coming on as Peggotty, Ralph Nickleby, Dick Swiveller, Wilkins Micawber, and some other characters, heavy or light. It was difficult enough to watch this tragedian playing all these parts, even the light Swiveller and the festive Micawber, in the same thunderous rolling tones, and flaunting in each character wearing his own very heavy moustache which he refused to remove!

Worse was yet to come however, for finally this classic actorrrrr . . . presented himself to us as Mrs. Gamp! There was the celebrated midwife frock, there was her battered bonnet, and there also alas was that heavy moustache, slightly soaped over in order to impart "realism" to the make-up!

Never shall I forget, when as Sarah Gamp, my tragic old pal boomed forth Sarah's words, in a tone deep enough to shake the very rafters, and said:

"Put it on the mantel-shelf, and I will—er—take—a little when—er—I feel so dis-poged!"

At this awful outburst I fled from the hall into the streets, despite the fact it was the rainiest day and night I have ever seen in London . . . or even in Manchester!

Chapter XVI

Various Ventriloquists—G. W. Jester, Lieutenant Cole and Lieutenant Albini—John le Hay, "Rotten Cotton Gloves"—Walter Lambert Painter, Inventor and Ventriloquist—A crowd of Conjurers—Professor Anderson, "The Wizard of the North"—Lafayette and Paul Cinquevalli—The Zancigs—J. Nevil Maskelyne, The Master Magician and his young assistant Brodribb, afterwards Sir Henry Irving.

"Vents" of course is the professional abbreviation of ventriloquists, of whom I think there was a greater supply upon the music-hall stage, than there is even now. Although I must say that your modern artist of the kind is much more finished and more amazing than in some cases of the past.

Yet I assure you we had in my young days some very clever "speakers from the belly," to give the word "Ventriloquism" its true Anglo-Saxon meaning.

When I was concerned as a child with the old Britannia Theatre, Hoxton, and its variety turns or "incidentals" as they were called, also with such semi-public houses as Sam Collins's at Islington Green; Deacon's (on the New River Bank facing Sadlers Wells Theatre,) MacDonald's Music-Hall in the long and unlovely Hoxton Street; "The Grapes" in Southwark Bridge Road and so on, one of the most popular ventriloquists of the time was G. W. Jester. He was always billed as "The Man with the Talking Hand," because he made up one of his hands to represent the face of an old woman, wagging his thumb as the under jaw and covering the improvised visage with a sort of widow's cap made out of a handkerchief.

Even then it was customary for the "vent" to indulge in the wildest of wheezes, which in those days mostly took the form of awful "puns." I remember particularly that Jester used always to work one wheeze, which as I grew up I began to find must have been used at least as far back as our old

Greek burlesque merchant Aristophanes, and which wheeze I have certainly heard in many a burlesque of revue since, and almost in every pantomime I have ever encountered.

If this wheeze may seem a little, shall I say "Out of Order," I hope I may be pardoned, for I use it only to mark historically the kind of humour which our comic vents were fond of exuding.

In connection with this wheeze ventriloquist Jester's talking hand old Dame remarked that she had just come out of an omnibus, where she had been compelled to stand most of the journey. She added that the conductor kindly said to her: "What missus, ain't yer got nothing to sit down on?" to which her ladyship replied, "Yes, young man, I have plenty to sit down upon, but nowhere to put it!"

Other celebrated ventriloquists of my earlier days included several who made it a habit of billing themselves as Lieutenants and so forth. As a matter of fact, I fancy that Lieutenant Cole, one of the best vents ever known, was really a Naval Lieutenant in his time. I am not sure whether he is still surviving, but a great many will remember him from the old Tivoli, Pavilion and Oxford days, as being a very cheery, handsome, nautical type of man, whose chief and sometimes only figure was a very little girl in a very dainty frock. The most popular catch phrase of my friend the Lieutenant's act, was to the effect that the little child was suffering great discomfort from sitting down to give her vocal turn.

"Oh, Mr. Cole," whimpered the little figure, "I'm sitting on a pin, Mr. Cole."

Of course the Lieutenant denied this assumption, whereupon the poor child after repeating her statement for many times exclaimed:

"Oh, Mr. Cole, if you were sitting where I am, Mr. Cole, you would soon know Mr. Cole."

Here again the humour, if not profound, always had a popular appeal.

Another popular loquacious Lieutenant is that still strong survivor Lieutenant Albini, who while many of these memories were running serially was often of great assistance to me in reminding me of sundry matters which had slipped me.

I think one of the best of the vents of what it is the fashion to call the old Tivoli days, was undoubtedly the brilliant actor John Le Hay, who met with such a tragic end not so very long ago. Le Hay was an anagram of Healey, which was John's real Irish name. He was long a comic operatic and straight part player with a singularly pleasing tenor voice, which he first used as far as any important London engagement was concerned, in the famous comic opera "Dorothy." It was rather late in life that John became a vent, a line in which he had only previously appeared in sundry private entertainments at the Savage Club, etc. It will be remembered that Ventriloquist Le Hay's figure was that of a grumbling old man with a comic growl as to being condemned to wear "rotten cotton gloves." This catch phrase uttered in varying tones of deeper and deeper misery never failed to evoke hurricanes of laughter. Like many another catch phrase or trick, as, for example, Chirgwin's white eye on his black face, this gag of John Le Hay's arose from an accident, which had compelled John himself to wear a pair of gloves of that kind, at some very extra special aristocratic function.

A fine vent who is still going strong is Fred Russell, born Parnell, who, when I first knew him, was a very hard worker in the newspaper offices, and afterwards became a very nimble journalist. Frederick has for years exploited a figure named Joe, a little Cockney, who emits all sorts of quaint and strange forms of slanguage, and of course like the rest of his tribe, also sings a good song when he's put to it.

Fred Russell, who worked so hard on behalf of the artists in the Music-Hall War, is one of the Founders and was long Chairman of the Variety Artistes' Federation. This fine organisation and its splendid charitable appanage, The Variety Artistes' Benevolent Association, were run by Vent Russell in conjunction with those other tip-top variety workers, Harry Marlow, Monte Bayley, and Albert Voyce, himself a very varied entertainer.

Coram of course, is one of our best ventriloquial artists, and he is very much in demand. I well remember however young Coram, who also I believe came out of the printing offices, coming to the Lyceum one night on trial, during an early part of the late Tom Barrasford's big, but not too bountifully blessed variety season at that huge playhouse.

It was Barrasford indeed, a fine manly sort of fellow, who helped to do away with the Irving Lyceum, and to rebuild it in its present huge, and one may say, highly coloured form.

Coram caught on at once at that sudden audition, as a sort of deputy on the night I mention, and since then he has as pro.'s put it, "never looked back."

But undoubtedly one of the finest types of the real versatile vent is that dapper little personage, Arthur Prince, whose cabin boy figure's, wild but often practical "service" wheezes, never fail to arouse such extreme laughter, not only among the general public, but even among naval and military experts.

Arthur Prince is one of those all-round comedians, who have been everything . . . everywhere, both in circuses and on shipboard, etc , and so forth. Therefore A. P. is able, as I have so often found to make his, or his figure's "gags" fit every occasion, and even to cover all sorts of sudden visitors in front from the "Services." Prince is married to that charming actress, (or diseuse, as it is the fashion to call them), Ida Rene.

And now for a vent, who is also like Le Hay and Prince, a trained comedian of the dramatic boards. This is Walter Lambert, who for many years did, and still does, a ventriloquial act for which he is billed as "Lydia Dreams," and appears as a very demure and winsome hospital nurse. Of later years "Lydia" has devoted himself a great deal to the invention of most remarkable figures, chiefly of a ventriloquial kind, but sometimes being life size; these dummies are able to startle all beholders by walking on and off in a play, and enacting this or that difficult character, and speaking in all kinds of dialects, all of course via this vent's own mouth.

"Lydia," Walter Lambert, has also invented sundry startling appliances and mechanical affairs for stage use both in the theatres, and in the halls, together with a remarkable specimen of quick change scenery, all intent on making you wonder "How it is done."

Ventriloquist Lambert has also very great gifts of another kind. He is a fine painter both in oils and water-colours, and has exhibited with great success on sundry occasions.

Perhaps Mr. Lambert's greatest achievement and certainly his most far-flung one is his wonderful composite picture, entitled "Popularity." It contains faithful portraits of every variety artist male and female at all known or popular at the time of the painting, namely 1903.

The original large oil painting is, I think, somewhere in the Provinces, but reproductions of it may be found in almost every town and district in the British Isles. This "Popularity" picture has also penetrated to the United States, as so many artists depicted therein have been known, and have become more or less popular.

MANY MAGICIANS

One of the earliest of the conjurers or Mystery Men Magicians, or to give them their favourite label "Prestidigitators" of my youthful variety days, was the great Professor Anderson, who, being Scottish, and rather fond of Sir Walter Scott's works, always billed himself as "The Wizard of the North."

Many a time have I sat and marvelled at the uncanny feats of this professor, whom I grew to know very well, and found him a very interesting if rather erratic-tempered artist.

Anderson was one of those wholesale wizards who travelled with entire companies for his job, such as some few other magicians afterwards did. In his time, however, this extensive form of conjuring production was rather a novelty, and certainly it helped mostly to fill those large theatres which the professor found so necessary for his purpose.

I have seen him sweep the boards in the financial sense at the Standard Shoreditch and similar popular playhouses and halls. He had a large family, and all these had to do something in the show. A couple of daughters I remember as being specially clever.

Ever and anon this Wizard of the North having been brought up as an actor in the "legit." would go in for some specially dramatic production. Mostly this took the form of "Rob Roy," which character (originating with the great Macready) our professor played somewhat brilliantly but barnstormily. I was not old enough, (in fact I was a babe in arms,) when Professor Anderson put one of his big dramatic productions on at Covent Garden Theatre, when, alas! that vast playhouse was burnt to the ground.

He went well into my time however, mystifying all and sundry. In fact, he died when I was twenty years of age, and even then after all his vast amount of work in all parts of the world, Professor John Henry Anderson was only fifty-nine.

Conjurer Carl Hertz, an American of German extraction, of course calls for special commendation in the ranks of Mystery Merchants. For many years up to his recent death, he held large audiences spellbound by his feats.

I have seen him perform extraordinary feats in ordinary rooms, not to mention refreshment bars. At the time of his death, Hertz was arranging for bringing out a vast production such as I have mentioned in connection with Anderson. Such indeed, as we have seen presented by those other famous spectacular wizards Rameses, the Egyptian magician; Oswald Williams, (who afterwards joined up with the Maskelynes), and especially by poor Lafayette. This Lafayette, who was of German extraction and named Neuberger, was one of the most terrific illusionists, and most spectacular producers. of his class.

Lafayette had a habit, which grew upon him, of engaging all sorts of wild and fearsome animals for his shows, turning his mystery work as it were, into a sort of travelling zoo. Many will remember what wonderful feats he used to perform with some of these animals. Alas, it was during one of his engagements with a more than usually unwieldy show, that his entire misen-scéne caught fire, and poor Lafayette, in rushing back to save the life of a pet performing lion of his, was himself burnt to death, with that animal.

The wonderfully varied, mystical and zoological work built up by Lafayette is now being carried on, with even more success by the Great Carmo, who is so ubiquitous that I need not dwell further upon his achievements, as they are so well known.

One of the greatest jugglers, at all events jugglers seen in English variety theatres, undoubtedly was Paul Cinquevalli. Well do I remember Paul, whose real name was something else, (also German) making his English début one night in the midst of a huge variety show which that Napoleon among variety managers William Holland, was then giving at the Royal Opera House, Covent Garden, if you please!

On that eventful evening, the then young very handsome Cinquevalli had hardly stepped on to the Covent Garden boards, when it was evident that here we had a genius in the juggling line. He then introduced those marvellous feats with the huge cannon ball and with billiard balls and cues . . . feats which for so many years mystified and astounded music-hall audiences at the Alhambra, Tivoli, Oxford and so forth.

Like many another big variety star, Paul was snapped up year by year for pantomime engagements at the most swollen salaries. For years he stood at the top of the tree in his own special department. In all those years I knew him most intimately, and found him always a singularly undemonstrative, unboastful alien and artist.

So merged did Cinquevalli become with British born artists of the variety stage, that it seemed very strange . . . (as strange as it was regretful) that when the War arose, this wonderful fellow . . . the friend of everybody . . . and one of the biggest benefactors the variety charities have ever had, was turned upon and in effect ostracised by large numbers of his fellow professionals.

Undoubtedly this revulsion of feeling against him told severely upon his health, and it was not long after that one Sunday night, when giving a little party at his house in Mostyn Road, Brixton, dear old Cinquevalli died almost at a moment's warning.

So much for one of the most brilliant entertainers that ever graced the variety boards.

There are many of our other conjurers, jugglers and prestidigitators who were of alien birth. The best of these included Horace Goldin, a Russian who used to utilise and appear to destroy a whole house and its furniture for one of his chief "Tricks." Also, perhaps, the still more wondrous Russian, Malini, who, for the most part, seemed to conduct his conjuring without props. In fact, I have seen Malini in this or that Club, or at Romano's and such like haunts of pro.'s and "sports," perform all sorts of tricks and feats while you were talking to him! Yea, including even the removing of a button from your coat . . . and putting it back, when he had worked his more or less wicked will upon you!

A modern conjurer who breaks forth ever and anon into this kind of card and other amazing prestidigitation is the funny Jewish comedian, Harry Green, whose whole life when not acting, seems to be devoted to performing sudden tricks in your house and elsewhere, with all kinds of domestic utensils. Young Harry Green, who, as all who have seen him act, know, is a true humourist, if ever there was one, always seems to me whenever I see him to be immersed in a kind of mystic and mystifying atmosphere.

Two conjurers who are also thought-readers of an extraordinary type, of whom I have seen perform incredible feats under one's very nose, and also at a vast distance from the "subject" were the famous Zancigs. Zancig and his first wife, both fellow natives of Hamlet's nation, came here some few years ago, and absolutely "paralysed" all who beheld them. I remember that on the first time I saw them, one night at the Alhambra, when they had recently made their début, I sat in the top-box, way up in the sky, with an ex-Mayor of New York, who happened to know these two great Danes.

A strange thing occurred as regards myself. Zancig, in making his rounds in the auditorium to find articles which were to be guessed at by Madam, struck our box, and asked me to show him something of the sort.

Now, I am always very cautious when I am watching conjurers and other such folk, as I have a dread lest I should say or do something which would upset some harmless "confederate," or in other ways "give away the show."

Zancig, however, persisted, and eventually I showed him a rather peculiar watch I was carrying. Zancig then asked Madam to name and describe the article. To my utter amazement the blindfolded lady, far, far, below on the stage, described that peculiar old lever exactly as to form, etc., and even gave its number and the name of its Scottish maker!

I made it my business journalistically to interview the Zancigs later at their house. They began to astound me with their deep knowledge of the lore of the Black Art generally, and especially by their extraordinary views and promises as to thought-reading of a startling kind.

Presently Madam left us and went to a distant part of the house, stating that she would on her return tell me what we had been talking about, reading, and so forth.

On the Danish sibyl's return she fulfilled her promise. She indicated the subjects upon which we had been conversing, and even pointed out to me a passage which I had read at random from one of Scott's novels !

The first Madam Zancig died a few years ago, but Zancig and his second wife still carry on this bewildering business.

Speaking of second-sighters and thought-readers, even the Zancigs are being run rather close, if not outclassed, by those modern magicians, Mr. and Miss Tree. Since this couple appeared at a recent Royal variety performance, they have been in great demand for public and private séances. The great feat in this case—the one performed by the lady—is the extraordinary one of playing (at second sight as one might say) any piece of music or popular song, indicated by the male partner, after he has been told by this or that member of the audience.

Miss Tree's performance of so many musical *morceaux* in one turn would be in itself marvellous as a feat of memory, but seeing that it is done by what is called thought-transmission, the performance is all the more wonderful.

It is, indeed, a most unique specimen of entertainment, and I remember especially how much it impressed the King and Queen at the aforesaid Royal show.

Harry Houdini, that strange little American Jew who made a huge sum of money all over the world, and recently left an extraordinary will concerning it, was one of those conjurers whose feats take the form of escaping from all sorts of tyings, bindings, and even the heaviest chains and fetters. Harry did all these things, including the breaking-out of a steel house, and all in the same manner as the Dibdin's Jolly Young Waterman feathered his oars . . . that is, " with skill and dexterity."

I have seen Houdini, in the midst of a private circle of friends, do all kinds of feats in escaping from bonds fastened upon him. Houdini's wondrous skill in this fetter-breaking regard are now carried on with even increased skill, and startling manipulation by that newest representative of the fetters and straight-jacket conquering kind—namely, Murray the Escapologist, as he calls himself, with something of Micawberian phraseology.

It is not always that your smartest of conjurers is also a most deceptive character actor, baffiing all attempts at identity, yet such a one was the late Chinese conjurer, Chung Ling Soo. Here was one of those feat performers who seemed to delight in being surrounded by props. In his case his props were almost as startling as himself.

Chung Ling Soo used to give us an entire scene or episode of a "Celestial" character, winding up with his being cannonaded as it were, and blown to pieces! It was a most thrilling act, and to those who had only seen this amazing wizard from the front of the house, it was evident that he was really a born Chink, who didn't know any language but Chinese. The acting of the character was the most perfect in an artistic sense that I can call to mind in any such connection.

One day, however, a strange thing happened with regard to this wizard.

A few of us were chatting in the London Hippodrome canteen, and our talk turned upon this Chinese conjurer. I happened to mention his extraordinary character performance, and to express the most profound belief that he was a born "Celestial."

Suddenly a gum-chewing sallow-faced American turned to me, and said: "I know *you*, sir . . . and I have read you for many years in the *Referee*, the *Era*, and especially in the *New York Dramatic Mirror* out in my own country, but *you* don't know *me*! *I*, my friend, am the Chinese Chung Ling Soo! And now I ask *you*, sir, as you have been very kind to me, without knowing who I am, I ask you to 'give it a name'."

This was certainly one of the most extraordinary surprises I have ever met in my life, and I was mentioning this fact only a week or two back, to Chung Ling Soo's charming widow, who used to help him in his act, and is now the wife of the celebrated Irish player, Tom Warden.

Alas, as in the case of so many of the other conjurers I have mentioned above, Chung Ling Soo met with a violent end. His being shot at in the episode indicated, owing to an accident in loading the rifles, resulted in his being shot to the heart, and falling dead upon the stage.

I apply the label of the Master Magician without hesitation to my late dear old friend, J. Nevil Maskelyne. J. N. M., not content with giving wonderful shows of his own also, as we know, founded a theatre or home of Magic, his specimens of which occupied the whole of the programme presented. This was first at the old Egyptian Hall, Piccadilly, where the famous firm, Maskelyne and Cook appeared for so many years, and where, indeed, Maskelyne used to cut off the head of Cook, and walked about with that head under his arm for many a scene!

Other startling, nerve-shaking feats were performed by Magician Maskelyne anon at his new home of Mystery—otherwise St. George's Hall—where this prestidigitatorial family have been in possession for many years past, and are still going strong in a most mystic manner.

Maskelyne Senior could perform all sorts of feats almost beyond comprehension. His vanishing ladies, his startling box-tricks, his dissection of human bodies, *coram populo* (after the fashion since adopted by Selbit, who "Saws through Ladies"); all these things, plus the making of numbers of huge wash-hand basins to dance to any tune; yea, all this and more Maskelyne, the elder, performed like the trapeze young lady, who, according to that comic singer, George Leybourne, "flew through the air with the greatest of ease."

This veteran wizard who went on until about eighty years of age, brought out other wizards in battalions, so to speak. These pupils of the old sorcerer, included David Devant (now, alas, retired through ill health), and, of course, the three or four male members of the family, who are mystifying audiences nightly at this Home of Mystery.

It was my privilege to know, and to have a good deal to do with, Maskelyne *père*, and many an hour have I spent in his sanctum, or down, down down, in his mystical workshops, among his lathes and his marvellous electrical and other appliances, which honeycomb all the available space under the St. George's Hall stage.

The roof of that underground dungeon, so to speak, which is the underneath part of the stage, is literally one mass of copper, steel, and other wires, contacts, etc., for the carrying on of the most astounding conjuring effects.

Ever and anon, when Mage Maskelyne lured me "below" to these uncanny regions, he would beckon me across to a very darkened corner, and tap mystically upon the wall. Then, to the shudderful glare of small green bulb lights, there would emerge from that wall, silently, and creepily, a kind of table top. On this table there would presently glide, several small wine-glasses and tumblers, followed by two or three tiny picturesque bottles or flasks!

Then, at a given sign Magician Maskelyne would tap the tops of these bottles with a small magic wand, and out of them would come, not Hippocras or Nepenthe, as one might suppose from such an environment, but samples of the best whiskey, brandy, etc., for the purpose of harmless necessary refreshment!

During the many hours I spent with my honoured, uncanny friend, he revealed to me, on occasions, the true inwardness of the wonderful feats he worked, when he performed such so-called spiritualistic marvels as those wherein he defeated and brought to naught sundry great spiritualists. These included a certain ecclesiastic, who professed to be able, like that Welsh Wizard, Owen Glendower, to "call spirits from the vasty deep."

Maskelyne's greatest feat, however, in this connection is not known to many, especially nowadays, yet in its time it caused a sensation throughout the British Isles, as well I remember, though I was a mere youth at the time.

It grew out of the notorious rope-tying and rope-escaping feat of the so-called Davenport Brothers, who went about ascribing their wonderful success in this regard to spiritualistic or unseen mediumistic powers.

Maskelyne, then a very young man, undertook to do every feat which the Davenports did without the aid of spiritualism or any such "influence." Travelling about to halls here and there in different parts of the provinces, Maskelyne performed these startling feats upon himself and his confederate.

It is not generally known that Magician Maskelyne's young confederate in these marvellous revelations, and indeed, one of the chief instigators of showing up the Davenport tricks, was no other than a growing lad, born Brodribb, christened John Henry, and afterwards known to fame as Sir Henry Irving, Actor-Manager!

CHAPTER XVII

Datas, the Memory Man—Some Pro.'s and their Prototypes—Sir Harry Lauder as an Irish Comedian—Will Fyffe and George Robey—Some Hibernian Entertainers—Charles Coborn and the Interrupter—Neil Kenyon—Milton Hayes, Little Tich, and Wee Georgie Wood.

The description of " A Marvellous Memory Man " obviously applies to Datas, who for so many years (a quarter of a century at least), has " answered questions," and in the process has lavished " dates " upon his amazed audiences.

When I first knew Datas he was a very young boy named Harry Bottles, and until that moment, when he suddenly bobbed up for a " try-out " at that old pub-saloon, the Royal Standard Music-Hall (now the Victoria Palace) the boy Bottles was still a kind of " fetch and carry " kid at the Anerley Gas Works.

It was while beer-fetching for his mates at an adjacent tavern that young Harry happened to " chip in " with a sudden correction or two in an argument then being conducted by a couple of customers in " the bottle and jug " bar.

One of these correctees, being rather astonished at the youthful corrector's cheek and knowledge, followed him out, and soon learnt his gaseous history. Also that the little fellow while a temporary cripple in his childhood had picked up and devoured all sorts of newspapers, magazines, etc., and had tried himself with remembering dates, just to ease his pain and soothe his loneliness.

This questioner, happening to be a music-hall agent, brought Boy Bottles to see the great variety manager, Charles Morton, and well do I remember the event.

Morton, who never missed a chance of discovering or fostering talent, arranged for the little lad to have a sort of secret try-out at the aforesaid Standard Pimlico, and came to see the result himself.

That night Manager Morton, labelling the lad as " Datas," engaged him to give off dates at the Palace Theatre, and there

Harry Bottles (Datas), engaged for a week, stopped about eighteen months!

I remember that towards the end of this unintentionally long engagement of Datas at this high-class variety theatre, a quaint incident occurred. A very distinguished looking military personage just in front of me, after fidgeting a little, suddenly arose in response to Datas's request for questions, and spoke as follows—

"Can you tell me, please, Mr. Datas, if there are more letters in the Bible than acres in Yorkshire, or otherwise?"

Datas seemed taken aback for a moment, but presently he retorted—

"I beg your pardon, sir, I'm engaged here to answer *dates*, Is your question a date, sir?"

"Well . . . er . . . No. Not exactly," quoth the military-looking gentleman, "but I thought perhaps that . . . er . . ."

"Look here, sir," resumed Datas, "if you really *want* to know whether there are more acres in Yorkshire than letters in the Bible . . . or vice versey . . . I'll tell you."

"There are three million, eight hundred thousand acres in Yorkshire, and three million, five hundred thousand letters in the Bible. And if you don't believe me, sir, *you go away and count 'em*!"

Datas, even now of "no age," continues all over the amusement world to roll off his dates, concerning say, the Derby Winners from the time that race first started 150 years ago (and recounted backwards); all sorts of dates of wars, earthquakes, and other cataclysms; all kinds of criminal and other trials, and even the dates of all the chief executions and their respective victims!

Just lately, being rather steeped for the nonce, in sundry criminal and murderous matters, I found Datas, swatting up his "executions" in . . . no, not even in the "Newgate Calendar," but in a mysterious and not too easily procurable publication called, "The Hangman's Record."

LAUDER AND ITHERS O' THAT ILK

Sir Harry Lauder is of course a commanding figure in the variety stage of to-day, indeed as he said in a speech a few weeks ago, perhaps with a dash of self ebullience, he started at the top twenty-five years ago, and is there still!

What friend Harry did not state however, is perhaps what would appear surprising to a great many of his multitudinous admirers, that he really started on the stage as an Irish comic singer. In fact, for a year or two, when I first knew him, he was singing Hibernian ditties only, and doing them in a very good brogue. His achievement in the Irish dialect is perhaps not surprising when one remembers that he spent a great deal of his time in Glasgow, where the Scotch and Irish populations are about equally mixed!

Harry, after working as a child in a flax mill most of the hours of the day, and afterwards toiling down a coal mine for still more hours per diem, found, by a few experiences in the sing-songs and free-and-easies in the mining neighbourhood, that he really might do fairly well in the halls.

Harry then toured a good deal round the provinces at very paltry pay, and eventually bobbed up in London. It was his idea, and that of his agent at the time, to warble lyrics of his native Caledonian kind. Tom Tinsley, then the burly chairman and manager whom many will remember at Gatti's in Westminster Bridge Road, at once put his veto on the Scottish suggestion. He pointed out that the halls had been overdone with that sort of thing, and that he, Tom, didn't mean to encourage any more of it.

Harry, however, was equal to the occasion; for, having, in several free-and-easies and also down the coal pit, mixed several Irish songs with his Scottish repertory, he at once offered to come out as an Irish comic singer, with some few Hibernian songs, including "Call Again, Callaghan." And so it happened that our breezy braw knight for some time was one of our numerous Paddies of the halls.

It was not until Lauder began to blossom forth in Caledonian carolling however, that he began to make his biggest hits and to draw his largest audiences, for as he soon found in travelling all over the world, that there is no town or city that does not contain fellow natives of the world-famous poet Robert Burns, not to mention Burns Lodges and Societies.

As a Scottish comedian Lauder soon gained fame with his different ditties, such as "Killiecrankie," "A Roamin' in the Gloamin'" "She's Ma Daisy," "Tobermory" and so on.

It may be said, and with some truth, that the Lauder lyrics differ very little in tone or tune, yet thanks to his canny artistry and rich sense of humour and expression, Sir Harry, our only music-hall artist knight, always achieves considerable renown, drawing undoubtedly the biggest salaries ever paid to a music-hall star.

Some of these large sums have accrued of course by way

of sharing terms. It is not so long ago however, as well I know, that Lauder, then rising to magnificent salaries, was compelled by old contracts of several years duration apiece, to fill all manner of dates, at sums varying from eight to twenty pounds per week !

That time has now passed, and Sir Harry is one of the richest men upon the stage, dramatic or variety.

I say dramatic because Sir Harry, like so many other variety favourites, has at times worked sundry big star theatre engagements. At the moment of writing, Lauder is deservedly adding to his well-earned lucre, by acting on the films, where of course, there is no scope for his comic singing, or his very fine ballad vocalisation. His chief screen work up to now, has been in that big production, " Huntingtower."

Speaking of Lauder's singing, it would perhaps surprise some to know that in his splendid baritone voice, and in the songs that he selects for serious treatment such as " Rocked in the Cradle of the Deep," Sir Harry echoes in a remarkable manner the same kind of ballad singing which ever and anon was indulged in, (often by way of a joke), by that otherwise frivolous and fanciful " Lion Comique," George Leybourne !

In this respect, the tall majestic George Leybourne was the exact singing prototype of little Lauder. In Lauder's other droller character songs and studies, his exact prototype was an extraordinary versatile Scottish comedian named Tom Maclagan, who, in addition to singing songs of Lauder's Scottish type, was a splendid artist alike in grand opera, and the wildest of burlesque.

The general legend as to Harry Lauder's said to be characteristically Scottish thrift or " nearness," is of course only a legend. Those of us who know him well, also know well that he is one of the most benevolent and philanthropic of men, who takes care never to let on regarding his benefactions. In fact, as he said the other day, when I had to put him an enquiry on this subject, from a *Referee* correspondent, " I dinna let ma left hand knaw what ma richt hand doeth."

Right away from the war time when like so many of us, he suffered a tragic blow, Harry Lauder has done a great deal for war sufferers and others ; and indeed it was for this, more than anything else, that the King made him Sir Harry !

Will Fyffe, that other tremendously favourite Scottish comedian, is more a versatile general actor and character impersonator than Lauder. Indeed Will, like many another variety star graduated in what some pro.'s still call " the legit."

I remember Fyffe enacting all sorts of characters of the so-called "regular" stage, and many a time and oft have we exchanged views and experiences of that stage, and of the many parts he (and some of us) had to study per week.

Will Fyffe varies his "business" so much both in manner and make up, that at first sight it would seem difficult to quote a prototype to fit him. On the Scottish side of course, like Lauder and Neil Kenyon, there is naturally a resemblance to the often mentioned, very varied Maclagan. I have long come to the conclusion however, that the nearest prototype to Fyffe was that also remarkably versatile acting comic singer and realistic monologuist, so long known as the Great Vance, whose full history and startling funeral, are treated elsewhere in this volume.

It is this extensive and varied ground work which enables Will Fyffe to impart such contrast to his character studies and musical monologues in the halls, studies which have won him fame and fortune in many a far flung part, of what Mr. Micawber called "the habitable globe." It is this versatility also which causes Will Fyffe to be sought for every Christmas for some big pantomime engagement, chiefly of course up in the North.

Did space permit, I could relate several quaint episodes and hard struggles and adventures undergone by favourite Fyffe on his way from one might call, "Busker-dom, and barn-storming in the Blood and Thunder" and other drama, on to what our American friends delight to call the "stellar firmament."

George Robey (born Wade), has won for himself so high a position as a variety comedian and comic singer, to say nothing of his theatre work, that he well deserves his somewhat strange poster label of "The Prime Minister of Mirth."

When I first met George it was on rather a peculiar occasion. It was at a matinée at the Oxford, and one of the turns was being provided by a then very popular, though somewhat crude, entertainer called "Kennedy the Mesmerist." Kennedy like most of his kind had quite a regiment of subjects or "mediums" on the stage, and these he put under what we called then the "Fluence," in such sort, that the subjects, or victims, on being "hypnotised" by Kennedy broke out into strange behaviour, not to say maniacal ebullitions.

One of these 'fluence folk was a growing boy who did all sorts of strange antics on being pierced with needles, knitting pins etc., and even consumed candles with a gusto, anon waking up into abhorrence at such fearsome food.

GEORGE ROBEY
(Stage Photo Co.)

MILTON HAYES
(Photo by Dawson Studios, Liverpool)

THE GREAT MACKNEY
(From the "Life of Mackney")

G. H. ELLIOTT

This especial boy became the comedian afterwards known as George Robey, and had his chance of becoming so because he showed such unquenchable humour and burlesque antics in his hypnotic sufferings, that the then Oxford manager promptly engaged that boy to come out of Kennedy's group, and to give a comic singing and comic acting turn on his own.

George Wade Robey had even then been to "college" (as they say in America) with intent to being trained as a scientist and engineer. Anon he returned to Jesus College, Cambridge, where he took his B.A. degree. Many a time have I been asked to state whether George was or was not a 'varsity undergraduate.

There are people who seem to think that because a man is a comic singer, (and George is of course one of the most comic, with a wonderful list of lyrics to his credit), it is impossible for such an entertainer to have been educated on a higher scale. Not only however did George E. Wade Robey win distinctions of this sort, he is also a very brilliant painter in water colours and oils, and has frequently exhibited with great success, gaining diplomas and so forth at the Royal Academy, the Royal Institute of Painters in water colours etc. Moreover, George is also a very fine cricketer and footballer, and is a member of the M.C.C.

During the War, George, ever a patriot, served with the Motor Transport Service, and also gave numbers of performances for War Charities realising about £12,000 in all. For these services, in doing which I have found him working day and night, he was created a Commander of the British Empire.

I may as well add that George Robey's other accomplishments include the writing of comic and other stories, both serially and in volume, and a deep and intense knowledge of Egyptology and Assyriology, and a wide acquaintance with the whole of the British poets! In each of these departments of knowledge my friend George has often held me spellbound.

George Robey's prototype in the halls looms up large in my memory. It was a very droll comic singing actor named Billy Critchfield, many of whose songs were of the Robey type, perhaps a little more sultry than even some of Robey's earliest ditties. I remember Critchfield especially scoring in a remarkable Tinker song, and above all in a satirical semi-topical musical monologue, called "Freedom of Opinion."

Robey the Roamer recently came back from a highly successful South African tour, during which he was made a chief of a certain savage tribe. At the present moment he is an actor-manager running "Bits and Pieces" at the Princes Theatre, London.

MORE PATS AND PADDIES

Undoubtedly at the head of the present day specimens of these carollers of Erin, stands Talbot O'Farrell, whose rich vein of humour and whose melodious voice, together with his voluble Irish patter, are in great demand in present day variety theatres. Here again is one who was richly experienced in other stage work before he took to the music-hall boards. In fact, T. O'F. was for a good while both an operatic singer, and an acting comedian. O'Farrell's most valuable asset in the halls is his ability to veer from the comic to the pathetic, especially in his ballad singing. In this respect he possesses an acting and singing vein which was wont to be labelled in the stage world not many years ago, as "Robsonian" because that swift change from side-splitting humour to heart-rending pathos was brought to such perfection by the renowned little cockney comedian and comic singer Frederick Robson, who was as a matter of fact born Brownbill!

Another notable Irish comedian especially on the comic side, but plus a genius for dancing, is of course Joe O'Gorman, who can jest and jig with equal dexterity, either as a single turn, or in revues. Joe's performance in one of the best revues I have seen namely, "Irish and Proud of it," is indeed a thing to remember. The O'Gorman name bids fair to be carried on to good sound comic singing and comic dancing heights by Joseph's sons, the well-known O'Gorman Brothers.

A Hibernian comedian and singer of the more pronounced London Cockney type is Tom Costello, who is now careering around with the "Veterans of Variety." Middle-aged music-hall goers, will still call to mind (and will e'en chorus for you), several of Tom's carols. The most memorable of these undoubtedly are "Comrades" and of course "At Trinity Church I met my Doom." Here again we have an artistic combination of humour and pathos, albeit of a rather rougher type than that of Talbot O'Farrell or Joe O'Gorman, but all the same always very successful.

I have spoken above of sundry prototypes of present day music-hall artists, Scotch and otherwise. As regards the Irish group, the most similar examples I can call to mind as prototypes to the last three named comedians, include the following: One, the late ever joyous, ever attractive comedian and wonderful dancer, dear old Walter Munroe.

Another prototype of our present-day variety humorists, was Pat Rafferty, a very comic comic-singer, who was enormously popular. But especially one's memory goes back in this connection to that really beautiful Hibernian artist, finished alike in singing, acting and dancing, the late Pat Feeney to wit.

Pat Feeney was strong also in the singing of Irish patriotic lyrics, especially at some outbreak of famine etc., in "the Disthressful Country," a kind of national appeal which was wont to be made contemporaneously by that other strong Irish favourite of the halls, Nellie Farrell, who was always billed, some will remember "The Glittering Star of Erin."

Feeney was really a patriot off the stage as well as on, and on more than one occasion of famine and other causes of unemployment in his native land, Pat collected for sundry charity funds for the relief of his distressed compatriots. Many thousands of pounds did Pat Feeney raise for this and similar noble causes.

But alas! like too many others of his profession, Pat died young, at thirty-eight to be exact, and he died poor. Not only was he not one of the swollen salary type, but he also gave largely of his earnings, and at the time of ill health and fell disease, poor young Feeney was "broke to the wide."

Not long after his death, Pat Feeney's grave was found to be in a disgracefully neglected condition. It was however speedily renovated, thanks to the care and cost of one who, also did the same service to the grave of the great favourite, but also unfortunate music-hall artist, the once swollen-salaried Charles Godfrey.

The man who performed this and similar kindly services alike to the living and the dead of the variety world, is my very old friend and fellow enthusiast, Sydney W. Page, who, at the moment of writing, is one of the most honoured members of the Middlesex County Council.

I may add that what that Councillor doesn't know about variety matters in general is not worth bothering about.

Hereby hangs a tiny tale. This same Sydney Page happened to be physically the exact double of the late Charles Godfrey; in fact no twins were ever more alike. As they were in the habit of travelling about a good deal, much confusion used to result.

I remember one night a very persistent bailiff, who had been pursuing Charles for some time for certain debts, started out and followed Sydney Page instead. Shadowing him all day long until at last he dropped upon his victim going into a music-hall, "Got him at last," he exclaimed, and at once showered upon poor Page quite a sheaf of writs intended for Charles Godfrey! Complications and curtain!

It is not often that stage folk, either theatrical or variety, run on so well and so successfully into the sere and yellow leaf period, as our old friend Charles Coborn, born McCullum.

I have not put this clever and canny Scot among the Scottish variety comedians, for I do not know, nor have I ever heard whether he has ever indulged in Caledonian carols. Like Will Fyffe and others Charlie served a long and strong apprenticeship on the "legit." stage. In that department he played a couple of very important characters in pieces of my own. One a musical burlesque, and the other a pantomime. But no more of that!

In the variety stage line Coborn made many a memorable song-hit. The chief of these of course included those popular lyrics, "The Man who Broke the Bank at Monte Carlo," and the perennial and linguistic "Two Lovely Black Eyes," which Charles can chortle in about nine different languages!

When Charlie was at the Palace Theatre, and chanced to warble a Bacchanalian ballad with the refrain: "Come Where the Booze is Cheaper—Come Where the Pots Hold More!" a man in front, rightly or wrongly, (but at all events, well within rights as a playgoer) audibly objected to the slang word "booze." Alarums and excursions of course ensued, the audience taking sides, so to speak.

It has always seemed to me that one could sympathise with the singer this time, especially as one remembers that at that period our music-halls were absolutely full of songs glorifying "booze." One need only recall that favourite chirruper, rough, but always rollicking, Harry Anderson to wit, who carried the ballad called "Beer, Beer, Glorious Beer" throughout the country like some conquering hero. Or James Fawn, that funniest of low comedians, one of whose most popular songs stating in a hiccup-y refrain the not too "refaned" line, "It must have been the Lobster . . . It couldn't have been the Booze." In fact, Jimmy's warbles and wheezes were all about drink in some slang form or another.

Anyhow, the courageous Coborn went on his warbling way, even as he does still at the age of seventy-six, adding to his warbling of late years, his wondrous walks from Land's End to John O'Groats or vice versa, stopping ever and anon, only in this or that town or village, to administer harmless amusement in song or jest.

But mark ye, always on the Sawbath, Coborn resumes his

McCullum-ship or clan, and makes straight for the kirk, there to act as sidesman or in some similar capacity.

In short, the dramatic and variety stages possess no cleverer or worthier member than Coborn of the Clan McCullum.

Another very renowned comic comedian, who still holds audiences as he has done for many years, is Neil Kenyon, (born McKinnon). Here is another case of one deeply versed and richly experienced in regular dramatic work taking to the variety boards.

I remember Neil figuring a good deal in touring and stock companies, at first with the blood and thunder drama, and burlesque, and afterwards making very marked successes for a long time in the Shakespeare revivals thirty years ago by that fine Bardic actor, Osmond Tearle, father of Godfrey Tearle. Even then it was a long while before N. K. took to the halls; for he put in some few years again in drama, and annually in pantomime. In that Christmassy form of work he has appeared nearly ever since.

It is a little over twenty years ago since he made his variety début at the London Pavilion, and since then he has given his famous songs and musical monologues, such as "The Caddy," "The Station Master of Dunrobin," "The Postie," etc., all over the world.

Perhaps the nearest prototype to Neil Kenyon in the music-halls were those two fine character actors, Fred French and Arthur Lloyd.

Another of the "legit." actors who, taking to the variety boards, swept the same with no uncertain broom is Milton Hayes, a Mancunian, who, in early life, like Man in the Seven Ages Soliloquy . . . played many parts!

He was, and is, also something of an inventor of a mechanical kind, and you would not think from his now famous disjointed asinine musical monologue that he is a deeply intellectual student of Mathematics, Philosophy, Ethics, Geology and "Faith! and Theology if he'd the call."

This young Hayes is also a very talented author, especially on the serious side. He has written many a rousing recitation, perhaps the most successful being his Bransby Williams specimen, "The Green Eye of the little Yellow God." You will also find, if you look for them, several novels from M.H's pen, and, even as I write, he is putting the finishing touches to about five plays. One of these I may tell you (entre nous) is of the most mystical character.

Milton Hayes's chief successes in the variety world, which

to my thinking, are his numerous puzzling political orations, all of which are written by him, bring to my memory a couple of prototypes of whom I told Milton a short while ago. He agreed that, although he was too young ever to have seen them, I was evidently right in my comparison, for I was able to quote from memory sundry wild orational examples to prove my case.

These two prototypes were respectively Marcus Wilkinson for the wilder type of monologue, and J. G. Forde, who was undoubtedly one of the greatest comic patterers ever seen on the music-hall boards. He never changed his dress for the stage. He always wore a long frock coat, a heavy black moustache, a little dab of red on his nose, and a mop of black hair (his own), which was agitated violently whenever he reached a certain point in a remark. Whenever George Forde spoke, say on marriage or other blessings of the kind, I have seen whole audiences rock with laughter.

It may be interesting to many to note that George Forde died a good many years ago, and left a son, A. G. Forde, who was for many years, until recently in fact, the stage manager at the Alhambra, Leicester Square. He was a relation of the late Sara Lane of the popular Britannia Theatre, Hoxton, and his daughter, now a revue star, keeps up some sort of connection with the Sara Lane family, by giving herself the stage name of Crawford. She is in fact that delightful young artist, Mimi Crawford, granddaughter of the late George Forde.

I am not ashamed to confess that it was I who wrote a line, often quoted in advertisements and posters, which ran as follows:

"One Tich of Nature Makes the Whole World Grin."

For can it be denied that Little Tich always has this effect upon his audiences? And these audiences Tich has played to with enormous success in every part of the world.

One peculiar thing with Tich in this regard, is that almost wherever he goes, Harry Tich, (born Relph) is able to speak and to play in the local language! I have heard him give off in this manner sundry songs and patter in French, German, Italian, and Spanish to name no other tongue. Very cultured also in other regards is Tich. He can argue with you for example on sundry philosophies and e'en upon the world's religions! I have known him also perform very remarkable feats in mathematics, and he moreover is always inventing something or other.

When I first knew this intensely funny droll and really

wondrous dancer, he was billed as Little Tichborne, and forsooth he was appearing as a blacked-up or nigger turn! In fact, it was as a "Nig" that our Tich first started his inimitable big boot dance, which, after so many years of doing, he still does with the same finished skill.

The Tichian studies of Station Masters, Sergeant Majors, fascinating feminine ballet dancers, and so on, will always be remembered as comic and highly humorous performances unexcelled by any other variety performer.

Like many others, Little Tich has rather an obsession for "putting a bit on," but it is not generally known that on one occasion he was very nearly arrested for making a bet with a pal at Romano's . . . a bet concerning the length of his shoes in his big boot dance. Happily he managed to escape the Law.*

A couple of other *multum in parvo* comedians, well known in the halls as well as in the theatres, are of course respectively Wee Georgie Wood, and of a somewhat larger type, Nelson Keys.

A very remarkable little fellow is Wee Georgie. He still looks like a tiny boy, but it is really infringing no confidence when I mention that he is close upon thirty years of age. Alike in sketches and in pantomimes and plays, Georgie has proved himself one of the most finished as well as one of the funniest of artists in his profession. Like Tich, Georgie is also a deep reader and a ditto thinker, and can discourse most eloquently on all kinds of subjects, esoteric, ethnological, and even ethical.

In fact, it was only a short time ago that the droll Wee Georgie delivered at the Kingsway Hall a very remarkable as well as very earnest and gripping address, entitled, "A Methodist Among the Mummers!"

I have before indicated where I have thought that a prototype of any certain present-day artist should be mentioned. In the case of Wee Georgie Wood, I can recall one equally gifted but even more experienced an actor of miniature stature, namely "Master" Percy Roselle.

I have seen Percy play an extraordinary variety of parts when he was supposed to be about twelve, but was really double that age, such characters as Hop O' My Thumb, Tom Thumb, Humpty Dumpty, and similar parts in pantomime. Also Prince Arthur in "King John," and similar Shakespearian characters with the great Samuel Phelps, all these being given at Drury Lane.

During one engagement of Percy Roselle's at the Brit. in Hoxton, I saw him star as Rob Roy in a burlesque of that name,

* Alas! Little Tich died as these pages were going to press.

and on the same evening, he played several scenes from "Macbeth." In this tragedy he enacted the name part, and the Lady Macbeth on that occasion was his younger sister, Amy Roselle, who was then about fourteen, but towered over him.

This was the lady who afterwards became one of our most artistic leading actresses. Alas! her end was very tragic, for she and her husband, Arthur Dacre, under stress of unemployment and other terrible anxieties, committed suicide in Melbourne some years ago.

Yes, Wee Georgie Wood and clever little Ivor Vintor are the only actors on the variety stage at present, who remind me continually of the very versatile Percy Roselle.

As to Nelson Keys, popularly known as "Bunch," undoubtedly it can be said that his versatility, like his vivaciousness, is boundless.

Whether in the halls or in the theatres, including even old Drury itself, young Key's singing, dancing, mimicry etc., all possess the inimitable Nelson touch.

Here again a prototype occurs to me. I allude to a young actor, who has long been dead, namely Fred Foster. Foster was one of the many East End favourites I have had occasion to mention, but there was a time eventually, when he was spotted for the West End. Alas! he died just before he could achieve that honour.

Fred Foster, who resembled "Bunch" facially and physically, could play all sorts of characters in sketches, dramas, burlesques etc. I do not forget seeing him enact the heroine Eily O'Connor in Byron's burlesque, "The Colleen Bawn." He did this at the Variety Theatre, Pitfield Street, Hoxton, between his engagements at the "Brit." in the neighbourhood.

I may as well mention here that the Variety, Hoxton, was a very peculiar music-hall entertainment house. It was run on the twice-nightly system long before even George E. Belmont did his twice-nightly stunts, first at the Seabright, a free-and-easy in the Hackney Road, and later at the Surrey and at Sadler's Wells, which he irreverently billed as "Sunny Old Sad's."

One thing which has always stuck in my memory regarding the Variety Theatre, Hoxton, which was one of my own earliest song-writing pitches, was that like a good many similar lower class theatres and music-halls, we never got our money on usual "Treasury" nights.

Our "sals" were always kept back until the bars there

opened on Sunday, when alas, very often the hard-earned wage was soon spent in treating one's pals.

This scandalous form of salary paying was so rife in certain theatres of the sort during my earliest associations with such places, that on becoming a journalist I showed up the scandal in *The Weekly Dispatch* of the period, in an article entitled "The Sunday Ghost." "Ghost," as will be remembered by many, is professionalese for salary. "Treasury" night, being always regarded as the time when "the Ghost Walks!"

CHAPTER XVIII

An untutored Genius—Some writers who became Song Sellers—The founding of Francis, Day & Hunter's—The Mohawk Minstrels—More Variety Stage Song providers—The romance of Lawrence Wright—Royal Variety Performances—The forerunners of the Victoria Palace—A manager descendant of Hereward the Wake.

An untutored genius. This label I apply without hesitation to Joseph Tabrar, the amount of whose lyrical output for the halls is as amazing as its abundance, and it is marvellous how he manages to do it all!

For as Joseph always confessed whenever he speaks of these musically metrical matters, he is totally unable to read and write.

And yet poet-composer Tabrar, e'en now when past his three score years and ten . . . continues to pour forth songs which are really good songs, and "poems" which are scarcely so good.

Out of his thousands, yea, literally thousands, of "lyrics," it is perhaps only necessary to inform my readers that Bard Tabrar here stands revealed as the author of "Daddy Wouldn't buy me a Bow-Wow"; and "Ting Ling, Ling, that's how the Bell Goes," which was the last song ever sung by the renowned "Lion Comique," George Leybourne.

Most of our music-hall stars, past and present, have made good with Joseph's always catchy, if crude, ditties. But alas! they have not always made payment for the same. This is owing to his financial laxity among his clients, and due partly to his own free and easiness.

Joe, like Browning's wise thrush "always can recapture the first fine careless rapture," of his songs and airs. I have never known him fail to recall to memory every syllable and every note of anything he ever wrote . . . or rather had had taken down. And lo, Joseph is still supplying all sorts of songs, "While you wait" . . . and very catchy carols too!

Of late, lyrist-composer Tabrar has become, (as he proudly described to me), "A Poet of the Pubs."

In soaring to these heights he has been subsidised by various "licensed premises." From these licensed victualler lays Bard Joseph recently quoted to me such picturesque fragments as the following :

> "Peele's ! Peele's ! That's the place for meals !
> Quite a blooming banquet with your Beer !"

And the following even more insinuating verselet:

> "If you want Whiskey without any smuts. . . .
> Go to the Cricketers, Newington Butts !"

Nay more, when a day or two before jotting these gems of poesy, I met old friend Tabrar, he crumpled into my pocket a lyric and score of a "Pub Poem" which runs thus :

I append the first verse and chorus :

"Adam and Eve"

> "I am weary, and sad, I am lone and forlorn !
> Well, I wish from my heart I had never been born !
> Thro' the solemn dictation of nature's decree
> Fate has always been cruel and most unkind to me.
> I have tried to be good, I've been taught to believe
> I am one of the off-springs of Adam and Eve.
> And as I've lived my life by the sweat of my brow,
> In a *spiritual* form I appeal to you now.
>
> *Chorus*—
> Adam and Eve, Adam and Eve !
> Why was I sent on this earth to grieve ?
> To struggle with strife in the battle of life,
> Where my brothers and sisters will lie and deceive.
> If I strike bright ideas, it always appears,
> That the fates have been sent here to wreck 'em.
> So I only believe in one Adam and Eve,
> And that's in High Street, Peckham."

Sometimes these lyrists and composers (especially when they are both), blossom forth as song-publishers, and run businesses, big or little, "on their own."

Joe Tabrar deviated into this kind of thing at one time, and had a big office or shop in the York Road by Waterloo Bridge. In those premises, which his lack of looking after himself caused him soon to give up, the enthusiastic Tabrar filled his shelves with large parcels of what was pretended to be correspondence from sundry well-known stage and literary lights. These big bundles were labelled respectively:

> "Letters from Henry Irving."
> "Letters from the Great Macdermott."
> "Letters from Hugh Jay Didcott."
> "Letters from George. R. Sims," and (please pardon me for adding)
> "Letters from H. Chance Newton."

Now I don't think I ever wrote to Joe Tabrar in my life, but certainly I had a good deal to do with him.

This took the form, chiefly, of arousing him out of his careless and foolish habit of giving away his ideas broadcast . . . and he was always . . . and still is . . . full of clever ideas. Apart from giving away his notions, he would always give away his songs and tunes. Anyhow he charged paltry prices till I made him cease to be a sort of bardic blackleg to himself as well as to others.

But Tabrar's best and most loyal friend and helper was a then young and still surviving brilliant song-writer, who after he and Joe parted, became a kind of regular poet.

Anon this friend, John P. Harrington, to wit, set up for himself, like those other clever and increasingly popular lyrists, George Arthurs, Worton David and Lawrence Wright. Of these more anon.

SOME SONG HIT FIRMS

That big musical publishing firm, Francis, Day & Hunter, really grew out of a single song writer. This was Harry Hunter, who wrote all songs and ditties for himself and others to sing with those popular "blacked up" entertainers, the Mohawk Minstrels who started at the Agricultural Hall, Islington, over fifty years ago. Later in their existence, they joined forces with those other noted "Nigs," the Moore and Burgess Minstrels.

Harry, a huge and portly personage, became a middle man or "Interlocutor" of the Mohawks, and during that long period he wrote all sorts of songs. Two of his famous "tongue twisting" specimens, will be remembered by middle-aged and mature minstrel and music-hall patrons.

Here are the respective refrains:

> I saw Esau kissing Kate, and the fact is that we all three saw;
> For I saw Esau, he saw me, and she and I saw Esau."

And the other chorus ran:

> "I knocked the knocker just as Enoch went to sup;
> Enoch he knocked me down, Enoch he knocked me up!
> Enoch knocked me over.
> Enoch knocked me sober
> I'd like to knock Enoch about as *he* knocked me."

With Harry Hunter there were associated two brothers, namely, William and James Francis, (also Mohawk Minstrels). These three, plus a very smart non-professional business man named David Day, founded the present great firm of Francis, Day & Hunter by opening a shop, chiefly for the sale of Harry's Mohawk and other ditties.

All but David Day have passed away, and if one may say so, earlier than they need have done. For alas, those Mohawks like most of the Moore and Burgess Minstrels whom they afterwards joined . . . were a very "Bohemian" band.

Two very facile lyrists who became merchants in the song-selling line, are George Arthurs and Worton David, both of whom contributed ditties not only to music-halls, but to many a musical play. Also upon occasions they have written the full grown librettos thereto. Both are now flourishing in or adjacent to that busy song-selling neighbourhood, Charing Cross Road.

Yet another song-provider, especially as regards the scores thereof, is Herman of the far-flung Darewski family. He too has furnished forth several complete scores of musical comedies and revues, and after travelling around the provinces with a very fine big band of his own, he is, at the moment of writing, conducting that band in connection with Covent Garden balls.

Perhaps one of the most truly humorous comic song-writers within the memory of music-hall going man, is Edgar Bateman, who happily is still going strong in that same line. He was at first a compositor on the *Referee* and other papers, but for many years past he has been connected with the staff of Francis, Day & Hunter. The student of comic songs and such-like lively lyrics, must perforce take account of the ditties of Edgar Bateman, especially for the many such which he wrote for the hereinbeforementioned Gus Elen, the long-popular Coster caroller, who, when I first saw him come out on the variety stage, was giving a very remarkable impersonation in song of a remarkable person called, "The Haunted Idiot."

Bard Bateman's songs for Elen included such really droll specimens as "She's too Good to Live is Mrs. Carter," "The Postman's Holiday," "If it wasn't for the 'Ouses in Between," and his unforgettable ballad in which the singer ardently wishes he'd got certain attributes of sundry animals in the Zoo!

One of the now famous firms for song-publishing, is of course that run by Bert Feldman, up in Shaftesbury Avenue. This house of song "hits" is in the habit of engaging all sorts of lyrists and composers, and sending their works around to be sung by special Feldman companies of chortlers in all the big provincial centres. Bert Feldman also runs, under the management of that very humorous ex-comedian Charles Warren, a big American branch, the songs and scores of which are supplied by the American firm of Witmarks.

There is another great song-hit firm, the rapid rise of which is what the newspaper reporters would of course describe as a "romance." I allude to the Lawrence Wright Music Co. If the word "romance" could be applied at all in this adjunct to the variety stage, it certainly could be used in reference to the rise and progress of Wright himself.

Starting in business as a very struggling youngster of eighteen, he soon began to spin ahead, and to write such popular songs in their day as "Blue Eyes," "Wyoming" and "Delilah." His one-room business, extended to one floor of the building, and then he took over the building itself. Not content with that, he then put up the large building, opposite the scene of his first venture in Denmark Street, which houses his business to-day.

Almost throughout the year, Lawrence Wright sends around the provinces, several companies of singers and musicians, who, making Blackpool their centre, pour forth upon the people the Lawrence Wright song publications embodying the most tremendously popular ditties of the day.

I don't know whether I ought to divulge this secret or not, but I feel that I must tell you that Publisher Lawrence Wright is also that fine ballad composer Horatio Nicholls!

I need hardly add that the Horatio Nicholls ballads, both humorous and serious, are not only the most numerous, but are also among the very best of all British song successes sung to us by the leading variety artists, for many years.

The old-established firm of Ascherberg Hopwood and Crew, primarily addicted to the wholesale publication of comic operatic scores, also run a large department in which variety songs, both comic and sentimental, figure very largely.

I have good reason for stating that this "side line," is being extensively increased, quite a little army of authors and composers, being "earmarked" for the purpose. Like sundry other firms, of course, the Ascherberg house is issuing a series of variety song albums, and such like harmonic collections.

ROYAL VARIETY SHOWS

Inasmuch as the last Royal Variety Performance took place at the Victoria Palace, it has struck me that it would form an interesting chapter in the history of the Music-Halls themselves to give herewith a little of the strange and chequered history of this popular resort in the days that were earlier . . . very much earlier.

For look you, few people who didn't know, could possibly guess at the kind of sing-songs, and free-and-easies, which materialised from time to time on the site of the Victoria Palace, which is now as gorgeous and gay as was the husband selected by poor Villikins' Dinah's proud Papa.

The building which was the immediate predecessor of the Victoria Palace, will of course be remembered by many as the Royal Standard Music-Hall, Pimlico, but that entertainment house had undergone at least a couple of re-incarnations, so to speak, before then.

Way back in the eighteenth century, if not earlier, stood a little roadside inn amidst beautiful country in almost the centre of what was called Pimlico, but which, it is necessary to note, was not the original Pimlico at all.

The original Pimlico was situated in Elizabethan times in what is still known as Pimlico Walk, and which is still a most peculiar winding alley of a thoroughfare, stretching from the side of the Britannia, Hoxton, (or Old Brit.) right into the New North Road.

In that still very unsalubrious thoroughfare, a Tudor restaurateur named Ben Pimlico started a pie-shop and general entertainment establishment, of which place one regrets to note that his pies were more delectable than his patrons. In fact, this resort of Pimlico's soon became famous, (or infamous) for shady characters, and for specimens of what might be called Elizabethan Raids, because of the behaviour of what even the thieves' slang of that period called " Blowens." So much so, that Ben Pimlico and his place presently gained the " honour " of being named by Elizabethan and Jacobean dramatists whenever they wanted to name any specially notorious haunt.

Now when Host Pimlico found his Hoxton neighbourhood, slummy though it even then was, becoming too hot to hold him, he took other steps. And he took them to what was then, and became still more so, a fashionable district subsequently known as Belgravia.

Here Ben acquired a good deal of landed property, and in the midst thereof, and apparently not far from the present Victoria Palace, he put up another entertainment place, and called that, and his new territory, again by his own surname—Pimlico.

And so you see this is really a case when, in defiance of Kipling's dictum, the East can meet the West . . . or at all events that the North East can meet the South West !

But to return to the little roadside inn which nearly two hundred years ago, gave good entertainment for man and beast, and was not long afterwards known as the Royal Standard Tavern.

These "licensed premises" (as the police always say, when they mean a public house), became, about a century ago, used for that class of musical entertainment which was given at taverns and pothouses twice or thrice weekly as a rule, under the name of Free-and-Easies, or Sing-Songs. By the time I used to haunt these go-as-you-please gatherings they had become known as "Select Harmonic Meetings" if you please, as was testified by the card to that effect which was always shown in the window of the pub concerned.

About eighty years back the Royal Standard Inn passed into the hands of a publican named Moy. Now Mr. Moy, the fully licensed man, who seems to have been a very worthy fellow, ran the premises partly on sing-song lines for a great many years. This manager-publican, evidently pining to do better things than were then current in such free-and-easies, from time to time engaged all kinds of music-hall stars of the period.

One of the stars of Moy's Music-Hall, and subsequently at the Royal Standard, was that brilliant, but alas often blasphemous, singer, G. W. Ross, at whose tremendous but unquotable song "Sam Hall," I have hinted aforetime in these "Memories."

Early in the last century's 'sixties, Moy's Music-Hall passed into the hands of another very worthy licensed victualler, R. A. Brown to wit, and it was about then that I began to haunt the "Stan. Pim." as we used to call it. Brown's régime lasted apparently for about sixty years when in came another proprietor, one surnamed Elliott.

Also well do I remember there Madame Pleon with her then tiny sons, Dot and Tom. The great Jenny Hill, (never beaten) Leybourne, Nash, Fred French, and the great Vance.

BILLEE BENNETT
(*Photo by Dawson Studios, Liverpool*)

GRACIE FIELDS

NEIL KENYON
(*Photo by Claude Harris*)

CLARICE MAYNE
(*Photo by Sasha*)

Facing page 212

Other favourites at the Royal Standard in my young days included the very comical comedian J. H. Milburn, father of the popular agent Hartley Milburn, and grandfather of the sweet Julie Hartley Milburn.

The later day programmes at the Royal Standard, Pimlico, immediately preceding its conversion to the Victoria Palace, will be remembered without my memorising them. I ought to mention, however, two of the most remarkable proprietors and managers who ran the Royal Standard, and made it one of the most reputable and most merry of music-halls.

The first of these two licensed victualler-lessees, was my late dear friend Richard Wake, who I think succeeded Brown, but there may have been two or three contemporary proprietors in between, for truth to say there are certain advertisements, etc., of that hall, which do not vouchsafe the name of the manager.

Richard Wake, a fine upstanding chap with something of a nautical cut about him, soon interested me very greatly by his far-seeing and courageous temperament. On noticing this, I soon put to him the question, (as a book-loving worshipping youngster would), as to whether he, Richard, was in any way connected with Hereward the Wake, whose exploits are so splendidly narrated in Kingsley's novel of that name. I might mention here that Hereward the Wake was the son of that great English heroine, Lady Godiva, and that the late Queen Alexandra was directly descended from Hereward.

Richard Wake told me that he was a direct descendant of Hereward, and indeed he soon gave me sufficient proof of his assertion. "And so you see," he remarked, "I am like Hereward, a yellow belly." This term I may remind my readers, is one always applied locally to all natives of the Fen Districts, wherein Hereward was so pluckily popular.

Good old Wake's successor was my still surviving friend . . . everybody's friend, Thomas S. Dickie, who carried on, and eventually even improved Wake's improvements at the Royal Standard. Dickie managed this famous establishment long described, and perhaps truthfully, as the oldest music-hall in London, right up to the time when he was eventually prevailed upon to sell his interests, and to allow the Pimlico Standard to be turned into the present magnificent Variety Theatre, at which our King and Queen were present at the great entertainment, given recently by Sir Alfred Butt, and R. H. Gillespie.

The foregoing Victoria Palace Royal Performance which took place on February 24th, 1927, was the last of the series up to the time of writing. It was the sixth year in succession that the King and Queen had honoured the variety stage by attending such performances, and thus helping, of course, to draw such splendid "returns" for the Variety Artists' Benevolent Fund and Institution.

The favourites appearing at this Victoria Palace performance were as follows: "Auntie" the comic cyclist and ditto character "actress" with a splendid Mrs. Gamp make-up; Mona Grey, described as the vari-voiced entertainer; Norman Long, labelled as usual "With a Song—a Smile—and a Piano"; Jack Edge, the Lancashire comedian; Lily Morris, the truly humorous actress-singer, Wee Georgie Wood, described as the Peter Pan of the music-halls, (ably assisted by Dolly Harmer and Tom Blacklock); The three Huxter Brothers, wondrous acrobats; Mr. Flotsam and Mr. Jetsam, and very rightly the Victoria Girls, trained by Rodney Hudson.

The two previous Royal Performances were both given at the Alhambra, and both were for the same good cause and under the direction of Sir Oswald Stoll.

At the performance on February 12th, 1925, under the musical conductorship of George M. Saker of the far-flung theatrical family of the same name, the stars appearing were in the following order to quote from the programmes which lie before me:

George Hurd, Australia's representative juggler; the hereinbeforementioned mystic couple, Mr. and Miss Tree; Will Hay, the scholastic humourist in "The Fourth Form at St. Michaels," (assisted by George Wilma, and Cyril Platt), Ethel Hook the famous contralto with Edith Page as her pianist; Milton Hayes, labelled as "The Laughsmith with a philosophy"; G. H. Elliott, the original Chocolate Coloured Coon; Talbot O'Farrell, the melodious Irish entertainer; Jimmy Nervo and Teddy Knox; and The Fantastic Follies, (assisted by Charles Rawlings), Harry Tate, his son Ronnie and Co. in "Broadcasting"; Will Fyffe, that versatile and truly humorous comedian, and J. W. Jackson's Twelve English Dancers, all tip-top Terpsichoreans.

At the Alhambra Royal Performance May 27th, 1926, the programme was made up of the following stars:

John Tiller's Twelve Famous Dancing Girls, who started the bill this time; Dick Henderson the Yorkshire singing comedian (with his Comic Cadey); Robb Willton the very droll comic actor, assisted by his wife Florence Palmer in that quaint sketch "The Magistrate"; Lillian Burgiss, billed as "An English Ballad Singer," the just then discovered brilliant

Houston Sisters, Billie and Renee; Conn Kenna, the funny airman, and his pilot; Carr and Parr, the very novel dancers; Bransby Williams in his delightful Dickens and other impersonations; Rich Hayes, the Crusoe-like conjurer; Billy Bennett, that voluble comic, who modestly describes himself as "Almost a Gentleman," and last but not least, Jack Hylton and his famous Band.

Other Royal Performances included those respectively at the London Hippodrome and elsewhere.

One of the most noteworthy of Royal Performances in Varietyland was given at the London Coliseum on July 1919 by desire of the King: "to show his appreciation of the generous manner in which the artists of the variety stage, helped the numerous Funds, helped in the War." The Royal Party included the King and Queen, Princess Mary, Prince Albert, Princess Victoria and Prince Henry.

Their Majesties were received by Sir Oswald Stoll, Arthur Croxton, the manager, and the house had been splendidly decorated under the direction of Val Prince. Alfred Dove's fine resident orchestra played several fine selections. The stars concerned comprised: The Flying Banvards, Ernest Hastings, George Robey, Violet Loraine, Sam Barton, Harry Tate in "Selling a Motor Car," Arthur Prince and his remarkable figure "Jim," Clarice Mayne and That (the late J. W. Tate) Du Calion, who does all his business on top of a ladder; and that funniest of all modern clowns, Grock. By way of finale, a Pageant of Peace written by Louis N. Parker, was presented with the contralto Ethel Hook as Brittania, was conducted by Sir Edward Elgar.

What is claimed to be the first Royal Command Performance in the history of the music-halls, was given at the Palace Theatre July 1st, 1912.

The King and Queen were attended by the Grand Duchess George of Russia, Princess Victoria, Princess Christian of Schleswig-Holstein, Princess Victoria of Schleswig-Holstein, Prince Arthur of Connaught, the Duke and Duchess of Teck, Prince Alexander of Teck, and Princess Henry of Battenberg. The building was handsomely decorated as a flower garden, the Royal Box itself, presenting a bower of roses.

The artists engaged included: Charles T. Aldrich, Wilkie Bard, the Bogannys, G. H. Chirgwin, Cinquevalli, David Devant, Happy Fanny Fields, Barclay Gammon, La Pia, Harry Lauder, Alfred Lester, Cecilia Loftus, Clarice Mayne and J. W. Tate, the Palace Girls, Anna Pavlova, Pipifax and

Panlo, Arthur Prince, George Robey, Harry Tate, Little Tich and Vesta Tilley.

The concluding item was a tableau representing "Variety's Garden Party." In this nearly 150 music-hall artists took part, the central position being occupied by Harry Claff, who took the solo part in the National Anthem.

This first Command Performance realized the sum of £2,738 13s. 5d. clear profit, and this, in accordance with the expressed wish of the King, was divided among the music-hall charities.

The attendance of Royalties at the above-named performance, makes a large and dazzling array. Or rather it did make, for alas since then, the intervening World Disaster has removed several of the Royal Personages then present, especially those occupying or intending to occupy, certain foreign Thrones.

A ROYAL PERFORMANCE AND A DITTO HITCH

The first visit paid by Royalty to a Variety Theatre or music-hall, took place at the London Coliseum soon after it was first opened by the then Mr. Oswald Stoll. The business manager at that time was the late Captain John Donald, who had fulfilled similar posts with Johnnie Toole and other renowned actor-managers.

John was a man well connected, and of some influence, not only in military, but in diplomatic circles, and it was he who suggested to Stoll the idea of getting a Royal visitor to make his first appearance as patron of a variety and music-hall show.

Thanks to influence in the proper quarter, Stoll and Donald contrived to capture the King himself, namely, Edward the Seventh.

As it had been suggested in the Royal Circles that His Majesty was not too anxious to be seen by crowds in his entering the Coliseum, Captain John had a brainwave. He got Stoll to let him have made a sort of private Box on wheels, which would receive the Royal Visitor, at his own chariot door, and "cart" him bang into the Auditorium!

Anon they deposited the Monarch into the movable box, but on its way into the theatre, this precious conveyance got stuck, and it was some time before it could be moved Indeed, eventually it was found advisable to dig our King out of the box and conduct him in another manner.

I was present at this Royal Performance, as at all the

others, and I well remember how, on this awkward occasion, King Edward showed that same kindly humorous tolerance, and even enthusiasm, which many of us have seen him display at so many theatres, and other places of entertainment.

A PEER'S ROYAL VARIETY SHOW

What was undoubtedly a unique Royal music-hall performance, was given a year before the War broke out by Lord Derby at his historical mansion situated in his enormous park, at Knowsley, about seven miles from Liverpool City.

This peer of ancient lineage and of great political and sporting renown, gave this entertainment to our King and Queen by way of celebrating the birthday of Lord Stanley, the heir to the great Derby possessions.

The special variety entertainment given was very wisely placed in the hands of the then chief directors of the Moss Empires Ltd., and included the following seven "turns": Tom Edwards, the "Huntsman" ventriloquist; David Devant, the great conjurer; Olga, Elgar and Eli Hudson; Frank and Vesta (whirlwind dancers); the late George Formby, Neil Kenyon and George Graves.

To this extra special, not to say memorable variety show, I had the honour to be invited, apart from my journalistic associations with that event.

I had the additional honour of being deputed by Lord Derby to attend to the seating and other arrangements of Their Majesties. At the end of this remarkable performance, the Queen graciously asked me to conduct her to the artists' dressing-rooms in order that she might congratulate those great favourites who had given such an excellent show.

Within a twelvemonth of this happy Birthday Celebration, the World Crisis broke out, and of course the twenty-one-year-old Lord Stanley was off, like the rest, to fight the foe. Happily, in this case, young Stanley was fighting for a King whom everybody loved. How unlike to what happened to a previous Lord Stanley, who found it his duty to do battle against a wretched sovereign namely Richard the Third. Also, to take the Crown from that Crookback King and hand it on the field of battle to his successor, the conqueror who thus became Henry the Seventh.

THE CHOSEN RACE IN VARIETY

As in the dramatic and musical and other artistic circles, so the variety stage can boast, and with good reason, of the large numbers of Israelites among the members thereof. It would be almost impossible to give a complete list even of the most favourite Jewish entertainers of the past and present. Perhaps however, the following attempt thereat will be found interesting alike to Goyim and to Yidden.

The Hebrew music-hall folk in the past certainly included Jolly Nash, Fred French, George Leybourne, Walter Laburnam, Teddy Solomon, (first a song composer, and afterwards very eminent comic opera ditto), also Teddy's first wife, born Isaacs, but known as a stage serio by the name of Lily Grey, his second wife, Lillian Russell, Teddy's brilliant daughter Claire Romaine, her husband Edgar. Also dear old Ben Nathan, the late conjuror Carl Hertz, and the famous Australian impresario, Harry Rickards (otherwise Ben Leete), for some few years a comic singer in England. The far-flung family of the Lauris had undoubtedly had an Israelite origin, and good old John Lawson, as we have seen, was confessedly half a Jew.

I have good reason to believe that greatest of past variety managers Charles Morton was also one of the Chosen. Charles' brother, William Henry, also a variety manager, married into the family of the Russell's. That is to say, William's wife was a daughter of the great old singer and song writer Henry Russell, the composer of "Cheer Boys Cheer," "There's a Good Time Coming" etc.

This Russell family of Hebraic stock, is now represented by its most distinguished member, namely Sir Landon Ronald, who in his time has composed sundry ballets and spectacles for the variety theatres.

It will be interesting to many to know that two of the afterwards most distinguished Israelites who tried their fortunes on the music-hall stage, with occasional flutters on the dramatic ditto, were the Brothers Barnato, Barney and Harry.

When I first knew these youngsters, (who were born Isaacs) in and around Petticoat Lane—of course long before they drifted into the Diamond Business—they were both very stage struck. Not being then certain of any special profession, they tried their respective luck at comic singing, acting, conjuring etc.

Barney, both in those days and years afterwards when he became a millionaire, would talk with me enthusiastically about his stage ambitions for hours and hours. Harry was however, the cleverer entertainer, especially in variety work and was in fact a smart prestidigitator.

Of course, when out South Africa way, their keen business faculties brought them fortune, they dropped their stage work, but poor Barney, whose end was so tragic, never got over what we pro.'s used to call "Rubbing one's shoulders against the Wings."

The Barnatos' subsequent fortune and the wondrous benevolence of that extensive family, (even for Jews) is a matter of history of another kind.

And now for a batch of Hebrew variety folk, who are happily still with us. These include the following:

Ada Reeve, Ethel Levey, Lily Morris, Lowenwirth and Cohen, Hayman and Franklin, Colonel Sir Walter De Frece, Colonel Harry Day, Mrs. Harry Day, (Kitty Collyer), Herman, Julius, Ernest, and Max Darewski, Lew Lake, Joe Peterman, Ernie Lotinga, and his brothers, the Lucks, and Julian Rose. Fred and Arthur Conquest certainly are descended from the race. I have reason also to believe that wonderful family the Lupinos, whom I have known for years from Clown George downwards, and including of course the gifted and versatile Stanley, Barry, Mark and several others, are descended from Jewish ancestors from an Italian side.

There are also several Jews of Spanish extraction on the variety stage. Among these are the various Espinosas such as Edouard, the brilliant dancer, pantomimist and terpsichorean tutor, his gifted choreographic sisters Lea and Judith, his smart young son Kelland Espinosa etc. These are all descendants of that most wonderful ballet and drama producer, the late Espinosa, who never had a front name, at least on the bills. This little marvel was for many years, producer and stage director for everything spectacular presented by the renowned actor-managers Charles Kean, Sir Henry Irving and Sir Herbert Tree.

I may as well finish this admittedly incomplete list of deservedly popular Israelites by mentioning the renowned Wiggist Willie Clarkson. He may deny this soft impeachment, but let him.

And what about Charlie Chaplin?

CHAPTER XIX

Some still scintillating stars—Dorothy Ward and Clarice Mayne—Kate Carney and Nellie Wallace—Violet Loraine and Marie Blanche—Some Music-Hall Sisters—Music-Hall Males—Wilkie Bard, Harry Tate and George Mozart—A further survey of Music-Hall Talent.

In view of the recent ever-recurring lamentations of pessimists, or mugwumps, to the effect that variety is dead—and some even go so far as to add and D——d—it is necessary to give some account, however brief, of the large number of great favourites, male and female, who are now delighting music-hall patrons.

Following the good old rule of Ladies First, one may place the modern stars, in the following order, of course " without prejudice," as the lawyers say. For example, there is Dorothy Ward, which lovely damsel both as regards her variety and pantomime work, stands in the highest esteem as a Principal Boy. As such, she carols and croons all kinds of delightful ditties, mostly in conjunction with a group of youngsters, known as Dorothy Dots.

Clarice Mayne, another strong favourite is also much devoted to Principal Boyhood. Ella Retford, again, is a star of great magnitude, both in music-halls and theatres, with perhaps a stronger infusion of versatility and truly humorous " character " acting, than is usual in that class of artist.

Lily Morris, one of the cleverest of variety soubrettes, is especially striking in the more low comedy form of impersonations, as exemplified in her perennial song, " He's only a Working Man ! " Wish Wynne, a most versatile actress and singer, has won deserved fame by her realistic monologues.

In this varied form of musical monologue act, one of the best and brightest of the " school " is Maidie Scott, whose recent romance of espousing her very early and long faithful wooer will be fresh in the memory of many. When the merry Maidie returns from Australia, whereto she has embarked with her bridegroom, we all hope she again will regale variety patrons with her clever acting and miming.

Among the still great favourites of the variety boards, in the low comedy line, Kate Carney still stands high in position if not in stature. Bonnie Kate's Coster Carols are among the best of their kind. After several years she is still able to bring down the house with her chief old numbers such as "Three Pots a Shilling," and "Oysters a Shilling a Dozen." Another feature which Miss Carney, (the wife of George Barclay, the well-known agent and racehorse owner) still continues with success, is her Friday night Song Competitions.

These strange exhibitions of Amateur exploits, sometimes of a very painful kind, are a revival of a very common form of Benefit attractions of the very early days of the music-halls.

Of all the low comedy ladies of the variety world, undoubtedly one of the very funniest is Nellie Wallace, whose slavey impersonations especially, are equal to the comic specimens which were given in the past by that great all-round artist, Jenny Hill, the so-called "Vital Spark." I can give no higher praise to Miss Wallace than this.

Just before writing these mems., Nellie Wallace told me a quaint little story which served to show how different she looks off the stage than what she does on, in her comic make-up.

Not long ago, Nellie had an invitation to a very swagger Park Lane mansion, where she was to be the honoured guest. On arriving there the parlourmaid kept her waiting in the hall for some time. Eventually on being reminded by Nellie that she was still there, the maid replied, "You must wait a little longer. The mistress is expecting a comic-faced actress, who I believe is called Nellie Wallace."

The family of the late, and up to now unreplaced Marie Lloyd, is well represented on the variety boards. These representatives include those bright and breezy belles, Alice and Rosie Lloyd, and Daisy Wood, all three sisters of Marie's. Also Marie's daughter who as Marie Lloyd Junr. (born Courtney), is cleverly carrying on the traditions of Mama.

Hetty King and Ella Shields can rightly be labelled as among the best of male impersonators of the Vesta Tilley type, plus of course Nora Delany, a very skilful versatile actress and singer, who recently married into the Peerage!

Among the solidly established favourites alike on the variety and theatrical are Marie Loftus, mother of the famous Cissie, (who is even more of a dramatic star), Marie Kendall, who still chortles cheerily of emulating the Ivy, in addition to sundry clever low comedy impressions ; Daisy James, always excellent in principal boyish rôles ; and Marie Dainton, who lately sandwiches with her variety mimicry sundry acting successes on the acting stage.

Vesta Victoria, recently returned to the variety stage in several of her previous successes.

Still among the top liners of course is Ada Reeve, who seems to be able to sing all kinds of songs, and to play all sorts of parts ; also May Beatty, a similarly versatile artist, who at the present moment is going strong in her native Australia ; Lily Burnand, so long billed as the Lovely Lively Lily, (a label which I gave her a good while ago) and that remarkably clever Israelite damsel, the character-acting, and Principal boy playing Claire Romaine, daughter of the late gifted young composer, Edward Solomon.

There are of course several special variety favourites who from time to time go into regular theatres not only for pantomimes, but for special revues. The chief stars in this special group include the merry Marie Blanche, who is a member of that distinguished theatrical family comprising Ada Blanche, the famous Drury Lane Principal boy ; Addie Blanche, a popular Principal girl ; and the late Mrs. Robert Courtneidge. This batch is also strengthened by the taking in of Violet Essex, the sweet-singing wife of Tucker the violinist ; and Violet Loraine, one of the best all-round humorous artists, that ever graced the variety or the theatrical boards.

When I spoke to this last named charming friend, just before writing these mems., she still seemed, I regret to say, resolved to remain in retirement at the fine old Northumberland Castle possessed by her husband, Edward Joicey. But as I said to the jubilant Mrs. Joicey at the time, I am quite prepared to find her exercising the privilege of her Sweet Sex and changing her mind !

Of course, one of the most versatile variety artists of the time is that young damsel Gracie Fields, who has just become Sir Gerald du Maurier's leading lady at the St. James's Theatre !

Two of the best and brightest of the newest variety stars, are of course the Sisters Houston, a couple of Scottish lassies, still very young, and improving apace from night to night. The rise and progress of these Houston girls form quite a romance in music-hall history.

Other "sisters" also highly popular, include of course the Sisters Trix, the Ditto Dolly's, and last but by no means least,

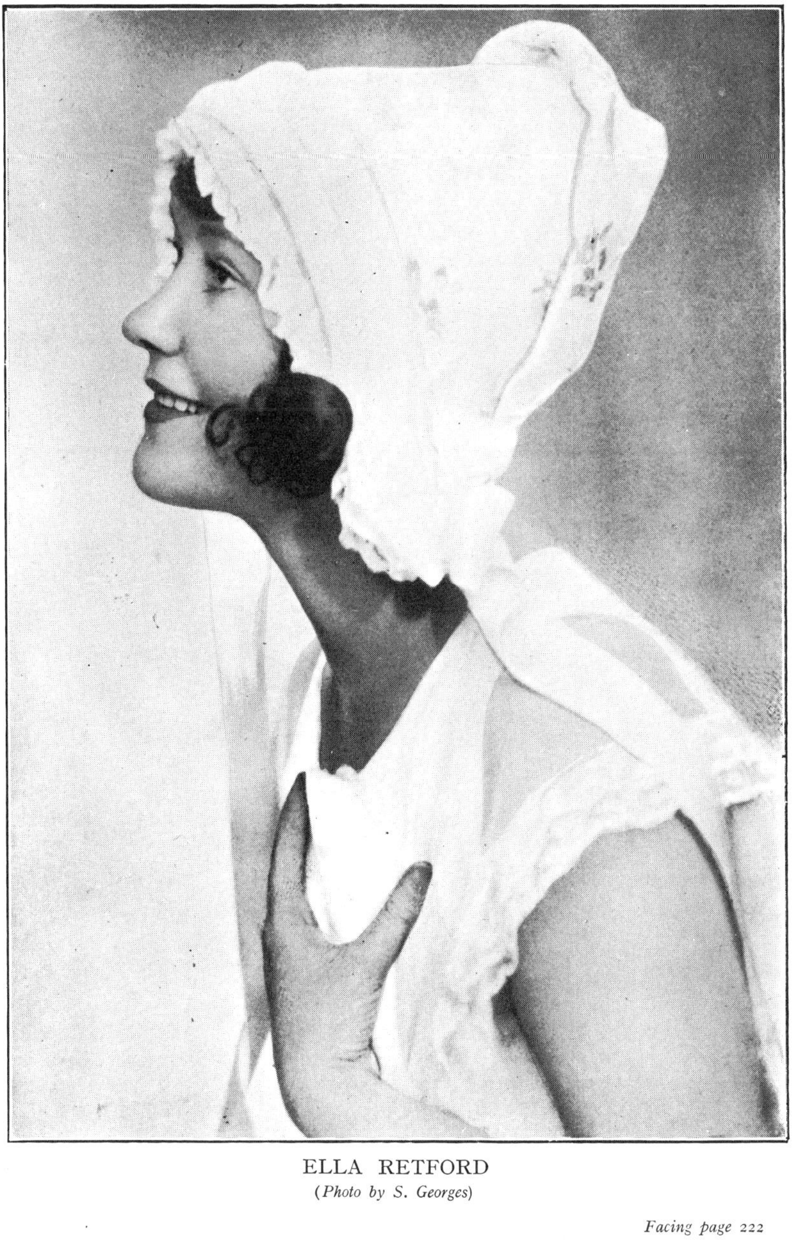

ELLA RETFORD
(*Photo by S. Georges*)

Facing page 222

those very smart Sisters, Lorna and Toots Pounds, who are among the lately very numerous variety stars, whom we have borrowed from "Down Under."

One of the biggest favourites that ever stepped upon the music-hall stage is undoubtedly Gertie Gitana, a very melodious singer and clever actress, who, after some years of single-turning, has acquired a habit of playing heroine in certain musical plays. In this line, Miss Gitana is achieving enormous success.

May Henderson, still young, has been on the stage a good many years, because of the fact that she started almost as a baby in arms. She was brought out at that tender age by her late father, who was the Henderson of the famous Henderson and Stanley quartette. Little May, on growing up, adopted coon carolling, after the fashion of that started by the late favourite Gene Stratton, and now carried on by G. H. Elliott. Miss Henderson dashes through the music-halls nearly all the year, the Christmas and New Year portions of which she spends making successes in pantomime. Her husband is the well-known comedian Bert Burnell of the Burnell Troupe, and a very clever chap he is!

I might of course add to the above list, several non-British artists, who are deservedly popular upon the British variety boards, but perhaps the above group will suffice for the nonce.

MORE MERRY MEN

Those feeble folk who think, or pretend to think, that we have no real music-hall comedians nowadays, deserve to be fed upon a list of current comedians of the sort. Herewith are some few details of the extremely numerous group thereof.

Among the chief of the older established merry-makers in the music-halls one of course places Wilkie Bard, whose musical monologues, even if sometimes of undue length, never fail to arouse the utmost hilarity. Wilkie (otherwise Billie Smith), one of the many variety recruits from that renowned old try-out tavern, the Slip Inn, Manchester, has always proved himself an excellent actor as well as a droll singer, especially in such impersonations as "The Night Watchman," the would-be Opera Singer, and the timorous henpecked husband in that very droll sketch entitled "Chrysanthemums."

Harry Tate of course looms large among the lively in his extraordinary domestic and realistic sketches such as "Motoring," "Fishing," "Billiards," and his latest strange mirth-provoking specimen called "Peacehaven."

Among the most nimble and comical actors of sketches and playlets comes George Mozart, who has had the most varied experience ever allotted to any stage player. There is not a line of business in which George has not figured, and I doubt if there is a musical instrument which he cannot play!

After some time passed in licensed victualling during the last few years, the merry Mozart has now happily reappeared on the variety stage. At the moment of writing he is doing a series of twice daily turns in connection with Maskelyne's Magical Mysteries at St. George's Hall.

A boy who was the protégé of Mozart's, and played the drum etc., as Black-Eyed Susan's William played the fiddle, that is "Like a Hangel," afterwards became a splendid variety artist himself, and is now the leading comedian of Drury Lane Theatre. I allude of course to that splendid actor and ditto dancer, Gene Gerrard!

Charles Austin (the "Parker" player), must also of course take a very high position among comic sketch artists, and so must Bert Darnley, a comedian of astounding versatility, who writes his own and other people's sketches and plays, and was the author of Dan Leno's most successful song hits. Herbert Darnley, born McCarthy, is descended on his mother's side from the great little Edmund Kean!

Often have I seen Herbert don the Hamlet dress of the electric Edmund's which "customary suit of solemn black," Bert has long possessed.

To carry on the Kean tradition still further, the droll Darnley has given the stage name of Nance Carey to his clever daughter, because that was the maiden name of Edmund Kean's mother, from whom Bert's Mama descended!

Quite a family group of a mixed theatrical and variety talents will be found in the Leonards, all blithe and busy artists. This batch includes Billy Leonard, who is equally funny as actor and dancer, and is now a popular comedian in the "Legit." Also Cressie Leonard, who is literally one of the most beautiful Irish colleens and principal boys I have ever met. Also that dainty little soubrette and musical leading lady, Billie Hill. These Leonards, together with the long popular couple called The Sisters Pine, are all offshoots of two of the most honoured and hard-working duettists of the earlier music-hall days, namely, Bob and Jennie Leonard.

Still strong-going comedians of the best brand include J. W. Rickaby, that brilliant character impersonator, who was wont to tickle all and sundry with his ditty entitled, "They built Piccadilly for Me." Also Charles Bignell, who may still be heard stating "What Ho she Bumps." Austin Rudd, whom I heard the other day still declaring that "Sailors Don't Care." Harry Ford, who may be described as the interrogative comedian; likewise Tom Leamore, a droll comic, and so clever a clog dancer that he once competed with the great Dan Leno himself, and I think, beat him!

And there is Albert Whelan who sings and "siffles," being indeed a wonderful whistler and altogether a brilliant artist. Also George Lashwood, who is perhaps nearest of all the latter-day comics to George Leybourne and such like "Lion Comiques."

Likewise, T. W. or Tommy Barrett, renowned for being, as he so often has told us, "A Nobleman's Son"; and Harry Champion the variety laureate of "Vittals." This is evidenced by his most useful culinary carols such as "Boiled Beef and Carrots," "Hot Tripe and Onions," and "Hot Meat Pies, Savoloys and Trotters" etc. Harry's commendations of these comestibles are always emphasised by his big boot battements!

More serious variety impersonators, who also however can be very humorous when occasion demands, include the herein-beforementioned versatile actor and mimic Bransby Williams, which artistic all-round actor was originally intended for a missionary. Also George Leyton, whose clever impersonations have included many an historical figure, and Hayden Coffin, who has often 'verted to variety from the musical comedy stage, and has always been a success in both departments.

Special mention should be made of the versatile and vivacious comic sketchist and monologuist Marriott Edgar, who not only writes all his own sketches, episodes and acts, but also pens many such for other artists. Marriott Edgar is another proof of the force of heredity, for he is the grandson of the wonderful tragedienne, Miss Marriott (Mrs. Robert Edgar), who was a great Shakespearian actress, and was certainly one of the greatest female Hamlets the British stage has ever known.

M. E.'s young son has also just taken to the boards, thus representing the fourth generation to figure thereon!

Another member of an ancient and accepted stage family, is the variety comedian Billy Danvers, son of Ramsey Danvers, one of the most side-splitting eccentric comedians of his day, and grandson of Edwin Danvers, one of the cleverest burlesque actors and drollest dancers of the early 'sixties. It was this last-named Danvers, who was the original representative of Dame Hatley, the mother whom the burlesque writer Burnand invented for Sailor William in his burlesque called, "Black-Eyed Susan or, the Little Bill that Was Taken Up."

A little band of dialect comic singers are appearing with marked success on the variety boards. These include Dick Henderson, the sweet-singing and wild-wheezing Yorkshire comedian, who has been scoring not only in the halls, in pantomimes and revues all over the Habitable Globe. It may not be generally known that Dick's comical hat (or cadey), which perches sparrow-wise upon his lofty brow, is a thing which cost him a few shillings and without which he will never go upon the stage, for, as he has told me, it is quite a mascot "tile."

This dialectical group also takes in George Jackley, whose thunderous voice resounds through many a theatre and hall, and who is a terrific favourite in both of those stage sections. Likewise Jack Edge and George Formby, Junr, a couple of popular Lancashire lads; and that great favourite George Bass, who also hails from Clog-and-Shawl Land.

Bass is also a musical devotee, as may be seen by his vocal and other treatment of his eternal flageolet, which instrument he so often starts to play but doesn't, but which he *can* play with no uncertain squeal!*

Two other dialect comedians deserve honourable mention. One is Sammy Shields, who so often has divulged the methods of a Goalie; and Harry Weldon, who so long informed vast audiences what he had "Done to Colin Bell!"

MORE OF 'EM!

Here is an additional and extra special survey of the inexhaustable talent of the music-halls. The exponents thereof include Billy Bennett, a mixture of comic singer and ditto reciter, who retails his wild wares with most side-splitting results. As a farcical monologuist he always recalls to me that old-time humourist of the halls, J. G. Forde.

Shaun Glenville, the Irish husband of the before-mentioned lovely Dorothy Ward, is certainly one of the most varied and gifted comedians of the theatres and the halls. He has learnt his "business" from a baby, appearing and playing in every kind of drama and pantomime. In point of fact, he started his stage career when he was a fortnight old in "Arrah Na Pogue," one of the best of all Dion Boucicault's plays.

G. S. Melvin is another of the wonderfully versatile "regular" stage folk who took to the halls, and continues to be in great demand alike for variety, pantomime and revue. Undoubtedly

*Mr. Bass is another who passed away as these pages were going to press.

he is one of the greatest quick change comedians and dancers of our time.

Another all round drama and farce actor, who is triumphing nightly in the halls, is Robb Wilton. So full of rollicking resource is Robb that he plays quite full-grown sketches by himself, but for the occasional smart intervention of his wife, Miss Florence Palmer. I understand that ere long the truly humorous Robb will be returning for a while to play an important part in a " Legit." production.

It is time now to consider two Roses, both of a fully blown humorous growth. One is Clarkson Rose, a very remarkable young comedian, who changes his very handsome appearance many times per night in order to impersonate all sorts of widely contrasted characters portrayed by him in song, sketch and revue. Alike in his appearance, his rapid and versatile method of acting, his first-class method of singing and his command of dancing and of dumb show, Clarkson Rose is the nearest approach to the great Fred Leslie of any I have yet met in that line of business. And *I* knew the great Fred well. Indeed, I wrote several of his biggest characters.

The other Rose is front named Julian, and like so many other stage dramatic, and variety pro.'s he belongs to the Hebrew race. Julian, whom I first saw in plays, musical and otherwise, has become a very alluring variety raconteur, his stories mostly being given in the character of a Yid. In this national (and natural) guise, Julian has won great praise both from Israelite and Goy audiences especially in the extraordinary brain whirling monologue entitled " Levinsky's Wedding."

Billy Merson, born Thompson, (and rather given to publish the fact), is indeed a many-sided purveyor of mirth. In the music-halls his Bandits, Toreadors, Pirates and other fearful wildfowl are all well known and highly appreciated. On the " regular " stage he has played many an important " lead," notably in " Whirled into Happiness," and subsequently in " Rose Marie," in which he was the original English Hard-Boiled Herman. Later Billy Merson-Thompson ventured on the perilous paths of actor managership, producing among other things " My Son John," at the Shaftesbury. Since then he has reverted to variety, and scoring amain again at such vast houses as the Alhambra and the Coliseum.

Just as we were going to press, " Billy " has again taken to the dramatic stage and is playing in Keble Howard's droll comedy "Lord Babs"—for another Howard—a celebrated many-companied manager—front named Bannister.

Once upon a time Billy was a circus clown and lately, for a series of charity performances, he returned with great success to his circus clownship.

Speaking of clowns, undoubtedly one of the greatest that ever appeared on the variety stage in modern times, is the great little Grock, who at the moment of writing is careering around the Continent.

No funnier or cleverer performer of the clown kind has ever been seen in the music-halls than Fred Griffiths (born Delany), who at the present moment is celebrating his sixty second year upon the stage ! I have only to mention Fred and his partner the original "brother" Griffiths, and their strange antics with those startling animals, the Blondin Donkey of old Tivoli days, and their present Blondin horse Pogo, to prove what I say as to that firm's championship among dumb-show music-hall entertainers.

Another couple whose extraordinary antics and gyrations I have seen send our King and Queen into shrieks of laughter, are the boneless acrobats who are billed as Nervo and Knox. These youngsters, emanating from an old time pantomimic family, are achieving popularity literally by leaps and bounds.

The other startling silent entertainers of boundless popularity, include the marvellous Craggs Troupe, in which Papa Cragg was continuing as Head up till his eightieth odd year recently ; the Musical Jees out of whom have come the Florador Troupe (which was connected with the Evans group) and has produced among others, striking successful comedians, George Gee, who is making such a huge success at the Palace in "The Girl Friend."

The Jees naturally bring into batch those deucedly comic couple, the brothers Egbert, (the Seth of whom is the husband of that dainty dancing soubrette Daisy Dormer) have been welcome for many years in every music-hall and in every available pantomime as "The Happy Dustmen."

The numerous niggers of the past are now no more. They have been reduced to one or two specimens. Of these undoubtedly the most popular is G. H. Elliott, who has so long billed himself as "The Chocolate-Coloured Coon." I have seen Elliott for many years in music-halls and in pantomimes, but even knowing his ability as I do, I must confess that I was utterly astounded a little while ago, when I struck him at the Bristol Hippodrome. So effective was his appeal to the vast audience of that beautiful Stoll house that he had to sing eight or nine songs before they would allow him to rest !

In olden days of the halls, it was customary to have all sorts of duettists, male and female. The former kind were mostly serious songsters, generally a tenor and a baritone or a bass. I remember also that generally they sang the same songs which included " All's Well," and " The Minute Gun at Sea." We have not many such duettists now, but the two best of these are Flotsam and Jetsam. These duettists not only avoid the threadbare ballads of the past, but even bring in all sorts or topical allusions. Altogether their turn is quite an amazing one, for apart from their change of carol, assuredly the bass partner is the most musical singer of the kind we have heard for years ; yea, even in Grand Opera.

Of course Kirkby and Hudson come into this category of the duet description. They lean mostly to the humorous order of song architecture, and they have become enormously popular and deservedly so.

It would be wrong here to omit mention of Ernest Butcher and Muriel George. This versatile pair have of late revived some of the most celebrated of the old-time folk songs and comic ditties, all tremendously popular in their day. It may be added, that when one is listening to this melodious couple, say in " Villikins and His Dinah," the listener can be assured that he or she is going straight back to the popular songs of the very earliest music-halls. And what songs they were !

Chapter XX

Strange stories of Stage sketches and sketchers—Fred Karno's sketches—The story of " Mumming Birds "—The Kitchens, Father and Son—George Gray and " The Fighting Parson "—A real Fighting Parson—John Lawson and " Humanity."

One of the many Fred Karno sketches which made history in the halls, was " The Dandy Thieves " sometimes called " His Majesty's Guests," and lately in revised form, renamed " Sergeant Lightning."

This sketch was one of a trio dealing with a set of crooks, some of a crib-cracking and some of a bookie brand. One of its principal musical numbers shows how " six little burglars went a-burgling," and how first one and then another got pinched " until there was only none."

This ditty was obviously based on the old Christy Minstrel catch, entitled " Ten Little Niggers," a terrific song hit in its day, which never failed to draw encore after encore when it was sung by " Pony " Moore, or any of his Christy co-corner men.

So it fared with the " Six Little Burglars," which had the additional advantage of a very remarkable treadmill dance for all concerned. I have seen this number used all round London and in the provinces, and always found it bringing the house down, so to speak.

The historical interest however, attached to the " Dandy Thieves," or " His Majesty's Guests," or " Sergeant Lightning," is bound up with the fact that in the character of the sergeant Impresario Karno brought out several of the most remarkable and gifted comedians of the day. These included Dan Rolyat, Alfred Lester, Syd Chaplin and his greater brother Charlie, otherwise the Kinema King.

Perhaps the biggest, best and brightest of the Karno concoctions is the old-established and still running " Behind the Scenes " sketch entitled " The Mumming Birds." This knockabout blend of burlesquery, helped to make the fame and subsequently the fortunes of at least two now very big salaried favourites. One of these was the above-mentioned Charlie Chaplin, and the other is an eccentric knockabout named Billy Reeves.

I may claim to have had some share in the "making" of the latter star, for on the first night of "Mumming Birds" in London some years ago, I pointed out in my *Referee* notice of the show that the great humorous hit of the piece had been made by someone who had played the drunken swell in a private box. This (to me) amazingly quaint actor was, I pointed out, not named in the programme, but nevertheless, that he had in one night become a fine variety star was undeniable.

My notice drew a very grateful letter from this "drunken swell" actor, who wrote to me somewhat as follows:

"I am the nameless 'pro.' who played the 'Drunk' in 'Mumming Birds.' My name is Billy Reeves, but up to the time when I went on in the part at short notice, I was Fred Karno's two-pound-a-week baggage man. Since your notice, I can get more than that."

My further notice and subsequent statement as to his identity drew much attention to Billy the Baggage Man from all sorts of managers, who began to fight each other in order to secure him. He soon had all sorts of big offers including one from America, where he went in due course.

There he speedily became a real star indeed, and now whenever Billy revisits the British Isles, it is with something of the effects and entourage of a big American potentate.

And naturally whenever I consider him, it is with something of journalistic or dramatic critical pride!

Here is another little tale about "Mumming Birds." It concerns the author thereof, namely Charles Baldwin, who wrote a good many other sketches for Karno, and indeed for all manner of other sketch purveyors.

Not that Charles has always confined himself to a concoction of sketches. I have known him do all sorts of strange work.

Once as a youth he was a combined actor and call-boy at the Old Princess's, and he bobbed up in all sorts of strange theatres and music-halls, not only in the play-acting line, but in assisting in scene painting, stage carpentering and what not.

There was a time also when C. B. got his living in the Air, so to speak, for he was for some time a parachutist! In fact, oftentimes has the cheery Charles come to me with stories of how he had soared up high with his kind of aerial umbrella, only to come down as he put it " Flop in some blinkin' canal."

It is however of " Mumming Birds," that I would tell a little tale, and as far as I can I will tell it to you in Charles's own words.

" I wrote 'Mumming Birds' for Fred Karno," said he, " for five pounds all at. But mark my doom! On the day I touched for the fiver, I went into Romano's. There I met a man who had lent me two quid, so I paid him straight away and stood him a drink. Shortly after, I met a cove who was bloomin' broke, so I gave him a quid. Then in the pride of my heart, at my great success and sudden wealth, I stood drinks all round to the extent of another jimmy o' goblin! I came out of the bar, and accidently dropped the last quid down a hole in the gutter. And that's all I got out of 'Mumming Birds.'"

Here is another Karno concoction and it is named " Moses and Son." It was quite a daring venture on the halls at the time, for mixed with its mirthful ingredients, there was, ever and anon, some patches of pathos. The great success of this sketch was undoubtedly achieved by a comedian, whom I have not mentioned up to now.

I allude to Fred Kitchen, who ever since he was a little boy has done most excellent acting work, not only in the music-halls, but also in the so-called " regular theatres."

It would be difficult to name a better all-round actor, both alike in the comic and pathetic vein than Fred Kitchen.

Here one may see again the effect of heredity, for Frederick is the son of a man whom I knew intimately when I was a youngster, a man deeply honoured by all who had to do with him. This was R. H. (or Dick) Kitchen, who, when I was concerned with him, was the leading pantomimist, and annual clown at the Old Vic . . . I mean the older Old Vic.

At that theatre and elsewhere, I have seen Dick Kitchen give most marvellous performances, especially in the dumb show drama, for example, his Dumb Man of Manchester in the murder melodrama of that name, remains in my memory as a performance of astounding intensity and harrowing pathos as well as of amazing agility.

I have seen many a Dumb Man of Manchester, all artistic pantomimists, but I have never seen one more dramatic or more appalling in the frightful fight that ends the play, than Fred Kitchen's father.

We live in a world of contrasts, and another proof of this

may be seen in the fact that Dick Kitchen, who taught son Fred all he knows, seldom rose to much above a fiver a week, while Fred can now command very often, a salary of at least £275!

Doubtless one of the most perennially successful pugilistic playlets ever seen in the halls was that entitled "The Fighting Parson," which was written by that still very skilful journalist and sketch writer Chris Davis, for George Gray.

Prior to this production, George Gray was one of the young minor actors, whom I used to see and consort with at that tip-top dramatic and blood-and-thunder theatre, The Pavilion, Mile End. I may re-mention that these minor actors of that period, and a little earlier included that afterwards tremendous music-hall favourite, the late Charles Godfrey, who strutted and fretted at that playhouse in all sorts of parts, for about five and twenty shillings a week.

Also there, engaged first as a young actor who couldn't act, but who showed great skill in scene painting and other painting, was the late Joe Lyons, afterwards Sir Joseph of the famous firm.

Another of the band was a youngster who is now the celebrated leading man, George Tully. And there were many others.

George Gray remained for a good while at this Mile End melodrama house, and eventually stepped Westward. Anon he had the good fortune to be engaged by Mr. and Mrs. Kendal, with whom George toured in America, Australia, etc. As indeed did another subsequently enormous favourite of the halls, namely, Albert Chevalier.

Being bitten by the bacillus of variety, like so many others, George Gray eventually went into the halls, and first of all chortled descriptive ditties of the Charles Godfrey type. Soon, however, he took to sketches and eventually struck oil with the above named specimen, "The Fighting Parson."

It will be remembered by music-hall goers that in this piece G. G. played a clergyman, who, at the crux of the playlet has to take off his coat and fight a professional pugilistic bully, in order to protect the heroine.

Naturally in order to be realistic, George engaged a well-known real professional "pug," to act as the chopping block for the cleric. All went well for a time, until one night this most practised scrapper got a little too much to drink, and also became very annoyed at Employer Gray taking him to task in consequence.

That night, alas, the dénouement of the play was reversed,

for the professional "pug," instead of allowing the ecclesiastical champion to "punish" him as per the script, landed poor George several smashing blows which floored him, and the curtain had to be rung down amid general chaos.

Happily my young friend Gray recovered sufficiently not only to resume his professional career with increasing success and ditto emoluments, but also to become what he still is, a Senator for the Island of Jersey!

A REAL FIGHTING PARSON

Yet another fistic champion. This one was a real Reverend, the late W. J. Waldron, who was for some years Vicar of St. Matthews, Brixton, and also a most diligent and earnest worker in the cause of Social Reform.

I knew the Reverend Mr. Waldron well, and anon I found that like so many others of his calling, he showed a leaning towards the drama. For a time he confined his stage work to writing sketches, including a very popular melodramatic specimen entitled "Should A Woman Tell?" He followed with two or three other playlets of a serious dramatic kind, and eventually he played in some of them, in the halls in one case enacting the part of a pugilistic self-sacrificing parson!

There was however one occasion when this Church-and-Stage comrade of ours, put in a very realistic pugilistic show of his own in the open.

He was preaching one Sunday afternoon in Brockwell Park to a large crowd, when a man constantly interrupted him. The Reverend Waldron repeatedly requested the interrupter to cease, but to no avail. At length the parson offered his annoyer one last chance, and pointed out that if he didn't take it, he would step down and punch the man's head.

The man continued to defy him, and so in due course the Reverend Gentleman carried out his promise, and having "pasted" the interrupter, resumed his parsonic address.

Mark the sequel.

A few weeks later, the Reverend Waldron was told at his church that someone wished to see him. He discovered that the caller was his old interrupter, who stated that he'd been thinking things over, and had come to the conclusion that he would call and apologise to the clergyman, who had given him such a dressing down, and moreover vowed to behave himself in future!

Poor Waldron continued to write for the variety stage and

to act therein, but I am afraid that on the whole, the stage life did not agree with him. Anyhow, his health failed, and he passed away at a comparatively early age, to the infinite regret of all who had the privilege of knowing him.

A fighter of another sort is the description I can apply to that very versatile writer for the stage, Harry M. Vernon, who, although he can say of his birthplace in the words of the coon song, "It's Kentucky sure's you're born," yet he is of British extraction and proud of it!

Before writing for the British variety theatres, H. M. Vernon was trained for the Army. He started his training at the Kentucky Military Institute, but soon went out upon the tented field to fight the foe. He fought them in the Spanish American War, and anon became a "Lootenant" in Roosevelt's Army Rough Riders, where in point of fact, he did deeds of derring do . . . and was Mentioned in Despatches!

When not thus actively engaged in warfare itself, the bold Harry went forth as War Correspondent for this or that American journal, and eventually did similar work for sundry English papers.

His stage sketches included "The Deputy Sheriff," "The Ten O'Clock Squad," "The Horse Thief," "The Third Degree," to name no others.

In due course he went in for the grown-up drama, and in collaboration with Guy Bolton he wrote "The Bamboula" which is still touring, and "Mr. Wu" (with Harold Owen), which has been played for years.

When I met H. M. Vernon a short time before writing these mems., he was engaged on two or three other "regular" stage plays, and some other big variety sketches.

ANOTHER VARIETY PARSON

One of the greatest and most courageous friends and advocates which the music-hall stage and kindred entertainments ever had was the late Reverend Stewart Headlam. When he was what W. S. Gilbert would call "a pale young curate, then" this ecclesiastic suddenly flashed forth as a champion of dramatic and variety stage folk, but more especially of the then certainly overworked and underpaid ballet girls of the period.

With this championing, the plucky parson also upheld what he regarded as the harmless necessary ballet form of show. Not only so, but likewise his reverence actually went among the players and ballet girls, and even formed clubs, tea rooms and other rest places for these often crushed down coryphees.

By this ardent advocacy the Reverend Stewart speedily drew down upon himself the ecclesiastical wrath of his Bishop under whom he served at Bethnal Green, also of vast numbers of the Puritanic and Unco' Guid.

But was that parson downhearted? . . . No! He continued his courageous warfare on behalf of the variety strugglers of all kinds, yea, even although he was inhibited, (or fired out) of his "Living."

The doughty divine was very soon helped by battalions of more tolerant persons, some of whom conspired to put him in a living in a kind of church of his own.

Here he worked with even increased zeal, not only for stage folk, but also for the under dog of every kind.

As years rolled on the Reverend Stewart Headlam wore down even the opposition of the Bishops and other church magnates, and also won for himself a far-flung admiration, in fact affection which was lavished upon him up to the moment of his death, a few years ago.

For some years before his "passing," this reverend fighter founded and became the President of the London Shakespeare League, in which department I always found him as learned as he was enthusiastic, and I had a good deal to do with him on several occasions. One of the greatest tributes however, which came to this pugnacious parson, was that for years in succession he was elected to the London County Council, in connection with which body he worked untiringly for the poor, and the suffering, the slum-crushed, and the starving, and for the downtrodden, and unemployed of every class.

It is however, for his fearless fighting for the needy and the oppressed that all who knew him, or have only read of him, will for ever honour the memory of the brave little Stewart Headlam.

A more peaceful playwright etc., is that very calm but very clever sketchwright, playwright, and author of innumerable songs, Charles Wilmott, whom I have known since he was a little lad, at the often-before-mentioned Britannia, Hoxton.

For many years past Charles has been the manager of that famous music publishing firm, Francis, Day & Hunter, and in that capacity he has had to judge and pass thousands and thousands of lyrics and scores.

He is the son of a combined theatrical and music-hall comedian named Wilmott who, when I was a mere kiddie in the halls, was half of the famous duet turn known as Connelly and Wilmott. Wilmott père resolutely set his face against young Charles having anything to do with the stage, but heredity, like murder, will out, and very soon Charles began to learn to act and certainly to scribble for the "Boards."

I remember that when he was just finishing his 'teens, young Wilmott, who looked even younger than he was, answered an advertisement issued by that tremendous Brit. favourite actor, J. Burdett Howe, who at that time was also like so many actors, bitten by the music-hall germ, and wanted sketches with which to strut and fret upon the variety boards.

When young Wilmott, turned up at the Brit. to see the great little Howe by appointment, Howe came into the room, looked over and through young Charles, and walked out again.

He returned after a time and exclaimed: "Who are *you*?" The youngster replied: "I am Charles Wilmott." "Oh," said Howe. "What message has your father sent? . . . I suppose you've come here for him." "Oh, no" returned Charles. "I am the Mr. Wilmott who wrote to you, and sent you some specimens of my work." Whereupon Howe exclaimed: "Do you mean to tell me that a kid like *you* wrote those three dramatic sketches? However did you learn even the technical requirements?"

"Please sir," said Charles, "My father is on the stage . . . he is with Mr. Connelly."

"Indeed," said Howe. "Then come along, my boy. Henceforth, you shall write all the sketches I intend to use on the variety stage."

And sure enough, Charles not only wrote those three sketches and many others, but practically all that J. B. Howe ever used in the halls, except (if I may say so), one or two I penned myself!

"ONLY A JEW" JOHN

Methinks the strangest sketches with the strangest of histories were those associated with that strangest of sketch producers and players, the late John Lawson.

Music-hall patrons will remember that the erratic but esteemed John's variety and other dramatic outputs in nearly every case took a Jewish form. Also that both the situations and the sentiments were always pro-Israelite and anti-Goy.

Before proceeding to indicate the stories of these often extremely Gentilephobe concoctions, it is perhaps fitting that

I should tell why my esteemed, but erratic friend John, presented such Yiddish propaganda playlets at all!

The reason was this, as I have heard Lawson assert more than once. His mother, up till then a "froom" Jewess, married a Gentile. So John was half Hebrew and half Goy. His father was a lovable and diligent man, and his wife was very proud of him. But as years rolled on, that wife grew more and more remorseful at having married a "meshumad" so to speak. In due course, as John began to adopt the stage as a profession, starting first as a trapezist in the halls, his mother with an increasing mental throw-back to the Judaic creed of her youth, took to persuading her bright boy John to seize the opportunity, whenever he had the chance, of advocating the Jewish faith and its ethical and social principles in his work, both behind and before the footlights.

Young Lawson's first chance of carrying out his mother's pleading in this matter . . . certainly his first chance of any moment, came with his music-hall production of what proved to be his most popular and most paying sketch, namely "Humanity." So financially successful did "Humanity" soon become, that in one of my early *Referee* notices thereof, I gave it a label which Lawson used for it throughout the remainder of his life . . . namely "The Moneyspinner."

The genesis of "Humanity" was most peculiar. It sprang from a five-act melodrama presented by the Brothers Douglass at their National Standard Theatre, Shoreditch. That melodrama was entitled "Humanity; or a passage in the Life of Grace Darling." It was really written around that famous maritime sailor-rescuing damsel, but through it ran a Jewish low comedy part.

On account of this character young Lawson, then a "Legit." actor, bought the provincial rights of this play, and toured it for a long while. John, however, didn't find this comic Yid rôle lend itself to the propaganda for which he pined being ever mindful of his vow to his mother.

A few years later however, there began to be a boom for music-hall sketches . . . especially as the insane persecution of the producers thereof, by the most bigoted of the managers of the so-called regular theatres was now slowing down.

Lawson speedily had a brain wave. Cutting away the first four acts . . . that is to say all the Grace Darling and the general interturned love-interests of "Humanity" and etc., he turned the final act into an eighteen minutes' variety sketch and called it simply "Humanity," which title now didn't fit at all!

For, look you, this act was simply a replica in melodramatic fight-form of that memorable real terrible struggle between the two notorious financial crooks, Murray and Roberts in Northumberland Street, Strand (later the site of the Grand Hotel), in 1861 culminating in the mutual murder of each miscreant!

John Lawson transformed one of these crooks into a very virtuous Yid, who conquered the remaining crook, and then bowed to the seated audience, from amid an awful and expensive mass of débris of shattered mirrors, vases, china goblets, and such like, which the Jewish and Gentile combatants had hurled at each other, with the fellest intent to slay!

Lawson played this Yiddish victor many years . . . and I must confess as I had stated in print . . . played it very badly . . . for, sooth to say, John, although sometimes effective as an eccentric or even pathetic character actor . . . (especially in "The Monkey's Paw,") was absolutely useless in heroic rôles. He was very proud, however, of his carolling, (or rather croaking) of a specially introduced song called "Only a Jew."

This reference was not, (as many seemed to think), of a highly religious nature, but was really pointed at Benjamin Disraeli, (Lord Beaconsfield) a character concerning whom John never rested till he played "Dizzy" in a sketch named after the great Disraeli scoring a magnificently picturesque failure!

Of my bizarre but benevolent and beloved friend, Lawson's other extensive . . . and always expensive variety sketch output . . . in many of which his wife, Cissie Lawson, often gave intensely dramatic performances . . . it must suffice to allude briefly to a few of the chief examples. Among these I may mention "The Shield of David," "The King of Palestine," (both literally packed with pro-Jewish propaganda), and "Vanderdecken-Todd."

The last named very sanguifulminous sketch in which, as in "The King of Palestine," I will shamefacedly confess, John lured me on to collaborate, was a compound of equal doses of the respective stories of "The Flying Dutchman," and "Sweeney Todd; The Barber Fiend of Fleet Street," plus a most startling and audacious innovation, the credit for the invention I cheerfully ascribe to John.

This precious idea was that whenever the otherwise virtuous Vanderdecken was moved to some vicious thought or deed, it was shown . . . plain for all to see, that the evil spirit of the Fleet Street Demon Barber . . . passed into the duped Dutchman's breast!

And it was also plain to see, because at that moment you saw a grim blue electric light gleam and glow in the fugitive sea-rover's heart!

Dear old John Lawson died far too young . . . and he died from overwork and over-speculation in various wild-cat schemes, theatrical, variety, commercial, etc.

Of all the people I have known throughout my long life, in every form of stage-life, I have never known a man more universally and deservedly honoured and beloved. He was as unselfish and generous as he was erratic and visionary . . . and that is saying a great deal. "After Life's fitful fever he sleeps well."

Chapter XXI

Some Strange Jewish Sketches—Lew Lake and "the Bloomsbury Burglars"—Joe Elvin, born Keegan—The Martinetti's—The Lauri's—The Conquests.

Another celebrated and quaint character of variety sketch-land is that still strongly popular actor and agent, now chiefly the latter stage, named Lew Lake.

For seven years the lively Lew toured a sidesplitting knock-about sketch called "The Bloomsbury Burglars." This in later years had a sequel or two, bringing in the same characters with sometimes a pathetic end to some of the leading parts, Nobbler to wit.

This character, which was always played by Bob Morris, was a kind of Jacques Strop to Lew Lake's Robert Macaireful burglar.

Little Lew in his boyhood's days was a kind of doctor's or chemist's boy, and I have often heard him tell how, even at that age, he became obsessed by a passion for the stage. This seems to have bitten him more acutely because his druggist employer knew the late Wilson Barrett, who used to visit him. It was characteristic of the benevolent Barrett, that when he did visit his pharmaceutical friend, he always gave little boy Lew at least five shillings for himself!

No wonder then, that before long I began to spot Lew bobbing up at the old "Brit." in Hoxton, growing up into all sorts of characters in pantos, etc., and being encouraged by that dearest of lady managers, Sara Lane, who was a kind of theatrical foster-mother of my own.

In due course Lew Lake, like so many pro.'s of the "Legit." stage, 'verted to variety and anon blossomed forth into such sketches as the one named above.

While mounting, however, to the variety pinnacle, Lew Lake and sometimes his afterwards music-hall comrade Bob Morris, used to haunt the fairs and boxing booths, on occasions running a boxing booth of their own.

This boxing game Lew often explained to me. "Was not all lavender, old pal. We charged tuppence a head for chaps to come in and scrap with each other, but sometimes we hadn't combatants enough to go round. So Bob and I often had to do a turn each as chopping blocks!

"This was all very well when we had to deal with beginners who didn't know much about boxing, but *my* word! When some of the knowing ones 'put em up,' Bob and I used to go home with chivvies resembling Christmas puddings! Still, Art's Art . . . so let it go at that!"

GOOD OLD JOE

I refer of course to everybody's old friend Joe Elvin, who really is not Elvin at all, but Keegan. It was when Joe's father, an old actor of the "Legit." took to the music-hall stage, that little Joe, then a mere boy, was re-named Elvin.

As Joseph grew apace he became a great favourite as a foil to his rather more serious papa, and in due course went into business for himself in the sketch line.

Joe's sketch material, mostly written or vamped up by that past master of sketch concoction, the late Wal Pink, mostly took the form of very old farces, plus a mass of wilder wheezes dropped in by Wal or by Joe himself.

Variety patrons will chiefly recall in connection with them such sidesplitting sketches as "The Hansom Cabby," (which was the old farce, "Turn Him Out,") and "Deaf, or I ain't Barmy," which had been rehashed up from that most famous of old farces "Deaf as a Post," in which the great John Liston if you please had performed the character of Tristram Sappy.

In fact, the old writers of curtain raisers were mostly utilised for the Elvin-ian output. But this didn't matter, for Joe was the chief ingredient, and he became very popular with these mixtures and their respective continuous catch-phrases.

The popularity even increased when Joe in due course turned on (per Pink and others) two or three Bookie sketches, which Joe was able from actual experience to enact with much realism, especially with regard to the aforesaid catch-phrases.

Unfortunately for Joseph he became a little too realistic in this bookie line, and as in the case of most honest people who "back 'em," he suffered accordingly.

It will, or should be always remembered, however, that most of the hard-earned money dispersed by Joe Elvin was spent in helping the poor and the suffering, not only of his own profession, but also out of it.

Many of us, (myself especially,) could tell many a startling story of Joe's boundless benevolence and glorious unselfishness. Joseph has now retired, but looking as fresh and acting as cheerily, and behaving as generously as ever.

I have told herein sundry stories about sketches and sketchers, but I think that I am here telling the best and noblest story of them all, when I relate the fact that out of Joe Elvin's earnings he not only helped so many in distress, but he also started and for some time subsidised that wonderful home for needy and infirm music-hall old people, the Institute at Brinsworth, up Twickenham way.

Dear old Joe! Often might he when helping many a poor fellow "Over The Sticks," say in the words of one of his most famous catch-phrases "I'm obliging My Brother I am."

SOME SILENT STARS

For many years one of the most popular group of pantomimic knockabout comedians, as contrasted with acrobats, was the famous Martinetti troupe. This was headed by Paul of that name, assisted by his very clever brother Alfred. They were descended from a pantomimic family of the same name, whose history extends back at least two and a half centuries. Paul himself was really a very great dumb show actor, and many will remember his splendid impersonation of the leading characters in "The Duel in the Snow," and in "Robert Macaire." In this he gave a side-splittingly quaint and finally pathetic performance of Macaire's foolish but faithful co-criminal, Jacques Strop.

This troupe never failed to "draw," wherever it appeared, and their performance was always followed with the most intense interest, even when, as I sometimes said to my late pal Paul, he spun out his own impersonation to the very extreme time limits!

A very interesting fact in the history of the Martinetti's is that Paul's wife, a very charming silent actress with him, was instrumental in causing the arrest of that unspeakable blackguardly murderer, the cultured Doctor Crippen. Students of criminology will find details in the proper reportorial quarters.

It should be noted with regard to Paul Martinetti that some time he occupied the throne as King Rat, in connection with that far-flung highly useful variety charity organisation, The

Water Rats, which like its fraternal body the Terriers, did most benevolent work among music-hall folk who had fallen by the way.

In both of these organisations, the hereinbeforementioned Joe Elvin and Joe O'Gorman were very much to the fore. So was another Rodentine monarch by name Charles Warren, formerly a very funny comedian, but of late years head man at the big song-publishing firm run by Bert Feldman.

Co-equal and co-eval in celebrity was the renowned Lauri troupe of pantomimists which band was run at first by Charles Lauri Senr., (so long clown at Drury Lane), and subsequently by his still more famous son Charles, who not only could clown with greater skill and comicality than his father, but who also became what his father never was, that is, a remarkable impersonator of dumb show characters and of all sorts of animals.

Young Charlie Lauri, who died too young, had put in a wonderful record of performances in pantomime, of such characters as Crusoe's Friday, the same wrecked mariner's parrot and goat, and any number of times as Mother Goose's and Mother Hubbard's dog, and especially of Whittington's Cat.

After this, young Charles went out with all sorts of animal sketches in which he played monkeys, opossums, alligators and every known kind of dog. In the latter canine department of dumb drama, Charles Lauri's latest, and if I may say so, one of the most successful of his silent plays, was written by myself.

It was based upon the fine old story of the Dog Gelert, and that animal's self sacrifice for his master's little child, whom it was thought for a while the poor dog had been trying to kill. But of course, that splendid animal had really fought a terrible wolf who had attacked the child.

Young Lauri's performance of this brave dog was as pathetic as it was realistic, indeed a memorable impersonation.

At the time of Lauri's death he was arranging to produce another dumb drama of mine, in which he was to enact a poor hunted-down little man who had sufficient strong and dramatic reason, (I think), for describing himself as a French Poodle. It was, indeed, a very powerful story, but alas! that wonderful zoological student and ditto actor did not live to carry out his promise.

Another Lauri—Edward Lauri, who married the brilliant musical comedy actress and sketch artist, May Beatty—was a cousin of Charlie's, and after a stiff apprenticeship in the knock-about line with members of his family he became a regular actor 'with words.' In fact, a very clever and versatile comedian and producer.

Poor Teddy, who was one of the most loyal workers ever met with on any stage, or off it, did absolute wonders as one of the chief special constables in the awful air raids of the War. So diligently did he do his duty that he died at a comparatively early age.

For some years in theatres and halls a considerable amount of pantomime and knockabout work was performed by Fred Evans, his wife Amy Rosalind, and their clever troupe. Fred's *métier* in this form of art was of the fantastic kind, and much akin to his celebrated impersonation of pantomime clowns, harlequins and sprites. He was a fine-figured fellow, and one of the best at his game.

Fred left behind him a still cleverer and more versatile son, namely Will Evans, seen in monologue and sketches equally compounded of diction and dumb show in variety houses. Of late years, in addition to playing in sundry pantomimes, Will has blossomed forth into dramatic authorship ; his chief achievement in this connection was his collaboration with the writer called "Valentine" in that still running tremendous financial success called "Tons of Money."

Will Evans, besides being a pantomimist, is a very fine instrumentalist. He still pines to follow his brilliant father as a clown, and as such to sing "Hot Codlins" and "Tipitty-witchet" in some big pantomime. To prove his fitness for the purpose, William, standing in his own dress on his own hearthrug a short while ago, gave me a most complete and artistic clown performance with "songs" as above.

To give any kind of historical résumé of famous dumb show and animal impersonators without mentioning the gifted Conquest family, would be, to use the trite illustration, like playing Hamlet without the Prince of Denmark!

I knew and was concerned with all these Conquests from the time of the father of the present group, the late George Conquest, who ran for so many years in turn, the popular Grecian and Surrey Theatres.

This Conquest was also a regular actor of spoken parts and a fine actor, too. His chief delight, however, was to pose as every conceivable kind of animal or insect. I have seen him play crows, ravens, eagles, many a monkey or gorilla, sometimes of a tragic type, and even spiders of a most fly-gobbling kind.

I have also seen him startle his audiences as a bottle imp, a vampire, a one-eyed demon-pirate and so on.

George père trained all his three sons (including the late George) to follow in his pantomimic wake and to play the same dumb animals, reptiles, and insects.

In this zoological and entomological regard, his surviving sons Fred and Arthur Conquest have achieved great fame. Fred's wonderful performance of a goose, for example, in recent pantomimes, will always be remembered by those who saw him.

As to Arthur Conquest, he, like Brother Fred, has often starred in certain of his father's most sensational animal characters, and also has figured in Drury Lane and other pantomimes now as Friday, anon as Whittington's cat, and later even as a Talking Tree.

Arthur was the original player of the terrible Wolf with Charles Lauri in the above named Gelert sketch of mine, and when Lauri died, this young Conquest took over this dumb drama, and starred very successfully for a long time as the Dog Gelert.

One of the cleverest as well as one of the most comical sketch troupes, both verbal and pantomimic is that run by Ernie Lotinga, who introduced his famous character Jimmy Josser, in quite a series of these side-splitting stage playlets.

Lotinga was really born Luck, and is one of the numerous family, The Brothers Luck, quite a happy Hebrew group, who are natives of Liverpool.

The actual Brothers Luck, apart from Brother Lotinga, are mostly of the dumb show kind, quite in the fashion for example of that other splendid acrobatic sketch troupe, The Bogannys, with their very mysterious Bakehouse.

AWFUL CONFESSION BY ME

I feel that I ought to conclude this series of sketches and sketchers with a very strange, or at least a disturbing, tale about myself. In any case, I can lay my hand upon my heart and say, with the manager in "Pagliacci," "And the story I tell you is true."

It fell out thusly: on two separate occasions I was commissioned to write sketches, one a slight musical scena, and the other, a full-grown musical specimen, and those who commissioned me turned out to be crooks, of a varied and versatile kind!

As I knew nothing whatever of these two people until the revelations at their respective trials, I can honestly say with the usual sentimental stage heroine, "I was inno . . . cent!"

Client Criminal number One was a handsome young fellow, who had fallen in love with a popular soubrette, whom, as he informed me, he intended to marry forthwith. He wished to appear with her first, however, in the halls, and he arranged with me to write the necessary sketch. He paid something on account, and I delivered the goods.

I did not get any further cash however, for alas! before the production could take place, this really delightful young fellow was arrested on several charges of embezzling his employer's money. So flagrant indeed was the case that he was sentenced to three years' imprisonment!

Criminal Client number Two was a charming young lady, for whom one of our biggest dramatic agents engaged me to write a very important playlet, for use in the variety theatres.

All went well for a time, the only drawback being that this young lady, who also had a fiancé who wanted to act in the play, developed a habit of not attending the rehearsals. Eventually however, they returned to the rehearsal fold, and they and I and our composer, (one of the biggest and best of his kind), got well to work and hurried on to the production.

Again however, before the production, the young couple, who played two nice young lovers, began to get very slack in their respective characters. The composer and I and the manager concerned advised postponement and more work for the happy pair. They were obdurate, however, and *on* the piece went . . . and *off* it went!

Yes! pretty quickly, but although I says it as shouldn't, it was really a very good little play of its kind, as the adjacent script still shows me.

Arrangements were made for the young couple to get to work properly, and to take the playlet on tour, when suddenly the Law stepped in, and the charming damsel was arrested on sundry charges of nefariousness . . . involving blackmail among other things!

There was a long and sensational trial, and eventually the little siren, as she proved to be, was sent away on a long sentence.

Of course I shall mention no names in either of these cases, as both of the delinquents indicated long ago served their respective sentences, and, as I have reason to believe, both have attempted to "Make Good."

I will only add this, that the case of the young fellow

proving a crook was an amazing surprise to me. In the case however of the beautiful young girl, I have never really recovered my astonishment at the revelations concerning her, for during the many weeks I was concerned in rehearsals etc. with that lady, I felt that I had never met a more modest, cultured, innocently charming damsel in all my life !

So there's my crook confession !

"THE LAST TURN"

By this phrase I mean of course the Tag or Curtain to my Music-Hall Memories.

I cannot expect a "Call," but I can at least, even in print, bow my acknowledgments for the kindness and patience my readers have exhibited in favouring me with a perusal of this book.

In conclusion, I think I may say that whatever else this volume may have accomplished, certainly it can claim, first, to be a comprehensive survey of the halls, their singers, and their songs, for more than half a century.

Secondly, I venture to hope that its latter and more modern portion will give the lie direct to those pessimistic anti-variety folk, who—alike for selfish and stuntful purposes—are so fond of asserting that the music-halls and their Art have passed away for ever.

In short, I trust I have made it plain for all who honour me by reading this volume, to see that Age has not withered nor has custom staled *our* Infinite Variety !

TOPOGRAPHICAL TIPS

The Sun, at Knightsbridge, was nearly opposite the Wellington Barracks. It was long ago absorbed—"Pub." and all—by the fine row of shops and flats there. The neighbouring Trevor, however, still stands—at least as far as its "licensed premises" are concerned—a little way westward, at the corner of Trevor Square.

The Raglan (or Lord Raglan) was in Theobald's Road, Holborn, and was long ago swept away for street improvements. The name "Raglan," however, was afterwards given for a while by the proprietor of that Holborn hall to the old Salmon Music Hall, in Union Street, Borough. I attended that Southside sing-song when it was called by these names, and also when it was renamed the Alexandra, the Borough, and so on.

The Winchester (with its old tavern, "The Grapes") was in the Southwark Bridge Road, near where the Marshalsea Road now is. It was called for a while the Surrey Music Hall. This once-popular hall has been *non est* for about forty years, I should think.

Wilton's (otherwise the "Mahogany Bar") was in Wellclose Square, E., and is now a mission hall.

McDonald's, another always crowded resort, was in Hoxton Street, on the opposite side of the Britannia Theatre, and a little more northward. For some years I saw all the star "comiques" and "serios" at McDonald's. That, too, became a mission or temperance hall for a while.

The neighbourhood of Shoreditch and Hoxton had a good many other music-halls and sing-songs scattered around. One of the most popular was Harwood's Varieties, in Pitfield Street.

In the Kingsland Road was the "Spread Eagle"—a very old-time tavern—and close by, at the beginning of Shoreditch, we had the "Gun" and the "Griffin," all three popular sing-songs, with what were called "Select Harmonic Meetings." On the site of the Griffin now stands the London, Shoreditch.

Still more renowned cheap music-halls were to be found in Shoreditch, namely the St. Leonard's Hall (or "Panorama"), nearly opposite the ancient church; the Cambridge (round the corner in Commercial Street, nearly opposite the present Shoreditch Olympia), and the Eastern Alhambra, which was a few doors cityward from the Olympia, then the Standard Theatre.

Further east there was the Eagle, Mile End, afterwards Lusby's, then the Paragon, and now the Mile End Empire; the Foresters, just off Whitechapel, a little way up the Cambridge Heath Road; the Eastern Empire, at Bow, afterwards the Bow Palace, and the still existing Queen's, Poplar. This hall I knew in my younger days as the Apollo, the Oriental, and the Albion.

Collin's is, of course, still on "The Green" at Islington. The Philharmonic Music Hall became the Grand Theatre, and is now the Islington Empire. Deacon's, also not far away from that ancient hostelry, "The Angel" (now Lyons's), was on the banks of the New River, facing Sadler's Wells. Deacon's—where all the stars scintillated, after they had "come out" there—has been defunct for about thirty years. I fancy that its last proprietor was my old friend Captain Davis, the now octogenarian co-manager (with Sir Oswald Stoll) of the Chatham Empire.

The two Regent Music Halls—the one off the Vauxhall Bridge Road and the one in Mile End Road—have long passed away—anyhow as "halls." That other long-famous Vauxhall Bridge Road old-time music-hall, the Standard, Pimlico is, as most people know, now the gorgeous Victoria Palace.

Among more westward halls of my youth, the "Met." is prospering, but the erstwhile popular minor theatre-cum-music-hall, the Cosmetheka, which was in Bell Street, Edgware Road, has long been (to quote Marie Lloyd) "a thing of the past, old dear." The old-time hall in Swallow Street, Piccadilly, is still there as a tavern, and I sometimes call in to refresh my memories (plus a little soda) of the days when I, too, worked there!

The two Gatti's (the one in the Road and the other at the Arches, Hungerford), like the neighbouring Canterbury, have become kinematised. The "Mogul," afterwards the Middlesex, is now the Winter Garden Theatre, and that extraordinary, but short-lived variety house, the Strand Musick Hall (don't forget the k!) became the old Gaiety Theatre!

INDEX